LEGACY ON TRIAL

JOE CARGILE

SEVERN RIVER
PUBLISHING

ALSO BY JOE CARGILE

Blake County Legal Thrillers

Legacy on Trial

In Defense of Charlotte

The Wiregrass Witness

To find out more about Joe Cargile and his books, visit

severnriverbooks.com/authors/joe-cargile

1

She awoke to the slam of car doors. The noise jostled the house. Sitting up in her bed, she peered through the darkness of her bedroom. The clock on the dresser read 3:15 a.m.

Outside, a low conversation began between two men, maybe three. The voices swam through the darkness. Unable to make out a single word, she sat there listening to the sounds. Unwilling to move from the bed, she waited.

More tires crunched the gravel in the driveway and slamming doors with new voices joined the conversation outside. The chirp of a radio cut through the night, and in a flash—blue lights filled the room. The light bounced off of the curtains in her bedroom and jumped to the walls. Zigzagging without direction, the pulsing of the police cruiser lights matched her racing heart.

She crawled to the window and counted the men in the driveway. There were at least nine. The flashing lights illuminated the faces of some as they milled around the front yard. Most wore blue or black police uniforms. Some had beards and dressed in jeans, bulletproof vests strapped around their chests. Then she heard the sound of a fist—*bang, bang, bang*—on the front door of the house.

"Open up, it's the police!" a voice called.

The doorbell rang, and she heard her mother's footsteps in the hallway. The fist banged on the front door twice more.

"Lee, we are coming through this door if you don't open up!" the voice yelled again.

The banging continued downstairs, and the group of men in the yard left her line of sight. From the window, she could not see the front porch of the house. A man stood in front of the garage door directly below her room. He held what looked like a black shotgun in his hands. A silver SUV with law enforcement insignia on the side blocked the driveway behind him. He stood there, coiled, waiting for movement.

She wondered if men with weapons were waiting in the backyard, too. Pulling her socks up tight, she slipped off the end of the bed. She slid her feet along the hardwood floor and down the hallway to her parents' room. This was her house, and she knew how to move about without making any noise. Two large windows in her parents' room overlooked the backyard. The drapes drawn, she pulled them aside for a look. On the patio bricks stood two more men, both in police uniforms. They peered through the back door, waiting, like their brothers out front.

The front door unlocked downstairs with a clank and the alarm system dinged twice, signaling an exterior door just opened in the house. She heard her mother's voice, calm and collected.

"He isn't here."

"Ma'am, we have a warrant, and we are going to perform a sweep of the home to confirm that is in fact the case," a man's voice replied. "We are coming in and will need you to step outside."

"My daughter is here with me. Can I—"

"Have her come outside with you while we search the house," he replied, cutting her off.

A moment passed and another radio chirped outside. A voice murmured into the radio out back but sounded as if it came from underwater. She listened as her mother let the officers inside the house. Creeping to the edge of the stairwell, she listened to the conversation in the foyer below. The man at the door began to explain that his name was Special Agent Tim

Dawson. He worked with the Georgia Bureau of Investigation, and they needed to locate Lee Acker. He was a suspect in their investigation.

"The GBI would like Lee to come into the office for questioning," the man named Dawson said in an even voice.

"Let me get this straight, you come to my house at three in the morning with all these men outside because you only want to chat with my husband?"

"Like I said, we have a search warrant for your home because we need to find him and discuss this investigation."

Dawson hadn't answered her question. A brief silence ensued until he began again.

"Ma'am, we need to begin, so please wake your daughter and step outside."

"Well, like I said, Lee isn't here tonight."

"Do you know where he is?"

"No, he left around lunch."

"Well then—" Dawson began.

"He told me he had to run up to Lake Blackshear to take care of a few things at our lake house that sold last week. The buyers took possession of the home, but there were a few things Lee wanted to grab out of the boathouse."

"What is that address?" Dawson asked.

"For the boathouse?" she asked, her comment implying she owned boathouses in the past with addresses separate from the vacation home. "This boathouse does not have an address."

"The lake house," Dawson replied, not taking her bait.

"The lake house is at 2002 North Valhalla Drive."

"What county is that in?"

"Crisp County, Georgia."

Special Agent Dawson made a call on his cell phone to the Sheriff's Office in Crisp County. They would send a deputy out to the lakeside address to see if Lee Acker's truck was there. Dawson already knew the make, model, and color of the pickup Acker drove. He relayed the tag number and asked that they be on the lookout. His voice faded in and out as he paced back and forth between the stairwell and living room area. When he ended the call, he said, "Wake your daughter and step outside, ma'am."

Footsteps began up the stairs and walked by in the hallway. Her mother's voice called, "Get up, Charlotte, some men are here to look around the house." The door bumped the wall in her bedroom as her mother pushed it open. "Charlotte, where are you?" Her mother's voice called again from down the hall—an edge of distress in her tone.

"In Dad's and your room."

She heard her mother's feet shuffle back down the hallway to the master bedroom. Turning the corner to the room, tears welled up in the eyes of both mother and daughter.

"Mom, what is going on? Why are these police officers here?"

"They are looking for your father."

"Is he okay? Is he in some kind of trouble?"

Her mother did not answer. She began grabbing a long-sleeved shirt and pants from the closet to change into.

"Mom, where is Dad?"

There are parents that lie to their children because it is best for the child's wellbeing. This approach to parenting is taken by all parents at one time or another. How do you tell a child that a car hit the dog? When is it the right time to talk about the reason you are getting a divorce? Where do babies come from? Parents choose to spare pieces of the truth. That is part of raising children. Grace Acker was a mother first, and she employed this strategy of sparing the truth only when it was appropriate. She paused and thought about the question. Her daughter, now a teenager, stood tall with both feet planted in front of her, demanding an answer. She deserved to hear the truth from her mother before hearing it from anyone else.

"He killed a man, Charlotte," she said, looking directly at her and whispering in fear of being overheard.

Charlotte Elmer Acker stood there in silence, examining her mother's face.

"You must never tell another soul that I told you. Can you promise me that?"

The two continued to stand in silence until the sound of an officer's footsteps started coming up the stairs.

"Promise me?" Her mother prodded again.

Another moment passed, then Charlotte nodded to her mother before making her way downstairs. The officers were beginning their search.

2

The sunrise looked orange and red as it filled the morning sky. He was ten miles west of Beaumont, Texas, and began looking at the interstate's exit signs for motels. There would be plenty of options as he approached the Houston metro area. This part of Texas looked no different than Louisiana. The Gulf Coast created its own unique blend of landscapes and culture along the coastlines of Alabama, Mississippi, and Louisiana. Its effect on Texas was no different, and it was not until you reached Houston that the influences of the Lone Star State started to take hold.

A blue-and-white sign for the Motorway Inn caught his eye. He signaled with the blinker and moved toward the exit ahead. He hoped for a breakfast diner, warm shower, and six or seven hours of sleep before moving on.

As he exited the interstate, he spotted the black-and-yellow sign of a Waffle House. The coffee would likely be terrible, but a waffle would hit the spot. He scanned the restaurant as he pulled into the parking lot. Seeing no one in law enforcement, he parked the car to head inside.

He wore a black baseball cap, jeans, and a blue button-down shirt. Walking through the parking lot, he felt the early September morning heat coming off the asphalt. The temperature would reach 95 degrees by 11:00 a.m., but he hoped to be sound asleep by that time.

His plan was to move during the night and sleep during the daytime. The larger hotel chains might find the early morning check-in unusual or suspicious. A bargain motel clerk would think nothing of it, though. He would hold a six-pack of beer in one hand and backpack in the other, signaling a need for a day away with one's vices. He would pay in cash for the room and be back on the road by that night.

The door chimed as he walked into the restaurant.

"Good morning, grab a seat where you like," called a voice from behind the bar.

Seeing plenty of open tables, he chose a booth by the window. It looked out at the side of the parking lot where he parked the vehicle. He smiled at the look of his borrowed Nissan Altima. It bore Mississippi plates and came with an Ole Miss sticker. Hotty Toddy, he thought to himself. Taking his seat, he removed his hat and pulled out his cell phone. A chesty waitress called from the restaurant's open kitchen, "You having coffee this morning, sweetie?" He nodded to her with a smile, and she grabbed a white coffee mug from the kitchen to take over to his booth. She wore a black apron and a name tag that said "Kim—Assistant Manager" on it. Pouring his coffee, Kim asked, "You know what you're having this morning?"

He did not need to look at the menu. It was all greasy diner food that tasted the same once you put it on a plate together.

"I'll have a waffle, two eggs scrambled, and a side of sausage."

"Patties or links?" Kim asked, her voice gravelly and Texan.

"Links."

Kim smiled as she took the large plastic menu from the table. She did not bother with the polite morning small talk. If he wanted conversation, she would oblige. She saw truckers, lawyers, cops, and deadbeats all day long. Some wanted to talk, but most wanted to eat and run. She scribbled on a pad and turned to the kitchen to call out the order to her line cooks. "We'll have it right out," she said with a wink, then walked away to check on other tables.

He pulled a cell phone from his pocket. He'd purchased it the week before from a prepaid, no-contract mobile provider. A backup sat tucked away in the vehicle outside. When the phone lit up, he stared at the generic background on the home screen. It looked similar to the one he'd left behind—it just didn't have his family photos on it.

With the phone on airplane mode, he connected to the restaurant's Wi-Fi to check the online version of the newspaper back home. The *Blake County News* was a small-town paper. Though not known for the tightest reporting, any local news of arguable importance would receive top billing and prompt updates from the newspaper's two reporters on staff. "Investigators Still Searching for Clues in Murder of Collins" read the lead story on the website. The date and timestamp showed the last update to the article took place the evening before at 8:50 p.m. EDT. He'd read it already, but he skimmed it again. Nothing new.

He closed out the article and typed in the information for his temporary email address with ProtonMail. The email service boasted the fact that no personal information was required to create a secure email account. He'd researched the service and found that by default, the service did not keep any IP logs that could be linked to the anonymous email account. As he logged in, "Your privacy comes first" appeared on the screen in sharp purple letters before fading to his inbox. There were two unopened emails.

The first email encouraged him to explore his new account's calendar and reminder features. He trashed it. The second email was from his contact in Laredo: *Loma Alta Motel $850.00.* It did not provide an address to the motel. He planned to arrive early the next morning and hoped that would not be a problem. He typed his reply—*Arriving before 5 AM*—and pressed send. He logged out and opened Google Maps. He entered the name of the motel in Laredo, Texas, as a plate with a golden-brown waffle arrived.

"Can I get you anything else, hun?"

Lee looked up from the image on his phone just as the travel route from Beaumont to Laredo finished calculating.

"No, ma'am, this is perfect."

"I'll top your coffee off and leave you to it, then."

3

The Southwest Circuit's Public Defender's Office was located two blocks from the Blake County Courthouse. The small government office's sign out front read: "Zealous, effective, and ethical representation to indigent people accused of crimes." The four attorneys on staff, along with one investigator, serviced the circuit's seven counties—Blake, Clay, Miller, Quitman, Randolph, Seminole, and Terrell. The western border of the circuit ran along the Alabama line, with tall pine trees and the Chattahoochee River serving as the boundary. The circuit's southern border butted up against the Florida line and its sprawling live oaks on the banks of Lake Seminole. The eastern and northern borders were as discernable as the property lines on family farmland, blending in with the expanse of rural South Georgia.

Some 95,126 people were scattered across the circuit's seven counties, but Blake County was the largest by far. With a population of nearly 38,000, Blake County was an economic jewel for a region that routinely ranked at the bottom of lists tracking education, employment, and economic growth. With no major interstate running through the region, the lawyers that worked in the Southwest Circuit's Public Defender's Office loaded up each week to ride the county roads or state highways to the rural courthouses peppered across the circuit. There the lawyers represented mostly Black and brown defendants, many facing hopeless cases.

Their office was led by Jim Lamb, an old marine that served in Vietnam. The draftee that fought for months in the Mekong Delta now ran his small office under the belief that they must test the system every week. He ensured his staff of underpaid lawyers maintained a fighting reputation, especially when their poor clients insisted on a trial. Lamb enjoyed the reputation of a true believer that had unshakable confidence in the constitutional safeguards of the system. The old marine embraced the mission of counseling and representing the indigent, even in the face of certain defeat. Still, when it became imperative that his office test the system by fighting fire with fire, Lamb ensured he kept a flamethrower on staff to handle the job.

Maggie Reynolds had plenty of fire in her, and she tested the system often for her clients. In her four years with the Southwest Circuit's Public Defender's Office, she'd tried forty-one jury trials—an unheard-of number for any attorney in a rural circuit. Of those forty-one cases, she'd acted as lead counsel on seven murder cases with four of those individuals receiving "not guilty" verdicts. Maggie was a talent unlike any other, but it was only a matter of time. She was a star quarterback on her last year of a rookie contract and was not long for practice in rural Georgia. With each win in the courtroom, more attractive job offers found their way to her desk. Offers that paid handsomely. Offers that could not be matched by an office that defended the indigent.

When Maggie Reynolds started working at the Southwest Circuit's Public Defender's Office, so began the busiest time in the office's history. The small sleepy judicial circuit in southwestern Georgia made headlines in 2012 when its homicide rate per capita spiked to bring it in line with some of the most dangerous areas in the state. The name Maggie Reynolds, counsel of record for defendants receiving acquittals in a number of these killings, began to garner attention from reporters looking for a story. Her prowess in the courtroom, coupled with her striking beauty, made her a media darling. Reporters from the *Atlanta Journal-Constitution* found their way to Blake County to write stories on Maggie, thus providing fertile ground for her legend to grow.

With each win at trial, Maggie's coworkers hung the news articles in her office and toasted to their local celebrity with cheap champagne. With each office celebration, Jim Lamb expected Maggie to sit down in his office—plastic flute of champagne in hand—to announce her impending move to a more exciting city and bigger salary. The months passed, though, the wins continued, and the conversation never came. If Maggie planned to move out into private practice, she did not let her boss or anyone else know it. "She keeps her cards close to her chest," Lamb once commented to a reporter from the *Tallahassee Democrat*. "She is a rising star with a genuine commitment to indigent defense," the quote continued.

Lamb knew the truth about Maggie, though. She liked to win, and that drove her to remain focused. Lamb suspected that she stayed working as a public defender not because of her passion for indigent defense, but because there would be an endless line of men and women with nothing to lose. People willing to roll the dice and take their cases to trial. He knew what she was about. For Maggie, every week—except this week—was just another opportunity to put another *X* in the win column.

4

Maggie Reynolds thought about the week ahead of cancelled hearings as she made the walk from her home to the Southwest Circuit's Public Defender's Office. She took the same route each morning and considered the short walk to be a sacred part of her day. Maggie had a '95 Saab 900 convertible that she loved dearly, but she preferred to walk. Going into the office each morning, she focused her intentions on the day's tasks ahead. When leaving the office, no matter how late, she left the stresses and pressures behind her for the evening. Maggie's ability to separate her work from her personal life was one of the many skills that set her apart from other lawyers.

As she walked into downtown Blakeston, Maggie stopped in Beans on Broad to grab her morning smoothie. The downtown coffee shop was her favorite morning pit stop, and it was packed as usual. She looked around at the faces circled about the coffee shop's small tables and suspected that many were quietly discussing the shocking news of the recent murder. After four years of picking juries in the area, Maggie knew the good people of Blake County. They only got riled up about local crime when a prominent member of the community was harmed in the process. It was the way of the world, and Blakeston was no exception.

"I'll put a Mean Green together for you," called the barista from behind the counter as soon as he saw Maggie standing in line.

The familiar voice broke her train of thought and stole her away from eavesdropping on the nearby tables. "Thanks, Dale," she said, flashing a smile in the direction of the busy barista.

A copy of the morning newspaper faced outward on the bar. The ongoing murder investigation splashed the front page, and Maggie picked one up, tucking it under her arm. She signaled to Dale that she was taking one with her, and he acknowledged with a nod as his noisy blender churned. The smell of coffee beans and biscuits surrounded her. It made her stomach groan and reconsider the choice of a smoothie that morning. As she inched closer to the end of the bar, though, she reminded herself that the buttered biscuits made her feel sluggish. She had work to do that day, so Maggie paid for the paper and smoothie. She flashed another smile to Dale and hustled to her office a block over, tangy drink in hand.

"Good morning, Maggie," the receptionist said as Maggie walked in the front door of the office.

"Morning, Lila," she replied.

"Coffee is fresh in the back if you want some."

"On my way now."

"All the court calendars are cancelled this week; do you think your clients will still be calling the office?"

"I bet they will give us the week off."

"Well, I'll just pack up and go down to the beach, then."

"Stick around until lunch at least, I am going to wade through my office and decide what needs to go into storage."

Lila chuckled. "Perfect, I'll take a load on my way to Panama City, then."

"Take Lamb with you. He needs a vacation," Maggie pleaded with her hands folded.

"Oh, sweetie, Lamb Chop wouldn't be able to handle the heat."

Not taking the bait with her receptionist's suggestive comment, Maggie gave a laugh and made her way toward the back of the building. She entered the building's main thoroughfare. A wide corridor of tattered green carpet made narrow by stacks of boxes. Fluorescent bulbs provided harsh lighting in the hallway, exposing the bumps and scuffs on the cream-colored walls. As Maggie made her way down the hallway, she glanced into the darkened offices of her colleagues—each as messy as the next. With court cancelled the entire week, she knew their stacks of paperwork would go untouched. Attention would be on the world outside the courtroom.

Maggie stopped in front of a picture frame in the hallway. The office décor needed work, but at least the walls weren't filled with inspirational quotes in cheap frames. Instead, the office's fearless leader chose what looked like motel paintings for the walls of the government office. Maggie commented to Jim Lamb on one occasion that Monet's Motel Series was accentuated by fluorescent lighting, so he'd made the perfect choice when picking out the paintings for the office. Lamb took the mocking compliment to heart and began adding bargain artwork to the walls every so often. Each time Lamb brought in a new piece from a yard sale, the two stood in front of it acting the part of art connoisseurs. The discount art now filled the hallway. Maggie enjoyed the game and did not care that the office looked dated. The appearance of the office mattered little to her clients. She spent most of her time meeting clients in court or in jail. That was the life of a criminal defense lawyer. A few green plants and her diplomas, for now, were good enough for any visitors that made it back to Maggie's office.

She poured a cup of dark coffee in her favorite mug and walked to her desk. She opened the newspaper and read through the latest on the murder investigation. The names of suspects, if there were any, had not been released. Maggie knew the high-profile case would garner interest from the media once the cops found their man—or woman. The article laid out the facts again and added little to what Maggie already knew about the killing. Law enforcement was "following up on leads" and "waiting on evidence testing to come back." The reporters did not know much. If investigators knew anything, they were not releasing comments to the local reporters yet. Lila, from reception, poked her head in Maggie's door. Maggie looked up from the newspaper and waited for the morning tidbit of gossip.

"You hear they went out to the Acker place last night to talk to Lee?"

Maggie could almost feel the juice spray off the latest slice of gossip in the murder investigation.

She shook her head. "That's the first I've heard of it."

"Wild, right?"

"I guess so," Maggie replied, not wanting to engage too much.

"I heard the cops showed up to the house with a warrant to search the place, and Lee was already gone. Can you imagine searching that house? It has to be at least a gazillion square feet. Anyways, I guess the investigators went up to Lake Blackshear this morning to check the Ackers' lake house out with some Crisp County deputies. Still nothing, from what I hear."

Lila's cousin's husband worked at the Blakeston Police Department. The cousins had been inseparable since elementary school, and Maggie often overheard the two talking about local gossip over the phone. Lamb brought the issue up in Lila's performance review last year, and Lila swore she would keep the personal conversations with family to a minimum while on the clock. Lamb let Lila walk all over him, though. The calls with her cousin continued, and they had obviously spoken or texted this morning about the details of the investigation. Standing in the doorway, Lila looked proud to have the latest intel.

"Must be nice to have a few houses to hide out in, right?" Maggie replied while folding the newspaper on the desk. She made a showing that she was going to begin work by opening the mail stacked in front of her.

"How crazy would that be if—" Lila began as the phone started to ring in reception. Lila stopped and craned her head in the direction of the front desk. Lamb managed the office and the employees that worked there. Maggie didn't boss anyone around, but it wasn't her job to answer the phones.

"I'll let you know what else I hear," Lila hollered as she hustled back to the front desk.

When Lila was gone, Maggie stared back at the newspaper's front-page photo of her friend and frequent adversary in the courtroom—Jake Collins. Found in the woods behind his house with three gunshot wounds to the chest. Dead at thirty-seven years of age. He looked tan in the smiling picture selected for the article. The headline above the picture read, "GBI Searches for Clues in District Attorney's Murder" in bold-type font. Nothing about a search for Lee Acker or about the family being under investigation, but she wasn't surprised by the rumors about the Acker family. This town loved to get the rumor mill going, and given the Acker family's recent history, they were an easy target.

Maggie had her own sources, though, and besides, a criminal defense lawyer rarely jumped to conclusions when the cops pointed to the first suspect. She knew the agents on the case were looking hard into Acker's whereabouts from three nights ago, but that didn't mean much to her yet. His problem was that they considered him a suspect avoiding questioning. In the world of law enforcement, that made him guilty as sin.

Maggie shoved the newspaper to the edge of the desk and sighed. She would have to wait for the juicy details like the rest of the town. Besides, no arrests had been made yet, and probable cause or not, no Acker would be walking through the doors of her office anytime soon.

5

It was a straight shot down I-10 from Beaumont to San Antonio. There he would merge onto I-35. That would take him into Laredo, Texas. He pulled out of the motel parking lot at 8:00 p.m. as the sun cast its golden hue across the streets of Cheek, Texas. The map he reviewed in his motel room that afternoon sat folded in the passenger seat of the Nissan Altima. He couldn't remember the last time he took a road trip without using his phone or Google Maps to track his route, but his temporary cell phone remained turned off in the center console. He knew where he was going, so it wasn't really about the lack of GPS. The real reason he wanted the cell phone on right now was to call his family. A short call to see how they were doing and to let them know that he was all right. That would come later.

The trip to Laredo would take him six and a half hours. Barring any delays, he anticipated he would arrive around 3:00 a.m. to the Loma Alta Motel. When considering his route, he weighed the path down I-10 with an alternate option through Victoria and Beeville. He knew that driving down I-10 in Southeast Texas had its risks. It would take him right down the gut of some of the largest civil forfeiture operations in the country, and law enforcement routinely looked for out-of-state plates passing through the area with cash, drugs, and other valuable property prime for the taking. A taking that many defense lawyers across the Southeast Texas courtrooms would argue was in violation of the Fourth, Fifth, Eighth, and Fourteenth Amendments to the Constitution. The seizures happened every day, though, and this was particularly worrisome given that under the rear seat of the borrowed Nissan sat four envelopes of neatly stacked cash. The manila envelopes each held twelve thousand five hundred dollars in hundred-dollar bills. Another one thousand dollars in twenties was tucked away in the center console.

In a routine traffic stop, a law enforcement officer could claim he or she smelled the odor of marijuana in the car or that the vehicle was stolen. With a gun on the hip—and authority to take anyone to jail that disagrees —the officer could then ask for "consent" to search the vehicle for evidence. The driver that disagrees is asked to step out of the vehicle. The driver that agrees is still asked to step out of the vehicle. Either way, law enforcement gets its search. Then the officer can comb through the vehicle for cash like a gold panner in a California riverbed, leaving the driver with one option— stand in shock as his or her civil rights crumble in front of their very eyes. People make for easy targets when you have the power of the US government or State of Texas behind you, and any whiff of a shady customer coming through the area brings the drug dogs out.

Once cash is located, law enforcement can perform a "currency investigation" in hopes that something—anything they can make a case on—pops up on a record. Every single year, millions in cash gets seized in roadside stops, and law enforcement can do it without ever bringing a criminal charge. Lee knew that a bogus search of his vehicle could reveal multiple cell phones along with the contents of the envelopes. An industrious officer would find a way to keep it, so the risk of a highway robbery by Texas law enforcement would remain a concern. At least until he reached the border. There he faced a new batch of challenges.

Though he was concerned about the ride down I-10, he still chose to stick with the route down the interstate for as good a reason as any— Monday Night Football.

The Houston Texans were playing the Dallas Cowboys. The rare regular-season matchup was just kicking off, and it would be on at every bar and restaurant in Texas. In 2002, the two teams played their inaugural game, and the Texans did the unthinkable—they humiliated America's

Team. Licking their wounds, the Dallas Cowboys proceeded then to do what every great brand does: protect its reputation. The two teams continued to face off during the preseason, but regular season matchups were out of the question. For those that love football, the preseason still meant little in the NFL. Unless you were a kid hustling to make the fifty-two-man roster, the main goal during any preseason snap was just to stay healthy and make it to the real games. That's what made this Monday Night Football matchup exciting. The regular season would be at full speed, and that meant plenty of prime-time intrigue that big-time sports were built to bring. It also meant plenty of after-work beers for football fans that loved to watch the games.

A route down back roads or state highways would pass through small towns that would consider setting out roadblocks to collect drunk fans off the roadway. Like civil asset forfeitures from "suspected drug smugglers," revenue derived from traffic stops and drunk driving arrests were just as crucial to a small town's bottom line. He didn't have a new ID yet, and providing the driver's license of Lee Acker risked an issue with a state trooper at a roadblock. He was not aware of a warrant for his arrest, but there was no way to be certain. I-10 and its risk of encountering the civil asset bandits enabled by state legislation would have to do tonight.

Lee's pulse picked up as he merged back onto I-10. He needed to be out of the country by sundown tomorrow, but speeding was out of the question. He set the Altima's cruise control at seventy-three miles per hour and flipped the radio on. He found a local FM station carrying the Cowboys' broadcast. He glanced again in the rearview mirror as he settled in with the broadcast. This was football country, and he hoped many of the boys in blue would be posted up watching the game or listening in their vehicles. As a college football fan with no allegiance to an NFL team, Lee decided he might as well root for the underdog. The commentator on the radio informed listeners that with 7:48 left in the second quarter, the Cowboys had just kicked their second field goal of the night to bring it to 6-0.

Lee gripped the wheel and thought to himself, Let's hope the underdog pulls this one out tonight.

6

Special Agent Tim Dawson sat at his desk in the GBI's Region 15 Investigative Office reviewing his notes on the murder of Jake Collins. He typed his handwritten notes from the crime scene into the digital case file and then scanned the notebook paper in as an attachment. He also removed his cell phone and replayed a short voice recording containing his thoughts about the crime scene. He'd recorded the voice memo that morning as he drove out of the woods where the homicide investigation continued. While not a meticulous notetaker when at a crime scene, Dawson's investigation habits required he return to the office each night to pour every bit of information he could remember into his digital case file.

He performed this act of discipline while the events were fresh in his mind to ensure his investigations remained tight. While the GBI did not teach him this specific process in his training, Dawson preferred this organization method because it forced him to reflect on the investigation at hand. He recognized early on in his time with law enforcement that his attention inevitably moved to the next day's crime du jour, and he found himself forgetting important details from a case that he worked only the day before. Dawson's structured approach to his work did not go unnoticed by his superiors. For that reason, he'd been named the point man on the investigation into the murder of Jake Collins—the highest-profile homicide investigation of his career.

Dawson looked up from his computer screen as a knock on the door broke his train of thought. Bernard Howard, a colleague, and friend, leaned against the doorframe.

"I'm taking it to the house, T.D."

"All right, brother, I'll be doing the same soon," Dawson replied as he rubbed his eyes. "Trying to knock out some work on this Collins case. Seeing the judge tomorrow morning to get a warrant to send over to Acker's cell provider."

"Guy still hasn't come back home, huh?"

"No, his wife knows where he is, though. She swears she hasn't seen him for two days, but I get the feeling she is protecting him. I told her we would put it out to the media that he is our key murder suspect if she doesn't tell us where he is, but I'm not sure she will crack. She is a cool customer, so I'll probably be calling Richard Montgomery over at the paper."

"Dicky will be ecstatic to get a call. He keeps sniffing around here asking for information on the investigation," Howard said with a laugh. "Do it quick, though. Acker has plenty of money, so you know he's running if no one has seen him in two days. You already send a notice to the State Department to revoke his passport?"

"Not yet," Dawson sighed. "I put a call in to Atlanta for some guidance on that this afternoon and haven't heard back."

"That's the mothership for you," Howard said, looking down at his cell phone in hand. "Cowboys are up thirteen to seven. I need Cooper to get a couple of TDs tonight. Three players on my fantasy team playing in this one."

"Exciting stuff. Get out of here and go home to your wife," Dawson said as he stretched his arms back behind him. He rubbed his left shoulder and pulled out a drawer to find his bottle of ibuprofen.

"Not all of us get a shot at the big time, T.D. Fantasy football is all us benchwarmers got left," Howard said, smiling as he looked up from the phone's screen. "You beat that shoulder up again?"

"Nah, just a little stiff from the workout this morning." Dawson paused, then added: "Or like my grandmother would say, it means it's probably going to rain tonight."

"You can still bust bad guys in the rain," replied Howard with a smile. "Your grandmother would approve of it."

"Oh, you know it. See you tomorrow, brother. Don't spend too much on that daily fantasy garbage."

"Have to do something with this big paycheck. See you tomorrow, T.D."

Shaking his head at the obsession with fantasy football, Dawson returned to his computer monitor. A dead prosecutor made for a long list of potential suspects, and he'd lined up a few dangerous individuals that paroled in the last month. Nothing tied those men to the crime scene, though. Nothing really tied anyone to the crime scene. All Dawson had was GBI procedure, and procedure dictated he look at ex-cons investigated or prosecuted by the decedent. The killing of someone in law enforcement required lining up those individuals sent packing to prison because, "Isn't that motive enough?" Still, out of the hundreds of individuals that Jake Collins put in jail, none made sense for this killing. None had motive that extended beyond basic hatred.

One case file fueled Dawson's theory of the case, though, but the conviction didn't belong to Jake Collins. He simply deserved the credit. Jake initiated the investigation and handed it off to the feds to get things over the goal line. The voluminous files the government compiled in *United States of America v. Clifford J. Acker* sat scattered around Dawson's office. "Was murder the price Jake paid for helping to put a childhood friend away?" To Dawson it felt like motive. Not that Cliff Acker was a suspect for the killing; he couldn't be. Dawson checked that afternoon to make sure. Cliff still sat tucked away in the Bay Correctional Facility in Panama City, Florida. He wouldn't be released for another eleven months.

Dawson rubbed his eyes and stared at the flashing cursor on the Word document. His affidavit that would accompany another warrant application contained the standard boilerplate information about his experience in law enforcement, but the facts section—the meat and potatoes of the affidavit—needed work. He wouldn't simply manufacture facts that were not at the crime scene. Other investigators included misleading and false information in affidavits to grab a warrant, to close a case. Dawson didn't build cases that way. He would include only the bits of information that pointed to the Ackers and leave it to the judge.

Jake Collins had been dead for three days now, and the Acker family was unwilling to assist in the investigation. The clock was ticking, and the funeral was scheduled for tomorrow. Dawson needed to show progress. He didn't know enough yet, but he knew Lee Acker running wouldn't look good to a law-and-order judge. He'd present the affidavit and proposed search warrant to Superior Court Judge John Balk tomorrow morning. Dawson prided himself on presenting paperwork to judges that was both organized and legally sufficient. Judge Balk would look it over and ask few questions because he was a former prosecutor that had little interest in reining in law enforcement. Lee Acker was a free man, and there was one reason his baby brother sat tucked away in prison. That reason was going in the ground tomorrow.

Dawson read through the affidavit one last time before shutting down the computer. He would add the finishing touches to it in the morning. As he stood from the desk, he heard the patter of rain begin on the roof of the building. "Figures," he said out loud as he grabbed an umbrella from behind his office door and switched off a lamp. He walked down the hallway past a clock on the wall that read 10:00 p.m. and flipped the last of the lights off in the office. Pushing out of the back door of the building that opened to the parking lot, he looked out at the downpour.

"Grandma, you called it," Dawson said with a groan and hustled through the rain to his SUV.

7

At 3:30 a.m., Lee pulled into the parking lot of a McDonald's on the outskirts of Laredo, Texas. He slammed the door to his vehicle and walked inside the dining area of the restaurant to order a cup of coffee. The empty restaurant looked spick-and-span—the night shift probably just having finished a deep clean. The sparkling appearance of the restaurant gave him confidence he could order something to eat. Staring up at the menu board, he added a sausage, egg, and cheese McMuffin to his order.

"*Un café y McMuffin*," called the cashier back to her two coworkers in the kitchen.

Standing at the counter by the "Pick Up Here" sign, Lee turned his cell phone back on and connected to the McDonald's Wi-Fi. He checked the *Blake County News* again for any updates on the investigation and noticed an article was up on the website about the funeral set to take place later that day. The funeral would be held at First United Methodist of Blakeston, the largest church in town. The article included new pictures of Jake under a heading that read "In Memoriam," and Lee scrolled through the photos. The funeral would be packed, and tears would flow as photographs— much like those in the article—faded in and out on a giant projector screen. The images of Jake Collins were from his childhood in Blakeston, graduations from The Citadel and University of Georgia's School of Law, the swearing-in ceremony after passing the bar, and another with his parents.

In the last photo in the article stood a group of four men on a deep-sea fishing trip. He recognized the trip to Costa Rica, but not the photo. Lee stood there looking down at the image of himself, tan and smiling, holding a massive sailfish. Jake stood next to him, a black marlin in hand. The other two men in the photo—Cliff Acker and John Deese—stood proudly next to the fish, beer bottles in hand. The photograph, most likely taken by the fishing guide, froze the group of young men in time. All strong, cocky, ambitious South Georgians spending five days on the Costa Rican shoreline. Fighting pelagic fish by day and bouncing from one beach bar to the next at night. "We have the world by the balls," would have been a fitting caption for the photo. It was a long time ago, though. Life eventually got its shots in, crumbling those friendships as the hits started coming.

A tray slid across the counter and the cashier said, "Cream and sugar over there," pointing at an area by the fountain drink station. A set of gold bangles clinked on her arm as she gestured. Lee thanked her and walked to select a seat in the empty restaurant.

Sitting down, he opened the wrapper on the greasy sandwich and dove in. The adrenaline from the ride down to Laredo had subsided, and his dampened appetite sprung to life after the first bite. He followed it with a sip of warm coffee. His hangover from the day's emotions welcomed the early morning meal, and he felt revitalized. He knew one should exercise caution when adding a greasy breakfast sandwich to an empty stomach, though. As he chewed, Lee conjured up images of a dash for the closest bathroom somewhere after the first few miles into Mexico, so he decided he would grab a protein shake to add something more substantial to his stomach later that morning.

Checking the time, Lee opened the maps application on his phone to scope out the next leg of the journey. The paper map also sat on the table so Lee could compare the two modes of navigation. He would be ready to revert to analog if necessary. The plan for the morning was to cross the border around 7:00 a.m. He would mix in with the commuters and continue south toward Monterrey. It looked like the journey could be done in around three hours, but Lee had no intentions to hammer the accelerator down once he hit Mexican soil. Nearly the entire ride to Monterrey would be on good road—a state-managed *autopista* labeled Carretera Federal 85. Confident the daytime drive would go without issue; he highlighted the path on the map and folded it up.

He sipped on his coffee and stared at the phone in his hand. Lee wanted to call home—just to see how they were doing. Instead, he pulled up Google and typed "Charlotte Acker Blakeston GA" into the search tab. A photo of his daughter and a link to her Facebook page popped up as one of the top search results. Clicking on the profile, Lee saw the information about her looked to be limited. He wasn't logged in to his own Facebook account, so the social media platform prompted him to set one up. Looking at her public profile, he could not see her Facebook wall with updates or flip through her pictures. He smiled at the fact that he, and her mother, fussed at her to always keep her social media pages as private as possible. "There is no reason to allow strangers to look at your photos on Instagram, Facebook, Snapchat, or whatever else is popular right now," he lectured. He wished now he could see what she put out to the world about her feelings. Teenagers are tied to their social media persona, and Lee imagined his daughter faced a conundrum as to how she should convey her thoughts to the world. Lee couldn't imagine how she felt nor the anger that would soon smolder inside.

Her mother would prepare her for the weeks ahead, though. The last forty-eight hours proved to be the most tumultuous of her young life, and the intensity would only ratchet up. Lee knew he would soon be identified, publicly, as the prime suspect in the murder. It was only a matter of time.

~

Lee knocked on the door of room 208 right at 5:15 a.m. He waited, listening for any movement on the other side of the door. Hearing none, he rapped on the door again and stepped to the railing overlooking the parking lot. A haze hovered in the dark morning sky. Sunrise wouldn't be for another hour, but the Loma Alta looked to be coming alive already. The motel, built in the late 80s, sat on the edge of one of Laredo's established industrial parks. Work trucks filled the parking lot with logos for linemen, welders, painters, and other trades that worked hard for a living. Men that woke up early—ate breakfast on the tailgate of a truck in a gas station parking lot—and worked an eleven- or twelve-hour day like warriors. A diesel engine cranked somewhere down the line of vehicles, and its engine sat idling in the quiet morning. The low, soothing sound intensified as its gears shifted and the driver let off the clutch, bringing the engine to life. Lee watched as the truck, a pump truck used for concrete work, moseyed out the back lot.

Lee turned back to the door and hammered on it again with his fist. This time loud enough to startle those in the adjoining rooms.

"Settle your ass down," came the voice from behind the door. "Give me a minute, man." A moment passed, then the chain on the back of the door clacked. The handle turned, and the door opened a few inches to reveal part of a man's face. "Who are you?" the man said in a low voice. The accent originated out of the Midwest—maybe Ohio or Michigan.

"Morning," Lee said before pressing against the door with his hand. "You going to let me in?"

"Are you the guy?" the voice asked.

Lee stood there staring at the man, four or five inches taller and only three feet away.

"Depends," Lee replied.

"Listen, man, it's too early to be standing out here in the corridor messing around."

"I am standing in the corridor; you are standing behind this door. I don't know what you have in the other hand or who else you have in there. Let me in and we can talk."

Both stood there in silence again—not offering to exchange names—playing an impromptu game of the man who speaks first, loses.

"You the guy crossing the border today?"

"That's right."

"You got the money?"

"You are charging me?" Lee replied with a smile.

"Great, a wiseass. Come on in."

The door swung open, and Lee stepped into the motel room. The darkness smelled of stale cigarette smoke and a hint of beer. A stream of light cutting through the motel drapes highlighted movement in one of the room's two queen-size beds. Covers ruffled and a woman leaned over to a lamp beside the bed. She turned it on and then rolled to the other side of the mattress before sliding off the end closest to the bathroom door. Keeping her bare back to the men, she stood up and stepped to the bathroom. Her figure was slender and attractive, Lee could not help but notice. The sound of the shower started, and the man turned back to him.

"Let's see the money."

"You have the passport and ID?" Lee replied.

"Settle down, man, this isn't some tough-guy movie. I've got them right here."

Lee reached into the back pocket of his jeans and pulled out an envelope with one thousand dollars in it.

"This is a grand," he said as he handed it to the man. "The extra one hundred fifty dollars in there is for some information on passing over the border this morning."

"*La frontera* won't be a problem, *güey*," the man said in a faux Mexican accent. The money was waking him up along with his sense of humor.

Pulling out the passport and Texas license, he tossed them to Lee and popped the envelope to inspect the contents.

"The passport and license are gold," he continued as he looked back up at Lee. "A customer has never complained."

"Anyone ever been held at the border on account of your documents not checking out?" Lee asked.

"Not because of my ID," he replied. "My stuff is the best; didn't your brother tell you that?"

Lee avoided the question. "I'll be coming through the border in a vehicle that isn't in my name, Mississippi plates."

"Is it stolen?"

"It is borrowed from a buddy in Biloxi. He doesn't know it yet, but if he knew the circumstances, he wouldn't care."

This was true. Lee grabbed the vehicle from Chad Day, his college roommate that owned a condo in Biloxi, Mississippi. Day, a degenerate gambler, left the vehicle there as his casino and beach wagon. Day was somewhere in Italy shooting dice and visiting vineyards. He wouldn't be home for another week. Lee knew the owner keypad code to a digital Kaba lock on the garage, and Day always left the keys to the Nissan Altima—a vehicle he won playing in some raffle—under the rubber mat on the driver's side.

"You ever cross the border before?"

Lee shook his head and said, "Never by ground."

"Well, regardless of the bridge you choose to cross over on, the border patrol will have a checkpoint set up that all vehicles have to pass through. When you pull up, you will see there are about five or six different lanes where they divide up cars, buses, and big trucks."

Lee nodded as he listened and opened up the passport to review the document. The sturdy blue booklet with the United States of America in gold lettering looked and felt identical to his current passport.

"All the lanes have license plate readers, and sometimes dogs are out walking the lines of cars."

"I am not worried about the dogs," Lee added.

"Either way, if they want to take a look at your vehicle or talk to you about something, they direct you to a secondary area where they inspect the vehicle. Take it from me; they will search that vehicle in and out. Make sure your 'buddy' didn't leave anything behind for you to worry about. The boys are not as concerned about what leaves the US of A, but they still shake drivers down to keep appearances up."

"Well, is the plate not matching my license and insurance going to be an issue?" Lee asked.

The Midwesterner leaned back, enjoying his newfound role as expert in the room. Lee didn't care; he needed the information.

"It could be," the man said, folding his hands.

"How do I make it not an issue?" Lee asked.

"You rent a car, or—" The door opened to the bathroom and the woman stepped out in her panties and bra, a towel wrapped around her drying hair. The man turned to her and said, "Baby, I'm conducting business over here, and you are walking around like this is some sort of a show."

The woman said nothing, flashing a coy smile as she grabbed what looked like a makeup bag from the top drawer of the dresser. Lee tried not to stare, but it wasn't easy. She returned to the bathroom and shut the door.

"Fucking unbelievable," the man murmured as he turned back to Lee.

"I love the girl, great ass, and smart, really smart, but Jesus Christ she likes to flirt. It's six o'clock in the morning and she is catting around."

Lee said nothing, unsure if the comment needed a response. The man reached into the front pocket of his shirt and pulled out a cigarette. He lit it and returned his attention to Lee.

"I can sell you a vehicle."

"Yeah? What kind of vehicle would that be?" Lee replied.

"Hypothetically, it would be a work vehicle that crosses the border every week. Back and forth, back and forth all the time. Company vehicle with company insurance and registration. Everything checks out—no problem, no worries."

"Wouldn't it be reported stolen before lunch?"

"That depends," the man replied.

He sat there smoking his cigarette, enjoying the control over the pace of the conversation.

"Depends on what?"

"Depends on who the guy is that drives the vehicle every day."

"What would that run me?" Lee asked.

"Ten thousand dollars."

Lee looked at the man and around the room again. Ten thousand dollars would cover the room fee in a place like the Loma Alta for at least six months. Maybe longer.

"I'll give you another five thousand dollars because that's all I have in cash," Lee began. "That's generous because I will only be able to drive the vehicle a few days. It'll eventually have to be reported stolen, so I'll dump it by Thursday at the latest. I am not too keen on spending any time in a Mexican lockup."

The man looked at Lee, evaluating him. The door to the bathroom opened again and the woman stepped out, this time fully dressed. The man nodded at Lee, then said over his shoulder, "Baby, can you go outside and grab the rest of our things out of the car? Cliff's brother here is going to borrow it."

8

Special Agent Dawson stood on Judge Balk's front porch with a borrowed travel mug in hand. It read "Go Dawgs" on the side in red and black—a detail he hoped would not go unnoticed by the judge. He rang the doorbell and stepped back a couple of paces. As he waited, he looked out at the dew-covered yard of the small farm and heard the low sound of a television going inside the home. It sounded like one of the twenty-four-hour news channels. "Breaking news" and chatter was all Dawson could make out.

The front door to the house was left open. A screen door covering the doorway allowed the smells of biscuits and bacon to seep out onto the front porch area. The smell activated Dawson's empty stomach, and it churned as a dog walked to the other side of the screen door. "You and I are just a couple of dogs scrapping for a meal, am I right, boy?" Dawson said in a hushed voice. The dog barked back at him twice, wagging his tail in agreement.

A woman in a dark dress approached the doorway and swung the screen door open with an enthusiastic, "Good morning!"

"Morning, ma'am, I am Special Agent Tim Dawson. I believe your husband is expecting me."

"Yes, sweetie, come on in," she replied. "He is just down the hall in the kitchen, finishing up breakfast."

Tim followed her down the hallway, and the smell of bacon intensified with each step, her perfume putting up a good fight.

As he turned into the kitchen area, Dawson found the judge seated at the end of his kitchen table, reading a newspaper. The front page showed color photos of Jake Collins throughout the years of his life. The story of a great man that was taken too soon.

"John, this gentleman is here to see you."

The judge looked up from the paper and extended his hand for a handshake, not leaving his seat at the table.

"Good morning, Judge," Dawson said as he shook the judge's hand. The judge nodded, chewing a bite of food.

"Now, Mr. Dawson, I am going to put a biscuit on a plate for you, and can I add some coffee to your mug?" asked Mrs. Balk.

Dawson felt like someone inserted him into an old-timey television show, and he wondered when the last time was that a Black guy came to breakfast in this little farmhouse.

"No, ma'am, that is not necessary. Thank you, though, I don't believe I should take up too—"

The judge pushed the newspaper aside. "That's nonsense, Tim, sit down and have a bite of breakfast with me."

Big John Balk, a man that stood at over six foot four, commanded attention in his courtrooms and any other room you found him in. The judge motioned to his wife to continue putting together the items for Dawson and focused his attention on the matter at hand. He sat there dressed in a dark suit, open collar. Freshly shaven and haircut trimmed tight. Swollen eyes, brown liquor still working its way out of his system.

Dawson took a seat at the table and found a place to lay his folder. "I appreciate you seeing me this early on the day of the funeral," he began.

"That's not a problem, Tim," the judge replied. "Honey, can you make sure Tim here has some butter and that peach jelly your sister brought down last time she visited." He didn't wait for a response.

A biscuit appeared in front of Dawson.

"Cream and sugar?" Mrs. Balk asked.

Seeing no creamer on the table or sugar grains scattered around the judge's coffee cup, Dawson said, "No, ma'am, this will be just fine."

Dawson began buttering the biscuit and rolled right into the task at hand.

"Judge, I'd like you to look at signing a search warrant for the investigation into the Collins murder."

He handed the judge a copy of the search warrant he'd drawn up along with his accompanying affidavit. As he did, Tim heard the clank of a few dishes being left in the sink.

"John," came the voice of Mrs. Balk. "I am going to finish getting ready upstairs and I'll be back down." She smiled at Tim and stepped through the doorway that led back down the hallway. The judge did not look up from the paperwork.

As Dawson waited, he heard a panel of political pundits discussing the crisis at the border on the television in the other room. Drugs, weapons, and human trafficking concerns were hammering the communities along the US border. "This is not an existential crisis," one panel member urged the viewers. "Mexico is taking advantage of America," added another pundit. Different voices made up the panel—they all held the same viewpoints. Dawson ate his biscuit, listening to parts of the news segment until it ended, and a commercial began urging viewers to put their money into buying gold. He glanced at the judge. It appeared he was reading every word in the paperwork. A good sign, Dawson thought to himself.

"You believe Lee Acker is involved in the murder of Jake Collins?"

"Yes, sir, I believe he may have killed him," Dawson replied.

"This is based on the fact that Lee has not made himself available to the GBI for an interview?"

Dawson recognized the tone the judge used when he called the prime suspect "Lee" instead of something more dehumanizing.

"Well, it is based on the fact that Lee Acker is on the run, avoiding questioning. I went to his office, and his staff says he is too busy to meet with me. I called his phone and left voicemails asking he come by for an interview. I went by his house and left business cards telling him to call. Nothing. So, I obtained a search warrant for his home, and his wife did not know where he was. She thought he went up to their lake house on Lake Blackshear. I asked that some deputies in Crisp County look for him there, but they were unable to locate him at the house. Apparently, the Ackers just sold their lake place, so we reached out to—"

"Who signed a search warrant on the Acker home?"

"The magistrate judge, sir."

"The chief magistrate or the assistant judge in that office?"

"The assistant judge, sir, Judge—"

"The one that isn't a lawyer," the judge said, cutting him off.

Dawson nodded and began again, "This warrant is also appropriate because Collins started the investigation that put Cliff Acker in prison last year on RICO charges."

"That case went federal, Tim. You know that," the judge scoffed.

"You are right, but what you may not know is Jake Collins pushed that investigation into Cliff Acker hard. He handed it off to the feds once there were enough legs to the case. The Ackers and Collins were longtime friends, and starting up the prosecution of Cliff Acker created a rift between them all."

"Well, I imagine it did, Tim."

Dawson noticed the patronizing tone and felt he already knew the judge's decision was made.

Dawson doubled down. "Words were exchanged between the two men —we believe threats were exchanged."

"Is there any evidence that you have found during your investigation that links Lee to this crime? Other than the falling-out between the Acker boys and Jake?"

"There is evidence, Judge, albeit—"

"Must I remind you, Tim, probable cause is wholly objective. You must look for facts and circumstances that are within your knowledge, that are sufficient to warrant a prudent person—or one of reasonable caution—in believing, in the circumstances shown, that the suspect has committed, is committing, or is about to commit an offense."

The judge handed the paperwork back to Dawson and began to stand. "It is not a high bar, Tim. You haven't met it, though. Come back with something more and we can talk again."

The judge pulled the napkin from his lap and tossed it on the table.

"My door is always open, Tim. I must start getting ready to take my wife to the funeral."

"I understand, sir. I just think that time is of the essence here and—"

"Not now," the judge said, holding out his hand in the direction of the hallway. "I may be a sitting superior court judge, but it's my bride that hates to be late."

9

The Rio Grande splits the border between Laredo, Texas, and Nuevo Laredo, Mexico. There are four bridges that one can use to cross the river. Three bridges allow noncommercial traffic to cross—Gateway to the Americas, referred to as Bridge I, Juarez-Lincoln International, referred to as Bridge II, and Colombia Solidarity, referred to as Bridge III. Bridge IV, the World Trade Bridge, permits the crossing of commercial vehicles only. Texas and US trade organizations estimated that in northbound traffic alone, the bridges handled around 2.3 million trucks and five million cars last year. On top of the cars, trucks, and goods, people crossed the border every day to work on Texas soil and return south at the end of the day. An estimated 3.7 million pedestrians crossed Bridge I, the only bridge that allows foot traffic. Another eleven million people crossed as passengers in vehicles over the four bridges combined.

The volume of traffic that crosses *la frontera* is big business, and over half of the trade that is carried on land between Mexico and the United States comes right through Laredo, Texas. The amount of goods, people, and money crossing the border each day makes the bridges over the Rio Grande the most important access points along the 1,254-mile Texas-Mexico border. The border agents assigned to the bridges are overworked, underpaid, and under constant scrutiny from the national media. Accounting for everything and everyone that is coming northbound into the USA would be ambitious. Sure, there are arrests—people are detained, and drug busts happen—but the partnership is vital to the economies of Mexico and the United States. The money heads north—the opportunists head south.

Lee sat ten cars back, waiting to cross the Juarez-Lincoln International. He wiped sweat from his brow as he watched the Tuesday morning traffic ease by the border agents. Cameras pointed down on the cars as they maneuvered through the plaza and over the speed bumps. Up ahead, a light signaled to drivers whether they would be required to stop at the secondary checkpoint for an inspection. A green light meant the driver could carry on south. A red light meant the border agents would take a closer look at the vehicle, documents, and any items on board. As Lee approached, he watched as a light turned red for the vehicle two places ahead. Lee looked over at the inspection lane where dogs circled a vehicle being searched. Growing up bird hunting in the woods of Southwest Georgia, Lee enjoyed working with dogs as they flushed a covey of quail or dove into a duck pond. A dog at work is a happy dog, and the dogs working the border were no different than those hunting in the woods back home.

Pulling to a stop, Lee held in hand his new passport. He'd memorized the name and identifying information while in line. Lee had on a yellow polo with a company logo that read "Móvil Red, S.A." in black lettering. The Mexico-based company specialized in cell phone tower repair, and the Ford Focus that Lee now sat in held a vehicle permit registered in the company's name. Lee's new friend—Móvil Red employee of the year and preferred guest at the Loma Alta Motel—decided to call in sick today. The "stomach bug" would keep him out of work for a couple of days. The wonderful couple Lee met that morning would take the six grand shelled out for the passport, ID, and unofficial rental car to play the tables at a nearby Indian casino. The Ford Focus would then be reported stolen a few days later. The good folks at Móvil Red would be none the wiser. It's business on *la frontera*—everyone gets a cut.

"Good morning," Lee said as he handed the agent the blue book. A young guy of Latino descent with *J. Velazquez* stitched on the breast pocket of his uniform and a silver-and-blue Cowboy's bracelet on his right hand. "You see that game last night?"

"Good *W* for The Boys," came the reply from Velazquez.

The Dallas Cowboys, affectionately referred to by its fan base as "The Boys," won big against the Houston Texans the night before.

"I think we might finally have ourselves a quarterback," Lee added.

"About damn time," the agent said as he opened the passport. He bent the book open twice and turned it over to look at the spine. He glanced up at Lee and back at the passport in hand.

"You working over the border today?" the agent asked, carefully paging through the booklet.

"Sales meeting in Monterrey."

The agent nodded as he continued to examine the crisp, fraudulent pages. He looked back at Lee, his gaze lingering now on the logo stitched to Lee's borrowed polo. He pointed to the shirt. "You a salesman for Móvil Red?"

Lee kept his eyes on Velazquez as he considered the question.

"Started last month," Lee replied, his pulse picking up. He stopped himself before adding more. He knew next to nothing about the company.

"They headquartered in Monterrey?" the border agent asked, bending down close to the open window of the vehicle to return the booklet. As he did, he peered inside. If he was looking for the body, it was a thousand miles away.

"That's what they tell me," Lee said after a long pause, his heart squarely in his throat. He coughed twice in his hand, then pointed to the dogs in the secondary inspection area. "You ever work with those shepherds over there?"

The border agent stopped his scan of the interior and looked over at the dogs. He smirked at the question, no doubt recognizing the change in topic. His eyes returned to Lee and stayed there for a moment more, considering his next move. "That's not what I do, sir."

"It's fun to watch them work, though, right?" Lee added, his eyes locked in on the agent, heart hammering away.

"You're right about that," Velazquez replied, recognizing the challenge.

A horn sounded from somewhere in the long line of cars, prompting another blast in response. The border agent looked back at those drivers that were waiting, then slapped the top of the vehicle twice. He had real work to do. "There's a different kind of dog south of here. Have a safe trip."

Lee exhaled as he pulled forward—free to run on Mexican soil.

10

Grace Acker sat in her vehicle watching three news vans unpack their gear. They sat under the shade of the old oak trees at the entrance to the church. All three local news affiliates had a job to do—grab a story. Groups of people walked from the parking lot to the church. Most she recognized, many she considered friends. The funeral would be filled with people she grew up with. People asking about her life and asking where Lee was. She did not know where he was but couldn't tell anyone that. She would tell them he was working and came down with the flu while on the road. Something fierce that had him held up in a hotel room in Nashville, Dallas, or Atlanta. It didn't matter what city she chose because it was a lie.

She unlocked her cell phone and pressed the call button beside Lee's name. The call went straight to voicemail, and she hung up, frustrated. Why hadn't he called? Lee had the reputation of a hardworking, successful, and above all, loyal family man. A fair description of her husband, though embellished to some extent. Still, his family needed him now. Grace needed him now. He had to know that, wherever he was. Checking the time on the phone, she stepped out of the vehicle and strode toward the church. Paying her respects to Jake Collins and his family felt right. Her history with him—with the Collinses—compelled her to be there.

Grace grew up in Blakeston, just like Lee, Cliff, and Jake. She wasn't born there, but she moved to town at nine years old from Birmingham, Alabama. Grace didn't get to know Lee and Jake until years after her arrival, but she remembered Cliff Acker being one of her first friends in elementary school. As a scrawny blond-haired new kid, she kept to herself in the first weeks of recess.

There are eerie similarities in the interactions that take place on a playground full of children and a prison yard full of inmates. Humans naturally group up with their own kind to prey on the weaker members of the herd. Not knowing any of her fourth-grade classmates, Grace brought books to read by the trees bordering the school's soccer fields. Isolated from the playground monitor's view, Grace became the target of taunting in the first weeks of school. Not rattled by the clique's attempts to intimidate her, she did what any inmate or elementary school kid should do when facing a bully. She stayed calm and did not let them see her cry.

One afternoon, as the group of bullies made their way across the soccer fields to Grace's spot, Cliff hurried over. He told the group of fifth graders, "Don't y'all keep pickin' on my new friend Grace or else I'll diamond cut all of your asses!" The group turned and laughed at their new challenger. A smaller, younger, and lone aggressor that did not stand a chance against the pack in a fight. For nine-year-old Cliff Acker, World Championship Wrestling—or "wrastling"—formed a big part of his identity. Grace remembered Cliff looked poised to imitate Diamond Dallas Page's signature move on the Blake County Elementary playground. Bowing up to the kids from the next class up, he walked toward the group, ready to defend her. He looked fearless, a quality that Cliff Acker continued to exhibit throughout years to come, but his fearlessness and assistance was not needed that day on the playground.

As Grace walked toward the church, she smiled at the old memory because before little Cliff could step in, the scrawny blond-haired new girl dove at the lead bully in the pack, spearing him to the ground in Goldberg's signature move. Teachers swarmed the incident as a melee ensued. Pulling children from the pile, teachers hauled them off in groups of two toward their respective classrooms. The PE teacher held both Cliff and Grace by the collars of their shirts as he walked across the soccer field and basketball court to the school building. "Just like Goldberg!" Cliff said in a hushed voice, smiling at Grace. Even at that young age, her history looked destined to become intertwined with the Acker boys. As she waited in line to enter the sanctuary for Jake's funeral, neither Lee nor Cliff would be by her side.

"Good morning, Mrs. Acker," the usher said as he handed her a bulletin. He looked familiar, but she wasn't sure how they knew each other.

"Thank you," she said, looking down at the smiling photographs on the trifold in hand. The usher held a clipboard under his arm and pulled it out to mark his list.

"Is that a guest list you have there?" she asked as the line stalled ahead of her.

"Sort of," the usher replied. "The family asked us to direct some people not on this list to the overflow room. They want to make sure there is enough space in the sanctuary."

"Makes sense," she replied.

"I guess it's also for security purposes. You know how Congressman Collins can be."

"That I do," Grace replied.

"The family missed you at the viewing this morning," he said.

"I hated to miss it. I had a few errands to run for my daughter, Charlotte." Grace hated the feeling of lying, and she sensed this stranger knew quite a bit about her and her relationship with the Collinses. "I'm sorry, but I can't place you. Do we know each other?"

"John Deese," he said, not answering her question. "Never seen the church this busy. Please grab a seat, ma'am."

Not one to be brushed off, Grace held the line up behind her by saying, "Wait, but how do I know you?"

John smirked at the question. "I'm Jake's cousin from Atlanta. I work for the congressman now. We met some years back. I know your husband and brother-in-law, too."

Grace looked at him, trying to place the memory. The line now backed up, causing congregants in the first pews ahead of her to turn to look at the two speaking. "Well, nice to meet you, again."

"You too, Mrs. Acker."

Grace walked down the center aisle of the sanctuary and felt the eyes looking on. The truth was, people in town already knew law enforcement

searched the Acker home. She felt it. Many would be digging for information. Some new comment to add to the rumors around her husband's
involvement in the mysterious killing. Though suspicious to some, skipping
the viewing that morning allowed her to bypass those prodding questions
and avoid a funeral ritual that always made Grace feel uneasy. The scene of
family and friends standing around the open casket—wallowing in the
grief that comes with the death of a loved one—while others stand off to
the side talking football or politics. The stilted comments made to family
members of the deceased by strangers filing by the casket for one last look
at the dead body.

The viewing, though painful, was mandatory at a Southern funeral. Its
practice one that was just as much about paying respects to the dead as
honoring those that knew the deceased best. She was sure the family
noticed her absence at the viewing, but Grace could not bring herself to
attend. She and Jake had a history—before she became Grace Acker—but
it was all so long ago.

Grace found a seat on one of the last pews, near the back left of the
sanctuary. Looking over her shoulder, she saw a security type in a dark suit.
She noticed the gold pin of the United States Secret Service. The sanctuary,
already packed, had cameras set up in the rear to broadcast the funeral into
an overflow room. Another camera leaned against the wall from a private
videographer hired to shoot the service. The footage would be reviewed,
edited, and then distributed for media coverage and other political
purposes. When a United States congressman's son is murdered, the political types within his orbit came out for support. They also came out to give
advice on how to present the tragedy to the voters. Out of respect for the
family, the political team asked that no cameras or cell phones be used to
take photographs during the service. Grace suspected this request was so
that the Collins family and the team around it could control the narrative
surrounding the family's grief.

Grace pulled her phone out. A notification read that CharlieGirl18
posted a photo on social media of her running shoes. The caption,
"Clearing my head" made Grace's stomach hurt. She texted her daughter.
Are you home from school yet?

The familiar dots appeared on the screen of Grace's cell phone, indicating Charlotte's fingers were typing away on the other side. *Yes, just got home and going for a run.*

Trail run or road run? Grace texted back.

The dots appeared, then disappeared. Charlotte Acker played basketball and ran track at Blake County High School. An excellent athlete with college scholarships rolling in from Division I schools around the country.

Charlotte? Grace added.

Road run, I'll be safe Mom. Heart emoji.

Let me know when you get back home, please. Love you.

Grace put the phone back in her purse and looked up at the screen at the front of the sanctuary. It cycled through photos of Jake Collins in his thirty-seven years of life. The screen transitioned to a string of images from the high school years, and the memories rushed into Grace's view. Lee and Jake both graduated from high school the same year—class of 1998. Both standout athletes and exceptional students. Great friends and destined rivals. The two fought over everything young men can find to square off on. Their coaches and teammates still told stories about the fistfights that broke out between the two in the middle of drills. Born leaders assigned to the same battleship, fighting to take the helm. Together—in constant struggle against one another—they achieved great success. The old men in Blakeston's breakfast diners still told stories about the football, basketball, and baseball seasons put together by the boys of the class of 1998, 2A state champions in football and basketball, first runner-up in baseball.

Jake Collins led the Bobcats football team under the Friday night lights and combined with his star receiver, Lee Acker, for twenty-eight touchdowns during the fall of 1997. "Collins to Acker" could be heard over the radio time and again as the two sliced defenses across the state. A photo faded in of Jake and his father standing on a football field after the state championship win, smiling, celebrating. During the 1997–1998 basketball season, Lee and Jake combined for nearly 1,300 points. Opposing coaches nicknamed the two "Double Trouble" as teams found it impossible to guard both players on the defensive end of the court. An iconic photo of the two cutting down the nets together after their state championship win in early 1998 showed on the screen. A photo the locals knew well—it was still hanging in the downtown breakfast diner.

Another photo faded to view from the duo's last baseball season together. Lee hit twenty-two homeruns and stole thirty-five bases. He earned all-state honors and looks from professional scouts. Jake pitched four shutouts that season, including a perfect game during the team's playoff run. A junior herself at the time, Grace remembered the feel of the late evening sun as she watched the team make its playoff run. She remembered the players lining up to shake hands after the Bobcats lost the state title and her tears shed for Jake that day, for all the boys on the team. When the high school baseball season ended, the two once-in-a-generation athletes went their separate ways. Lee went on to Vanderbilt University in Nashville, Tennessee, on a baseball scholarship while Jake went on to The Citadel in Charleston, South Carolina, to play quarterback.

～

The lights in the sanctuary dimmed, and the Collins family filed in from a side door. William H. Collins, US Representative for Georgia's Second Congressional District, held hands with his wife, Lucy Kelley Collins. The congregants in the pews ahead lifted slightly from their seats to catch a better glimpse of the grieving couple. Congressman Collins in his dark suit, shiny hair. Lucy in a black designer dress, tears in her eyes. They stood at the front of the sanctuary as the pastor assumed his post at the pulpit to offer a greeting to the congregants. The organ groaned to life, and the pastor raised his hands, inviting everyone to stand and sing "Make Me a Channel of Your Peace," the opening hymn.

Maggie Reynolds, in her slender black dress, turned to Jim Lamb to say, "Is that Jake's actual mother?"

Lamb nodded.

"Babe alert," Maggie whispered.

"She was beautiful thirty-five years ago; she may be more so today."

Maggie looked over to Lamb to gauge his expression. With a look of stoic resignation, he said out of the corner of his mouth, "Reynolds, this is a funeral. Show some tact, will you?"

"Settle down, sergeant."

"It's gunnery sergeant."

Maggie noted the hint of a smile in Lamb's expression, and she turned her attention to the other attendees at the funeral. She spotted Grace Acker and said, "Lamb, did you see Grace Acker made it? Looks like her husband is not with her."

Lamb sighed as a lady in front of Maggie turned to give her a motherly eye. "Grace Acker and Jake Collins were high school sweethearts. Hot and heavy until he went off to school at The Citadel. She knows the family well."

"How did I not know that?" Maggie whispered to Lamb.

"Lousy research on your opposing counsel is how. You missed the intel on Jake's high school romance. It'll be your downfall in the end. Your career might already be over. Pack your shit, Reynolds, you're fired."

"Language, counselor," Maggie quipped. "While I appreciate the sarcasm, you know I like to be prepared."

The hymn ended, and the pastor motioned for those in attendance to take a seat. Maggie looked back over at Grace Acker and wondered about the history that existed between her and Jake Collins. A gorgeous woman, there was no denying that. Her conservative black dress with a high neckline did not hide her figure. Maggie met her once at a party, a charity event for the humane society. Smart, attractive—drank bourbon and had a wonderful laugh. She could see the appeal. If the rumors were true, the investigators could say Lee Acker committed the murder out of jealousy. It would not be a stretch for the prosecution's theory of the case if they could find evidence of Jake and Grace rekindling their old high school flame. Give the jurors one look at Grace Acker on the stand—without her uttering a word—and she would prove problematic for the poor bastard employed as defense counsel.

The pastor invited an uncle in the family to read a word of scripture from the Bible and then a poem by Alfred, Lord Tennyson. Maggie shook her head, half listening to the pastor's words as she thought. The story of Lee Acker intrigued her. Especially since he was now apparently on the run, evading questioning. The problem that all criminal defense attorneys have when representing clients charged with a murder is they never get to meet with the client soon enough. People commit the crime—allegedly— then commit a series of stupid acts thereafter. Whether it's simply interviewing with the investigators without seeking advice from an attorney or not burying the body deep enough, your average murderer is an idiot. Maggie represented people every day that were smart enough to cover up petty crimes, but when it came to her clients charged in shootings or homicides, they always had to tell someone that they did it—it baffled her. Maggie always said, "If I snap and take someone out, I'll never tell a soul—that's half the battle."

Maggie turned to Lamb and asked, "Who is the family attorney for the Ackers?"

"Bruce Tevens."

"He doesn't know the first thing about trying a criminal case."

"Tevens is light on his feet, Reynolds. Careful with those assumptions."

Maggie shot him an eye. "You ever seen him slumming it with the rest of us working the criminal trial calendars?"

"The family refers out all of their criminal defense work. That's what they did for the younger Acker, Cliff, when he got tangled up in that mess a few years back. The family would do the same for anything Lee gets accused of. Tevens advises them on who to hire, then acts as family counsel through the process."

Maggie mulled this over as she thought back to a few years ago when the federal indictment came down against Cliff Acker. The Acker family hired a defense attorney from Miami, Florida, that specialized in RICO defense. Maggie, early in her career at the time, went to a hearing to watch the Floridian handle a pretrial motion on an evidentiary issue. She left the courtroom of the federal courthouse in Albany, Georgia, thoroughly impressed.

"What was that lawyer's name that handled the defense for Cliff?"

"Can't remember. Hell of a fighter, though," Lamb replied. "Can we continue this chat later, Reynolds?"

She leaned to the side toward Lamb and gave his shoulder a light bump as the pastor asked everyone to bow their heads for prayer. Maggie closed her eyes and ran through the advice she'd have given Lee Acker before he decided—like a fool—to take off and run:

"You have plenty of money, and you can fight this case. We'll hammer the prosecution with the best defense experts in the game. Experts in ballistics, fingerprints, toxicology, pharmacology—you name it, your budget can afford it. The value of not spending life behind bars is priceless, am I right? We can hit them with resources the State does not have, and the prosecutors will not be prepared to confront. When they issue a warrant, you turn yourself in and you don't say a word. Not a word. You have ties to the community; you have never committed a crime in your life, and you are not a flight risk. We will get you a bond, and you will fight this thing from the outside. I am the best there is, and I win cases every day with less. You follow my advice and I'll keep you out of prison."

11

The graveside ceremony would be held at Kelley Hill Plantation, and Grace followed the funeral procession as it snaked its way through town. Her emergency blinkers engaged, she kept the windows rolled up on her vehicle to allow the cool air conditioning to do its work. The sound of the blinkers clicked away as she looked out on the rows of people standing on the sidewalks. The entire town stood behind the Collins family. Storefronts with signs out that read, "Thoughts and Prayers for the Collinses" and "RIP Jake" to show support. The local VFW stood in salute as the hearse drove by; American flags resting on the rear of their motorcycles waved in the breeze. A large sign erected nearby read, "Thank You for Your Service, First Lieutenant Jake Collins" in red, white, and blue lettering.

Jake Collins entered the US Army after graduating from The Citadel, and then served two tours in Iraq, his second tour cut short by shrapnel from a roadside bomb. The explosion knocked Jake unconscious and lodged ball bearings, rocks, and a nail in part of his right leg. The great runner, elusive as a deer moving through the South Georgia woods, walked the rest of his life with a slight limp discernible only to those that remembered the gait of the cocky boy. The IED also took the lives of two soldiers in his platoon—a tragedy that forever changed Jake as both a leader and a person.

The procession headed out of town and picked up speed on GA 39. Grace tapped the voice command button on her steering wheel and said, "Call Charlotte" in the direction of the touch screen. The phone rang four times and went to voicemail. "This is Charlotte, I can't get to my phone right now. Leave a message and I'll call you back."

Grace thought about leaving a voicemail but decided against it. She would send her daughter a text message when she parked, as that seemed to be the only way her daughter wanted to communicate these days. She tapped the voice command again. "Call Lee," she said. The call went straight to voicemail. "This is Lee Acker; you know what to do." The voicemail was full.

Grace turned at the entrance to the plantation, and the tires transitioned from the smooth asphalt to the unpaved road. She rolled the windows down in her vehicle to take in the smell of the woods. The warm air rushed in and felt comforting on her arms and face. As she followed the clay path that wound to the backside of the property, she tried to remember the last time she'd ventured out there—maybe seventeen or eighteen years now. Back in high school. Back when she and Jake were together.

The road opened up to a grassy field, and a man in a suit and bowtie pointed her into a makeshift parking spot. Grace texted her daughter, checked her lips in the mirror, and grabbed her sunglasses from the center console. As she stepped out of the vehicle, her heels sank a bit into the field. She looked up at the hill and heard the whine of golf carts carrying attendees to the small family cemetery on the other side. A voice over her shoulder said, "Hey there, Mrs. Acker, need a ride?"

Grace turned and saw John Deese at the wheel of an all-terrain-style golf cart. "That would be great. Thank you, John, and please call me Grace. Aren't we the same age?"

He shrugged. Something about his presence made her feel uneasy, but she climbed into the golf cart that seated four. They stopped to pick up an older couple exiting their vehicle and then headed up the hill.

"I thought it was a nice service," John said, clearly trying to make conversation for the new riders.

"Reverend Moon is truly gifted," Grace replied. "Jake would have enjoyed his message this morning. He would have hated all the sappy things said about him, though. He was not much for the mushy stuff."

"He was such a sweetheart, though," said the woman riding on the back of the golf cart.

"Big-time sweetheart!" John added with a sarcastic grin.

"Is this Kelley Hill?" the woman asked.

"It's called Parker's Knoll," Grace said, feeling a bit like a tour guide. "Lucy's family—that is, Lucy Collins—has owned this land since the 1870s. Kelley Hill is another half mile up the river."

"This is probably the largest slice of privately owned land in Georgia," John added.

"It is beautiful out here," the woman remarked. "Jake was a good man, and I guess this is as good a place as any to lay to rest."

They all nodded and continued in the polite conversation that takes place at funerals.

When they reached the top, John helped the older woman from the cart and returned to his place in the driver's seat. He looked at Grace, arms draped over the small steering wheel of the golf cart. "Must be a little strange coming out here today?"

Grace narrowed her eyes at him from behind her sunglasses but said nothing. He held the gaze, then, with that smirk, he turned the wheel and headed back down the hill.

～

Congressman Collins—Bill, as everyone called him—walked to the front of the small gathering to thank everyone for being there. The casket, now closed behind him, sat under a small tent that provided shade to a handful of the people seated in the front row. The hill looked out over a bend in the Chattahoochee River that set the boundary between Alabama and Georgia. Its water glistened in the sunlight, and Bill turned to take in the view before beginning his second eulogy of the day. His first, at the church, was nothing short of spectacular. His words moved the sanctuary to tears. He showed the hurt of a father grieving the loss of his only son. He did so without anger—but the cameras were off now.

When he turned back to the group, he began with the poise and control of a seasoned politician—but tears in his eyes began to run, and he balled his fists in front of him. "When Jake was a boy, I'd take him up on this very hill every now and then to talk about a man's legacy. I explained to Jake that it was not enough for a man to simply be a good person. A man must do great things to be remembered. He must do such great things—feats that involve risk, hardship, and tragedy—so that those who write the history books are compelled to include his name. My son, Jake, was a great man and was not done with his contribution to history."

Sniffles in the group could be heard, and Lucy Collins cried harder under the shade of the tent.

"Jake understood at a young age that it would take grit and sweat to cement his legacy in this world. That it would take courage and sacrifice to do the things required of his destiny. He recognized his responsibility."

Bill Collins then began to move from his position at the front of the group and walked along the grave markers closest to the seating. "You may recognize some of the names on these headstones, but most you won't." Pausing, he squatted down in a catcher's stance in front of one weathered marker—the gifted presenter understood the theatric use of his body—and said, "Here rests former Colonel Nathan J. Parker himself, 1837 to 1873." He grabbed a handful of grass from beside the headstone and tossed it into the breeze as he stood to look back up at the group. "He is gone," he said with a shrug. "Most of you today don't know the history of Colonel Parker. Most of you don't know that this very hill we stand on is named after Nathan Parker.

"He farmed most of his life on a piece of family land outside Darien, Georgia. When the War Between the States broke out, he joined the Confederate Army to fight for the cause. Colonel Parker, by all accounts, fought gallantly in the war. His men participated in the Seven Days Battle and proved instrumental in the South's victory in Chancellorsville." Men in the group that knew their Civil War history, or wished to portray that they did, demonstrated their approval by nodding noticeably at the mention of the battles.

"When the war ended, Colonel Parker moved with his wife, Sarah, to

Blakeston. He started in on the timber business, and Sarah had their first child in 1866. He partnered with those in this area and lifted the town up with his efforts. He employed those around him and helped them feed their families. In a relatively short amount of time, Nathan grew to be wealthy."

Bill Collins looked out into the group to find the eyes of Grace Acker. "His great efforts did not come without opposition, though. A rivalry developed as Nathan Parker amassed land and resources with his timber business. Parker's competitor, a man by the name of Joseph Cobb, began buying timberland on the other side of the Chattahoochee. Like Parker, Cobb moved to the area after serving a short stint in the war with the 5th Alabama Infantry. Most accounts indicate Cobb deserted his company and resorted to robbing Southern farmers during the war."

Bill Collins shook his head and pointed out across the river as he recounted the story to the captive audience. Stepping aside to give the attendees a full view of the landscape, Bill Collins pointed to a rocky set of rapids at the foot of the hill. "Sometime in the fall of 1873, Nathan Parker and Joseph Cobb met down at this rocky spot to discuss a partnership going forward. See, opportunists from the North were flooding the area. Cobb's operation cut and sold timber to the highest bidder. Cobb didn't acknowledge the threat of these outside interests on our soil. Interests that wished to disrupt our Southern way of life. Cobb did not recognize the need to form a cooperative effort with the political powers of that time."

Bill shoved one hand in his pocket and talked with the other, palm up, pleading his case. "The men could stall the profiteers' advances on Southern resources. Cobb just had to agree to terms. Parker presented a joint scheme to Cobb that ceded some control over Cobb's operation to Parker and his affiliates. They would all make more money and keep the carpetbaggers from encroaching any further.

"However, reason did not prevail. Cobb insulted Parker by spitting at his feet," Bill said with a shrug. "The two wrestled in the rapids of the river until men from both outfits rushed in to separate the pair. Soaked in river water, the two groups exchanged threats from their respective riverbanks. Guns drawn, the parties backed away into the woods to avoid bloodshed."

Bill Collins paused, unbuttoned the top button of his dress shirt, and loosened his tie. He found Grace Acker's eyes again. "The following morning, as Nathan Parker trotted his horse down the tree line between his family's property and the river, a bullet ripped through his back." Bill turned to point at a hill on the other side of the river. A fire tower peeked up from the trees. "Most believe the bullet came from the high ground. A crack shot from just below that tower across the way." Almost on cue, a glint of the sunlight illuminated the metal hooding on the tower. "A second shot missed Parker but struck his horse in the flank. The reins, wrapped around Nathan's arm, jerked as the horse felt the sting of the bullet. Scared, the horse drug Parker along the ground back to the family's barn. His wife, Sarah, found him hanging lifeless from the horse. Her diary recounts the event. She described his face as being scraped and bloodied, nearly indiscernible."

Removing his jacket, Bill Collins hung it over the rear of the chair next to Lucy. He rolled the arms of his dress shirt up and pulled an empty chair close to the casket. He sat down in the chair, sweating. He stared at the ground in front of him and said, "Kelley Hill Plantation is named after Arthur Kelley. Many of you probably know the name.

"Arthur Kelley was a great man. Sarah remarried to Arthur in 1875, and they had a child together, lost another during childbirth. Arthur served four terms in the Georgia House of Representatives and grew his timber business to one of the largest in the industry at the turn of the twentieth century. He made decisions for his family and for this community that are still felt today."

He set his hand on the casket beside him and rubbed a smudge off the box's oak exterior. "Everyone remembers Arthur, but what about Nathan Parker? Why would a patriot that was murdered just down this hill be forgotten?" Bill Collins stared at the casket that his son lay in. "We remember him, though, don't we, Jake?" The orator paused, and a silence blanketed the group. "We know they couldn't prove it back then, but Cobb shot and killed Nathan Parker on his own farm. Cobb shot him in the back, like a coward." The weight of the silence glued the family and friends to their seats as the one-man act unfolded in front of them. "We know the reason people remember Arthur Kelley, don't we, Jake? Not because of his work in the state house or his business deals. No, none of that. We remember him because he finished what had to be done. Arthur shot and killed that son of a bitch Joseph Cobb for what he did.

"I won't let them forget you, son. I won't let anyone forget the man that you were."

12

Lee sat at a picnic table outside a gas station twenty minutes north of Monterrey. Droplets beaded on a bottle of beer that pinned the corner of his map to the table, leaving wet rings at its edges. He'd backed the Ford Focus up to the table so he could listen to music on the radio while enjoying the sunshine. Off in the distance, he spotted a small mountain range. He found it on the map—*Cerro de la Silla*. Monterrey's urban sprawl enveloped the short ridge that towered above the city's millions of residents.

Lee understood *cerro* to mean "hill," and he smiled to himself. In South Georgia, this "hill" might be the highest elevation point in the state. He tried to imagine the tall pine trees and wire grass at its foothills, changing the identity of the rural landscape he grew up on. It would bear the name of a long-forgotten Confederate soldier or ousted Native American tribe— both troublesome chapters in the history of the South. Chapters Lee's vision for the South conflicted with. Staring at the mountain, he decided it was better suited for this landscape. The stark contrast of the green elevated peaks against the blue Mexican sky made quite the welcome card for first-time visitors. Its beauty could not stay hidden. Not today, there wasn't a cloud in the sky.

Lee stretched his arms behind him to twist a few times and loosen his back. The toll road down from Laredo made for an easy trip, but fatigue crept in during the last stretch. His body felt tight. The fresh air and cold beer helped a little. Lee found the roadway that the gas station fronted and traced a route into *San Pedro Garza García*—a quiet neighborhood outside Monterrey. He planned to find a hotel and stay there for a few nights before moving on south. Somewhere with Wi-Fi and a warm shower. Somewhere that would not require he hand over a credit card for incidentals.

Stripping off the work polo, he tossed it in the back seat of the vehicle to change into one of his own button-downs. He reached down under the seat and popped the metal clasps on one of the manila envelopes. Each envelope held twelve thousand five hundred dollars, bound together with rubber bands. Lee felt inside the envelope and pulled a roll of five hundred out along with one stack of a thousand. He fastened the envelope again and slid it back under the seat. Walking around to the rear hatch of the vehicle, he opened the suitcase to grab the new shirt, some deodorant, and a ball cap. He rechecked the location of his Beretta 92FS and slammed the hatch shut. He finished his beer and walked back toward the gas station to grab a coffee for the road.

As Lee crossed the parking lot, a pickup truck with a gold star on it pulled up to the fuel pumps closest to the doors. The words *Fuerza Civil* straddled the insignia. Two men stepped out of the truck and onto the hot pavement. Each wore aviator sunglasses and bulletproof vests. As Lee passed them, he nodded. The older of the two nodded back. They were members of the state police in Nuevo León. A police force charged with protecting Nuevo León's residents and investigating criminal activity taking place within the state.

When Lee reached the door, he held it open behind him as the younger police officer approached. The man said nothing and then ducked into the store as the sound of gunfire began—*pop, pop, pop!* Three rounds went off from across the road and pinged against the side of the officers' pickup. The shrill sound against the metal reverberated throughout the store in slow motion, and Lee dropped to the ground while glass sprayed from another bullet's impact on the front window of the store. Screams from people in the back of the building erupted, and Lee looked to the officer some ten feet away to see if he was hit. The officer looked frantic, scrambling around the floor. He was unhurt but searching for something he'd dropped. Lee scanned the tile and saw the officer's fallen sidearm had slid under the edge of an energy drink display case. The two men made eye contact as Lee put his hand under the case and slid the weapon back to the officer. This time the young man nodded in gratitude.

Three more rounds went off, pinging against the pickup truck again. The radio on the officer's hip lit up with conversation from dispatch. Lee crawled up to the front wall of the store and crouched beside the officer, both low under the front windows. The officer began to say something when another cascade of glass erupted. Lee pulled the brim of his cap low to shield his eyes. Four more shots—*pop, pop, pop, pop!* The sound came from a large-caliber weapon, Lee knew that much. All from the same position with no return volleys from the other officer out at the pump—he had to be wounded. Lee peeked up above the window and saw a body lying on the ground between the truck and fuel pump.

"Your partner," Lee said, tapping the young officer on the shoulder, "he's hurt, *está herido.*" Lee gripped his side to illustrate.

The young officer reached for his radio and called in to dispatch an update. He waited, crouched with his pistol at the ready.

Lee turned to the officer and with exaggerated hand motions said, "Cover me! *Cúbreme!*"

The young officer reached out to grab Lee and said, "No, no, you stay."

Lee pointed to the open window, courtesy of their shooter, and made a gun symbol pointing out toward the direction of the bullets. The officer understood and flashed Lee the bird with a grin.

Good sense of humor, Lee thought.

Then, walking like a duck, Lee shimmied his way to the swinging front door. *Pop, pop, pop*—return shots went off feet away from Lee. Lee pushed the door and bear-crawled out onto the pavement of the parking lot, head low with his cap turned backward. Glass covered the ground, and he tightened his fists to avoid cutting the palms of his hands. Instead of making his way around the truck, he opted to crawl under the chassis. The truck felt hot above Lee's back as he slid across the oil-smudged pavement on his stomach. The older officer, now within arm's reach, lay on his side gripping his left thigh.

"Can you crawl?" Lee yelled.

The older officer turned toward Lee, startled. Lee made a crawling motion and pointed to the gas station.

"*No, no puedo,*" the older officer exclaimed.

Lee crawled closer and then rolled out from under the pickup. "*Su pistola, dame su pistola.*"

The older officer shook his head.

"Give me your damn gun, I am trying to help!"

The older officer understood and unclipped the sidearm—a Heckler & Koch USP9. Lee heard over his shoulder more rounds from the young officer in the store followed by a response from the shooter across the road. Lee moved to the edge of a pump and decocked the lever on the left of the weapon. He saw two men standing in the roadway in black masks. *Pop, pop, pop, pop!* Two shots pinged against the pickup, feet away. The other two careened overhead. Lee went back to the edge of the pump and fired five shots in the direction of the men. The shots felt good, and the smooth weapon performed as intended. *Pop, pop*—two more from the young officer, and Lee sent another three shots across the road. Lee peered around the corner again, and one of the men at the roadway knelt, gripping his shoulder. Lee's adrenaline brimmed, and he felt his heartbeat in his ears. He fired three more shots and tried to remember how many remained of the fifteen rounds in his clip.

"Can you stand?" Lee shouted back to the older officer. "If I help, can you walk at all?" Lee said as he made a stick-walking motion with his index and middle finger.

"*Sí, con su asistencia.*"

Lee turned to the road again, fired three more shots, then shimmied back over to the older officer. Sirens in the distance whined. "Your friends are on the way? *Sus amigos?*" Lee asked.

The older officer nodded, and Lee hoisted the man up on his feet. A tailgate slammed and tires squealed across the road. The older officer hobbled over to get a view of the pickup truck.

"They are going north," Lee said.

The older officer said nothing but nodded.

"Who were they? *Quienes eran ellos?*"

"*Lobos*," the older cop said.

"Wolves?" Lee asked, clarifying the response.

The older cop nodded again as Lee helped him around to the tailgate of the police truck. The younger officer joined them and looked concerned. Blood seeped into the older officer's pant leg, and the younger officer pulled a medical kit from the rear of his truck to begin administering first aid. Lee wiped the gun in his hand down with his shirt and set it on the tailgate beside the older officer's boots. As he turned, the older man grabbed Lee by the elbow. The grip felt strong, and it surprised Lee.

"*A dónde va?* Where are you going?"

"I can't stay. I have to go. Do you understand?" Lee replied. "*No me puedo quedar.*" Lee added, unsure if the older man understood, "*Entiende?*"

"You can't stay?" the younger officer said as he bit white medical tape from a roll with his teeth. "Why? We need to ask you questions."

"I need you to understand, I can't be involved."

The younger officer looked to the older officer. "*Dice que tiene que ir y que no puede estar involucrado.*"

They both paused—the whine of the sirens grew louder—and the older man said, "*Está bien.* Go."

"What's your name, cowboy?" the younger officer said, with that same smile from inside the gas station. His thick accent naturally looping the words together in his native Spanish tongue.

"Lee."

"Lee?" the older man asked.

Lee nodded and shook hands with both men.

"*Gracias.* Go, go," the older officer said with large hand motions. "Go, go, *amigo.*"

Lee hustled to his vehicle as two state police trucks whipped into the parking lot, late for the party.

~

Lee sat on the edge of the bed in his hotel room staring down at the cell phone in hand. He tossed it onto the bed. An article from the *Blake County News* was still open on the screen. He walked into the bathroom, stripped his shirt off, and started the water in the tub. Looking in the mirror, he needed a shave. Flipping the knob on the tub's faucet, he engaged the shower and undressed while waiting for the water to warm. The watch on his wrist read 5:45 p.m., but the local time was an hour behind. He adjusted the hour hand and then set the watch on the bathroom counter. Stepping into the warm water, it felt good to wash the sweat and motor oil off. As he stood under the warm showerhead, he mulled over the top story from the newspaper back home. "Authorities Look to Question Suspect in Death of Congressman's Son," read the first headline on the website that evening. It would be on the front page of the newspaper tomorrow. The town would be abuzz. Charlotte's friends from school would whisper behind her back. Grace would face stares from strangers. Their world would be upside down, and Lee stood miles away.

Lee stepped out of the shower and dried off. He turned the television on in the bedroom area and found an English-language news channel. He turned the volume up to be able to hear the commentary from the bathroom and collected his Dopp kit from the suitcase. The Beretta peeked out from the bag. Lee decided to move it to the drawer in the nightstand by the bed. Wildfires raged on in California that week, and the correspondent on the screen detailed the experiences of those fleeing their homes and businesses to avoid the spread. Her British accent made the events in California seem as if they were happening on the other side of the world. Lee shaved and listened to the news flip between international soccer, immigration issues on the US-Mexican border, and the upcoming elections in the United States.

International news organizations covering US politics rarely engaged in the partisan discussions you find on the domestic juggernauts like Fox News, CNN, and MSNBC. They presented the news, without slanted opinions, and Lee appreciated that. He stepped out of the bathroom to better listen to the reporter on screen as she went over the upcoming campaign events leading up to the presidential election. Both the nominees were slated to appear for a debate on the campus of the University of Texas at El Paso that week. Then they'd continue on to hold rally after rally across the country. The "battleground" states, as they were often called, were the focus of both candidates' schedules. The correspondent did not mention any of the seats open for election in the Senate or House of Representatives.

Lee dressed and grabbed his room key to head downstairs. He took the stairs down from the fourth floor and walked through the main lobby of the hotel. Approaching the hotel's front desk, he asked for a dinner recommendation.

The concierge smiled. "*Muy buenas tardes, señor.* There are many good options that you can walk to from the hotel. Of course, you can also dine here at the hotel tonight. Should I provide you the dinner menu to review?"

"No, thank you. I've been traveling today, and the fresh air will do me some good."

"Of course, sir. In that case, I recommend *Quinta Real.* The chef is a friend of the hotel, and his menu is one of the best for visitors to this region."

"Can you mark it on a map for me?" Lee asked.

The concierge nodded, then signaled with his hand that Lee wait a moment. The gentleman stepped to his side to pick up a ringing phone at the desk and began speaking French into the receiver. He spoke with patience, and Lee appreciated the concierge's command of his craft. With Monterrey playing an important role as a hub for business in Mexico, the hotel received international guests year-round. Its hospitality staff appeared well prepared to cater to businesspeople from all over the world. As the concierge hung up the phone, he apologized for the wait and then pulled a glossy map from under the counter. He pointed to the recommended restaurant's location and traced a walking route for Lee to follow. Lee thanked him, then asked to exchange out one thousand dollars as he placed the stack of bills on the front desk.

The concierge obliged. "Here you are, sir, your map and pesos." He smiled again, then asked, "Are you here for business or pleasure?"

"Both," Lee replied, placing another hundred-dollar bill on the desk for the man. "What's your name?"

"Eugenio," the concierge said as he pulled the bill from the counter. "Anything else I can help you with, sir?"

"I'd like two newspapers brought to my room in the morning. The best Mexican newspaper in Monterrey and a US paper as well."

"I'll have someone bring them up in the morning," the concierge replied.

"Also, I need help finding someone. This person is someone I have business with, and I'd like to do some preliminary research."

The concierge paused a moment as he evaluated the request. Guests from the United States frequented his hotel, and he found the businessmen to be presumptuous, ignorant at times. This guest was an American but seemed sincere. "I can get you some recommendations for a private investigator, sir."

"Thank you, Eugenio."

"Of course, sir. *Buen provecho.*"

13

Three days had passed since the funeral. As promised by Judge John Balk, the courts in the Southwest Judicial Circuit held no criminal proceedings that week. The judge issued an order effectively memorializing the decision to undertake a week of mourning in observance of Jake Collins's death. The order, now dubbed by the local members of the criminal defense bar the "Sitting Shiva Order," stalled an already backlogged criminal docket. The judge mourned from golf courses around Destin, Florida, and would return to the bench Monday, tanned and reinvigorated.

Maggie Reynolds pictured the judge having his customary "back nine" cigar as she sat in the attorney visitation room at the Seminole County Jail waiting for two clients to be brought up. Both Black men in their early twenties facing gang-related charges, both being held without bond. She doubted the judge cared much for the plight of her clients, and that, unfortunately, fit perfectly into her clients' expectations for the justice system in rural Georgia.

A knock on the open door caused her to raise her eyes to the hallway.

"Hey, Reynolds," called a voice as it passed the open door. Maggie recognized it.

"That you, Dawson?"

Tim Dawson stopped and backpedaled a few steps to look into the visitation room. "You know it. Who is the lucky dog that drew you as his attorney this week?"

"Hopefully someone you arrested. Tends to be shoddy work."

"Hey, now!" he said with a grin. "Let's see how much trash you are talking when we have a hearing on that Strickland case."

"If we have a hearing, Special Agent Dawson," she responded, wagging a finger.

"Your client decided to just plead guilty? Excellent decision, if you ask me."

Maggie raised her eyebrow at the agent. He looked sharp today. Black slacks and a blue polo made of some dry-fit material. Their paths had already crossed on a few cases in Dawson's first two years on assignment with the GBI's Region 15 Investigative Office. Dawson's work tended to be thorough, and Maggie enjoyed his even-natured sense of humor. Maggie dealt with cops and other lawyers all day, men mostly. They excluded her, whether intentionally or unintentionally, from the local boys' club. Dawson never gave her that impression.

"Are you prejudging my client?" Maggie said with a smile. All cops, even the good ones like Dawson, considered their suspects guilty upon arrest.

"Damn right I am," Dawson remarked. "But hey, if your boy wants a trial, we can give him one. DA will have him put away for ten years minimum."

She crossed her legs and made a note, mumbling to herself, "Minimum ten years, plead guilty, Tim Dawson does not support Americans' right to a fair trial."

"Don't say I didn't warn you."

"I have a little surprise ready in that case," Maggie said, grinning from her chair. "Just watch your six, Dawson."

"Okay, okay, counselor," he said, backing away. "I'll be on the edge of my seat until then."

"That's what I like to hear."

"You going out to play volleyball tonight at the Sandbar?" Dawson asked, pivoting subjects.

"You one of those volleyball nuts, Dawson?"

"Only when there are pitchers of beer on the line," he said, swinging his arms as if warming up to hit the court.

As his arm swung, he nearly hit the young man walking in behind him. Maggie's client, Eli Jones, stepped to the side, nearly missing a backhand to the side of the head. He wore an orange jumpsuit and held a spiral notebook in his hand.

"Whoa, sorry, my man," Dawson said, patting the young man on the shoulder.

"You strike my client?" Maggie said, teasing.

Eli stood there, unsure whether to wait in the hall until the back-and-forth concluded.

"Have a seat, Eli," Maggie said before Dawson could reply. "I'll report Special Agent Dawson to the appropriate parties after our meeting."

Dawson backed out of the room and mimicked throwing a ball into the air and spiking it down the hall. "I'll see you out there, counselor."

Maggie stood from her seat and pushed the steel door closed. The room had cinder block walls, two beat-up office chairs, and a square wooden desk. There were no recording devices, at least there weren't supposed to be, and cell phone reception was sketchy at best. She turned to Eli and apologized for not having visited him recently. He shot her a suspicious look, mostly due to her joking demeanor with a law enforcement officer.

Arms folded in front of him, Eli said, "Don't sweat it. I know you're busy." Maggie nodded and opened Eli's file on the square table beside her chair. He understood she had hundreds of files she was responsible for. Even though it was something she wouldn't be able to change, she still apologized to clients frustrated with the lack of communication with her directly.

"My momma called your office. You getting her calls? Nobody calls her back," Eli said.

Maggie nodded again as she handed a packet of discovery documents to him. Clients got frustrated waiting for her to visit. Waiting in the belly of the county jail with no call or visit, they pounced on the first opportunity to chew her out. When she first started practicing, she tried to quiet their concerns about not seeing her. She would explain in detail how many clients she has to see on a weekly basis. How many hearings she had to attend. How a trial would tie up an entire week. It never worked. Her clients only cared about one case—their case.

"Ms. Maggie, what's going on with my case? You aren't doing anything, it feels like to me. I know you're supposed to be good and all. They just got me locked in here four months now. I haven't even been to court. I see guys every day walking out on bonds. Dudes charged with shit way worse than what they're sayin' I did. A white boy walked out yesterday on some charges for touchin' some kids. That's some bullshit. I'm tired of not knowing what's going on, and I need someone who is serious about getting me out."

Maggie sat, legs crossed, listening to her client.

"I mean, we don't have a lot of money, Ms. Maggie. If we have to go hire a lawyer that will fight, I just need to tell my momma. I know you work for the judge and all. I heard in the—"

"I don't work for the judge," Maggie interjected. She held her client's gaze, challenging him. His eyes flicked away to the cinder block wall.

"Okay, well, the government pays you like they pay the DA and the judge."

"I work for you, Eli," Maggie responded. "That's my job."

Unconvinced, Eli continued, "I heard in the back that this judge thinks I'm a thug. That he doesn't let anybody out charged with gang shit. I'm not in a gang, Ms. Maggie. How are they keepin' me in here on gang charges when there is no gang?"

Eli was almost done with his tirade, and Maggie sat with a confident, knowing expression on her face. She'd earned a reputation for fighting for her clients during her short time as a public defender. Her results in the courtroom were second to none. She knew it. The prosecutors and judges knew it. Still, she was a public defender, and her work came without an invoice. Her client was rightfully skeptical about her motivation. Money motivates—especially attorneys.

"Eli, I am here today to talk about your case. You can sit here and act like a jerk, or we can be productive with this time."

"I want a bond, Ms. Maggie," he said, his arms still crossed.

"I am working on your bond. The judge denied you bond last time because the investigator testified that he couldn't find you for over two months. The judge cited concerns with you showing up to court."

"I was at my momma's in Albany. They never looked there, never called any of my people. They went by my girl's place twice, and she told them I wasn't there. I wasn't."

Maggie could feel her young client's resentment as it radiated off his body. Eli did hide out in Albany whether he wanted to admit it or not. That testimony was not what kept him from getting a bond in front of Judge Balk, though. No, the problem for Eli was the stack of photos the investigator brought with him to the bond hearing. All photos of Eli, and other young Black men, throwing up signs with their hands—gang signs, the judge deduced. The investigator got a warrant to search Eli's social media accounts, and the evidence was not good.

"Look, these photos and messages they got out of your accounts are going to be a problem. The grand jury indicted you last week, and your arraignment is scheduled for this coming Monday."

"Will we be able to go for a bond Monday?" Eli asked, maintaining his focus on his pretrial release.

"No, you won't get a hearing on the bond issue Monday," Maggie said, trying to steer her client back toward her goals for the meeting. "Your arraignment gives you the opportunity to hear the charges read aloud to you in open court. All you can do that day is enter a 'guilty' or 'not guilty' plea to the offenses in the indictment. We will enter your 'not guilty' plea on the record, and I'll tell the court that you demand a jury trial."

"How long till I get a trial?" Eli leaned forward in his chair and started flipping through the packet his attorney handed over to him. "And what is all this mess in this cop's report here?"

"That is your discovery packet. I filed a demand for discovery in your case, and that required the prosecutor to hand over all the information, good or bad, that they are going to use against you in the case. That report you are pointing to is the investigator's summary of what he did during the investigation of your case. Let me make something clear, Eli. That's law enforcement's version of how they see your case. That is not a summary of what really happened."

"Seems like the judge and prosecutor already got together and decided what is going to happen," Eli said, flipping through the photos in the packet. "How'd they get all this mess? I had my accounts set to private, and these messages are supposed to be private, too."

"The warrant, Eli. Judge Balk signed a search warrant that made Facebook and these other platforms produce downloads of what was on the accounts."

Eli shook his head and pointed to a row of messages with his girlfriend's name on them. Photos accompanied her explicit comments. "They printed my girl's naked photos in here? This is messed up."

"I am going to file some motions requesting that this information be excluded from your trial. I'll give you copies of what is being filed next week."

Eli reached the section of his packet with the indictment. He turned the page around to Maggie and pointed to the three counts he faced in the indictment. "When the hell did I get charged in a robbery?" Eli said, now standing.

Maggie let Eli pace a few steps to the steel door in the silence. Laughter from a few inmates echoed down the hall, and she waited for Eli to turn around.

"The messages from your Facebook account discuss a robbery that took place out on 27—a gas station three miles from the Alabama line. They implicate you in the incident."

Eli tossed the packet toward the table, and half the pages caught the edge, causing the packet to fall to the floor. He cursed under his breath and sat back down in his chair, rubbing his forehead with his hands. Looking down at the floor, he mumbled, "Whatever you say is best, do it."

Maggie put her hand on her client's shoulder. She thought of her boss's rules for representing people with compassion. "Personal contact with your clients that are in jail is crucial to forming trust and calming their concerns." Jim Lamb told this to Maggie in her first weeks with his office. "I know it can be awkward sometimes, especially with most of your clients being men in jail and you being a woman and all. I am not telling you to do something you are uncomfortable with, but our clients in jail miss people. They miss their families and friends. That handshake or pat on the back, even a hug, is important. It gives them some contact with the outside world."

The hug was one of Jim Lamb's signature moves. His passion for combating the issues in Georgia's jails and prisons stemmed from Lamb's concerns with the inhumanity of it all. "These are men and women just like you and me," he would tell judges. Lamb believed that as soon as a man was locked up, the system, and those desensitized from being around it for too long, began treating the person as a second-class citizen. Lamb would often say in his Alabama drawl, "Injustice may be all around us, but keeping innocent men and women locked away waiting for their fundamental right to go to trial is one form I will never tolerate." Injustice and its many forms were Lamb's war now—one he would never win. So, for Jim Lamb, the hug was more powerful in that fight than his words in court could ever be. Maggie preferred winning.

Eli looked back up at Maggie with tears in his eyes. She squeezed his shoulder and gave him a reassuring look. "I'll have ten days from your arraignment date next week to file the pretrial motions in your case." Eli leaned back and wiped his nose on the sleeve of his jumpsuit. Maggie continued, "I'll challenge the warrant that was issued to get downloads from your social media accounts, and I'll ask the judge to exclude the statement you made to the investigator that interviewed you the day you were arrested. I'll also demand that you get a speedy trial."

Eli nodded and said, "Okay, I trust you. Can you call my momma? She is worried."

"I'll call her as I am driving back to the office." Maggie stood and extended her hand. "I'll see you Monday, Eli."

~

The Sandbar—known mainly for the taste of its cold beer—sat on the eastern bank of one of the wide bends of the Chattahoochee River. The wooden restaurant's elevated back deck looked out on the river water as it drifted by. On summer nights, those congregating around the outdoor bar could watch the sunset to the west while boats coming in from an afternoon of fishing or skiing tied on at the restaurant's docks. Families and couples would line up outside waiting for their party to be called while kids trounced around the two sandy volleyball courts that paved the way for the Sandbar's weeknight success.

The Chattahoochee Beach Volleyball Club held two seasons on the Sandbar courts. League matches started every Tuesday and Thursday night at 6:00 p.m., and on Monday and Wednesday nights, players could drop in to play pickup games between 5:00 and 10:00 p.m. The serious players, or "Hoochies" as they were often referred to, would stop in to practice after work, changing from their office attire to athletic shorts and T-shirts. Players travelled in from nearby towns to take part in the games and socialize on the Sandbar's back deck. On warm nights, when the daylight extended well into the evening, there would be groups of people looking on with "downs" until the sun dipped below the horizon.

Maggie knew that for true Hoochies, a pitcher of beer was the only currency for wagers on pickup games. She slid a twenty-dollar bill into the back pocket of her workout shorts and closed the trunk to her blue Saab 900. She tightened her ponytail and walked across the gravel parking lot to the steps of the Sandbar. The rocks crunched under the soles of her running shoes as she made her way between the lines of vehicles parked outside. Jimmy Buffett–type music played from the speakers inside as she pushed through the front door. The inside tables were mostly empty, but Maggie could see the back deck through the rear windows, and it was packed.

She waved to the hostess leaning against the bar and walked through the island motif dining area to the rear doors. Maggie spotted two of her coworkers, Chris Owens and Jenny Marsh, as she opened the rear door to the deck. The Parrot Head music blared through the speakers out back and mixed with the laughter from the tables of people enjoying the September evening air.

"Hey, Mags, over here!" yelled Chris from a table near the back railing.

She waved from the door and walked in his direction. She recognized a few of the people seated at the tables around the deck and smiled at those who met her eyes.

"Hey, Chris. Hey, Jen. This place is busy!" Maggie said as she approached. She walked to the railing beside the table to look down on the volleyball courts. "Is it always like this?"

"It's a league night," Chris said, standing to grab a chair from a nearby table for Maggie.

"Yes, it's always this busy on Tuesdays and Thursdays," Jenny said, clarifying the answer to Maggie's question. "You look sporty tonight."

Maggie shrugged. "More like comfortable. I've been down in Seminole County most of the day meeting with clients. I jumped at the opportunity to lose the heels."

"You were working today?" Chris said, returning with a chair. "Come on, Maggie, you aren't supposed to be working this week. Making me look bad. Ol' Balk gave us the week off to mourn. I intend to take it."

"By mourning, Chris means he is fishing and drinking all week," Jenny added, slapping Chris on the rear as he sat down.

"We all grieve in our own way," Chris said, sliding his arm behind Jenny's shoulders.

Both Jenny and Chris worked as public defenders and had been an item for the past two months now. They were well ahead on the bar tab and looking cozier by the minute.

"You get this chair for me, Chris? Or are you two going to lie down and make out right here on the back deck?" Maggie said, smiling as she sat down beside the two lovebirds.

"Nah, it's not like that, Mags," Chris replied.

"That's right, he is a gentleman. Until it comes to the bedroom," Jenny added with a laugh.

"Gross!" Maggie remarked. "Oh, how you have corrupted my dear friend."

"I am sorry, Maggie. I meant well," Chris chimed in.

"Not you, Chris. I mean Jenny. She is the one you have to watch out for. Don't let her take you down the wrong path." Chris nodded and scooted closer to Jenny. Not that there was much space left. "Chris is just a simple boy from Arkansas, Jenny, he doesn't know any better. You big-city Atlanta girls swoop in and just cause trouble."

"Tell me more," Chris said as he grabbed a glass from the table and poured Maggie a beer.

Hollers erupted from one of the volleyball courts below, and Maggie looked over the railing to see what was going on.

"Playoffs start next week, and that team in green down there is the crew to beat," Chris said, handing Maggie the glass. "Long-time Hoochies, all of them. Bankers and insurance guys."

She sipped from the glass and pointed at the teams on the next court over. "Is that team in blue all law enforcement?"

"Yeah, the 'Boys in Blue' are all cops."

"Original," Maggie replied.

"Good team. I think they won the Hooch two years ago."

"The Hooch?" Maggie said, turning back to Chris with a puzzled look.

"Yeah, the Hooch is the ultimate prize, Mags. The league trophy. Championship team takes it home with them for a year."

"It's made to look like an old moonshiner jug," Jenny added.

"Thing is beautiful!" Chris said, playing along. "We were on the precipice of glory last season, and the Green Weenies out there snatched it away."

"You are going to need to dream bigger, Mr. Owens, if you want to keep your big-city girl around." Maggie grinned at Jenny.

"It's a summer fling," Jenny added, rubbing Chris's shoulders. "Already looking for my exit plan."

"Well, the Hooch would never leave me," Chris said with a wink to Maggie. "To the Hooch!" he roared.

The group sharing the other end of their table laughed and joined in the toast. "The Hooch!" they echoed back. They all clinked glasses, and Maggie shook her head, smiling at the absurdity of it all.

Chris stood to step away and mix it up with a table of friends nearby. He left the table carrying their empty pitcher, no doubt going for a refill.

"Did you go to the funeral yesterday?" Jenny said, scooting to the chair closest to Maggie. "I didn't see you in the overflow room."

"I sat with Lamb in the sanctuary."

"Oooh, Ms. VIP. Well, I thought the service was nice. Didn't you? Lots of Washington types in attendance. CNN did a nice piece on the Collins family."

The music paused, and a voice over the speaker announced the names of the two teams in the next match. A Dave Matthews Band track resumed on the speakers, and chairs scraped against the deck as people at nearby tables shuffled toward the steps that led down to the volleyball pitch.

"I mean it was a nice funeral. Whatever that means, you know," Maggie said with a shrug. "I still can't believe it all. He was such a pain in the ass to try cases against, but he was a really good guy."

Jenny nodded. "Total pain in the ass to deal with on cases."

"Principled, though, and I always respected that. Didn't matter if you had five bucks or five million. You broke the law in one of his counties, he'd prosecute you for it." Maggie clasped both hands around the cool beer glass as she spoke. "What bothered me about the funeral was that it felt too political at times. I know his dad is up for election, but there were comments here and there that made me uncomfortable. Jake had political aspirations, but he told me on a number of occasions that he would never play the game. He wanted to fight against corruption, regardless of party."

"I felt that way, too," Jenny replied. "I think that is just how these people are wired."

Maggie shook her head and took another sip from her glass. "Never miss an opportunity to campaign, even at your own son's funeral."

Maggie noticed Chris across the deck telling a story to a table full of firemen and EMTs. Jenny motioned for him to come back over to the table, and he waved her off. He loved being the center of attention. Sloppy lawyer, preparation wise, but excellent at picking a jury. He knew everyone.

"Did Jake ever tell you what his plans were at the end of his term?" Jenny asked, returning her attention to Maggie.

Maggie looked out at the sunset over the river and thought a moment about her answer. "No. I did ask him about it, though. Back when he decided not to qualify for reelection as district attorney."

"Come on," Jenny prodded. "He must have said something to you about it."

"All he told me was he wanted to focus on fighting corruption. I never got the details."

Chris returned to the table. Maggie was grateful for the interruption and the familiar face that stood next to Chris. Tim Dawson wore shorts, a blue tank top, and a backward baseball cap. Standing a few inches taller than Chris, he held a bottle of water in one hand and frosted mug in the other. He was still sweating from his team's game and wiped his brow as he said, "You defense attorneys have some room for one more?"

"That depends," Jenny said.

"Here we go," Dawson replied, sipping from his beer with a smirk.

"We need to know what it is going to take for you to leave your team to come play for Chris."

"You are the missing link, T.D.," Chris added.

"That's a heavy ask," Dawson replied. His strong shoulders flexing slightly as he shrugged. "I'm on a two-year deal with the Boys in Blue."

"Name your price, Dawson. We will buy your contract out. I am not above bribing an agent."

"Terms are pretty straightforward. I'll leave my team right now; I'll just tell the boys you bought me off with dinner."

"Done," Chris said. "I'll go grab us some menus."

"Nah, Chris, I'm thinking about dinner somewhere else."

Dawson's eyes locked in with Maggie's, and he held them until she looked away.

"Well, you name the place," Chris said as he refilled glasses on the table.

"I have somewhere in mind," Dawson replied, readjusting his hat as he grabbed a seat across from Maggie. "I'd even settle for going Dutch."

14

"All right, is everyone on the call?" Bill Collins said, looking at the core of his campaign staff on his laptop's screen. The group of six, four men and two women, nodded back from their respective offices around the Southeast and Washington, DC, area.

"I want to thank all of you for your support this week," Bill began. "Y'all shuffled around what needed to be moved from the calendar, and that freed up time for me to spend with my family here in South Georgia."

Bill had spent the week in the main house on Kelley Hill Plantation with his wife, Lucy. The two saw a few friends in the area, tended to their son's grave, and mostly disconnected from the expectations of Washington. Lucy would remain at the family home on Kelley Hill for two more weeks —Bill planned to get back to business.

"It is September twenty-fifth, and I intend to be back on the campaign trail next week," Bill said to the group. "We are just under forty-five days until the election, and this is do or die time."

Bill's campaign manager, George Dell, cringed at his candidate's use of phrasing. "Bill, the official statement that we released from the campaign says you will be suspending all campaign events until the end of the month."

"I know what the statement says," Bill snapped.

George could tell his candidate had grown antsy from sitting a week at the family home. Bill enjoyed action. Making deals and meeting with people. In the entire time George had worked for the congressman, some ten years now, he had never seen his boss step away from politics for ten days straight. George knew his candidate, though, and he knew what mattered most: winning.

"We polled the campaign's statement, and your decision is playing well to potential voters. Especially among those suburban women included in the sample."

Bill's face on the screen looked pleased as he took a sip from a coffee mug.

"Listen, George, I don't want to stay away from the trail for too long. We are nearly at the finish line here. You put me in front of a group of voters October one, is that clear? I want the media and the voters to know we are not letting up. Understood?"

The group nodded, almost in unison.

"Absolutely, sir."

At age sixty, Bill Collins had his eye on the United States Senate. He'd served his time in the United States House of Representatives and now wanted this new challenge. Even though Bill was a seasoned politician, his campaign staff still considered him old-school. He fed off being out in front of an audience, pleading his case to the electorate. Relationships, real relationships, were forged face-to-face, not on a video or phone call. That was his way of doing business, but he understood the power of social media and refused to be left behind. He knew his path to being named the next senator from Georgia would require the power of technology on the campaign trail, so he hired the best for his campaign. Mercenaries of political marketing that consulted for the highest bidder. They pushed the social media front in his campaign, and it proved effective. Clips of his speeches, interviews, and insights on issues that mattered to Georgia voters flooded the feeds on phones and laptops across the state.

Bill Collins, a man of revered work ethic, would not let younger, better-equipped opponents have the upper hand on any playing field. While Bill took his hiatus from rustling up votes, the social media machine within his campaign continued to connect with the voters. As it turned out, Bill's gravitas and gifted leadership transitioned well to a screen. The Georgia voters mourned with him, and the outpouring of support from followers on social media astounded him. His opponent led by a six-point margin before his son's murder; now Bill was gaining in the polls.

"How much do we know about the opposition's approach to my son's death?"

The question left a silence over the videoconference. Bill was looking for a fight.

"Jill Hollister's campaign issued a statement on Monday, the day of the funeral, expressing condolences for your family and condemning the senseless killing," George said with an even voice. "She also pledged fifty thousand dollars to the Wounded Warrior Project in honor of Jake."

"Trying to cover up her shitty voting record supporting our military," Bill added.

"Probably."

John Deese was on the call and chimed in his support with: "There is no doubt that's what it is for, George. She is just trying to generate some press for her campaign by hitching her wagon to a Collins family tragedy. It's despicable, if you ask me."

George Dell toyed with the idea of pointing out that John Deese had made a career of hitching his wagon to the Collins family. There was no point; everyone else on the call already knew that. In a calm voice, George said, "We are still behind in the polls, Bill, but I see no reason to be anything other than gracious. The attention is on you now—that's what matters."

Bill rubbed the stubble on the side of his face and said: "Well, I haven't watched the news since the funeral. Lucy and I haven't turned on the television. I can't bear to read anything on it. Especially not from some hack in New York City that believes he knows my family's history."

George sensed his candidate didn't want to ask the question, but he knew the direction Bill Collins's mind was heading.

"The public support has been incredible, Bill. Kind words from just about everyone in Washington, the press included. The numbers are through the roof."

Bill went silent for a moment, shaking his head. "Politics are a funny thing, folks."

"I agree, sir."

With steepled hands, Bill nodded in approval at the rising numbers in the polls and closed discussion on the matter without a word. George Dell took the seamless handoff and ran the meeting from there. Bill noted the optimism in his team. They were a talented group. Win or lose the election, he would miss the campaign.

For Bill, campaigns and politics were about making history. No other aspect of his life felt that way. Even more so now with Jake being gone. He'd built businesses, started a family, and contributed time to worthy causes. Those actions would be forgotten, most already were. His time in office—this senatorial election—would be his legacy.

"That's all we have for today, Bill," George said, evening up a stack of notes from the meeting in his hands.

Bill thanked his team and told them to enjoy the weekend. They would work most of it, as would he. "Everyone go ahead and step out of the call. John and George, you both stay on for a few minutes more."

Bill waited as a few of the windows on the video call disappeared from his laptop screen. He saw both John and George readjusting their earbuds. The men were both in their late thirties. Competitors at heart that felt they still had much to prove. They stayed hungry and had a slight disdain for one another. Bill liked that.

"All right, men, what do you have for me as far as updates on the murder investigation. Has anyone tracked down Lee Acker?"

15

She opened the glass door to the restaurant at 7:20 p.m. and eased through a large party milling around the front bar area. A path cleared, and she made her way past the hostess stand to the far end of the bar. From there she could scan the restaurant.

"Can I get you something to drink?" a voice asked over her shoulder. Maggie turned and saw the bartender looking at her. He collected a glass from under the bar and pulled the tap to pour a beer.

"Maybe in a minute," she replied. Maggie surveyed the tables in the room and then pulled her cell phone out to check for any messages.

"You meeting somebody?"

Maggie turned back to the bartender. He had his sleeves rolled up on his button-down and was now adding vodka, vermouth, and ice to a metal shaker. For style points, he held the spouts of liquid a foot from the container, then topped the mixture. He pressed his index and middle fingers down over the top and shook the ingredients. A quiver of arrows tattooed on the inside of his left forearm came into view as he slung the shaker back and forth.

"I am meeting a friend. I am a little late, but I don't see him here yet."

The bartender had a line of patrons. Maggie looked down the bar, and a few people had their hands up, trying to signal his attention. He took his time pouring the vodka mixture into a chilled martini glass. "You meeting Tim?" he said, looking down as he worked.

"How did you know that?"

"Tim came in the front door alone about twenty minutes ago wearing a black sport coat. He comes in here alone from time to time, never on a Friday night, though. Never dressed up. Always sits at the bar." The bartender dropped a spiral orange peel into the martini glass and picked it up along with the chilled beer.

"Where is he now?" Maggie asked.

"One second," the bartender said as he walked the glasses down to the end of the bar. He handed a couple their drinks and told them something amusing, because they laughed over the noise of the already crowded restaurant. He refolded a towel over his shoulder as he spoke. Maggie watched with interest as he appeared unhurried by the Friday night atmosphere. A few people stopped him on the way back, and he took their drink orders with the tempered enthusiasm of a pro.

When he returned, he said, "This a date tonight?"

"Kind of a nosy question?" Maggie responded, smiling.

"It's my job to 'nose' things," the bartender said, pointing to his large nose with a smirk.

"Where is he? Do I have to bribe the staff around here to find my table?"

"Couldn't hurt, and it looks like a date," the bartender said.

Maggie pursed her lips and shrugged, prepared to wait him out.

"He is out back on the patio."

"See, that wasn't so hard," she responded.

Signaling the hostess, the bartender said, "Can you walk this nice lady out to the patio seating area? She is late for a date."

Maggie stuck her tongue out at the bartender in a childish manner, and he responded with a dismissive flip of the hand.

As Maggie followed the hostess, she ran her fingers through her dark hair. Her blue dress was one she wore occasionally to court, but the black heels were brand new. The hostess, probably in high school, commented on the shoes as she opened the back door of the restaurant. A short flight of wooden steps led to the brick patio seating area. Music played over the speakers, and the seven or eight tables were all full, consumed in conversation. She spotted Tim, and he stood to greet her. The black jacket and fashionable sneakers looked good on him.

"I thought you might stand me up, Maggie Reynolds." Tim extended his hand for a handshake. Professional as always.

"I know I am late, sorry! I had to pay the bartender off just to find out where you were," Maggie said, taking her seat. The hostess handed her a menu and stepped away.

"Who's working the bar tonight? Kevin? I bet he was just giving you a hard time."

"He has a bunch of arrows tattooed on his forearm, blond, big nose."

"That's Kevin June. Guy owns the place with his brother. Careful with his nose, he's sensitive about it. He means well when messing with people. That's the test. If he is screwing with you, it means he likes you."

Maggie looked around at the patio area. "Well, I have to admit it's a nice place. Good choice, Dawson. Maybe I will let you pick up the tab."

He liked the way she called him by his last name. "In that case, let's stick with appetizers and beers," Tim replied, laughing as he said it.

They were both early in their careers as state employees, so neither could flex a large bank account. They ordered cocktails, and the conversation came easy. They worked in the same industry, so to speak. They knew a lot of the same people, and she recognized that he was not boastful in his description of his work. Like a good investigator, he focused on questioning her. He eased her away from talk of the criminal justice system by asking about life before the law.

Tim remembered reading a feature story that the *Atlanta Journal-Constitution* did on Maggie last spring. The article followed a Miller County jury's decision to return a "not guilty" verdict for her client—a twenty-year-old seasonal worker from Mexico. Tim remembered the case well and the firestorm that enveloped it. For a certain brand of politics, the kid from Mexico represented all that was wrong with undocumented workers living and working in Georgia. Charged in a robbery turned murder, the entire trial fell victim to the polarizing state of politics. The media fueled the outrage. The liberal news networks propped the defendant up around an incomplete narrative that screamed the migrant worker was a victim of his circumstances. The conservative networks spouted hateful rhetoric to stir its viewers into believing the young man was another reason to fear foreigners south of the country's border. After the four-day trial ended, Maggie walked her client out of the courtroom and into the waiting arms of US Immigration and Customs Enforcement. The media loved her and the meager beginnings that formed part of her story. Tim remembered the gist of her background from the article, but he wanted to hear it from her.

Growing up in Tampa, Florida, Maggie's family did not have a lot of money. Her father drove a school bus and her mother waited tables at a diner in Ybor City. She attended public school at a large high school and graduated as the valedictorian of her class. With scholarship offers from all over Florida, she chose to attend the University of Florida in Gainesville. "Go Gators," she said and gave a short gator-chomping motion with her hands. She spoke with modesty about the hard work she put in while in college. She waited tables and busted her tail in the classroom. "It was not a glamorous college experience," Maggie said as their server returned for orders. "I made it out, though."

Tim selected two hearty appetizers from the menu, and they both ordered a second round of drinks. Their server left the table, and Maggie talked more about her childhood. No one mentions life's struggles on a first date—or whatever you would call this. So instead of talking about her mother drinking too much or her father's obsession with the local dog tracks, she told Tim about the trips to Clearwater to see the Philadelphia Phillies play spring training games. She talked about the tourists coming to town for the mayhem that surrounds the Gasparilla Pirate Festival every year. Tim listened and nudged her along with innocent questions about her past. She soon recognized she was doing all of the talking—the hazard of spending time with a lawyer—and made an effort to steer the conversation in his direction.

"What about you, Mr. Dawson, what's your story?"

"Oh, you know, just a Black kid growing up on the streets of Fort Morgan, Alabama," he smirked. "That's right, just down the road from a tough little beach town by the name of Gulf Shores."

"Sounds pretty intimidating," Maggie said, eyebrows raised. She'd visited Gulf Shores last year for the first time over the Fourth of July. "You sure you aren't mischaracterizing something, Special Agent Dawson?"

"Oh, am I on the witness stand now?" he replied, sloshing the cubes around in his glass. He played along as if he were squirming and looked over at the patio door. "Ma'am, I may need to expand on my last answer."

Their server pushed through the doors and headed in their direction. She placed the plates on the table, and the smell of the food shook Maggie from her line of questioning. They ordered their entrees—two specialty salads at Tim's recommendation—and dug into the starters.

Tim, after some prodding, explained that he was born in New Orleans, Louisiana. Adopted at age two by a couple in Fort Morgan, he lived on the quiet Alabama peninsula until leaving for college. His family owned a seafood restaurant in Gulf Shores, and his dad ran the volunteer fire department a half mile from their home. Tim described life growing up in the small beach town. He toddled and played around the family's restaurant until his teachers started to require homework after school. By age thirteen, when he wasn't at football or baseball practice, he bussed tables. He seemed to know all there was to know about running a restaurant in a tourist town. When he wasn't working or playing ball, he scuba dove and fished the Gulf Coast waters.

"You left out your early training in competitive beach volleyball?" Maggie teased.

Tim laughed and said, "I didn't catch on to the volleyball thing until moving here—I swear. I went up to Auburn University on a football scholarship and played on the team for three years. Rode the bench mostly. Tore my shoulder up my junior year playing special teams and decided to step away from the game. Rehabbing it was going to be a long road and, yeah, I just wanted to be a college student."

"That's a tough break," Maggie said. She could tell the injury was still a tender subject.

"Shit happens," Tim said. "I love what I do, and I wasn't going to play in the NFL or anything."

Maggie nodded, and they both sipped their drinks, thinking for a moment. Their salads arrived, and they both switched to wine. They took their time picking through the leafy entrees.

"So, I hear they assigned the Collins murder to you?"

Tim nodded and said, "Yeah, been working on it all week."

"Burning it at both ends, I bet. How's that going so far?" She was unsure if he would be willing to discuss the ongoing investigation.

"It's going," he said. "Went to see Judge Balk on Monday to get a warrant signed, and he wanted to see more."

"That's saying something for Balk. I've seen him sign warrants on less than nothing. That client you saw me with the other day, Eli Jones, is sitting in jail tonight because of a bogus search warrant signed by the Honorable Balk."

"Not a *scintilla* of evidence, as you lawyers like to say."

"Very nice. Someone is listening in court," Maggie said in response.

He gave a half-cocked smile, then said, "Yeah, well, the judge decided to go dick around at the beach all week, so it is making it a little difficult to get the job done. Gave whoever did it a nice head start."

"Get a magistrate judge to rubber stamp it. The warrant is for Lee Acker's arrest, isn't it?" Maggie asked in a conspiratorial tone.

Tim eyed her from across the table. Her face flushed from the wine; she knew why he needed the superior court judge's signature. He didn't have enough evidence for an arrest warrant. He needed access to Acker's digital footprint. The cell phone companies and social media sites wouldn't accept the magistrate court judge's signature—they wanted the big judge to sign off.

"Reynolds, you know we don't have to talk shop."

"True, but I am pretty sure Lee Acker won't qualify for the services of his local public defender's office. He will hire some heavy hitter from out of town."

"If he did it," Tim said in an even tone.

She smiled and after a brief pause said, "That's right. If he did it."

Tim clasped his hands together and said, "Well, enough of that. How about dessert?"

16

Lee sat in a corner of the hotel lobby drinking coffee and reading the morning edition of *El Norte*. Four days now he'd scanned Monterrey's newspaper for any mention of the shootout at the gas station north of town. The paper published articles every day about investigations taking place in Nuevo León and incidences of violence, but nothing about the blatant attack on local law enforcement. He folded the newspaper in front of him and looked around the quiet lobby to the front desk area. At seven thirty on a Saturday morning, most of the hotel's guests were lounging in bed. He raised his hand to get Eugenio's attention. The concierge nodded in his direction and collected a small black tablet from his post behind the hotel's front desk. He strode to the corner seating area with his shoulders back, chin elevated.

"*Buenos días, señor.* How is your stay going thus far?"

The concierge's dark eyebrows bobbed as he offered a good-natured smile. His pressed black jacket, slacks, and starched white dress shirt were tailored to his frame. The heavy gel in his jet-black hair held every strand in its place, and his dress shoes shined against the lobby's floor.

"Excellent, thank you. I need to hire a car to take me to Querétaro."

"Of course, sir," Eugenio responded. He pushed a button on the tablet and began typing away. "What time do you plan to leave?"

"This morning. No later than eleven."

"I will make a phone call. It should not be a problem."

Lee pulled a fifty-dollar bill from his pocket, folded it in hand, and passed it to the concierge. Eugenio slid the bill into his back pocket and looked around the quiet lobby. One couple sat on the other end of the seating area; they spoke quietly in Spanish to one another.

"Were you able to get in contact with the investigator I recommended?" Eugenio asked.

"Yes, thank you," Lee responded. "Your recommendations have been spot-on."

"He found the people you are looking for?"

Lee needed an address that proved impossible to locate. He had convinced the concierge that the assistance of an investigator—someone talented and discreet—was necessary for a potential business deal.

"Yes, he found a phone number and an address for me," Lee said, leaning forward in his seat with his arms resting on both knees.

"You are going yourself to this address?" Eugenio asked, his face concerned.

"Yes, I plan to, eventually."

The caterpillar eyebrows lifted slightly as the concierge exhaled, "Oof! Well, remember that business and the politics of dealing with outsiders can be complicated in Mexico."

"Business and politics are complicated everywhere," Lee said. "One debases the other."

Eugenio nodded and said, "I must notify the car service. I'll mark your room when I settle on a time with the driver."

"No later than eleven," Lee said.

"Yes, sir," the concierge replied as he started to walk away. Mid-stride, he turned and said, "I am glad the information has been helpful. *Cuidate.*"

~

Bay Correctional Facility in Panama City, Florida, permitted visitation on Saturdays and Sundays. Grace Acker visited her brother-in-law once when he arrived at the facility and had not returned in eleven months. The two-

and-a-half-hour drive down to the federal prison made for an easy trip, but she'd chosen to avoid seeing her friend and brother-in-law behind bars. Her husband, on the other hand, had visited his brother twice a month, without fail. She never asked about the visits, and Lee shared little.

The building felt cold as Grace waited in line at the security checkpoint. The air conditioning pumped chilled air down into the cinder block room, and she gripped her light fleece jacket against her body. She'd felt silly hoofing it across the scorching Florida parking lot with a light jacket in hand but now did not regret the decision. Security waved at her to step forward, and she greeted the officer with a warm smile. The officer confirmed that a visitor's application was on file and reviewed Grace's driver's license. Grace signed the visitor's log and wrote out whom she planned to visit and her time walking into the facility. A guard then led her through a metal detector and directed her down the hall to the visitation area.

The rows of cloth-covered chairs in the lobby looked stained and dated. She found the cleanest in the bunch and sat to wait. The room's flat-screen television played an old *Batman* episode. The spy-themed music clipped along as Batman and Robin raced down a California highway in the Batmobile. Grace watched as a fight scene ensued between Batman and Mr. Freeze's henchmen. The words "Bam" and "Pow" flashed on the screen as Batman made quick work of the bad guys. Without her cell phone on hand to peruse the internet with and refusing to touch the magazines on the lobby's end tables, Grace watched in amusement as Mr. Freeze evaded capture.

A guard stepped into the waiting area with a clipboard and called her name. As she walked down the hallway to her assigned visitation area, she heard, "Tune in tomorrow—same Bat-time, same Bat-channel!" She knew Batman would get the villain in the next episode—she'd seen it all before.

Grace turned the corner and stepped into a space the size of a phone booth. A metal desk, split down the middle by a plastic divider, separated her from Cliff. As soon as Cliff saw her, he stood from his metal stool and placed his hand against the divider. He flashed a crooked grin, emblematic of the Acker boys, and rapped his knuckles twice against the plastic before sitting back down. He picked up the receiver, and Grace did the same.

"Well, well. Look who finally made it back in here to see me," Cliff said as he leaned against the metal table, still grinning.

"I don't make a habit of coming to Panama City to go to the beach. What makes you think I would come visit my family in prison down here?" Grace replied, playing along.

"Well, I happen to enjoy the Redneck Riviera myself," Cliff remarked. "Not so much this stay, but I always had a good time in the past."

"They didn't let y'all out for spring break? I thought this was one of those cushy prisons, Cliff. Do I need to go talk to the warden and make sure he knows you deserve special treatment?"

"You are convincing, Grace. It's Ms. Warden here, though. You won't be able to flash those long legs and a smile to move that negotiation."

"Well, in that case, how much longer do you have?"

"Should be three months. Depends if I can get all my classes done."

"Homestretch, though," Grace said, patting the table.

"Uh-huh, it's not too bad." He ran his hands through his long hair. He'd spent time in the weight room, and his frame looked solid, like it did in college. "Won't be soon enough, though."

"You doing all right?" she asked, her voice sincere.

"Don't worry about me. I am doing my time and keeping my nose clean. Sober now for fourteen months." Grace nodded and he continued, "I consider myself lucky given the deal I got in court. There are quite a few guys in here serving longer stretches. A couple of the lawyers locked up in here told me that my attorney did a hell of a job." Cliff could talk all day if you let him. "Speaking of attorneys, sounds like my brother might need one?"

The two looked at each other through the divider. Grace knew the phones recorded all visitor conversations. Cliff knew that, too.

"Your niece asked about you the other day," Grace said, sidestepping Cliff's question.

"How is little Charlie girl?" Cliff had started calling Charlotte "Charlie" when she was a baby. The nickname stuck.

"Not so little anymore. She's starting to want to do what seniors in high school do. Go to parties, date boys, and stay out later. Missing her family, though. Her uncle is locked up in prison, and her dad has been out of town for almost a week now."

"He hasn't called?" Cliff asked.

Grace shook her head. "She is doing great in school, though, top of her class. Athletics are going well, too. She wants to run track at Oregon or the University of Southern California. Somewhere out west, far away from home."

"Can you blame her?" Cliff said.

"No," Grace replied. "Not one bit. It'll be far away from her momma, though."

Even if asked, Cliff would not try all that hard to convince his niece to attend a college closer to home. He wanted the same thing when he gradu-ated high school. The opportunity to get miles away from small-town Georgia—to step away from the shadows cast by his family name.

"Maybe you can talk to her about it one day?" Grace said. "The Univer-sity of Florida wants her to run for them. Gainesville is still four hours away; it's plenty far."

"I don't know, Grace. I'm kind of riding this cool prison uncle thing at the moment."

"I'm just asking you to help nudge her in the right direction," Grace pleaded.

"I guess my story does give her a worst-case scenario to consider." Cliff smiled. "Look where leaving the pews of the First United Baptist Church of Blakeston got me?"

Grace laughed. "Oh, is your situation a result of the Lord's smite now?"

Cliff loved her laugh. "No, no, I'm just saying a little help from the man upstairs would have been nice."

"So, you'll talk to her?" she prodded.

Cliff nodded. More silence.

Cliff looked at his childhood friend through the divider. Her pert nose and killer eyes scrunched as she made a face at him in the awkward silence. Her sense of humor remained unchanged, but he could see the pain in her eyes. The need for answers motivated her visit today.

Tim Dawson had called her that morning on the drive down and scheduled a meeting for next week. The investigators wanted to meet with her again to discuss Lee's whereabouts. She needed Cliff's help.

"Do you know where he is?" Cliff asked.

Grace shook her head again, unwilling to answer audibly over the recorded phone.

"Well, you know I love my brother. He can be a self-righteous prick at times, but I would never accuse him of being a coward. He does not run from a fight," Cliff said. "I have the scars to prove it."

"What are you saying?" Grace asked.

"I'm saying my brother has a reason for the decisions he makes. You know that. I know that. Hell, anyone that knows Lee Acker knows he doesn't make decisions on a whim."

Grace waited as Cliff set the receiver on the desk and rubbed his temples. He pulled a rubber band from his wrist and put his hair into a manbun, then pressed the receiver back to his ear.

"I've read the papers, Grace. Looks like the cops think he is running. Lee isn't running. He wouldn't run from something like this."

"Then what is he doing?"

"He is looking for someone," Cliff replied. "He is looking for her."

17

The drive from Monterrey to Santiago de Querétaro took close to ten hours. Lee traded off between reading newspapers and pulling the brim of his hat down to nap. He admired the landscape that whirred by in the windows and thought of home. He missed Grace and Charlotte. He missed Saturday night dinners and talking to them about their work and school. His stomach hurt thinking about the conversations that had taken place since he left. The things that were said—the things that were left unsaid. He hated the position that his family was in, and he felt the early pains of exile.

The driver spoke little, other than the occasional mention of a notable mountain ridge or river as it passed. The two stopped once for coffee in San Luis Potosí. Lee grabbed two more newspapers, *La Jornada* and *El Universal*. The driver had no interest in stopping to eat and insisted they keep moving. He preferred to travel during the day, and that was fine by Lee.

When they arrived at the hotel in the center of Querétaro, the driver unloaded Lee's bag and accepted a few pesos without a smile. Eugenio had insisted that Lee pay for the car before leaving the hotel in Monterrey. Tucked away inside Lee's bag was the paid invoice. Before departing, the concierge had admonished the driver, the way a father would to his son, to ensure expectations for the trip were clear. There would be no dispute with the driver as to the cost of the trip. The men, both Mexican, adhered to a rigid hierarchy. Eugenio considered his work at the international hotel to be above that of the driver. This gave the concierge license to set the boundaries for the trip. He threatened discontinuing the partnership between the hotel and the driver's company should any unprofessionalism arise. He demanded a level of service from his staff, and those that the hotel partnered with, that would be second to none.

Lee entered the lobby of the hotel and made his way across a tile floor with rich blue accents. He showed the passport he purchased at the Loma Alta Motel to the hotel clerk and asked for two keys. She expected his arrival and flashed him an attractive smile. Lee paid cash for his room and handed over a thousand dollars to exchange for pesos. He tipped the clerk and headed for the room to change.

When Lee stepped back out on the street, he pulled a map from the rear pocket of his jeans to orient himself. The doorman, some ten feet away, smoked a cigarette and listened to a soccer match on a small radio. A serious expression on his face, he listened to the voice providing the play-by-play commentary as it recounted a near miss over the top of the goal. Lee nodded at the man and then mixed in with the traffic on the sidewalk. Meandering through the packs of teenagers and couples out strolling, he made his way to the *Plaza de Armas*. The restaurants that opened out onto the historic city square were filled with groups enjoying an evening dinner. Conversation and laughter filled the plaza.

Lee pulled out the prepaid cell phone and dialed the number given to him by the investigator in Monterrey. Lee wore a short-sleeve button-down, dark jeans, and a baseball cap. He looked American. The Beretta in his waistband felt tight against his lower back, and he readjusted it as the phone rang.

On the fourth ring, the call connected, and a voice said, "*Bueno?*"

Lee's heartrate picked up. He listened to the breathing on the other end of the line.

"*Sí, bueno?*" the voice said again, agitated.

"Alex?" Lee said. He looked out on the square as children ran around chasing each other, laughing. Bubbles floated by from somewhere around the corner.

The line was silent. Lee pulled the phone away from his ear and checked the screen. The call had not disconnected. "*Quién habla?*" the voice said. "Who is this?"

Lee waited, then said, "It's Lee. I'm in Mexico."

More silence. "How did you get this number?" the voice said in a cool tone.

"I paid for it," Lee replied.

Another pause. "Are you here on vacation?"

"No, I'm here to see you."

"*Por qué?*"

"The lawyer is dead. Yes, *el fiscal*. I need to talk to you about it," Lee said, trying to remain calm.

"No," the voice said. There was no pause in the response.

"No?" Lee replied.

"No."

Lee looked over as a large party filed out of the outdoor seating area at one of the plaza's restaurants. The sign outside read "*La Dahlia*" in yellow font. He sighed and said into the phone, "Well, I am here, and I need to see you in person. I'll come to you, just tell me where."

"Are you as dumb as your brother? If you come here, you may never go back home."

"I thought you might say that. Not the dumb part. I thought you knew my mother dropped Cliff on his head. That's just the way he is."

"Is that supposed to be funny?"

"It's an expression, Alex. And well, yes, Cliff is a dumbass."

"Where are you staying?"

"Are you going to send someone to kill me?"

There was a brief silence. "No."

"Promise?" Lee said.

"I'll find out where you are staying so you can just save me the trouble of having my people call around."

"*Casa del Obispo*. Room 414."

"Okay, I'll call tomorrow night."

The call ended, and Lee stared down at the screen. He contemplated making one more call. A call home to talk to Grace. He decided it was too soon. He tossed the phone in a nearby garbage can and walked toward *La*

Dahlia. A good dinner was in order—his days alive or as a free man were numbered.

~

Charlotte Acker crept down the stairs and out the side door of her home. The soft morning glow and dampness of the cool air greeted her as she closed the door behind her. She took a knee to tighten the laces on her shoes, double knotted on both sides, and then stood to stretch. Looking out onto the woods behind the house, she listened as the forest started to come alive. It would be October next week.

As she stood at the edge of the trail, she tightened her ponytail and adjusted the tank top under her Nike jacket. She looked out into the darkness of the forest and set her intentions for the run. Charlotte then closed her eyes and said a prayer for her family. She'd prayed a lot that week—no one answered.

She pushed through the rear gate and set out at a jog. No earbuds, no music. Only the sounds of her breathing and running shoes against the trail. Charlotte loved to run. She was seventeen, fast, and competitive. She liked the medals around her neck, the scouts at her meets, and the photos in the newspaper. She liked seeing her dad beaming from the bleachers. She liked pushing her limits. She liked all of it, and it was enough. Then the murder happened, and she realized she needed running—so Charlotte ran.

She came to the clearing and slowed to a stop. Yellow police tape still marked the boundary around the crime scene. She breathed heavy and put both hands on her head as she walked in the direction of the house. The morning sun still sat low, and its light slashed through the tall pines' sparse canopy. She pulled a pair of latex gloves from the pocket of her jacket and rolled them over her hands. Walking to the edge of the house, she peeked around the corner to the front drive. No deputy appeared to be watching the house, so Charlotte began checking the doors to the home. The patio door, garage door, and front door were all locked. Same with the windows on the first level.

Charlotte spotted an old farm truck parked out back and walked in its direction. She mashed the button down on the driver's-side handle, and the door creaked open. She surveyed the cab. Paperwork, dip cans, and Mountain Dew bottles cluttered the floorboard. A worn baseball cap sat on the dashboard along with a set of work gloves. Then, she noticed the silver keys tucked under the driver's-side visor. Charlotte pulled the set down and turned back toward the house.

Jake Collins was never married. The news articles didn't mention anything about a girlfriend either. If he had a dog or a cat, the family would have already moved it to a new home. The small two-story house in the woods was quiet.

Charlotte stood at the back door and slid the key into the deadbolt. Her heart started to race as she felt the lock turn and she entered the dark room. She found a light switch and turned on the hallway's fluorescent light. It buzzed as it kicked on. She followed the hallway into the kitchen and noticed the cleanliness of the home. There was no clutter on the countertops, and the kitchen table sat bare.

The small den off the kitchen was just as tidy. Charlotte walked through the ground floor rooms and looked at the artwork and pictures on the walls. The sunshine through the large windows provided plenty of light. Every single room was in perfect order.

Charlotte came to a door that was closed and turned the handle. It opened to what looked like the home office. The curtains were drawn, so she flipped on the light. The walls were bare. Large frames that held black-and-white photographs and certificates leaned against the walls. Half the room was already in boxes, neatly labeled, stacked one on top of the other.

The boxes read, *Acker I, Acker II, Acker III, Acker IV*, and *Acker V*. Another set of boxes read, *Collins I, Collins II*. Charlotte crouched down to look at the thick masking tape that covered the edges of the boxes and then stood to find something sharp. She moved to the rolltop desk and pushed the cover open. She spotted a letter opener. It looked sharp enough to slice the tape on the boxes, and she collected it from the desk. As she did, she noticed one color photograph remained on the desk. Charlotte picked the frame up with her gloved hands and stared at a smiling image of her father. He stood next to Jake Collins, her Uncle Cliff, and a man she did not recognize. They were on a fishing boat with bright blue water in the background. They held beer bottles and large fish up for the camera. They were all young, smiling.

Charlotte cut through the tape on one of the boxes that sat on top of the heap. The *Acker V* box held rows of documents, divided by different color tabs, and Charlotte started pulling the documents from the box. She laid them out on the ground and sliced open two more boxes. The contents of *Acker IV* and *Collins II* appeared similar to those in the first box. They held certificates of organization, operating agreements, articles of incorporation, bylaws, and other memoranda. Charlotte only recognized two of the companies in the Acker boxes: Acker Farms, LLC and The Acker Project, Inc. The Collins box held aerial photographs, bank statements, tax forms, and stacks of handwritten notes. She browsed the contents of the three boxes. There were plenty of notes about her Uncle Cliff, but she couldn't find any mention of her father. She sat cross-legged on the floor and read the handwritten notes of a man that died only nine days ago. His neat handwriting was easy to read, and each page was dated in the top right corner. Most notes were from before her Uncle Cliff's arrest. She found nothing dated within the last twelve months. Frustrated, she began stacking the paperwork back into the boxes. Then, she stopped—the sound of gravel crunched outside.

Charlotte's heartrate jumped, and she went to the window. A black SUV with two men in the front seat pulled to a stop in front of the house. She turned to the boxes on the floor and knelt to grab the remaining documents, cramming them into the boxes. She heard the doors on the vehicle slam shut outside, and her mind raced. What the heck was she thinking? Her mom was going to kill her if she got arrested. Charlotte scrambled over to the rolltop that sat open and yanked on the handle to close it shut. The cover slammed on the desk and caught the fingertips of her opposite hand. She grimaced and suppressed the need to scream out in pain. Eyes watering, Charlotte turned to listen for voices outside—nothing.

Rubbing her hand, she stood and noticed a black USB drive on the floor by her feet. The label read "Collins III" on the case. Not remembering where it came from, she tucked it away in the pocket of her jacket and headed for an exit. Charlotte heard the garage door on the other side of the house open, and she dashed upstairs. Standing at the edge of the top step, she listened.

"Let's get this packed up and get out of here," a deep, country voice said. "I want to be back in Atlanta before the Falcons game kicks off."

"You grab the boxes from the office, and I'll give the house one more look over," the other voice replied. "He asked us to get all of it, and I am not making another trip down here for this."

Charlotte stepped back away from the landing as the men passed the bottom of the stairs. She heard the door to the study open and thought, Is the light off? She couldn't remember.

"That's not how it works, big guy. You go wherever he tells you to," replied the deep voice. "It's called having a boss."

"I'm not his damn errand boy. We have you for that."

"Watch your mouth, Deese. You think I won't—"

"Shut up," the man called Deese said. "Something isn't right."

Charlotte's knees almost buckled. She looked down the hallway and saw light peeking from a window. Maybe she could make the jump from the roof to the ground out back.

"Didn't you tape all of these boxes up yesterday?" Deese asked.

"Yeah, I taped them all shut. Real tight. It's just a bunch of paperwork."

"I took a photo of the room before I left late last night. These boxes were in a different order."

"Dammit, did the cops come back through here?" the deep voice said. "They told me they were done processing the crime scene."

"No, not the cops. Not between midnight and early this morning. They would have called before coming by again. That agent on the case, yeah, Dawson, that's his name, he's a Boy Scout. He would have reached out to the family before cutting boxes open in here."

"I'll call the congressman," the deep voice said.

"No, you won't," Deese replied. "Let's look around first and see if anything else looks out of place. Then I'll call him if there is a problem."

"This isn't some redneck robbing the place, Deese. The house would have been trashed. Plus, the TV and computers are still here. Call that guy Dawson, ask him if he has been here."

"Do you think before you talk? No, I'm not calling the investigator about this," Deese replied.

"All right, man. Well, you do what you have to do. This wasn't some random break-in. If the congressman asks me about this shit, I am telling him I voted that we call the cops."

"This isn't a democracy," Deese replied. "Load the boxes."

Charlotte stood there, frozen. The screech of masking tape being pulled from a roll could be heard downstairs as footsteps made their way across the hardwood floor. She waited and heard the second set of footsteps begin the path to the other side of the house. She backed away from the stairwell and moved to the light at the end of the hallway. The small room's window looked out onto the woods behind the house. She opened it and swung her legs out onto the short roof. The drop couldn't be more than ten feet. She could make it, so long as she didn't break an ankle.

She crept to the edge of the roof and put her hands down to check the backside of the house. The grit from the shingles dug into the gloves on her hands. Seeing no one, she jumped to the ground below. She landed hard, but both ankles felt good. She did not turn to look behind her and eyed the farm truck some fifty feet away. Charlotte made a dash for it. Nearly tripping as she turned the corner around the truck, she spun her head to see who, if anyone, might have seen her. No one stood out back. She was sweating and breathing hard from the short sprint. She removed the gloves from her hands, stuffed them in her pockets, and spotted the entrance to the trail leading back into the woods. She wiped her forehead and took one last look toward the house. A man with a phone pressed to his ear stood at the kitchen window. Had he seen her? She couldn't tell from his movement. Wouldn't he come outside to confront her? Charlotte watched as the man disappeared from the window, and she made a break for the woods.

Charlotte knew the trails well. She'd pushed her body up and around the curvy paths since her parents started to let her run the woods. That morning she put together a personal best as she ran, wide open, toward home. How could I be so stupid? she thought, lungs burning against the morning air. What would they have done if they'd caught her?

Thin streams of tears trickled across her face, but she pushed on down the trail. She felt drained and dizzy. No one followed her, but if they tried, they wouldn't catch her. Had they seen her, though? She couldn't be sure. As she approached the rear portion of her family's property, she began to relax. She stopped at the gate and put her hands on her hips.

No one was out there watching her, but she scanned the woods, searching. It would be a while before she'd return to run the woods. She'd always felt safe running the quiet trails that zigzagged along the edges of the Collins and Acker properties. Thousands of acres that she used as a private training course, a place to run or walk when she needed to get away. Her dad's only two conditions were that she not set out on a trail run within an hour of sunset and that she not run the woods when deer or turkey were in season. It was easy to get lost in the woods at night, and the large swath of private land attracted trespassers every year. She had never gotten lost in the woods or come across a trespassing hunter. Charlotte still followed her dad's instructions, though.

The only person she ever came across while running the trails was a runner as well. He had a nice smile and ran with a slight hitch in his step. She looked out into the woods once more and walked toward the house. She was the only one that would run the trails—Jake Collins was gone now.

18

Tim stood in front of the open fridge and surveyed the options. A pot of coffee brewed on the countertop behind him, and the clock above it read 9:00 a.m. Maggie was still in bed, but he figured the smell of eggs and coffee might coax her into the living room. He'd stayed over two nights in a row and performed at the top of his game. Now it was time for the second half of the Dawson one-two punch—showcasing his skills in the kitchen.

He pulled a carton of eggs, milk, and half a watermelon from the top shelf of the fridge. Music played from his cell phone on the countertop as he rummaged through the cabinets, grabbing flour, sugar, baking powder, and the other ingredients for his homemade biscuits. He found what he needed and got to work.

The biscuits went in the oven, and he filled a mug of coffee. Sitting at the kitchen table, he waited with his bare feet propped up on the chair next to him. His feet and shoulders ached. He was grateful it was Sunday, a rest day. The morning before, he'd grabbed his gym bag from his SUV and jogged five miles before Maggie woke up. Rain or shine, with the exception of Sundays, Tim trained first thing in the morning. He loved his job, and discipline in one's physical training was a requirement. Still, rolling out of bed to train proved harder with Maggie in bed next to him—so yes, he was glad it was Sunday.

The timer dinged. Tim pulled the biscuits from the oven and began scrambling eggs in a skillet. A pair of long legs walked through the door, wearing only a T-shirt.

"Right on time," Tim said as Maggie walked toward the coffeepot.

"Morning," she said as she put her arms around his waist, kissing him on the cheek. "I see you decided not to dash out the door this morning."

"Rest day," Tim replied, looking down at her.

"You sure you aren't just worn out?" she said with a smile as she moved toward the mugs in the cabinet.

"I'll go right now."

"I bet you would, stud. Let me try these biscuits and see where that leaves you."

"My biscuits have never let me down before."

Maggie flashed him a playful smile. "Is this the Tim Dawson Sunday special?"

"Family recipe," Tim said, sidestepping the question.

Maggie bit into the biscuit. She slowly nodded her head in approval and added some eggs to a plate. "I'm on to you, Dawson."

The two sat at the table and talked as they ate. When the plates sat empty, Maggie draped her legs over his knees. Tim rubbed her legs as she told him about her week ahead. She loved her job, and it consumed her life. Tim admired discipline and commitment—Maggie exhibited both.

"What's your plan this week?" she asked.

"Collins case and more Collins case. It'll be like that until we get it solved."

"I bet," she said. "I still just can't believe it all."

"Yeah, the shock will wear off quick, though. People want answers. Hell, I want answers. Jake was a driven guy, but he didn't seem to have any enemies. He really hadn't been at the job long enough to prosecute a long list of hardened criminals. Not a lot of candidates for people that would come back out of prison looking for revenge."

Maggie nodded along and took another sip of her coffee, listening.

"And to me, that angle doesn't make sense, really. The killing went down early in the morning, right in Collins's own backyard. We found plenty of gunshot residue on the body, and all three shell casings were found nearby. The shooter couldn't have been more than maybe twelve feet from Collins when it happened."

"So, maybe he knew the shooter well?"

"He had to," Dawson replied. "No defensive wounds. No signs of struggle."

"What does his family think happened?"

Tim paused as he considered the question. "Well, this is us talking here, but I think the family is pretty focused on the Acker angle. They are distraught. I've seen it before. I haven't been doing this for twenty years, but I deal a lot with families that lose loved ones to violence. They want to focus that anger on someone."

Maggie enjoyed seeing him open up about his work, about the investigation. She listened as he discussed his approach to the case. He cared about the integrity of his investigation.

"I have a conference call with Congressman Collins on Wednesday," Tim continued. "He asked for weekly updates on the case. We don't have any other suspects, but I don't have anything linking Lee Acker to the murder."

"Other than him just disappearing?" Maggie said.

"Right, other than that. Which is pretty damning, in my opinion," Tim responded. "The job was clean, though, and we combed that place over for other evidence. The house is already out in the woods. Nice place, secluded spot out there off of 131. Maybe a quarter mile from the river."

Maggie nodded. "So no neighbors around to see or hear anything."

"That's right, nothing in the way of witnesses," he said, draining the rest of the coffee in his mug. "He was either coming in from or leaving for a run. He had on workout gear and running shoes when we found him."

"Who called it in?" she asked.

Tim paused, and she could see he was contemplating his answer again. "That's the thing. The caller was a secretary from the district attorney's office. I've listened to the 911 call seven or eight times, and the woman can barely hold herself together."

"Why was she out there?"

"Collins hadn't shown up at the office for his morning meetings. He wasn't picking up his phone, so she dropped by to check on him."

"She didn't see anything unusual out there?"

"Nope. Well, other than the dead body."

"Right. So, what are you going to do?"

"Keep investigating it. Nothing else I can do. I am meeting with Lee's wife again tomorrow. Yeah, Grace Acker. I don't expect much, though. She hasn't been all that cooperative."

"Can you blame her?" Maggie said with a grin.

Tim laughed now. "Hell yeah I can blame her. If her husband didn't kill the guy, I need her to come out and say it. If she knows where he is and she isn't telling me, I am going to charge her with hindering apprehension."

Maggie didn't say anything and did her best to leave the comment alone. They could agree to disagree, she thought. Maggie knew that cops had a sense of entitlement when it came to questioning people. Law enforcement treated unwillingness to cooperate in an investigation as evidence of guilt. A witness that tried to protect a family member always risked becoming a target.

"Well, at least you know where one of the Acker brothers is at the moment," Maggie said. "You should go talk to him."

"Seeing that Cliff Acker is already in prison, I don't get the feeling he will be all that helpful," he replied.

"You never know, might be worth a shot."

19

The water felt cool as he waded into the shallow end. Lee found an open spot against the wall and sat his beer on the edge of the pool deck. Families with children played in the water while others sat off to the side, relaxing in the sun. From behind his sunglasses, he scanned the faces of the hotel guests. He didn't recognize anyone, and no one seemed to pay attention to him. He removed his sunglasses and dipped his head under the water to wet his hair. When he came back up, he slicked his wet hair back and replaced his shades. A group of three women on lounge chairs talked behind him. Lee sipped his beer and listened as they recounted their Saturday night out on the town. He tried to follow the conversation. They spoke quickly and used plenty of words outside his limited Spanish vocabulary. He turned for another look at the group of nicely assembled bikinis, and one of the brunettes caught him. Lee grinned at the woman as she readjusted her long legs, giving him a playful smile in return that said, "Busted!"

As Lee returned to his lounger, the poolside server stopped him to ask what his room number was. He looked at the young man and replied, "Four one four."

The waiter pointed at the bar on the other side of the pool and put his hand to his ear, mimicking a phone call. *"Señor, tiene una llamada."*

Lee nodded and handed the waiter the empty beer to dispose of. "*Sabes quién es?*"

"*Su esposa,*" he replied.

"My wife?" Lee asked, confused.

The young man nodded and motioned to the bar.

Lee thanked the waiter and patted the young man on the back as he passed. Wrapping a towel around his waist, Lee made his way around the pool and over to the outdoor bar. When Lee approached, the barkeep handed over a cordless phone. With one hand cupped over the bottom half of the receiver, Lee said, "*Me da otra cerveza, por favor? Y un espresso, también.*"

The barkeep collected a Mexican lager from the cooler behind the bar and popped the cap. Handing it to Lee, he asked in a heavy accent, "Four one four?"

Lee nodded as he put the receiver to his ear.

"Hello, sweetie," Lee said into the phone.

"You shouldn't be checking out other women at the pool when you are away on business, *cariño,*" the voice replied.

Lee smiled. "What would give you that idea? Are you watching me, Alex?"

There was a slight pause. "If you are in my city, there will always be someone watching."

Lee took a sip of the beer and leaned with his back against the bar. He heard the bartender set the small plate and cup of espresso down behind him. Lee lowered his voice and said, "You are calling a little early. Everything all right? I wasn't expecting to hear from you until this evening."

"Everything is fine."

"When do I get to see you?" Lee asked.

"I'll send you an address tomorrow morning. Don't hire a car. I'll send over transportation."

"Okay," Lee said, his tone cautious. "So, I'll wait to hear from you. That's it?"

The response was quick and curt: "Yes, that's exactly what you will do."

Lee turned to the bar and added half a packet of sugar to the small white cup. He stirred it with the spoon, thinking about his response. He gave a sigh into the phone.

"If I get picked up, this is on you," Lee replied, sipping the warm espresso.

"None of this is on me, and it'll stay that way," Alex said, frustrated. "I am not talking about this over the phone. Go to the address tomorrow. We will discuss whatever it is that you want to discuss."

"Okay, okay, don't get so fired up. I'll be there," Lee replied.

"Good boy. And Lee? Be careful with the Mexican women while you are here."

Lee noted the playful tone in the threat and turned to look at the brunette across the way, a yellow bikini tight to her figure. She eyed Lee from her seat while sipping from a straw.

"Your source for information on my whereabouts is a looker."

"I can assure you, Lee, they won't all be that nice to look at."

"Understood," Lee said.

"See you tomorrow."

"Yes, see you tomorrow, Alex."

He placed the phone back on the bar. Only the froth of the espresso remained in the small cup. Lee thanked the barkeep and turned to admire his lookout. She'd already thrown a cover-up on and was walking down the pool deck with her friends in tow. She gave Lee a small wave and disappeared back into the hotel.

~

Charlotte sat on her bed with a laptop open. She clicked on the browser and typed "Deese" and "Georgia" into the search tab. She hit enter and reviewed the search results. Most articles were from years ago, but Charlotte clicked on each of the top results. She scanned the articles, reading bits and pieces while looking for photographs. Nothing resembled the man standing in Jake's kitchen window that morning.

She performed the same search on standard social media platforms and found next to little. Charlotte still clicked on a few of the profiles that matched the search terms, but it was hard to tell. *I got a clean look at the* man in the window, didn't I? Charlotte thought. She couldn't be sure. "Come on, Mr. Deese, where are you?" she murmured out loud, looking at each profile picture, skipping over images of men that looked too old or too young. After twenty more minutes of sleuthing, Charlotte abandoned her search. Could he be in some kind of law enforcement? Charlotte thought. He didn't seem like a cop—her gut told her he was quite the opposite.

Charlotte exited the browser and stood up from the bed. She found her running jacket and pulled the flash drive labeled *Collins III* from the pocket. Turning it over in her hands, she walked back to the bed and stuck the small black drive into the side of the laptop. Charlotte waited for a folder to appear on the desktop of her screen, but instead a window popped up. It prompted her for a password to access the contents of the storage device. She could do a lot on a computer, but she was not about to start hacking into password-protected devices.

As she stared at the screen, Charlotte heard footsteps coming down the hallway. Her mother rounded the corner into the bedroom.

"Charlotte, what do you want to do for dinner?"

"I am not all that hungry, Mom," Charlotte replied.

"Have you eaten today?"

"I had a big lunch," Charlotte responded, lying.

"Yeah? You still need to eat something for dinner. You put in a long run this morning, right? I saw you come in the door, and you looked tired." Her mother was clearly trying to make conversation. Charlotte glanced down at the thumb drive sticking out the side of the laptop. The side labeled "Collins III" was facedown.

"It wasn't a bad run this morning, Mom. Nine miles in the woods. Also did some core work and an active warmup."

"Are you still doing the core routine Dad showed you?"

Charlotte winced at the sound of "Dad." They hadn't mentioned his name since the night the police searched the house. Charlotte and her mother had not talked much since that night, certainly not about her father's absence. "Yes, ma'am, and I added a few more moves to the end of the routine. It's helping. I am definitely getting stronger."

The two sat on the bed together in silence. Grace noticed the family photo sitting on the nightstand, their last trip to Key West. The three of them smiled back at her. Grace looked away from the photo.

"What are you working on?" Grace asked.

"Research for a project that's due next week in psychology class," Charlotte said.

"Do you want any help? I loved psychology when I took it. So interesting."

"Maybe later."

"Well, let's have dinner together tonight. I want to talk a little bit about what's going on with everything."

"When you say *everything*, you mean Dad. What's there to talk about?" Charlotte replied, her voice cold. "I have called him probably fifteen times, and I've texted him, too." That was all true. "He isn't responding, and the newspapers keep saying they are looking for him. I don't care what you say, he didn't do this. He wouldn't do this. I can't believe you think he killed someone."

Grace sidestepped the affront from her daughter. "The news hasn't said they are going to arrest him for anything. If the police had an arrest warrant, they would come to the house first," Grace said, trying to reassure her daughter. "Let's order dinner, and we can talk more about this."

"Whatever you want to do," Charlotte replied.

"Listen, they are not going to arrest your father until some kind of evidence comes to light. That has not happened. If it does, we will handle it. They are going to interview me tomorrow, and I bet they will ask me to let them interview you," Grace said, a strong tone to her voice now. "We need to talk about this before any of that happens, do you understand me?"

Charlotte closed her laptop. Unbelievable. Her mother wanted to coach her on what to say to the police. Is this real life? She thought to herself. Her mind raced with a thousand more questions. Tears welled up in her eyes, and she pulled the thumb drive from the side of the laptop, clasping it in her hand. Charlotte looked back at her mother and wiped her eyes.

"I need you to listen to me and understand what needs to be done on this," Grace said again. "This is our family."

Charlotte wiped her eyes and nodded. "Can we order from Gallinari's Pizza?"

20

"This is a great town, but Washington will never be home," Bill Collins said as he closed the vehicle's door behind him. His driver, Geoff Bailey, gave a knowing nod as he eased the black SUV away from the curb and through the parking lot traffic. Eight minutes remained in the football game, but fans already trickled out of the stadium. The driver was careful as he nudged through the packs of discouraged pedestrians.

"Mr. Collins, do you mind if we put the game on the radio?"

Bill rolled his window down and let the warm evening air drift into the vehicle. He leaned his head back against the headrest and closed his eyes. "Go ahead and turn it on, Geoff," Bill said, eyes still closed. Geoff had played as a backup defensive lineman in college and was a longtime fan of Washington, DC's only professional football team. Bill wasn't about to deprive him of listening to the final minutes of that night's game.

Geoff tapped a button on the steering wheel with his thumb. The local sports radio station came over the speakers, and the two men sat listening to the broadcast. Both the play-by-play and color commentator sounded frustrated. The home team's performance that night showed the fans little to get excited about, and their division rival, the Philadelphia Eagles, had a fourteen-point lead. Only three games into the regular season and the team was on the verge of an 0-3 start.

"The backup is getting the next series," Geoff said over his shoulder as the SUV turned out of the parking lot. The vehicle pulled to a stop behind another row of traffic. "Hopefully the kid can show us something."

Bill had watched most of the game that night from one of the stadium's luxury boxes. He shook hands and chatted with executives in town for a conference geared toward American manufacturers. The group of mostly men ate well and drank plenty, their spouses far away in Nebraska, Indiana, or Michigan. Bill knew the group would enjoy themselves and all that DC had to offer. As soon as the comeback became improbable, he made his exit. Donor money was important, but he needed to get back home. Back to his voters. The polls still showed him trailing by four points.

"Everybody likes a comeback story," Bill said over the noise of the radio.

As the second-string rookie quarterback stepped under center, the commentators rattled off the statistics from his college career. Washington had drafted him in the fifth round, and the consensus among the diehard fans in DC was that the newcomer wasn't ready for the next step.

"Here we go," Geoff said as play resumed.

A roar erupted from FedExField, and Bill opened his eyes to look back over at the lights of the stadium. The commentators' voices on the radio picked up their pace. The new signal caller had just completed a twenty-two-yard strike across the middle to Washington's star receiver. The team reset its offense for another quick play, and the rookie dropped back again. He connected with the tight end on a flag route for another eighteen yards. The Eagles' defense called timeout, and the excited voices on the radio chatted away during the break. A comeback was mounting.

The cell phone vibrated in the pocket of Bill's blazer, and he checked the call. It was John Deese. Bill asked his driver to turn the game down. Geoff, reinvigorated by the late-game heroics, replied with an emphatic, "You got it, boss!"

"What do you have for me, John?"

. . .

"We collected all of the boxes from the house and delivered them to the storage container in Atlanta."

"Good," Bill replied. "Anything else at the house?"

"Nothing of interest, sir. We thoroughly checked all of the rooms and did not find anything else. The local authorities have his laptop, but my understanding is that the security on the computer is pretty tight. They can't access it."

"Well, then that should be it, right, John? As long as the laptop is clean, there won't be any other concerns."

There was a pause, and Deese said, "I do want to bring to your attention something strange today."

"Yes?" Bill said, shifting his weight. The vehicle picked up speed as game traffic loosened up.

"We left the boxes and other material packed up at Jake's house Saturday night. They were taped up and stored in the office."

"These are the documents that you found hidden in the shed? Go on," Bill prodded.

"Well, the boxes were taped Saturday night. All of them," John reiterated, his voice quick and already defensive. "When we got to the house again this morning, someone was there. Three or four boxes looked to have been cut open and—"

"What do you mean cut open?" Bill said.

"Like someone had been looking through the documents in the boxes," John said. "Before you ask, we know it was not the investigators."

"How do you know that?" Bill asked.

The vehicle approached the Taft Bridge, and Bill eyed the large lions standing guard at the bridge's edge. "John, who was in the house?"

Deese paused on the other end of the line. "Well, sir, I don't know who she was, but I think I got a good look at her."

21

"How did you and Mr. Acker get together?" Tim Dawson asked, leaning back in his chair with his hands in his lap.

The question caught Grace off guard, and she smiled at the young investigator. She considered his angle with this opening question as she stirred sugar into her coffee.

"Do you need anything else with your coffee?" Grace asked, stalling.

"No, ma'am, this is perfect, thank you. And I don't mean to necessarily pry into your personal life. I am just curious."

"Yes, you do—mean to pry, that is. It's fine, though. Coffee and a talk about my love life. No different than any other Monday morning playdate with a girlfriend."

"No, it's just for background and—"

"I am teasing, Special Agent Dawson. I'll see if I can remember. It has been a little while."

Tim nodded along. "I get it. How long have y'all been married?"

"Eighteen years in November. Time flies."

Tim looked away from her blue eyes. The cell phone poking out of his chest pocket would record the words of the conversation, but not the calm image of the woman that sat across from him. She had control of the situation, and Tim admired her easygoing nature. Here he was, sitting on the patio of her beautiful home, drinking coffee, and openly investigating her husband for a crime. No attorney sat next to her to stonewall the questioning. She made no stilted attempt at small talk or flattery—just her calm blue eyes staring back at him.

"This is a two-way street, Special Agent Dawson. I expect to hear something about your love life before you leave."

Tim half laughed and said, "There isn't much to tell, ma'am."

"I doubt that," Grace replied. "There has to be someone."

"Nothing steady, ma'am. My work is my focus in life right now."

"Is that so?" Grace replied, her eyebrow raised.

As Tim nodded, Grace picked her cell phone up off the table and fiddled with the screen for a moment. She turned it around and showed him a picture. A wide grin came across his face, but he reined it in. "How did you get that photo?" he asked, staring at the snapshot of his weekend. She'd seen it come across social media. The photo was taken Friday night at Juno, the restaurant he and Maggie met at for dinner. Half of the restaurant's chairs were on tables in the background. They closed the place down that night. In the photo, he and Maggie stood close together, leaning against Juno's amber-colored bar. A laughing Kevin June stood behind them, wineglasses in hand. Tim vaguely remembered huddling together for the picture.

Grace turned the phone back around and hit a button on the side that locked the screen. "I am friends with Kevin June. Chipped in some capital when he got Juno started."

"It's a great restaurant. The food is excellent, and the June brothers are good guys," Tim replied, uncomfortable with his lack of control over the meeting.

Grace tapped her index and middle fingers on the side of her coffee mug, blue eyes resting on him. "It's a nice picture of the two of you. I'll share it with you. You never know, it could turn into something long-term."

Tim stayed off social media. He loathed the constant sharing of photos and locations on the various platforms out there. It all seemed unnecessary to him.

"Was this a date?" Grace asked, enjoying the ambush.

"Now who's prying?" he replied with another half-laugh.

Grace rolled her eyes. "Like I said, this is a two-way street!"

"No, ma'am, it was not a date. Just friends." He sounded unconvincing.

"She is gorgeous. How do I know her?"

"Her name is Maggie Reynolds. She is an attorney here in town. Works with the public defender's office."

"There have been some news articles about her, right?"

"Quite a few. She is a good lawyer. I've seen her work in the courtroom firsthand," Tim said, giving as professional a response as possible—knowing everything was being recorded.

"So, work friends?" Grace asked.

"That's right."

Grace smiled again. "Well, that's how everything began with Lee and me. Not work friends, just friends friends."

Tim nodded to show he was listening, grateful the conversation was moving away from his personal life.

"Lee and I started dating during the summer of 1999. It started on a trip to the lake with friends. A summer fling, really."

"How did you know each other?" Tim asked, although he knew the answer.

"High school. Lee was a year ahead of me."

"Same class as Jake Collins?"

"That's right," she said. "Jake and my husband both grew up here. I've lived most of my life here since moving to town in elementary school. I'll never be from here, though. Are you from this area, Special Agent Dawson?"

"No, ma'am. Alabama. Now, both the Collins and Acker families seem to have deep ties to this community," he said, redirecting the conversation back to his investigation.

"That's right, they are both 'old money' families, as people like to say. They are really just farmers that found some success years ago. Their great-grandfathers and grandfathers turned business owners or politicians some-where down the line. The legacy was in place well before Lee and Jake were born."

"It's an interesting family history, though, right?"

"You could say that," Grace said, a smirk on her face. "There are plenty of stories about the colorful characters in both families—war heroes, politicians, rural tycoons, and a few outlaws mixed in."

"My understanding is there is a long history of men that muddied the line between the legal and illegal." Tim was genuinely interested.

"There are plenty of stories. It's local folklore, really. There are black sheep in every family."

"Uh-huh," Tim said, sarcasm heavy in his voice.

"There is a dichotomy that exists in us all," Grace added.

"Some would say that," Tim replied, raising his eyebrows. "Pirates, bandits, and bushwhackers are still criminals in my book."

"Then you need to update your book," Grace said, waving her coffee cup in a dismissive manner. "The histories of these families have been distorted over the years, but I think we know that's not what you came to talk about today."

"Well, what did I come to talk about today, then, Mrs. Acker?"

"You want to know Lee's and my story. Then you want to know if any of that fits into Jake's death, right?"

"Something like that," Tim said, holding Grace's stare from across the table.

"Well, I can assure you, Jake Collins did not die over some dispute to do with me."

Tim noted a hint of self-deprecation in her words—a touch of honesty, maybe. He shifted in his seat, waiting for her to continue. He didn't want to say anything that would disturb her train of thought. He'd learned that witnesses and suspects would often provide the best information when faced with silence.

"Lee and I never dated in high school. We shared friends in social circles that overlapped, but there was never anything romantic between us. My ties to the Acker family at that time were through Lee's brother, Cliff."

Tim nodded.

"Cliff and I went to part of elementary school together. Then we were as close to friends as boys and girls can be during those early middle school years. By high school, we ran with the same friend group all the way through graduation in 1999."

Tim made a mental note. That put Grace Acker at somewhere around thirty-six or thirty-seven years old.

"Cliff went to Texas to play football, and I went off to Auburn for my freshmen year."

"That's right. I remember watching those Texas teams that Cliff played on." Tim hesitated. "And the play in the USC game."

"Every college football fan does," Grace said with a sigh.

Tim nodded. He remembered that Rose Bowl game well. Fifteen at the time, he was working a shift bussing tables. He watched parts of the game from the kitchen of his family's restaurant as he hauled plates from the dining area to the dish pit. The University of Texas and University of Southern California played in one of the greatest games in college football history that night. The Longhorns topped the Trojans in the last seconds of the game with a thrilling touchdown run by the UT quarterback. A mass of fans swarmed the field and helped the team celebrate under a shower of confetti. All the proud players, coaches, and fans were dancing on the field that night, except for the redshirt senior, Cliff Acker. He watched the on-field celebration from a small television in his team's locker room. Ejected from the game, Cliff formed what would become a small footnote in the history of the Texas Longhorns' championship run.

With 6:42 left to play in the fourth quarter, the Trojans held their biggest lead of the game. They trotted out their special teams' unit to kick off to the waiting Longhorns' return team. The score 38-26 burned bright on the scoreboard above the field as the players took their positions. The Trojans' kicker, a finalist for college football's prestigious Lou Groza place-kicking award, booted the ball four yards into the end zone. A touchback on any other night, the Longhorns' returner opted to take it out into the field of play. Cliff Acker helped lead the way up the sideline as a seam opened in the sea of bodies. A clear lane down the right side of the field held firm, and the return went for fifty-four yards. The game-changing play electrified the Longhorns' sideline, and the crowd erupted in cheers until the referees' yellow flags cluttered the field.

Twelve yards behind the play stood Cliff Acker. A referee barking in his face, Cliff pushed the striped official away as he started toward the Long-horns' sideline. The body of the Trojans' prized placekicker, Martin Cruz, wrenched in pain near midfield, his left leg broken in two places below the knee. Medical staff rushed on, and the crowd fell silent. The officiating crew huddled on field for a conference and then ejected Cliff for the dirty hit. It cost the Longhorns' needed field position, but they still found a way to win the football game.

"Did he ever get a ring for that national championship?" Tim asked.

"I don't think so," Grace said. "Even though he didn't have any eligibility left, the University of Texas kicked him off the team and banned him from ever coming back to any of the football facilities."

"Wow," Tim said. "Harsh."

"It was a dirty hit," she said. "Martin Cruz never got to play again either. I still don't know why he did it."

She paused to glance at the investigator's notepad. Not a single line scribbled on the front page. Grace made the choice yesterday not to call Bruce Tevens, the family attorney. She would call him later. She thought about her words as she slid her coffee cup off to the side. Picking up her phone, she checked the time. The screen read 10:15 a.m.

$\sim$

"Before I dated Lee, before I went off to college, before all of that, I was in love with Jake Collins."

Tim nodded. No surprise in her revelation. Still, he hoped the microphone in his chest pocket would capture her every word.

"Looking back, we were still kids at the time, high school love and all, but it is part of the story. We 'became an item' during the fall of my sophomore year of high school." Grace rolled her eyes as she said this. "I was fifteen."

Tim listened. He'd seen the high school yearbooks and old photos. All buried in a box of keepsakes that Jake Collins had stored in his study. An investigator with the office even found a prom photo of Grace and Jake together. A copy of the photo sat in one of the investigative files back on Tim's desk. Two high school kids, skinny and smiling, standing in front of a makeshift Eiffel Tower. "A Night in Paris" scrolled in gold lettering on the banner behind them. Jake wore a black tux, sized too large for his frame. Grace wore a pink dress with rhinestones across the high neckline.

"Jake checked all the boxes. He was popular and the star quarterback of the football team. Good-looking and a great student. All the girls wanted to date him."

"Tough competition for Lee at the time," Tim added.

"Sort of," Grace replied. "Lee was no second fiddle by high school standards. A great wide receiver and free safety on their football team. Better than Jake at basketball and baseball. Lee was wilder back then, but he finished as the salutatorian of his graduating class."

"All-American guys, right?" Tim said, arms crossed.

"They both were given a lot, certainly privileged upbringings by local standards. Still, they worked extremely hard to achieve success. It sounds ridiculous to say this, but they were kids that came with that extra gear built in. Do you know what I mean?"

Tim nodded. "I do. It's no coincidence that high achievers have an extreme work ethic. Rich or poor, discipline doesn't discriminate."

"I agree," Grace replied. "My husband is still driven to this day."

In the ten days since the murder, Tim asked nearly everyone he knew what their thoughts were about the victim and his main suspect. He'd spoken with countless friends and family. Everyone went on about how great both of the men were. Tim was growing tired of the narrative—every man has faults.

"Hardworking, high achieving, and a local boy, but where is he today, Grace?" Tim spurted out. He immediately regretted the comment.

Grace didn't blink as she resumed her narrative, "Like I said, they were both hardworking, and they went head-to-head in everything. They were fiercely competitive, and more so against each other. It was a recipe for conflict between friends, but sports defined them. It bonded the two together."

Tim nodded again. "No animosity between the two?"

"To me, animosity implies that there is some dislike or hatred involved. That was never the case. They were close friends. We spent many weekends together during that time in high school. So no, I don't think there existed any animosity between them."

"Did he attend your wedding?"

"No, he did not. Lee and I understood at the time."

Grace looked away from the investigator, and he could tell she was thinking. There were things she wouldn't tell him. He knew that was the case with anyone he interviewed. All witnesses lied. The lies were often small or immaterial, but Tim constantly looked for the witness that lied. Not because he wanted to catch that person being untruthful. No, that was not what mattered—what mattered was why that person would lie.

"When I say they were close friends, I mean it. I remember when Lee's father committed suicide in the spring of 1998. That was Lee's and Jake's senior year of high school. I remember exactly where I was when I heard about it. Jake and I were sitting on the beach in Panama City, Florida. We'd made a day-trip down there and had just settled in. When we got the call, Jake insisted we jump in the car to head back. We drove straight to the hospital. Jake was that kind of a friend."

"That's terrible," Tim said, unsure why he wasn't aware of this part of Lee's background.

"It was awful."

"That was in 1998? Do you remember the month?"

"It was baseball season. The week before the high school playoffs started. Middle of April, I think."

Tim pulled a pen from his pocket and noted the date on his pad. The sunlight felt warm on his face as he scribbled a few lines about the incident. He'd check on it later.

"So, they were friends, you were dating Jake, and then what happened?" Tim said, returning his gaze across the table.

"Life happened, I guess," Grace said, cradling the coffee cup in her hands.

"No, I mean what happened with you and Jake?" Tim prodded.

"Jake went off to college, and I started my senior year of high school. We dated for a short while into that school year, but Jake was at The Citadel on a football scholarship. He had his responsibilities as an athlete, and the cadre is hard on cadets during their first year. Even when I went up to visit, the rules were strict around when and how long he could leave campus."

"It is a military college," Tim added.

"I know that, smartass," Grace said with a smile. "We just drifted apart, you know? We were a couple of kids still and we wanted different things in life. Jake focused on playing football and getting ready to join the military. I focused on life back here."

"I get it," Tim said. He did.

"I don't think our story is all that unique. I mean, did things work out between you and your girlfriend in high school?"

"Of course not."

"That relationship still felt real, though, right?"

"It did," Tim replied, the response instinctive. It surprised him.

"Love at that time in life leaves an imprint on you. Wherever you go, whomever you love after, the mark from that early love still stays there."

"I don't disagree," Tim remarked. "It becomes part of our history."

The two sat there in silence, a natural break in the conversation. Tim looked out toward the woods as the sounds of birds chattering filled the void.

"So, you and Jake break up. Where was Lee?"

"Out of the picture. He was up in Nashville playing baseball at Vanderbilt."

"Scholarship athlete?"

"That's right, also studied economics and history while he was there."

"So how did your paths cross again?"

"Not until the spring of my senior year of high school."

Grace looked down at her lap and tightened the cloth belt on her green dress as she spoke. The color looked nice against her tanned skin.

"I went over to Auburn for a visit and to look at housing for my freshman year. My dad was with me, and he wanted to see a baseball game while we were there. A lot of people from Blakeston were at the game because Vanderbilt was in town."

"The Lee Acker fan club?"

"That's right, the hometown boy returns," she said, smiling. "Lee spotted me from the field, and in between innings, he walked over to the edge of the stands to get my attention. Asked me to come out with the team after the game."

"Guessing your dad wasn't having it."

"Absolutely not. My parents were strict, and Lee had, let's say, a reputation. My dad and I got in the truck and headed back to Blakeston that night after the game."

"Smart move by your dad," Tim laughed. "I take it Mr. Acker was persistent, though?"

"Right again," she said. "In his defense, he didn't have to try too hard—I was flattered. He came home for the summer after his semester ended and kept asking for a date. I'd graduated by then and started working a summer job. It was an amazing summer together."

"I am not the best at math, but you mentioned your daughter is now a senior in high school, right?"

Grace smiled. "We don't have to beat around the subject, Special Agent Dawson. Our daughter was conceived at the end of that summer. She was born in the spring of 2000. I found out I was pregnant my fourth week as a freshman at Auburn."

"Wow," Tim said, shaking his head. "That's a lot to handle at eighteen."

"Little bit. I called Lee before I told my parents."

"What did he say?" Tim asked. "If you don't mind me asking."

She sat back in her chair and readjusted her legs. The sun bearing down on them felt hot. Grace couldn't remember the last time she'd talked with anyone about that moment in her life. She smiled at the memory of Lee's response. The feelings of terror and excitement coursing through her body as the phone rang.

"The funny thing is, it took me a little while to find him so I could tell him the news. I called his house in Nashville, and his roommate said Lee was fishing in Costa Rica. He didn't know where, with who, how long, or anything, really."

"Helpful," Tim said, grinning.

"So, shit, I call Cliff's dorm in Austin, Texas, thinking he will know where his older brother is fishing. Cliff's roommate doesn't know where Cliff is. Tells me that Cliff had some family emergency with his parents."

"Well, I know the senior Acker had passed away at that point," Tim said.

"And Mrs. Acker died when Cliff was nine," Grace quickly added. "A car wreck."

"Jesus," Tim said, rubbing his head.

"So, I knew immediately that Cliff told some story so that his head football coach would let him have a leave of absence from the team."

"Wait, back up, the Acker boys lost both parents before the end of high school?"

Tim jotted more notes on his pad on the table.

"It was tough on them," Grace said, turning back to her story. It was clear she didn't want to dwell on that heartbreak. "Well, I call over to The Citadel and get the number for Jake's room in the dorms. His roommate knows my name and seems intrigued by the call. He tells me he knows where Jake is but that he would be in deep shit if anyone found out."

"Swear your friends to secrecy and they'll tell your ex-girlfriend where to find you," Tim remarked playfully.

"Whose side are you on?" Grace said, smiling.

"Well, I am going to say yours even though I am here performing a murder investigation, Grace."

"That's what this is? Seems like you just came by to talk about my love life," Grace replied, teasing him again.

"Yeah, yeah, get to the point."

"Well, the roommate in Charleston gives me the number for a travel fishing company in Costa Rica. I call the number and leave a message for Lee to call me as soon as possible."

"How did he handle it?"

"Better than most twenty-year-old guys would."

Tim nodded, listening.

"I finally get him on the phone, and he tells me they are flying back the next day. He went up to Nashville, withdrew from his classes at Vanderbilt, and moved home to Blakeston to work in the family business. He finished college online and never looked back at baseball."

"Wow, so this is a trip with Jake Collins. I assume your ex found out about the pregnancy around the same time as Lee?" Tim asked, leaning forward in his seat.

"Yeah, he found out the same night."

"How did that go over?"

"There was never an argument that I was aware of. Lee and I both moved home to Blakeston, we got married, and started our life together."

"I understand all that, but how did it impact the friendship with Jake?" Tim prodded.

Grace paused, then said, "He never talked to me again."

"Never?"

"We passed in public a few times over the years, and he was cordial. I tried to call, but he never called back. We invited him to the wedding. I sent him cards when he returned home from the Middle East. Nothing."

"What about Lee?" Tim said.

Grace thought about the question. She looked across the table at the investigator and sighed.

"Lee understood that us getting married changed things between him and Jake."

"How?" Tim said, needing something for the recording.

"I don't know, it changed the dynamic, you know. Lee and I spoke about it a few times, and he assured me that Jake would always be a friend. That he would come to us if he ever needed anything."

"Did that ever happen?" Tim asked, now on the edge of his seat.

Grace nodded across the table, her face somber.

"When?" Dawson prodded.

"Two weeks ago," she replied. "He called me and told me he needed to see Lee."

22

Lee heard a knock on the door of his hotel room. His wristwatch read 11:30 a.m.

"Who is it?" Lee called as he approached the door.

"Delivery from the front desk," called a voice with a heavy accent.

Lee checked the peephole and saw a short round man in a bellhop's uniform. He opened the door, and the man greeted him with a smile. He handed Lee a box that was taped shut and added that the package arrived earlier that morning by courier. Lee placed the box on the dresser inside the hotel room and returned with a few pesos. Thanking the man, Lee closed the door behind him and returned to the box.

Lee found a letter opener on the nearby desk and slashed into the tape. He popped the top and found a black motorcycle helmet inside. As he pulled the helmet from the box, a pair of riding gloves, keys, and a GPS spilled out onto the dresser. A rectangular piece of stationary, taped to the inside of the box, caught his eye. He pulled the note free and read its contents.

"I trust you have enjoyed your stay in Querétaro, and I look forward to hosting you this evening for dinner. The GPS device included with this note will guide you to one of my family's estates. You will find a black motorcycle parked at the edge of the *Plaza de Armas* that has sufficient fuel to make the journey. Depart from your hotel no later than 4:00 p.m., as the trip will take at least two hours. Please understand that this invitation is extended to you alone. *Cariñosos saludos, Alex*."

Lee turned the note over in his hands and placed it on the dresser in front of him. He went to his bag and retrieved his map along with a black marker. Sitting at the small desk, he turned on the GPS to begin reviewing the route. The coordinates, already entered into the device, led to the southeastern corner of the Guanajuato state—a patch of dirt in the middle of nowhere. Lee marked Alex's family's estate on his map and scanned the surrounding area. The banks of the Lerma River were ten miles to the south, and the foothills of a small mountain range—*Sierra de los Agustinos*—looked to be only a few miles to the north. The closest town of any significance, Jerécuaro, sat ten miles to the east.

Lee felt a knot in his stomach begin to tighten as he stared at the map in front of him. The surprise location outside of the city worried him. He touched his forehead and noticed the sweat forming above his brow. He folded up the map and grabbed a bottle of water from the mini fridge. He turned the GPS off and placed it inside his bedside table, next to the Beretta. Stretching out on the bed, he pulled his one remaining cell phone from his pocket. With a web browser, Lee attempted to research the area around his new destination in rural Mexico. He found little of substance. It was safe to assume that this was the way Alex's family liked it.

Tossing the phone aside, he decided he needed to eat. It was lunchtime. Food would help his stomach and his nerves. He would eat well. There was no telling what would be served for dinner.

~

Bernard Howard eyed Tim Dawson walking past his office with his head down. He hollered from his desk chair, "Hey, Dawson, come in here and check this video out!"

Tim kept walking down the hallway, headed in the direction of his office. His headphones were in and the recording of his interview with Grace Acker played in his ears. He felt a pat on his shoulder, and it spun him around. Bernard stared back at him with a wide grin on his face.

"T.D., I've got something for you!"

Bernard was on the balls of his feet, bouncing no more than two feet away. He looked like a boxer as he clapped his hands together in front him and pointed both index fingers at Tim's chest.

Tim laughed as he pulled an earbud from his ear. "What'd you eat for lunch, man? You are wired up."

"Nothing yet, been working on something for you. We can go grab a bite, but I want to show you this video first."

"Nah, I already ate. I'm just grabbing some paperwork and heading to the gym at three. Can the video wait? I'm going over a few things in my head on the Acker case."

"This video has to do with the Acker case. You are going to want to see it."

"What is it?" Tim asked.

"Surveillance footage from a gas station in Mexico. I can't be sure, but I think your guy is on it," Bernard replied, excited.

Tim pulled his second earbud away from the opposite ear as he followed Bernard back down the hallway. As they walked, Bernard explained that there was a website he checked out from time to time that showed footage from shootouts with law enforcement.

"The videos are uploaded from all over the world. Good guys and bad guys have cameras now. These videos come at the shootings from all angles," Bernard said, sitting down in the chair behind his computer. "Some of the footage can get pretty crazy, especially the bodycam footage."

"How often are videos uploaded to the site?" Tim asked.

"There is something new up every single day. Most of the graphic stuff gets taken down once it's flagged, but it doesn't stop people from trying to get it out there for a while."

Tim stood behind Bernard's chair and stared at the computer monitor. Bernard had the video queued up, and he pressed play. The date and location of the shootout—September 22, 2016, Nuevo León, Mexico—scrolled across the screen as the video started. Tim watched as the surveillance footage showed two police officers step out of a marked pickup truck. A row of fuel pumps ran along the far side of the vehicle, and the angle from the

surveillance camera showed a wide view of the road fronting the convenience store.

"Do you know when this video went up on the site?" Tim asked.

"Only a few hours ago, must have been added earlier this morning,"
Bernard said, pausing the video while they spoke. He right-clicked on the
username—*El Mariachi*—that uploaded the video. The profile information
popped up in a separate window, and Tim squinted to read the screen.
"There is nothing about this user," Bernard replied. "We'd have to get some
kind of warrant or subpoena to get more information."

Bernard pressed play again on the video. A man in a baseball cap
entered the frame. The brim from the baseball cap covered his face, but
Tim could tell it was a white male, medium build, with a wedding ring on
his left hand. As the man passed the truck, one of the officers followed
behind him.

"Watch the guy in the ball cap," Bernard said, leaning back in his swivel
chair.

Tim nodded. "The image quality isn't bad, but what am I looking for?"

The camera angle switched to a view from inside the convenience store.
The video had no audio, and they watched in silence as the front windows
to the store were blown out one by one. Both the officer and the man in the
cap remained in the frame. The image showed the man in the cap slide
what looked like a handgun across the tile floor of the convenience store.
The Mexican officer picked it up, and they both crawled to the front of the
store. The officer fired volleys through the windows as the man in the baseball cap exited the front door, crawling on his stomach.

The video continued rolling from inside the store until it switched to an
angle directly above the first row of fuel pumps. The man in the ball cap
reappeared from under the officers' pickup truck and began talking with an
injured officer lying near the fuel pumps outside the store. They could see
on the video that the officer's right thigh was dark from blood, and he
appeared unable to move. The injured officer passed a handgun to the man
in the cap, but the video angle switched back to the view from inside the
store. The healthy officer, now repositioned on the other side of the door,
continued to fire from his covered position behind the cinder block front
wall.

"Do you have a shot of the—" Tim began but stopped himself.

The video switched angles again, and a clear image from above the fuel pumps appeared on the screen. The man in the ball cap crouched behind the pump, firearm in hand. Tim watched as the man fired a few bursts from the weapon and returned to cover behind the pump. Then the man readjusted his cap, and the individual's full face came into view.

"Pause it right there!"

Tim and Bernard stared at the screen in silence.

"Have you compared the image with any photos we have in our system?" Tim asked.

"I can run it if you think it might be him."

"It's him," Tim said, smiling. "That's the son of a gun right there. What the hell is he doing getting involved in gunfights in Mexico, though?"

Bernard made copies of the images on the screen and pressed play on the video again. The two watched as the camera angles flipped back and forth twice more. Unknown gunmen across the street jumped into a truck with what looked like a wounded comrade. Acker helped the wounded Mexican officer to the bed of the patrol truck and began talking with the two officers.

"That has to be him," Tim added again. "Pause the image there where they are talking at the tailgate of the truck."

They zeroed in on a still image of Lee Acker wiping down the law enforcement–issued handgun.

Tim turned to his buddy with a smile. "Bernard, did I ever tell you all that time you waste screwing around on the internet is valuable to this department?"

23

Lee rolled off the throttle as he crested a high hill and pulled the clutch in with his left hand. It quieted the engine. He could hear the sound of the tires running against the road below as the motorcycle angled down the other side of the hill. He tapped his foot twice on the gear shifter and let off the clutch. The tachometer jumped, and the bike groaned as it slowed against the steep grade of the road. He removed his left hand from the grip on the handlebars and placed it in his lap. The Mexican wind pressed against his chest as he coasted down the hill. It washed over his bare arms and, from time to time, kicked the back of his T-shirt up. Lee glanced at the GPS on the handlebars; it showed fifteen miles remained until he reached the destination.

As the bike rolled into the outskirts of the town of Jerécuaro, Lee spotted a group of kids playing soccer in a field by the road. He gave the throttle a few quick clips as he passed—*brap, brap, brap!* The throaty sound of the engine caught the attention of a few of the boys standing along the sideline. They raised their arms in excitement, confirming the universal truth that boys are born to love fast cars and loud motorcycles. They excitedly waved as he zipped by the makeshift soccer pitch, and he gave a short wave in return.

He continued on to the city center and slowed his speed. Unclasping his helmet, he slipped it off and placed it on the metal gas tank of the motorcycle. He ran a gloved hand through his hair, combing it back. Sweat had built up in the helmet during the last hour-and-a-half ride, but the sunshine and breeze on his face would dry it in minutes. The knobby tires bounced along the rough street as he crept past two- and three-story buildings painted in bright colors.

To Lee's surprise, thick traffic appeared ahead at the city's main square. Cars and mopeds lined the road, and a barricade blocked the street some fifty yards ahead. Above the barricade, an orange banner read *Feliz Día de San Miguel* in sparkling letters. Must be a festival to celebrate Saint Michael's Day, Lee thought, setting one foot down occasionally to balance the bike as the pedestrian traffic forced him to slow to a snail's pace. In predominantly Catholic countries like Mexico, the celebration of the patron saints of cities or causes throughout the calendar year was customary. Lee's church back home probably didn't care that Saint Michael's Day existed.

Lee pulled the motorcycle to a stop to review the route on his GPS. He cut the engine on the bike and leaned it on its side stand. He'd have to skirt around the traffic and street closures. As he looked for the best alternate route, groups of people dressed in festival attire walked by on the sidewalk. It was not uncommon for a few tourists to visit the city for the festival. They'd mix in with the locals and spend money with local vendors and businesses, a welcome influx of cash for the small town. A few festivalgoers nodded at Lee when he looked up from the screen on the handlebars. The men wore hats and donned colorful jackets, while the ladies wore bright dresses with their hair in high buns. Lee nodded back. He looked like an *extranjero*, a foreigner, but the locals greeted him with smiles.

Lee slid his helmet on and pressed the start button on the motorcycle to fire it back up. The rhythmic *pat, pat, pat* of the exhaust clipped along as the bike idled. Lee pressed the shifter down with his left foot and heard the familiar click as the transmission transitioned from neutral to first gear. The sound from the engine competed briefly with the festival's music ahead. Its rumble echoing off the walls of the stone buildings that lined the street. Slowly letting the clutch out with his left hand, Lee pulled away from the curb. He wove his way down a side street and circumvented the festival with ease.

As Lee made his way to the other side of town, he found himself again on a wide stretch of road. He glanced at his watch—it read 5:45 p.m. "Plenty of time," Lee told himself. He opened the throttle up and sped toward the unknown.

~

A stone wall with a wrought iron gate came into view, and Lee slowed the motorcycle as he approached. The bumpy trail was covered in small stones and gravel, dusty from a lack of rainfall. He steered the bike, avoiding the ruts on the trail. Two men appeared ahead, leaning against a beat-up Land Rover from the mid-90s. They smoked cigarettes and listened to a regional rock station on the radio. Standing up straight as Lee's motorcycle came closer into view, they waved him over to the vehicle.

Lee obliged, pulling the motorcycle to a stop some ten feet away. Metallica blared from the speakers of the Land Rover, and the shorter of the two men reached inside to turn the volume down. Both men had long hair and mustaches. They wore tactical boots and clean fatigues. Lee killed the engine on the bike and removed his helmet.

The taller of the two men spoke first.

"*Señor Acker?*"

"That's me," Lee replied, running his gloved hand through his hair to smooth it down. He readjusted the weight of the bike between his legs, and he felt his feet scrape against the stones on the ground.

"*Bienvenidos a La Finca,*" the man added. Welcome to The Farm.

Lee nodded, and his eyes flicked to a firearm resting on the hood of the Land Rover.

"I am the Olivera family's head of security. My name is Roberto," he said, taking another step closer toward Lee. "You must ride with me."

Lee looked at both men and swung his leg back off of the seat of the motorcycle. "Fine by me, boys. My ass could use the break."

Lee tossed the motorcycle's key to Roberto's sidekick and headed toward the Land Rover. Lee opened the passenger door, and it gave the creak of a beater vehicle meant for work on a farm. He slammed it shut, stowing his bag at his feet. He felt certain they would search it.

"*Señorita Olivera* is running late," the man said, taking his seat on the driver side.

"No worries," Lee responded. "I'm on vacation."

Roberto mashed the clutch in and started the vehicle. It struggled to start, groaning to life on the second try. He looked over at Lee as the Rover lurched forward, "She asked me to take you to your room here on *La Finca*. You'll be comfortable. You can shower and relax before dinner."

"That's mighty kind of you," Lee said, playing up a down-home accent. The sarcasm was lost on his driver.

The sidekick stood by the gate, and its two black panels opened to allow the Rover to pass through. A dirt road snaked its way ahead through the woods. Roberto changed the station on the radio and hand-cranked the window down on his side.

"How was your ride from Querétaro?" he asked, pulling a smoke from his chest pocket.

"Nice," Lee replied, rolling the window down on the passenger side. "Been years since I've ridden a motorcycle."

"Your wife won't let you?" Roberto chided, lighting the cigarette and taking a deep drag. He smiled at his own comment and blew the stream of smoke out his window as the vehicle bumped along the trail.

Lee wasn't surprised his captor was talking shit. Mexican men were proud and particularly skilled at trash-talking. "No, Roberto, it's your mother and sister that have the problem with it."

The sidekick zipped by the vehicle on the right side, the motorcycle fishtailing as it climbed a steep hill ahead. Roberto smiled. He was in no hurry and drove the Rover as if he'd bought the vehicle the weekend before.

"Tsk, tsk, tsk, Señor Acker. You insult my mother. You are in Mexico, don't you know that is, how do you say, out of bounds?" He made the comment with an easy tone in his voice. "I left home at fourteen and joined a group of guerillas in my home country of El Salvador. I haven't seen my mother since."

Lee looked over at his driver, unsure if he was joking. Roberto held a solid poker face. Lee decided to counter with honesty. "I'm sorry. I lost my mother when I was eleven."

Roberto stared ahead at the trail and took another drag on his cigarette before tossing it out the window. He rubbed his head and squinted at the road in front of them. The trail needed work. Rainwater appeared to have washed out large sections, making it impassable without a truck or SUV. Roberto kept both hands on the wheel as he navigated over a severely rutted area.

"The Olivera family brought me on to handle part of their security two years ago. There won't be any problems as long as you follow the rules of the home."

Lee expected this type of arrangement. He knew he would likely become a quasi-prisoner during his time on Alex's family's property. "I don't foresee a problem, Roberto."

"Good," he said, still looking straight ahead.

The vehicle entered into a clearing, and a large ranch-style home came into view. Pastures surrounded the residence, and Lee spotted a small airstrip running along the back of the property. A metal hangar of sorts anchored one end of the runway, and a red barn sat at the other. Horses stood under a nearby grouping of shade trees and stared at the Rover as it pulled to a stop.

"I am sorry about your mother," Roberto said, pulling the parking brake back with a crank.

"It was a long time ago, but thank you."

"I have worked for the Olivera family for a short time, Señor Acker." He paused before opening the door to the vehicle. "They have reminded me, though, of something that I forgot many years ago."

"What's that?" Lee asked.

"*La familia lo es todo.*"

Lee nodded and proceeded to step out of the vehicle.

Family is everything.

24

Fronteras Force, S.A., started calling itself "The Force in Border Labor" when it began doing business in 2008. An obscure outfit based out of Mexico City, Fronteras got its start facilitating the exchange of labor between Mexico and its two closest neighbors to the south—Guatemala and Belize. The initial group of investors that formed Fronteras recognized that their own businesses faced two major concerns. The increasing regulations on the kind of labor they could employ and the vicious drug cartels. The investors' businesses, located in various Mexican states situated along Mexico's southern border, needed to exercise better control over the cartels and the disenfranchised people working in those areas. The investors were a collection of established Mexican families disgusted by the pervasive cartels intertwined with the Mexican identity. They formed Fronteras to lobby and advise governments to the south of Mexico on how best to monetize the exchange of labor. Every day, thousands were crossing the borders across Central America looking for work. Fronteras positioned itself to capitalize on those individuals that were trying to survive.

Since its inception, Fronteras had grown exponentially each year, and the talented teams of Fronteras' advisors were known to be both resourceful and aggressive. The leadership within the organization maintained open lines of communication with the offices of key advisors in governments and major corporations across North, Central, and South America. When governments or private companies faced labor disruption or a labor crisis, one of the first calls they made was to an advisor with Fronteras. Former politicians and prominent businesspersons from Mexico, Brazil, and the United States sat on Fronteras' board of directors, and Fronteras boasted an impressive cache of Fortune 500 clients. Fronteras was considered by many to be a unique business and rising star in a burgeoning industry.

On top of the organization's success, it was also considered to be quite progressive in the male-driven Mexican business community. The Fronteras' board selected Alex Olivera Calderon to serve as the organization's chief executive officer in January of 2016. She was the highest-ranking person in the organization's leadership and the first female CEO in Fronteras' history. Those in her business respected her, and she had shown herself capable of navigating the tumultuous relationships Mexican business owners often had with the cartels and Mexican government.

"This is her plane arriving now," Roberto said, pointing to the lights of a small aircraft making its approach on the airfield.

The last light from the day dipped behind the short line of mountains in the distance. Lee watched as the small plane bounced twice, landing some two hundred yards from the back of the house. Lee sat in a patio chair facing the airfield, and Roberto stood ten feet away, slightly behind Lee's chair. He watched Lee's every move.

"How often does the family use this property?" Lee said, looking over his shoulder to make conversation.

Roberto shrugged. "I work for Señorita Olivera, that is all I am concerned with. I don't deal with her family's whereabouts."

"Fair enough."

Lee understood the family's need for discretion. The Olivera clan, made up of successful businesspeople with skilled lawyers and established relationships in the banking community, had a nefarious element to the way it did its business.

"How long do you plan to stay?" Roberto asked.

"Not long."

Roberto nodded, and they waited in silence. The two men watched the lights of a newer Land Rover swing around the far side of the airstrip's hangar. The beams from the headlights flitted about as the vehicle bounced along the road leading to the house. As Lee waited, he thought of his brother and wondered if Cliff ever made it down to *La Finca*.

The Rover stopped twenty feet from the stone patio, and Lee stood to greet his host. Alex Olivera stepped out of the vehicle and gave Lee an immediate reminder of why his brother remained enthralled with her. She wore a dark pantsuit and red high heels. The silk scarf around her neck and short hairstyle made her look as if she fell off the cover of a fashion magazine. She didn't smile at Lee when exiting the vehicle but turned to her driver and thanked him for the ride over to the house. She moved intentionally, and Lee waited until she was within feet to say anything.

"My brother wishes he could have made the trip."

She lifted her eyes to his and held his gaze, her blue eyes those of a bona fide knockout. "I thought Southern men were supposed to be gentlemen," she replied, brushing a strand of hair from her face. "It seems you are trying to start a verbal confrontation with a lady before a dinner engagement?"

Lee had forgotten how proper Alex's English was from years spent studying at the University of Cambridge in England.

"I'd never do that sort of thing, ma'am. I was just sending along the warm regrets of Mr. Clifford J. Acker."

She carried her overnight bag in hand, and her cell phone began buzzing in the other. She checked the screen and silenced the call.

"Busy as always, I assume," Lee added.

"*Por supuesto,*" she replied.

Alex turned to Roberto and asked him to ready one of the vehicles. They were going into town. Roberto nodded and slipped inside the back doors to the house without a word.

"Are we hitting the town tonight?" Lee asked, surprised she was planning to turn around and leave after just having arrived.

"We are. *El Día de San Miguel* is an important day in Jerécuaro. Saint Michael is the patron saint of the city, and the *Jerecuarenses* host a *charreada* each year on this day."

"A rodeo?"

"That's right. My family sends someone to attend each year. I'll be taking you as my guest."

"I noticed that a festival looked to be going on when I drove through town."

She nodded. "We should have traditional clothing available, something my brothers have worn in years past. I'll have someone carry a jacket and hat to your room."

"Will this not work?" Lee said, looking down at his button-down and jeans.

"No, this is Mexico, Mr. Acker, and you are going as my guest. Take some pride in how you look."

"I understand, but I've been to a rodeo before, Alex."

"*La charreada* and your country's version of a rodeo are not the same. Attire matters at any event. Even more so at a traditional event in Mexico."

"I'll still be a gringo in disguise," Lee said, giving her a sharp wink.

"Don't sell yourself short, Mr. Acker. You have made it this far." She returned the wink. "We will leave in thirty minutes. I'll meet you out front."

~

Tim sat on the first row of the small stadium's bleachers. He waved at Maggie as she came into view from the football field's adjacent parking lot. She wore workout gear, yoga pants, and a tank top. Tim gave a loud whistle from his seat.

"I have to know, is this where you take all your girls, Special Agent Dawson?"

"To an outdoor track for a workout?" Tim asked, standing from his seat.

"To a high school football field to relive your glory days," she chided.

"Well, since you mentioned it. I played for the mighty Dolphins of Gulf Shores High School and—"

Maggie cut him off, "I've checked your stats out. You had a decent high school career. Your junior year was your best season, numbers wise."

"Decent?" Tim said, rubbing his chest. "Ouch!"

"You didn't think I'd look you up? Check you out to make sure your backstory lined up."

"Well, Detective Reynolds, how about I show you how to put together a workout? Then we can trade notes," Tim said, swinging his arms to warm up.

"Trading notes? Is that what we're calling it? I'll have you know I am more than a pretty face. Don't make me show you up out here." Maggie smiled and leaned over the bleachers' railing for a kiss.

"That may be the sweetest trash talk I've heard today."

"You get a lot of trash talk from women that look like this?"

"Only if I am lucky," Tim said, laughing.

He hopped the railing, and his feet landed on the synthetic rubber surface of the high school track. Maggie stood much shorter in her running shoes. Tim bent down and tightened his shoelaces under the stadium lights.

"So, what's on the workout agenda tonight?" Maggie asked.

"We can warm up with a mile, and then I have a sprint workout put together. Then it's core work and a little bit of strength training. It shouldn't take more than an hour."

"Sounds a little light to me?" Maggie replied, slapping Tim on the rear.

"Well, that's just the first phase of the workout. I'll walk you through phase two at my place later tonight."

"Presumptive, aren't we?"

They grinned and stretched together like two kids in high school. They talked about their workdays, and Maggie detailed her approach to a string of cases she had on the preliminary hearing calendar that day in Seminole County. Preliminary hearings in criminal cases were an opportunity to challenge probable cause and ask for reconsideration on most bond issues. The routine hearings rarely resulted in a dismissal of the criminal case. Still, Tim admired Maggie's fire, and he listened to her approach to representing her clients. Tim had little doubt her clients were guilty, but she presented interesting arguments over and over that law enforcement lacked probable cause to arrest. Though he would not admit it to her, her arguments were rather convincing.

"It isn't as if an arrest happens and the officer's perspective is the only one that matters."

"It's the only one that matters to me!" Tim added with a grin.

"Well, think about any football game you have been to," Maggie said, standing in a runner's stretch and pointing out to the football field in front of them. "You and I are seated on opposing bleachers. We root for different teams, and we have varying levels of expertise around the rules of the game of football. More importantly, we have varying opinions on how the game of football should be played."

Tim nodded, thoroughly enjoying the sight of his running partner lecturing beside him.

"Imagine that we are watching a game from our respective bleachers. We both see the ball get snapped at the line of scrimmage and watch as the quarterback drops back to throw a high arcing pass to one of his receivers."

"Wheel route?"

"Sure, any route you want."

Tim faked as if he were running the hypothetical wheel route, and Maggie tossed him an imaginary ball.

"Say, the quarterback in our hypothetical completes the pass to his receiver and the play goes for a touchdown. One half of the stadium goes crazy, cheering and chanting. The other half looks forward to the next offensive series. Then, the fans see yellow flags tossed out onto the field—two penalties on the play."

"That's the worst. Pass interference?" Tim asks.

"Uh-huh, offensive pass interference. On the wide receiver."

"That's unusual," Tim added, speaking like a former member of the defensive secondary.

"The second flag is for roughing the quarterback. A defensive end came off the weak side and drilled the quarterback three Mississippis after releasing the touchdown pass. The quarterback in this hypothetical is still on the ground, waiting for the trainers to rush to his side."

Maggie stepped out onto the grass of the field and pointed at one side of the stadium.

"Let's say I am sitting over there. I see the play unfold and I am pulling for the visitor team, the team on defense. I followed the play on the ball, so I missed the late hit on the quarterback. In fact, I am unwilling to believe the defensive end would have hit the quarterback late because I know the player personally. We are friends."

"Okay?" Tim said, confused.

"On top of that, because my team is the visiting squad, I believe the home team probably got a favorable call from the referees because it's their home turf."

Maggie then turned to point at the other set of stadium bleachers on the far side of the field.

"You, on the other hand, are seated on the home team's side. You played college football and are a student of the game. You saw the play unravel and noticed an offensive tackle lose his footing right as the ball is snapped. You know to look for a big hit, so your eyes stay with the quarterback after he releases the ball."

"I see the hit?"

"That's right. In fact, you are able to call the penalty out before the referees' yellow flags litter the field."

"I am guessing I am unwilling to believe offensive pass interference took place on the play," Tim said, legs feeling nice and warm now.

"That's right. Even as a former defensive player that has seen wide receivers take advantage of rules that favor the offense, you are still unwilling to give any credence to the pass interference call."

Tim nodded and listened as the two started to jog at a light pace around the track.

"Perspectives on an arrest, just like a play in a football game, can vary greatly," Maggie said as she bounced along beside Tim. "Arrests happen, and I either want as many spectators as possible or none at all."

"Why is that?" Tim asked.

"Because the more people that see an arrest or crime go down, the easier it is to show the judge that there isn't just one version of the story. The recollection of how things went down will be fluid, and that creates issues for any judge or jury."

"What about when no one sees something happen?"

"Well, that's the situation we just talked about in our hypothetical game. People already form their conclusions based on their rooting interests. They come to flawed conclusions through conjecture and bias."

The buzzing of the stadium lights above and the patter of their feet against the track filled a brief pause in the conversation.

"So, you are saying even if I don't see a crime take place, and don't have any witnesses to a crime, I will still believe it took place because of my rooting interests in law enforcement?" Tim asked in a skeptical tone.

"No, but I believe you are more likely to believe the crime could have taken place even though you don't have any witnesses or credible evidence. That belief is not based on sufficient evidence, it's based on conjecture."

"Let's agree to disagree," Tim said, starting to pick up the pace. "I gather that the judge ruled incorrectly in your hearings today?"

"Twelve different cases, all different facts, all officers with varying perspectives or levels of expertise. Probable cause to arrest existed in every single one. That's a system with issues, Tim."

"Maybe they were all solid arrests?"

"Maybe, but that's not what I am getting at. You have to understand that people facing criminal charges, especially those that are poor minorities working from a disadvantage, they are already considered members of the 'visitor team' when they walk into a courtroom."

Tim nodded, and they both pushed the pace around the track.

"The judge, law enforcement, and the prosecutor all see the arrest from the perspective of the 'home team.'"

Tim was impressed at Maggie's speed around the track and tried to remember whether she mentioned she was a runner.

"Pick an issue that would have some bearing on a criminal case. Profiling of the defendant, overreach in the search, outright bias, any option will work."

"Okay."

"If any issues occurred during the arrest, if any penalties or personal fouls could be assessed against the home team, no one in law enforcement or the district attorney's office will be willing to believe it, and the judges aren't far behind."

"Well, I'm not sure that's going to change anytime soon."

"I know," she said, shaking her head. "I am just venting here."

"No, I get what you are saying, and I admire the commitment to your job."

Tim changed topics. He gave her the scoop on the video he and Bernard came across from the gas station shooting in Mexico, and it piqued her interest. She listened to Tim explain how he planned to approach the search for Lee Acker. How he thought Lee venturing to Mexico may fit into the death of Jake Collins.

"Have you followed up on any other leads with the murder?"

Tim shook his head. "We don't have any other leads."

After clocking a little over a mile on the track, they did some pushups followed by core work. They were both single and driven in their small-town professions; exercise served as a close friend. The two cooled down and talked until the stadium lights dimmed above.

As they walked away from the track, sweating and feeling the rush of endorphins, Tim took a shot at extending the evening. "Do you want to come over to my place?"

"I'd like that."

Tim's knees about buckled. "Good, well, you can follow me over, or I'll shoot you the address by text."

"I'll follow you. You can't keep me up too late, though. I have an early morning breakfast meeting with another lawyer here in town."

"I make no guarantees, Ms. Reynolds."

"Typical!"

"Are you meeting with someone at the DA's office?" Tim asked.

Maggie paused a moment. "No, I am meeting with a civil practice guy here in town—Bruce Tevens."

25

Lee woke up and tried to remember where he was. His forehead ached as if someone hit it with a hammer the night before, and his throat felt dry. He tried to decide whether the trek to the bathroom faucet would be worth the energy. It wasn't. Lee noticed his shirt was off. He still wore a pair of jeans from the night before, no boots or socks. He ran his hands along the jeans and felt the dirt caked on the front of them. Rolling over on his side, Lee slid his hands through the soft sheets of the large bed. He felt the grit of dirt scattered about, but no one lay beside him.

The rodeo, they'd attended the rodeo in town, Lee thought, trying to piece together the night before. How much did he have to drink? He'd blacked out. Hard.

His wristwatch was still on, and Lee squinted at the hands on the watch face—6:10 a.m. He closed his eyes and listened to the quiet in the house. The pounding in his head seemed to emit the only sound around him. It pounded, and he buried his face in the pillow to apply pressure to the self-inflicted injury.

"Jesus Christ," Lee murmured into the pillow as he proceeded to curse tequila, Jake, and Cliff in one succinct tirade. He'd remember the night before long. The cobwebs just needed clearing.

Lee willed himself to a seated position on the edge of the bed and looked around the dark room. He flipped the lamp on beside the bed and found his clothes strewn around his suitcase. There was a fifty-fifty chance that either Alex's security people ransacked the suitcase, or the mess was simply the work of a drunken Lee staggering in late last night. Regardless, his few belongings looked to all be there—including the Beretta.

Then he noticed the device on the bedside table. The remaining cell phone. It was right there in a spot that left no doubt it had been used last night. Why else would it be sitting out?

Lee picked the phone up and tapped a button on the side. As he suspected, the device was already on. Lee's stomach sank. He paused and took a deep breath in before pressing the green phone icon on the screen. It pulled up the call log, and he saw the list of outgoing calls. There were five calls made to two separate numbers. He didn't have any contacts saved in the phone, but he recognized one of the numbers offhand—Grace's number. The first two calls to Grace at 1:40 a.m. and 1:42 a.m. went unanswered. The third, a call at 1:45 a.m., connected. He opened the call details and about dropped the phone. "Fourteen minutes! Sheesh." Lee grunted, shutting his eyes and struggling to recall the conversation. Nothing.

Lee's heart pounded, and he stood to walk to the bathroom. He felt sick and shuffled along with the cell phone in his hand. His legs felt sore. So did his ribs. Then he sat the phone on the bathroom counter and started running the water in the sink. Cold water. Cold as he could get the faucet going. He soaked his face and massaged the cool water into his eyes, trying to remember the night before.

The phone vibrated on the bathroom counter. *Buzz, buzz, buzz.* Lee about knocked it into the toilet reaching for the device. The number wasn't Grace, but the area code was from a local number back home. He let the call go unanswered, returning to the cold water still running in the sink.

Buzz, buzz, buzz. The device rumbled on the counter. The noise sounded loud enough to wake anyone else sleeping in the house. It was the same number calling as before, another number Lee called twice that morning while plastered. It would get the nondescript message from the mobile provider and no option to leave a voicemail.

. . .

The device then emitted a sharp ding. A tone he didn't recognize, but one that twisted the threads of his hangover deeper. Lee rubbed his forehead as he stared at a text message on the screen in hand. *Heard you might be in a jam. Give me a call. BT.*

Lee knew the Acker family attorney, Bruce Tevens, rose early in the morning. He represented farmers and businesspeople across Alabama, Florida, and Georgia. Bruce prided himself on rising before his clients that farmed in the morning and still putting away more brown liquor than his corporate clients in the evening. A classically trained lawyer in his twentieth year of practice, Bruce proved instrumental in advising Lee on most of the major decisions Lee confronted during the last decade. The mysterious death of Jake Collins would be no different. He mashed the number for Bruce and listened as the phone rang.

~

"Well, how are we doing, young man?" Bruce said as he picked up the phone, his voice enthusiastic as always. "I'm sitting here at a breakfast meeting. Give me one moment so I can step outside."

"That'll be fine, Bruce," Lee replied.

Bruce excused himself from the table, and Lee could hear what sounded like the noise of Blakeston's busy downtown diner in the background. Lee listened to the other end of the line as his lawyer made it toward the front door of the diner. Lee's stomach growled. He could almost smell the pancakes through the phone.

"I'm glad you called, you crazy son of a bitch," Bruce said, obviously outside of the diner now. "Half the state seems to be looking for you."

"What do you mean, Bruce?" Sarcasm heavy in the response. "I'm out of town. Tell them that."

"I have, knucklehead. The cops have been by my office three times in the last week, and they keep asking when you will be back."

"You tell them you aren't a travel agent?"

"I actually did. The investigator didn't have much of a sense of humor."

"Well, that's unfortunate."

"It is. Listen, this thing is not going away anytime soon. They seem to think you have something to do with this Jake Collins mess." Bruce's voice trailed off in a hushed tone as someone walked by on the sidewalk. "Where the hell are you? Every time I called this new number, the ringer switched to the international tone."

"Mexico."

"Mexico? I take it you are down there fishing."

Bruce Tevens was a local boy that went off to college at the University of Georgia. He graduated top of his class and went on to law school at the University of Virginia. Top of his class again and a speaker at his law school graduation in 1997. As sharp as they come, Bruce received all the generous offers from large firms in the big cities up east. He'd considered the big first-year salaries and weighed the promises made in his interviews. The interviewers assured him that in five to seven years, he'd litigate head-to-head with the best lawyers in the world. The big show for those lawyers that can hack it. Bruce liked the idea but knew a penance as a big law associate would have to be paid first. The young Bruce balked at the idea of grinding away the rest of his twenties in the big leagues in hopes of taking on a meaningful role in his thirties. He loathed the idea of camping out in the basement of a monster New York City law firm, so he opted to return home to play in the minor leagues. A decision he rarely regretted and one that brought him together with the businesses and affairs of local royalty—the Acker family.

"That's right, Bruce. I'm trying to do a little fishing."

"Those are dangerous waters you are in, Lee. Why don't you pump the brakes on trying to meet with any folks down there?"

"Too late."

"Would it have been a good idea to roundtable the idea of taking this little trip?" Bruce said with a chuckle.

"I already knew what your advice would have been."

Bruce paused and thought for a moment. If his clients always sought his advice before making bonehead decisions, he'd have a lot less business.

"Well, all right, boy. What's the play here? You coming home anytime soon?"

"It depends how the week goes, but I plan to soon. I miss Grace and Charlotte."

"And?"

"And you of course, Bruce. Listen, I need you to go check on Grace for me. She has an envelope that I need you to get from her. When you have it, call me back."

"What's in the envelope?"

"Just grab it and it'll make more sense."

"All right."

Lee stood in the bathroom still. He stared at his reflection in the mirror. Both men let the silence sit for a moment until Lee spoke again.

"Well, I don't want to keep Mr. Bruce Tevens from a breakfast meeting with a client."

"It's no client, Lee. I'm meeting with your new attorney."

"Oh, yeah? I hope he is good."

"It's she. And she is very good."

"All right, then. You know I'll follow your recommendation. Call me later when you have the envelope."

"Be safe down there, and good luck."

Bruce pocketed his cell phone in the front of his jacket and headed back through the front door of the diner. Shaking his head at the audacity of his client, he worked his way back to the breakfast booth. Bruce glanced at a copy of the morning newspaper that sat on the front bar. On the front page was a somber picture of Bill Collins. The headline read, "With a Heavy Heart, Collins Returns to the Campaign Trail." The death of Jake would, one way or another, be politicized for the candidate's benefit.

"I apologize, Maggie. I had to grab that call," Bruce said as he sat back down in the booth. "You know how things can be."

"Of course, Mr. Tevens. I know how it is. Once people get your cell phone number, they can find you anywhere. Everything all right?"

"That's a tough question to answer. That was your potential client on the phone."

Maggie knew better than to ask if that was the first time Bruce had spoken with his client since the murder. "What's his plan?"

"I'm not sure he necessarily has one. I'd like to tell him we have something in place, though. Part of that plan is to have you lined up to handle the case once the you-know-what hits the fan."

Maggie understood the urgency. "Well, like I was saying, I know law enforcement found a video of him in some shootout in Mexico. Apparently, the video quality is pretty good."

"Still no arrest warrants, though," Bruce said, taking a bite of his egg white omelet. "That's all that really matters."

"I tend to agree," Maggie replied. "They are trying to flush him out by any means necessary. I'm surprised the national media hasn't made this a bigger story yet."

"It'll blow up once there is an arrest," Bruce said. "I think the Collinses and local law enforcement are getting dangerously close to a defamation lawsuit by pushing this garbage that Lee Acker is a prime suspect in the murder case. I don't remember a newspaper ever doing that without even having information from an arrest warrant."

"True," Maggie said, sipping her coffee. "I think they will have a warrant today, though. A judge is going to look at that video and will hear testimony from the lead investigator that Lee has been dodging questioning since the murder."

"I'm no criminal defense attorney, but that still seems like a weak argument for probable cause."

"Well, I am, and these judges don't need much."

"So, you are in?" Bruce asked, somewhat eagerly.

"Let me think about it another day or two."

Bruce pulled a credit card out of his pocket to pick up the check for breakfast. He wanted an answer to his proposal. If Maggie Reynolds didn't want to handle the case, he would have to move on to options in Atlanta, Birmingham, and Miami.

"That'll be fine, Maggie. But let me know this week. If an arrest warrant is issued, I want the face that'll be seen in court ready to give a statement to the reporters."

"I understand," she replied. "I'll let you know by Friday."

26

As Maggie lugged a crate full of files up the steps of the Blake County Courthouse, she admired the old building. The courthouse was her favorite of those across the circuit. Designed in the neoclassical architectural style, it anchored the small downtown with its porticoed entrances facing all four sides of the city's main square. Its tall slender columns looked reminiscent of the Old American South, and the main courtroom had served as the stage for every momentous legal event in local history for more than a century.

As she started through the doors, she looked down the line of mostly Black and brown faces that waited to enter the building. Maggie knew that for many of those in line, the handsome old courthouse represented only the latest chapter in a struggle for equal footing in America. Enslavement to mass incarceration, and all they could do was continue the fight.

Up the steps to the second floor, Maggie made her way to the main courtroom. The area around the bench bustled with activity, and the noise echoed around the large wood-paneled room. The regulars from the criminal defense bar were scattered about, talking with each other or the families of their clients. The prosecutors, huddled around their table stacked with files, made last-minute plea offers to lighten their load.

As Maggie set the crate full of files at her feet, Chris unloaded the news of the day. "Did you hear they issued a warrant for Acker?"

Maggie raised her eyebrows and tried to act surprised as she fell into the chair. This would change things. Bruce Tevens would want an answer today. "No, when did that happen? This morning?"

"Yep, I guess Judge Balk signed it about an hour ago," Chris replied, proud as hell that he had the inside scoop.

"They'll have to find him first, though, right?"

"True, and who knows where the guy is. He certainly has plenty of money to hide out for a while. He may be sitting on a beach somewhere without extradition drinking a mai tai."

"I doubt anyone knows," Maggie said, still processing the news. "Have you seen any investigators here this morning?"

"A couple were here earlier. Dawson and another guy. Why, who are you looking for?"

"Never mind, don't worry about it," Maggie replied.

Maggie turned to survey the crowd behind her and made sure her clients were all present that morning. Lawyers would often stand at the front of the courtroom and call off their list of clients like a starting roster for a basketball game. Not Maggie, though; she had a knack for faces. She had twenty clients on the upcoming trial calendar. Ten of those faces were expected to be in court that morning for the calendar call. The other ten were being held in jail without bond and would only be transported over to the courthouse if slated for a guilty plea. Maggie scanned the crowd and counted the faces of her clients that were present. Nodding at those that caught her eyes, she counted nine.

"Somebody is getting a bench warrant," Maggie said as she turned back around to the table.

"Someone always does," Chris said. "I just prefer it not to be my clients."

"I'm missing a client by the name of Tareka Miller." Maggie stooped down to the floor and dug through the crate to find the Miller file.

"How do you do that?"

"Do what?" Maggie asked.

"Remember what all of your clients look like," Chris replied. "I can't remember half the people I met last week, much less a client I haven't seen in two months."

"Commitment to the craft, Owens," Maggie said, winking at him as she flipped through her client's file to find the most recent phone number.

"What I would give to just have a few clients to worry about," Chris said as the bailiff stood to make his booming announcement to the packed courtroom.

Maggie didn't respond.

"All rise now for the Honorable John Balk; this court is now in session."

"Be seated, everyone," Judge Balk said as he took his seat behind the tall desk that looked down on the courtroom.

As he walked through the customary introductions to the defendants and family members seated in the courtroom, Maggie texted her client, urging her to hurry to court. Having sat through countless calendar calls with Judge Balk, Maggie knew it would take him ten minutes to make it through his standard introduction and any questions to the attorneys. Though she often disagreed with Judge Balk's rulings, she appreciated the manner in which he handled his courtroom. He had the patience and skill of a seasoned jurist.

Once finished with his introduction, Judge Balk turned and asked the attorneys seated in the courtroom if anyone had matters that should be taken up before the call of the trial calendar.

Without hesitation, Maggie stood from her chair. "Judge, may I approach the bench on one matter?"

The judge looked over at Maggie and replied, "Very well, come on up, Ms. Reynolds."

As she walked by the prosecutor's table, Maggie patted the assistant district attorney on the back to let him know he didn't have to get up. It was customary for opposing counsel to be present at any bench conferences taking place in a courtroom, but she was not planning to discuss the specific facts of any case with the judge.

"Good morning, Judge," Maggie said as she eased up to the side of the elevated bench where the judge sat.

He swiveled his chair in her direction. "Morning, Ms. Reynolds," he said, smiling. He held a University of Georgia travel mug in his left hand and took a sip from it while he waited for her to begin.

Maggie skipped the pleasantries. After all, a courtroom full of people sat waiting behind her. "This is unusual, Judge, but I've been offered a job that would start next week."

The judge took another sip of coffee and nodded his head, listening.

"I have twenty cases on your trial calendar. Some cases I hope to resolve today, but all, of course, cannot be closed out. I intend to ask for a continuance on those cases that are near the top of the trial calendar to allow the public defender's office time to reassign counsel."

"I see."

"This is all very new, Judge. I have not formally accepted the job, but I will later today."

"Have you talked to your boss, Mr. Lamb, about this decision to leave the office?"

"Well, that's the thing, Judge. You are the only other person that knows right now." She hoped the bit of secrecy might endear him to her cause. "The offer was just made to me this morning. I'd appreciate you understanding this is news I'd like to deliver to Jim myself. He hired me out of law school, and I am grateful for the opportunities he has given me."

"I understand. Where will the new endeavor take you?"

Maggie paused and thought for a moment. "I am not sure I am able to disclose that at the moment, Judge. I hope you understand and can keep this in confidence for the time being."

Judge Balk nodded again.

"I did not want to misrepresent my clients' position to the court this morning, Judge. And—" Maggie felt like she was talking too fast.

Judge Balk stopped her. "Well, as you would expect, the DA's office is scrambling to account for the loss of Jake Collins. I don't foresee there being any trials next week. I appreciate your candor, though, Ms. Reynolds."

"Thank you, Judge."

"Ms. Reynolds, I assume this job offer requires you to stay local. You will continue to handle criminal cases in my courtroom?"

Maggie noted the judge's steady gaze on her. He was watching for an

expression, a reaction. His gaze told her that he knew what she was planning to do.

"Absolutely, Judge. I expect you will see me soon."

As she turned to walk back to her seat, Maggie saw her missing client
slide through the double doors at the back of the courtroom. She gave
Maggie a small wave and found a seat along the back row. Maggie returned
the gesture. No bench warrants for her clients today.

~

Lee opened the door to his bedroom and walked down the hallway toward
the back patio. The events from the night before were foggy, and he didn't
remember what the plan was for the day ahead. He'd showered and shaved,
but the hangover remained. He hoped a coffee and something to eat would
help clear the cobwebs.

"*Buenos días, señor*," a voice called as Lee turned the corner into the
kitchen area. It was Roberto. He sat with his black boots propped up on the
table, reading a newspaper.

"*Buenos días*, Roberto."

Roberto made a dramatic showing of looking at his watch and said, "I
trust you slept well. Unfortunately, it's ten a.m. and our chef that prepares
breakfast has already left for the morning. This is a farm. We rise early for
the day's work ahead."

"Coffee will be fine, if there is any left."

Roberto pointed to a silver coffeepot on the banquette behind him.

"Where is Alex?" Lee asked as he made his way over to a stack of mugs
and the coffeemaker.

"She returned to DF first thing this morning."

Lee nodded. Although the capital of Mexico formally changed its name
to *Ciudad de México*, many still called the sprawling city the *Distrito Federal*,
or DF.

"Will she be returning to the farm today?" Lee asked as he sat down at
the table, two chairs over from Roberto.

"No, you are to meet her in the city in two days."

Lee sat there thinking—he didn't remember anything about a discussion around him travelling to Mexico City.

"Very well, if your man has the keys to the motorcycle, I'll leave later this morning."

Roberto sat the newspaper down in front of him and looked across the table at Lee. "Señorita Olivera asked that we fly to the city. We discussed this last night," he said, giving Lee a smirk. "I take it you thoroughly enjoyed the mezcal at the fiesta last night."

"It appears so, Roberto," Lee replied. "I sure could use a Bloody Mary or one of those famous micheladas right now."

Roberto's smile widened, and he sprang to his feet. "That is the best idea I've heard all morning. Come with me."

Lee followed Roberto through the double doors into the kitchen. They found the fridge humming on the back wall, and Roberto pulled out lime juice, chile peppers, tomato juice, and two tall beer bottles. Roberto selected two wide glasses from a nearby shelf and began squeezing the lime juice into both. He whistled as he worked an assortment of sauces into the glasses and popped the tops on the beers. He added the tomato juice and beer to both, stirring the glasses with a long spoon. Roberto handed one of the chilled concoctions to Lee, and they clinked glasses.

"*Salud*," Roberto said.

"*Salud*."

Lee took a long sip from the cold glass. The sauces tasted like a mixture of Worcestershire and hot sauce. The beer and tomato juice felt like the elixir Lee's body needed to shake the awful aftereffects of the night before.

"It's good, right?" Roberto asked as the two walked back to the seating area.

They assumed their seats again at the table, and Lee gave the chief of security an approving nod. He took another sip of his michelada and asked, "Have you been to the United States, Roberto?"

"A few times. I'll go where the Olivera family needs me, but Mexico is my home now. I prefer to be here."

"In what city do you live?"

Roberto smiled at the question. "I live wherever the mission takes me."

"That sounds like a line from an old *Rambo* movie," Lee replied.

"*Rambo*?"

Lee nodded. "That's right, *Rambo*. You know, John Rambo. Vietnam veteran. Total badass played by Sylvester Stallone."

Roberto looked confused.

"Get the hell out, you don't know *Rambo*?" Lee exclaimed.

Roberto shook his head and took another sip from his drink.

"That's a shame. Well, you watch it one day and call me to let me know what you think."

"Do they take international calls at American prisons?" Roberto chided.

"Eh, *cabrón*, that's uncalled for."

The two men laughed, and then Lee gave the old guerilla fighter the overarching plot from the franchise of renowned action movies. Roberto's demeanor relaxed as the two spoke.

"If you wish to ride to the capital, I'll return the keys to you," Roberto said. "The trip should not take you longer than two hours."

"I appreciate it. It won't put you in hot water with your boss?"

"You let me worry about that," Roberto replied with a wink.

The two men discussed the trip from *La Finca* to Mexico City, and Roberto provided Lee with an address for a hotel. A room had been reserved under the name on Lee's fake passport. A name Lee was certain they pulled from searching his suitcase the night before. Roberto reiterated that Lee would not see Alex until Friday. She had other pressing engagements with her business.

"She maintains a busy schedule," Roberto said. "The company requires her attention at all hours of the day."

"Well, she certainly subscribes to the work hard, party hard approach to life, then."

"That is customary in Mexico. The fiesta usually continues late into the night."

"I certainly enjoyed my first *charreada*, but I'll have to keep it to once a year," Lee replied with a laugh.

They replayed the night at the rodeo and the colorful characters that participated in the rural *charreada*. Lee remembered arriving at the event and pushing through the mass of people crowded around the railings of the arena. The Mexican cowboys wore flashy outfits and put on an entertaining show, a spectacle that put the rodeos back home to shame. Lee's ears still rang from the speakers that blasted Mexican music from the stands. A sound that was only drowned out by the crowd as it erupted in cheers when the wranglers avoided injury or downed a calf. Lee watched most of the event from a private box with Alex. She spoke with the locals brave enough to approach the railing of her private seating area while the two sipped chilled tequila and beers. He remembered that at some point late in the evening, the arena floor cleared to make way for a band and dusty dance floor. With the lights low and Alex pulling his hand out into the grinding crowd, his memory went dark.

"We returned to *La Finca* around one thirty this morning," Roberto said, placing his empty glass on the table. "I noticed you were *un poco ciego*—a little blind—from the mezcal. You spoke clearly and walked without assistance, but I could see it in your eyes."

Lee listened to the uneventful narrative and sipped what was left of the cold coffee in his mug.

"I left you at the back door of the main house with Señorita Olivera. She insisted I not escort her into the house," Roberto explained. "The two of you went inside, and I drove the truck down to the barn."

Lee shrugged. "I made it to my room without issue, at least."

Roberto nodded. "I performed a security check of the premises around two fifteen and made sure to check on my team."

"Uh-huh, I was probably dead to the world at that point."

"No, well, I am not certain."

Lee looked across the table at the expression on the head of security's face.

"What makes you say that?"

"You must understand, there are certain things in my work that require discretion," Roberto said, deflecting the question.

"What requires discretion?"

He gave Lee a shrug. "I performed my last sweep of the house at two twenty a.m. I saw Señorita Olivera leaving your room at two twenty-two a.m."

27

"I'll have some polling numbers to you by the end of the day tomorrow," John Deese said as he pointed a remote control at the television screen.

A familiar intro and the voice of the cable news network's primetime personality filled the room. Bill Collins stood by a large window listening to the coverage. He watched the traffic pass by on the street below as an aggressive recap of the day's news stories began.

"I don't care what these people say about my family," Bill said over the noise of the television. "They didn't know Jake."

Deese looked over at his candidate and back at the television screen. The issuance of an arrest warrant for a suspect in the brutal murder of the sitting congressman's only child was leading the conversation that night. Bill would soon be surging in the polls. Deese tried his best to offer some reassurance.

"They drive the conversation, though, sir. Plus, they are honoring Jake. The poll numbers will be through the roof by the end of the week."

"I know, John," Bill said, eyes still staring out the window. "Nothing is private anymore. The sacrifices we make..."

"All the great men do," John said, unsure what else to say. "You will make a great senator, sir."

Bill nodded, and the men listened as the news segment on the Collins tragedy drew to a close.

"Any news on Lee's whereabouts?"

"The investigator believes Acker is in Mexico. There is a video posted online of a shootout outside some Mexican gas station near Monterrey. Lee has been identified as one of the individuals involved. Inquiries are being made to the police department there in that area."

Bill turned away from the window and stared at his young advisor. "A shootout? Have you seen it?"

"Not yet, but we should have it soon."

"These videos from police shootings can be gasoline on a fire," Bill added. "It is going to be on tomorrow night's news segment if the media gets ahold of it. Are they saying Lee attacked some cops?"

John shook his head. "That's not what I'm hearing."

"Then what?"

"Apparently, he stepped in and helped save a policeman's life. Fended off the attackers along with another officer that wasn't wounded."

Bill smiled and nodded as he listened. "That sounds like something Lee would do."

John thought about saying something but bit his tongue. It troubled him that Bill still cared so much for the Acker boys.

"I remember taking Jake and Lee hunting together when they were kids. Both were crack shots. They would compete for hours shooting cans, clays, and targets. I'm glad I never tallied up the money we spent on shells and bullets to fund their competitive spirits."

Bill stood there. Silent and reflecting on the implications of a warrant being issued for Lee, the childhood friend of his only son.

"Lee's daddy was a nice shot too, wasn't he?" John said, interrupting the congressman's train of thought.

"That's right," Bill replied, his gaze resting on his young advisor. "Champion target and skeet shooter."

"A shame Lee's daddy had to go the way he did," John added in an even tone.

"Yes, it is, John. A damn shame."

～

Lee left the windows open in the hotel room and listened as the rain began to fall outside. He'd arrived on motorcycle an hour before, racing all the way into the city against the clouds that now hung above. He opened a newspaper and lay in bed reading. The breeze from the windows felt cool and smelled of a city. It reminded him of the last trip he and Grace took to New York City together. Summertime in 2015. After dropping Charlotte at a summer camp in Alabama, they flew direct from Birmingham to JFK. They stayed in the East Village in a small rental for two weeks straight.

He wanted to go to the shows on Broadway and take in the museums. She wanted to eat great food, laugh at comedy clubs, and shop Fifth Avenue. The streets were hot, and the two small-town Georgians rambled around the city for thirteen days, taking in the sights. At the end of each day, they'd lay in bed naked with the windows open, listening to the sounds of the cars and foot traffic outside. They often talked of home and always of how they missed their daughter. Each night he asked Grace if she was happy; she promised she was.

Lee smiled at the memory and checked his watch—it read 8:15 p.m. He folded the newspaper in front of him and pulled the cell phone out. He dialed Grace's number and waited as the phone rang.

"Hello?"

Lee waited a moment. "Hey, Grace."

"Why are you calling?" she asked. "We talked about this."

"I know," Lee replied, though he didn't know what she was talking about.

The two listened to the silence. Lee had to assume there was some way the authorities could be monitoring the calls to Grace's phone.

"I miss you," she said.

"I miss you, too," Lee replied.

"When are you coming home?"

"Soon, I hope," Lee replied. "I have some more work that I need to do."

"All right, well, Charlotte is doing okay. She misses you."

"Good," Lee said. "I love you both."

Grace paused on the other end of the line. Enough of a pause that Lee could tell she was thinking about what she wanted to say. "We love you," she finally said. "Have a safe trip and come home soon."

"Bye, Grace," Lee said.

"Goodbye, Lee."

Lee leaned back on the bed and shut his eyes. His boots were still on his feet, and dust from the ride earlier that evening covered his jeans. He breathed in deep through his nose and slowly exhaled through his mouth. His stomach hurt, and he beat his fist twice against his chest, telling himself not to break down. He could feel the tears begin to well in his eyes, but now was not the time to break.

The rain picked up on the street outside, and the sound poured into the hotel room. The month of October signaled the beginning of the dry season in Mexico City. Tonight's rain was one last cleanse. Lee listened and breathed in deep one more time before drifting off to sleep.

28

Maggie made two phone calls that morning as she walked from her home to the office. The first was a call to Bruce Tevens. She accepted the job and would agree to represent Lee Acker in connection with the murder investigation and his eventual trial. Bruce sounded pleased on the other end of the line. Maggie confirmed the salary amount of $120,000 for the first eight months of the case. A handsome offer for rural Georgia that would nearly triple her monthly income. "We can discuss the money again after the first eight months," Maggie said, a firmness in her voice. "I'm the best person for his defense, and he will value my work even more so by that time." Bruce agreed, and the two planned to meet first thing next week to discuss her transition to his law office. Maggie hung up the phone and gave the air a quick fist pump.

The second phone call was to Tim. The phone rang four times and went to voicemail. Maggie left him a message asking that he call her back. Her stomach hurt as she crossed the street toward the coffee shop. The connection with Tim was still new, but the news of them squaring off against each other would force the relationship to crumble. He would find out soon enough, and she wanted to deliver the news herself. Is he dodging my call because he already knows I plan to handle the Acker defense? Maggie thought as she pushed through the front doors of Beans on Broad.

She knew if Judge Balk whispered anything about her taking a new job, the rumor mill would find a way to tie her to the Acker case. That kind of news would make it to Tim Dawson's office in no time.

"One Mean Green for Maggie!" the barista called out from behind the coffee bar. Maggie grabbed her smoothie and thanked Dale with a smile. As she turned to leave, he looked as though he wanted to strike up more of a conversation. But Maggie was immersed in her thoughts. She told herself she was being foolish with her concerns about ending the relationship with Tim. Why should she feel guilty about anything? This was a great opportunity, one she'd earned through her performance. Besides, she planned to go into private practice soon enough, and the State of Georgia against Lee Elmer Acker would be one of the highest-profile cases in the country. How could I pass it up? she thought, hustling out the door of the coffee shop. Win and start raking in the job offers from firms in the larger markets— Miami sure would be nice.

As Maggie continued her walk to the office, she refocused on the tasks left for the day ahead. Sure, she always liked the idea of practicing in Miami, but daydreaming would get her nowhere. There were things to do, and the first task at the office would be her hardest.

"Morning, Lila," Maggie said as she walked through her office's reception area. Lila was on the phone, talking with what sounded like a disgruntled client. She gave Maggie a small wave and a frustrated smile. Maggie knew that if the gossip mill was running around her representation of Lee Acker, Lila would already know about it.

"Is Jim in yet?" Maggie asked.

Lila nodded and pointed down the hallway in the direction of the offices.

Maggie poked her head into Jim Lamb's office and saw him seated at his desk reading the newspaper. She knocked on the open door and said, "Good morning, Jim."

He looked up from the paper and replied with a distracted, "Morning, Mags."

"You have a few minutes to talk?" She walked a few steps into the office.

Lamb lowered the newspaper again and looked back up at Maggie. He had his feet propped up on the corner of the desk and looked like he hadn't shaved all week. Rubbing his stubbled face, he said, "Absolutely, come on in and see if you can find a spot to sit."

Maggie smiled at him and surveyed the classic Jim Lamb organization method of client files strewn across the office floor.

"What's up?" Lamb said as Maggie grabbed a seat.

"Well, first I want you to know that I appreciate everything you have done—"

"Where's the new job, Mags?" Lamb interjected.

"I mean if you would let me finish," Maggie replied, prepared to defend herself.

"You are leaving my office, right?"

"Yes, I am taking on some work in private practice. I'll be working with Bruce Tevens."

Jim raised an eyebrow and smiled. "You are taking on Lee Acker's defense?"

Maggie nodded across the desk at her boss and mentor. He looked pleased to hear the news of her departure. The trial, if there was a trial, would be the largest in Blake County's history, and Lamb's young protégé would be at the center of it all.

"How do you feel about it?" Lamb asked.

"Excited, a little nervous."

"No, how do you feel about the fact that you personally knew the victim in this one?"

Maggie paused. She had not thought much about that aspect of the representation. She'd never had a personal relationship with any of the victims in her clients' cases—much less the victim of a murder case. "It'll be strange going through the photographs and other evidence in discovery," Maggie replied.

Lamb shrugged. "I think it's something you should at least be prepared for."

"I'll still be picking your brain on strategy."

"As long as I have a job, the door is always open."

"Thanks, Jim."

"So, when can I expect you to pack your shit and get out of here?"

"Well, it appears my new client is not within the jurisdiction of the court, so that'll make it difficult to meet with him. I'll talk to Tevens this week about the timetable to get started over there."

"Can you give me a week? Maybe two?" Lamb asked. "Jenny and Chris are pretty swamped already, and I'd like to get as much work out of you as I can. Especially with all that big money I've been paying you."

"I'll see what I can do. I'll try to make two weeks work," Maggie replied.

Lamb smiled and stood from his seat to shake her hand. "Congratulations, Mags. This is a huge opportunity."

"Do you think I'm ready?"

"No doubt."

"Thanks, Jim. Can we go out for cocktails tonight?"

"I'll be getting everyone out of the office by 3:30 p.m. so we can head to the Sandbar to celebrate."

"That'll be great," Maggie replied. "Besides, one of the great things about leaving your tutelage is the fact that I can knock off early every Friday."

"Be careful what you wish for," Lamb said with a laugh. "Now get out of here and get some work done."

∼

It was race weekend in Mexico City, home of the Mexican Grand Prix. Of the twenty-one tracks on the FIA Formula One World Championship Race Calendar, *Autódromo Hermanos Rodríguez* sat at the highest altitude. At over a mile above sea level, fans from all over the world flocked to the Mexican capital to see how race teams and their drivers fared in the thin air.

As Lee waited on the packed platform of the *Zócalo* stop, a central station on the Mexico City Metro's blue line, groups of strangers decked out in race gear stood shoulder to shoulder. They conversed excitedly in Spanish, Italian, and French while they waited for the next underground train to arrive. Most of the Italians wore red in support of the Ferrari drivers, and Lee noticed that many of the Frenchmen wore yellow for the Renault F1 Team.

When the train arrived, Lee and the other race fans pushed into the waiting car. They were all going in the same direction. Down the blue line to the *Chabacano* stop, a station that intersected with the Metro's brown line, and over to a train that would take them to the stations nearest the *autódromo*, the speedway. Crammed up against a group of Germans, Lee stayed silent and listened to the men talk in harsh accents. He pulled his hat low over his eyes and withdrew a local city map from his back pocket to study. There were thousands of internationals in the city for the race, and Lee hoped he could drift easily through the touristy areas of town.

Still, he'd checked the news the night before, and it wasn't looking good. Lee's face now appeared in major news stories that provided continual updates on the progress of the murder investigation. A video from the gas station shootout outside Monterrey had gone viral, and he suspected his anonymity in Mexico had been compromised. On top of the nightly expert panelists commenting on the developing investigation, surging senatorial candidate Bill Collins was getting plenty of face time on the major networks. In each interview, he urged law enforcement to work together in the ongoing search for his son's killer, and he humbly asked for the support of the American people come November.

The train slowed to a stop, and Lee exited with the other passengers. The mass of fans and commuters snaked through the tubes of the Metro station and made the exchange for the brown line bound for the racetrack. Lee held in hand a laminated pass for the speedway and directions from Alex on where to meet her. He'd attended NASCAR events in Talladega, Alabama, and Atlanta, Georgia, but this would be his first experience watching Formula One in person.

As he climbed the steps of the station and returned to street level, the racetrack came into view. Cheers could be heard ahead from the other fans that were walking toward the gates that surrounded the steep stands of the track. Lee couldn't help but smile as he pulled the lanyard over his head and hung the race pass around his neck. If today was his last day as a free man, watching some racing wasn't a bad way to spend it.

~

At 11:00 a.m., the GBI's acting director, Don Malone, walked through the front doors of the bureau's Region 15 Investigative Office. He asked to speak with Special Agent Tim Dawson and informed a young intern at the front desk, rather loudly, that he needed an update on the investigation surrounding the murder of Jake Collins.

"Do you have an appointment?" the intern asked, failing to recognize Malone's face.

Malone gave the kid an incredulous look and said, "It's an unannounced visit, young man." He then started down the hallway and said over his shoulder, "Tell Special Agent Dawson that Don Malone is here for an update. I'll be waiting in the main conference room for him."

The bewildered intern called twice before Tim picked up.

"This is Dawson," Tim said.

"Mr. Dawson, there is a guy here at the office waiting for you in the main conference room. Says his name is Don Malone, and he wants an update on the Collins case."

Tim took a deep breath in and said, "All right, this is an ambush, you understand me? Malone has a reputation for doing this sort of thing."

"Yes, sir."

"He is mostly bluster, but tell him I'm on my way. Get him some coffee, and then get the main conference room prepped for an interview."

"Video interview?"

"That's right, I'm bringing a witness in now."

Tim Dawson checked the time on his cell phone before returning it to his chest pocket. He stood in the parking lot of a truck stop on the outskirts of Blakeston. A red pickup truck with the name "Acker Farms" printed on its side entered the back of the lot. Tim waved to the driver, an older man by the name of José. When the truck pulled up alongside Tim's SUV, he told the man to follow him over to the local GBI office. The man nodded, and Tim hopped into his own vehicle to lead the way. Tim rubbed his forehead as he made the drive back to the office. An impromptu meeting with the GBI leadership had been sitting in the back of Tim's mind for the past week or two. Malone couldn't have picked a better day to stage his ambush, Tim thought to himself. He knew if José's interview went as planned, Malone would be impressed with the progress in the case.

Don Malone was sipping coffee when Tim entered the main conference room. Tim extended a hand and gave Malone a firm handshake. "Good morning, sir."

Malone stood from his chair and responded with a gruff, "Good morning, Dawson."

"I see you have some coffee. Anything else we can get you?"

"This isn't a bed and breakfast, Dawson. Let's get down to business. Where are we with the investigation on Collins?"

"We are running down every lead," Tim said, preparing to lay the cards on the table for his boss. "I have a witness here ready to go today. He may have found our murder weapon."

Tim's pointed approach out of the gate piqued Malone's interest. "You don't say?"

The intern walked through the door with a tripod and video camera. He started to set up, trying to make as little noise as possible. "That's right, the guy works for the Ackers on their property that is just over the state line, in Henry County, Alabama. Apparently, Lee Acker left his work truck there almost two weeks ago. The guy says he found it in the toolbox of the truck."

"Seems like a pretty stupid place to hide a murder weapon," Malone replied, somewhat suspicious.

"Not if you think no one will suspect you committed the crime."

"True," Malone said.

"I am going to bring him in. You are welcome to sit in on the interview, if you'd like."

~

"This is the interview of José Valdez Bisbal," Tim said, a video camera rolling over his left shoulder. "Did I pronounce your name correctly?"

"It's close enough," José replied, a good-natured smile on his face.

"Now, this interview is being conducted in English. It is my understanding that this is not your first language, Mr. Valdez?"

"Uh-huh."

"Are you agreeable to proceeding in English, or would you like for an interpreter to be involved?"

"No, English is good," José replied.

Tim nodded and looked over at Malone. The acting director held the case file in hand and flipped through the material.

"Okay. Now, I am Special Agent Tim Dawson, and I am the lead case agent on the investigation into the murder of Jake Collins. Seated to my right is the acting director of the Georgia Bureau of Investigation, Don Malone."

José nodded. His eyes moved between the two men and the lens of the small video camera. He'd removed a red ball cap when he sat down and held it in hand. Fidgeting with the bill of the cap, he listened.

"You called me this morning and wanted to talk about something you found in your boss's truck?" Tim began, his voice slow and steady. Tim preferred to give people an opportunity to warm up in an interview. He found it made things easier for the people sitting on the other side of the camera.

"Yes, sir," José replied. "I called this morning. I have been watching the news and the reports about Mr. Acker. A reporter on the local news said you were the person running the investigation."

"That's right, and I am glad you called. There have been a lot of things put out on the news about this case, but you being here today may be important," Tim said, trying to sound as complimentary as possible.

José nodded again. His hands shook as he reached for a bottle of water at the middle of the conference table. His anxiety was obvious, but a nervous witness was not unusual for Malone or Dawson. In a murder investigation, they expected it.

"I've worked for Mr. Acker for seven or eight years now. I run his family's farm in Alabama. I live on the property with my family. We don't pay rent, and I earn a good salary. Yes, Mr. Acker is a fair man to work for. I handle anything he needs, and there are almost six hundred head of cattle on the property, so something always needs to be done."

"How often do you talk to Mr. Acker?" Tim asked.

"Once a week in person. He drives over from Georgia, and we go over what needs to be done the following week."

"You call him on the phone much?"

"Only if there are problems. Normally, if it can wait, I wait until he comes by the farm to discuss anything with him in person."

Tim looked over at his boss again. Malone was still reviewing the case file and making notes on a notepad, seemingly ignoring the interview taking place.

"When is the last time you talked to your boss?"

"I saw him about two and a half weeks ago. He came by to check on things, and he brought roofers with him."

"Roofers?" Tim asked.

"Yes, sir. The farmhouse I live in with my wife and children, the roof was beginning to leak. I asked Mr. Acker about it, and he put a new roof on."

"And that was the last time you saw him?"

"That's right."

"Did you two talk about him going on some sort of a trip?"

"No, sir. Nothing about a trip."

"Would he normally say something to you like, 'Hey, José, I am going to be out of town for two weeks, so call me if you need me' when he planned to go on vacation?"

"Not usually, no," José replied, looking down at the crinkled ball cap in his hands.

"Mr. Valdez, I need you to help me out here. Are you saying there was not anything strange about the last visit Mr. Acker made to his Alabama property?"

José Valdez tossed his cap on the conference table and gave a long sigh. Born and raised in a small town near the southern edge of Guanajuato, Mexico, José valued his family and friends above all else. In his home country, he had little use for law enforcement. That opinion had not changed since his arrival to the United States. Lee Acker was a friend and man he respected deeply—José would do what he had to do, though.

"I did not notice anything strange when Mr. Acker came by, sir."

Tim nodded, listening and maintaining eye contact with his witness.

"Mr. Acker came by the farm, and it was a normal meeting day. He asked about the work trucks, and he wanted to know which ones were running without problems. I told him that the Dodge needed to go to the shop again. That Manolo, one of my helpers, had been having problems

with it when he used it around the farm. I told him the other trucks, especially both of the Fords, were running good."

"Okay," Tim said, leaning back to look at the screen of the video camera
to make sure it was still recording.

"Mr. Acker and I'd discussed buying another truck for the farm. The
Dodge is a piece of shit, and we are always working on it. Mr. Acker goes to
an auction in Florida from time to time to pick up used trucks, and I
assumed he needed to know what was going to have to be replaced. We
decided the Dodge needed to go."

José paused for a moment, and Tim waited for the witness to continue his
story. José Valdez would not be in the GBI's conference room, helping to build
a criminal case against his boss, if he didn't know something damning. Tim
wondered if the man held documentation to be in the United States—Tim
suspected that José did. Based on Tim's experience interviewing undocumented men and women, he knew how rare it was for someone to voluntarily
get involved with a police investigation without some legal status in the US.
The fear of deportation or removal from the country was simply too much of
a factor for those that had overstayed a visa or crossed the border illegally.

"I remember it was a Saturday night, almost two weeks ago. I took my
family to dinner in Dothan. We got home around nine that night, and I
went over to the barn to check on a calf that we were bottle-feeding. The
calf's mother wasn't feeding him any milk, and I wanted to make sure he
was all right."

"Sure," Tim said, no experience whatsoever working in the world of
cattle farming.

"When I got out to the barn, I noticed that one of the Ford pickups was
gone."

"One of the good work trucks?" Tim said.

"That's right. Probably our most reliable truck."

"Did you see Mr. Acker?"

"No, sir, but Mr. Acker's truck was parked there behind the barn."

"Sort of hiding behind the barn?" Tim prodded.

"Not really," José responded. "It wasn't in Mr. Acker's normal parking
space, though."

"Did you call him?"

"No, sir. It is his property, and if he wants to take it, that's not my place to say anything."

Tim nodded. It seemed plausible given the witness's obvious respect for his boss.

"Well, Mr. Acker doesn't come by as he normally does that week after. And then last week I didn't see him either, so I called him to ask about putting up another line of fencing. Cows keep crossing the creek and escaping on the eastern edge of the farm. Mr. Acker and I had already talked once before about adding some new fencing and a hot wire. I called to confirm that we could purchase the material and start work. Mr. Acker's phone was not turned on, so I called him again the next day and then the day after that."

"Were you worried?"

"No."

"So, what did you do?"

"I bought the fencing."

Tim smiled and folded his hands in front of him. His witness was a farmer. He was not going to just blurt out something damaging about a man he respected. José was going to make Tim ask.

"Mr. Valdez, you called our office and said you found a weapon in Mr. Acker's truck last night, did you not? Tell me about that."

José nodded and shifted in his seat. "I was watching the news last night, and it didn't make any sense, this whole story about Mr. Acker attacking someone."

"Murdering someone," Malone added, still reading the reports in the case file. His first words of the interview.

José didn't acknowledge the comment. "I tried to call Mr. Acker again, but the phone went straight to voicemail, and his phone would not let me leave a message. So, I went out to Mr. Acker's truck and opened the door. I thought maybe he left his cell phone behind. I figured I'd call Ms. Grace and let her know there was some misunderstanding."

Malone looked up from the case file and set the documents on the table. He leaned forward in his seat and rested both elbows on the conference table. Malone knew the meat of the interview was ready to be served. He interjected with a forceful, "Mr. Valdez, where did you find the gun?"

"I opened the center console and the glovebox. Went through the back seat and the rest of the cab. Nothing. Then I found the truck keys under the driver's-side visor. I don't know why I decided to open the toolbox, but I did."

"Okay, what did you find?" Tim asked, frustrated.

"A handgun. A Beretta handgun."

Both men were pleased by the revelation, excited even. A handgun matched the theory that was in place for the murder weapon involved.

"Have you touched the gun, Mr. Valdez?" Malone asked.

"I picked it up to look at it. I removed the magazine to see if there were any bullets loaded, and then I set it back where I found it," José replied.

"Jesus," Malone murmured. "Did you have work gloves on or anything?"

"No, sir. Don't worry, though, I wiped the places I touched the gun with my handkerchief."

Both agents didn't say a word. They were thinking about how to proceed. There would be little doubt that José Valdez tampered with the murder weapon—a team needed to get out to the truck immediately.

"Is everything all right?" José asked.

"Other than the fact that you may have wiped the killer's fingerprints off of a murder weapon, everything is just dandy," Malone replied as he stood from his chair.

Tim leaned back in his seat and rubbed his forehead. He switched the video camera off and turned to Malone.

"Let's get a team over to Alabama."

29

A short security guard in a baggy dark suit motioned for Lee to lift his arms. Lee obliged and the guard began a slow pat-down, then a once over with a metal detector wand. Appearing pleased, the dark suit checked the laminated pass around Lee's neck and pointed toward a bank of elevators. Lee thanked the man and continued along the wide hallway that ran behind the speedway's main grandstand.

As Lee made his way to the elevators, a whine from the vehicles echoed down the hallway with each pass the drivers made around the track outside. The smooth sound of the gearboxes upshifting signaled to Lee that this particular grandstand fronted a straight section of the track. He'd studied the layout of the speedway, and his ticket granted him access to a premium skybox that provided the perfect view of both the start and finish of the race.

Like all sporting events, though, the passion and energy would emanate from the cheap seats. Lee was particularly interested in an area of the track labeled *Foro Sol Norte*, a tricky section known for drivers' gutsy attempts to overtake one another while they tackle turns thirteen through fifteen. Formula One drivers compete in open wheel racecars and the vehicles aren't equipped to withstand the "rubbing and racing" approach found in other forms of automotive racing. The drivers rely first on qualifying well for the competition. Then, once the positions are set in the field of drivers, they attempt to execute highly technical and strategic passes throughout the seventy-one laps of the Mexican Grand Prix.

The race weekend would span three days of events, but the main competition would not be held until Sunday. Today, the Friday schedule permitted the drivers and their teams to engage in two practice sessions—both one and a half hours. The practice sessions proved crucial each weekend of the race calendar because they allowed teams an opportunity to make adjustments to their race cars and to test new pieces sent over from the racing teams' factories.

As Lee stepped out of the elevator, another security guard stood waiting to review Lee's ticket. Other than the security personnel, the hallway was empty. The sleepy guard appeared surprised to see someone, but he reviewed the laminated pass and directed Lee to a door thirty feet down the hallway. A placard on the door read, "Fronteras Force VIP." Lee knocked and waited a few moments for the door to open. He knocked again and listened. Hearing no one, Lee checked the handle and walked into the suite.

"Hello!" Lee hollered as he walked into the empty skybox.

The high-performance engines from the practice outside crescendoed as a group of race cars flew past on the straightaway out front. Like a kid on Christmas morning, Lee crossed the empty room toward the floor-to-ceiling windows at the back of the box. With rows of private seating just outside, the location provided a sweeping view of the entire track.

"The seats aren't bad, right?" came a voice over Lee's shoulder.

Lee recognized the voice and turned to find Alex standing in the middle of the box's interior sitting area. She wore a flowy blouse and a yellow skirt that stopped just above her knees. Her short dark hair, styled fashionably, left her tan neckline and the tops of her shoulders exposed.

"Not bad at all. You have quite the setup here," Lee replied. "This is all on Fronteras' dime?"

"Business development, *cariño*," Alex replied with a wink.

"Ah, yes. Well, new business isn't free."

"Neither is old business," she replied. "Especially when it keeps coming back in the picture and demanding payment for services already rendered."

Lee looked around the skybox and spotted an open door off to the side.

"Where did you come from?" Lee said, changing the subject. "I didn't see you when I came in the door."

"The bedroom," she responded, a coy smile on her face.

"Well, this suite really does have it all, then."

"Do you want the full tour?"

Lee noted the sarcasm in her voice. He knew Alex was cutthroat in her business, but he was beginning to understand how much she enjoyed making people squirm. He wondered where the inclination stemmed from. Maybe it was the confluence of beauty, intellect, and growing up in a family that thrived on the fringes of criminal activity. Regardless of the reason, Lee had no doubt she crushed her rivals without quarter.

"Not right now. I thought we were here to watch some racing?"

"Be my guest," Alex said, waving her hand in a dramatic fashion toward the outdoor seating of the box.

Lee turned to head toward the glass-paneled door, but Alex tapped him on the shoulder.

"We need to discuss your situation back home, but I need some assurances."

"What kind of assurances?"

"Assurances that it is just you and I in this conversation," she replied, a serious tone in her voice now.

"Why would I be wearing a wire?" Lee said, shaking his head. "You just saw me two days ago. You know the story of what's going on back home. The cops want me in custody for the Collins hit. You know that. I know that. Hell, most anyone with a television back home knows that."

"My head of security, Roberto, told me you wouldn't fly over from *La Finca*."

"Yeah, that's right. I preferred to ride."

Alex stared at him for a moment, evaluating his response.

"Still, show me there isn't a wire."

"Fine," Lee said with a shrug. He unbuttoned his shirt and showed a wireless chest.

"Okay," she said, pointing to his belt.

"Really?" Lee said with a laugh.

Alex nodded.

Lee dropped his pants to the floor and stood with them at his ankles.

"All right, I showed you mine," Lee said. "It's only fair that—"

"Tsk, tsk, Lee," Alex said, wagging her finger. "You can't ask a lady something like that."

Lee smiled. "I'll take your word on it, then."

"That's a good choice."

Lee pulled his pants up and buttoned his shirt. Alex headed toward the glass doors of the skybox, and Lee followed behind. They took two seats next to one another and watched as the vehicles wound their way around the track. A giant digital scoreboard counted down the time left in the practice session, and small groups of fans dotted the stands around the raceway. Lee leaned over the railing of the box and peered down the line of luxury suites. Most appeared to be empty.

"There is one of our drivers now," Alex said, pointing to a white race car as it passed. The green-and-blue rear wing had the word "Fronteras" emblazoned across the top. "We hope he'll be competing for a podium spot this Sunday."

Lee nodded and watched as the vehicle whipped into the pit lane and slowed to a stop for the team to make adjustments.

"I wouldn't mind going down to see the pit area."

"You are a wanted man, Mr. Acker. You sure seem casual about showing your face wherever you go. Do you think no one watches the news in Mexico?"

"I'm not hiding," Lee replied, leaning back in his seat. "I told you that at the farm."

"Well, that doesn't mean you shouldn't be hiding," she replied, gazing out onto the track. "I'll take you down to the paddock area to show you around, though. We can go once the practice session ends."

The two sat in silence, thinking about what should be said. The clear blue sky above made for a perfect Friday at the track, and Lee took in the view, determined to remain comfortable in the uncomfortable.

"I owed your brother a debt," Alex said. "There are few people in the world that I will ever say that about."

Lee nodded. "I can understand that. I don't like owing people either."

"Cliff is a lot of things, but he never betrayed me—even when baited to do so," Alex continued. "He is in prison for his connection to me, to my family. I have people working for me now, people I have known since I was a child that would have crumbled under the pressure put on Cliff to cooperate."

"Cliff is a dumb, stubborn son of a gun, but he is one of a kind," Lee said. "He is loyal and tries to do what is right. I've seen him about every other weekend since he went to prison, and he hasn't complained one time. It's incredible, really."

The throaty growl of an engine came to life again in the pits below, and one of the red Ferrari drivers returned to the track. The pit crews scrambled back to their monitors that collected countless data points around the performance of the race car. That information would be used to get every ounce of productivity out of the driver and the race car come Sunday. It was advanced metrics at its best.

"Did you ever find out how much information Jake Collins collected around the nature of our business relationship?" Alex asked.

"It's hard to say," Lee replied, readjusting the cap on his head. "He started his own investigation up after Cliff went off to prison. It apparently got nasty between Jake and the Attorney General's Office when he found out the prosecution would not go beyond Cliff."

Alex nodded. She knew all of this.

"With his family's political ties, Jake tried to call in some favors at the Department of Justice—a move that was completely out of character."

"He was a Boy Scout, from what I know."

Lee paused. "Jake was certainly principled, but it was well known around town that he was dissatisfied with the extent of the DOJ's investigation into the business ties between Cliff's work and your family."

"So, he started digging?"

"That, he did," Lee replied, stretching his legs out in front of him. "Eventually, he came to talk to me about it."

Alex turned in her chair to face Lee. With her elbow on the arm of the chair, she balanced her head in her hand. She leaned in close, like Lee was about to dish on the latest gossip.

"What did he say?" she asked, her eyes trying to capture his gaze. Lee returned his focus to the track below.

"I hadn't spoken with Jake in years. Sure, we had seen each other around town and all, but not once in the last sixteen or seventeen years had Jake Collins struck up a conversation with me. Known the guy since close to birth, and then he goes incommunicado as soon as I get married, start a family."

"Wasn't it with his, how do you call it, grade school sweetheart?" Alex said, raising a manicured eyebrow.

"It's high school sweetheart, and that's a bullshit reason. We could have gotten past that."

The digital clock on the scoreboard arrived at "00:00" and a horn blew, signaling the end of the first practice session for the day.

"What did he say, Lee?" Alex asked again.

"He asked about your family first," Lee replied. "He'd come across some records in his investigation that suggested you were still doing business with someone in Blake County. He asked me if I picked up where Cliff left off."

"What did you tell him?"

"I told him the truth, Alex."

Lee watched for a reaction. Her face revealed nothing.

"Did he ask you about anything else?"

"He asked about my father," Lee replied. "He'd come across some interesting records in his investigation into my family's businesses."

"Like what?"

"Well, for starters, a coroner's report. That's the person that comes out to a homicide and helps determine the cause of the death."

Alex nodded. "What did it say?"

Lee sighed. "It was more about what it didn't say. The official report had been amended or doctored."

"The report that concluded your father's death was a suicide?"

Lee nodded. "That's right. The initial report by the detective and coroner stated that my father's death was suspect. That it was likely a murder, not a suicide."

Alex stared at him, unsure what to say.

"Why would that report about your father's death be in some old business records?" she asked.

"I asked Jake the same thing."

Alex kept her gaze fixed on Lee, listening.

"The report itself popped up when Jake started looking into a series of land transactions that occurred between our families."

"Yours and mine?" Alex said, confused. "We don't have any—"

"No, Jake's family and my family," Lee said, cutting her off. "The Collinses and the Ackers."

Lee stood from his seat and started to pace along the railing as he spoke.

"We were brought up to believe that our families have always competed against one another. The stories go all the way back to just after the American Civil War. Both families started in on the timber business, and soon after that, pine tar and turpentine. A dispute arose between two of our long-lost relatives, Joseph E. Cobb and Nathan J. Parker. With slavery officially abolished in the South after the Civil War, the Reconstruction effort was going on to try to help, among many things, former slaves' transition into a free society."

Alex checked the watch on her wrist, listening as she watched the activity in the paddock area.

"My grandfather told my family's history to me when I was young. He explained that Joseph Cobb embraced the new laws and Constitutional amendments handed down after the War. That Cobb believed the freemen, equal under the law, deserved the same respect as any other man."

"What about the women?" Alex asked, sarcasm heavy in her tone.

"Are you going to let me tell this story?" Lee replied.

"Go ahead," she said, impatiently.

"Well, this didn't comport with Parker's view on how the businesses should be run in the South. Though both men were making money hand over fist, Parker wanted to ensure that the profit continued without much competition from northerners or the Black man. He proposed a partnership of sorts, backed by political support, but Cobb refused. The men go back and forth about it, and Parker eventually ends up getting shot in some mysterious incident along the banks of the Chattahoochee River."

Lee leaned against the private box's railing, his back to the racetrack.

"An investigation of sorts happened for a few months, and Joseph Cobb is put on trial for the murder of Parker. Well, a jury acquits Cobb of the charges. He walks out of court a free man. Then, a few months after the trial, a man by the name of Arthur Kelley hunts Cobb down deep in the woods of South Alabama and kills him in retaliation. They never prosecuted Kelley for the murder, and those years forever shaped the dynamic between the family lines that eventually lead to present day."

"So, because of all of this, over one hundred years ago, your families still don't trust one another?" Alex asked.

"That's right. At least not until my father and Bill Collins, Jake's dad, decided to start buying up land together again. They decided it was time to smooth over the history between our families."

Alex sighed and stood from her chair, not saying anything. She walked to a small fridge in the private box and collected two beers. She returned and handed one to Lee.

"Where exactly did Jake Collins find this coroner's report, then?" Alex asked.

"He went into his father's study out on a piece of family property. They own an estate of sorts, a hunting preserve, really. It's called Kelley Hill Plantation. Jake told me he knew how his father preferred to keep his records, so he went to the house out on Kelley Hill. He opened his father's safe and found some files tied to the strange land dealings. There he found the report from my father's suicide investigation."

"So, Jake's father killed your father?"

"We don't know that. He may have covered it up, though," Lee replied. "What we know is that the story has always been that there was no doubt my father took his own life. Now there are doubts that is true."

They both sat in silence for a moment and sipped from the glass beer bottles. The action in the pit areas below continued as teams worked on the vehicles still cooling from the afternoon's practice session.

"What does that mean to you, then?"

"That someone killed my father and covered it up. Now, they killed Jake Collins and are trying to pin it on me."

30

With the second practice session closed for the day, Alex decided to take Lee down to the paddock area. Situated behind the garages and pit lane, the area looked like a small village erected within the speedway. They talked as they walked alongside the racing teams' motorhomes. Alex acknowledged a familiar face every now and then as it passed and explained to Lee how the teams go about moving the cars, equipment, personnel, and even buildings to the twenty-one races on the season's calendar. She knew an incredible amount about the logistics of moving the teams around the world and estimated that they travelled close to sixty-two thousand miles in a season. Though she loved the racing, Alex admitted she enjoyed the business of Formula One even more.

"Your company should buy one of these teams," Lee said, unsure of the price for such an endeavor.

"Right now, it is something my board is considering," she replied. "Many of these race teams break even or lose money during the year. This can be unappealing to a board of directors concerned with shareholders and their own money in Fronteras."

"I can understand that. I assume the money isn't in the actual racing, though, right?"

She nodded. "For the owners, the racing is about the competition. It's about signing the right drivers to be the face of the team. It's employing successful team principals and building a culture of winning within the team itself."

"With winning comes money," Lee added.

"That's right," she replied, that coy smile on her face again. "Money in this sport comes from the brand exposure and the sponsorships from other companies that want to be associated with an image that inspires winning. People like winners, and companies will pay good money to partner with those that do."

"It makes sense," Lee said. "F1 is a global sport, and your company strikes contracts with foreign governments. The more people that see Fronteras, the more trust the brand garners to provide labor services, right?" Lee said this as he eyed the pit lane area. He watched as a group shuttled a car back into a service bay. They would work late into the night to get the car set for the Saturday practice session and qualifying.

"I should have you on my board," Alex replied. "Ownership of an F1 team makes Fronteras a global brand."

"Well, you are very convincing. I trust your board will come around," Lee replied, still looking over at the faces of those standing nearby the pit lane's activities. He'd seen one of the faces before.

An SUV pulled up in front of one of the modern buildings peppered with sponsorship logos. Lee could see two individuals seated in the front of the vehicle. A young man with a thin mustache sat in the driver's seat, and Roberto sat next to him on the passenger side.

"That man over there, the one talking with some of the crew members on the blue team," Lee said, pointing with his right hand.

"That's Williams Racing," Alex replied, distracted.

"Yes, but the man there in the dark sport coat. He is walking with a limp now. Do you see him?"

Alex placed her hand above her eyes to shield the sun. "That's Martin Cruz."

"That's how I know him," Lee said, snapping his fingers. "He was a placekicker for the University of Southern California some years ago."

"I know," Alex replied. "Your brother snapped his leg for me."

Lee stood there, stunned. He stared at Cruz as he continued discussions with what looked like Williams Racing's team principal.

Alex noted the surprise on Lee's face. "Martin Cruz is a sports agent now. He represents two drivers that have seats on Formula One teams. He is a reasonable man that comes from one of the oldest families in Mexico. My family and his have an understanding now, but years ago that was not the case."

"So, let me get this straight. My brother was thrown out of the biggest football game of his life for executing a hit for your family?" Lee somewhat regretted the tone in his voice, but the connection was shocking.

"No," she said, turning to face Lee. "I did meet your brother a few days before the game. It was New Year's Eve, we were at a bar on Sixth Street in Austin, Texas."

"I know how the story goes," Lee interrupted.

"Then you know Cruz made a big scene at that same bar?"

Lee stood there, listening.

"Martin was in town with some teammates. He recognized me and came over to the table that I was sitting at with Cliff. He was drunk and mouthing off. He and Cliff exchanged words."

"That sounds like Cliff," Lee said.

She nodded. "I never told your brother to do what he did, though. I explained the feud that existed between Martin's family and mine. Cliff told me he understood an old rivalry between families all too well. Martin was an asshole that night, yes, but at the time, I believed that would be the end of it."

"So, you are telling me that a few days later, on one of college football's biggest stages, my brother performs one of the dirtiest hits in college football history as an act of love?"

"My family saw it more as an offering," she replied, sidestepping the question. Lee cringed at her nonchalant attitude around the hit that ended a promising kicker's hopes of a career in professional football. "After that hit, Cliff was invited to join the family business. He and I started spending more time together."

"Until he got arrested," Lee replied.

She nodded and looked away. A fan in the waiting SUV kicked on high as it struggled to cool the interior of the vehicle.

"I have to step into a meeting now," Alex said, brushing a stray strand of her dark hair back behind an ear. "We will talk more, but I trust you and I have an understanding now."

Lee held her gaze and heard one of the SUV's doors open behind him. "You will help me?"

Alex nodded. "Your pass will give you access for tomorrow's practice and for the race on Sunday. Let's meet at the same time tomorrow. We can talk more about what I may be able to do for you."

"Thank you. I'll be here tomorrow, then," Lee said, turning toward Roberto, who stood waiting by the rear passenger door of the SUV.

"Has the Olivera family repaid the debt to your brother, to your family?" Alex said to Lee's back as he strode toward the waiting SUV.

Lee turned. "We are getting close to squared up, Alex."

~

Heavy metal played on the radio as the SUV picked up speed along the city streets. Race fans in bright-colored jerseys dispersed from the speedway and walked along the sidewalks, headed toward the restaurants and bars that formed part of the capital's burgeoning culinary scene. Roberto turned around to look behind his seat at Lee.

"I have been meaning to ask, isn't your name more of a woman's name?"

Lee tilted his head back a bit and smirked. "It can be a woman's name," Lee replied. He knew Roberto intended for this comment to get under Lee's skin. "My name is spelled *L-e-e*. Often times when you see a woman with my name, it will be spelled *L-e-i-g-h*."

"People can confuse your name as that of a woman's, though, right?" Roberto said, returning his gaze to the road in front of the vehicle.

"I dislike the name, yes," Lee replied. "Not for that reason, though. It was the name my father chose for me."

Roberto turned to his driver. *"Dice que su papá le dio el nombre de una mujer."*

The young driver laughed at the comment as he meandered through the city traffic. Lee unbuckled to move over to the center rear seat and leaned forward between the two men up front.

"My father did not give me a woman's name."

Roberto, the comedian, turned and said, "Then why do you dislike the name, Lee?"

"I'm named after a rebel general—*un guerrero que era rebelde*."

Roberto reached over and turned the radio down. The aging guerilla fighter looked intrigued and asked, "Should I be familiar with this rebel?"

"Maybe," Lee replied. "Some of his earliest appearances in history were in battles here in Mexico. He participated in the Battle of Veracruz, scouted enemy positions on reconnaissance missions, led soldiers in the Battle of Cerro Gordo, and marched into Mexico City's Grand Plaza—*El Zócalo*—after the Battle of Chapultepec."

"These are all battles that formed part of the United States' invasion into Mexico," Roberto said, hinting that he, too, was a student of military history.

"The Mexican-American War is what we call it back home."

"I am from El Salvador, as you know, but here, that war is considered a scar on Mexican history."

The SUV slowed to a traffic light, and Roberto leaned his head back, rubbing the stubble on his neck.

"The soldier that you speak of. It is General Robert E. Lee—leader of your country's southern states' rebellion in the American Civil War?" Roberto asked this while still looking ahead at the red light in the intersection.

"That's right."

Roberto smiled, no doubt pleased with himself. The light turned green, and the SUV continued down the road. They were still in the capital. It gave Lee some comfort.

"In my home country's civil war, we were considered rebels, too," Roberto remarked. "We fought against our federal government for twelve years. I was too young in the beginning, but I joined in the last years of the war."

"The Salvadoran Civil War was different than the American Civil War," Lee replied.

"No," Roberto said, wagging his finger. "War is about power, always. There are no other reasons to send your countrymen into bloodshed."

Lee listened and thought about Roberto's words.

"My country's civil war was about redistributing power, representation, and wealth to the poor," Roberto said with authority. "Your country's civil war was about holding onto that power, representation, and wealth that came from enslaving the Black man."

"Then you should understand my dislike for a name that serves as a symbol for the fight to preserve slavery."

"You are your own man, Lee. It's your name, not your father's. I am sure your father had a reason for choosing the name he gave you. It doesn't have to be to ensure some old rebel's legacy continues to present day. You can choose to assign your sense of morality to those men that are dead and gone if you wish, but I won't," Roberto said. "The Mexican-American War, American Civil War, and Salvadoran Civil War were led by men who wanted power. That's it."

"Maybe the politicians," Lee replied. "The reason the people—the soldiers—join to fight in wars is not for the power. It is for the cause."

"That may be true," Roberto replied, thinking on the subject. "When I joined the fight, I had my reasons. I see war for what it is now, though. For that reason, I have little appreciation for your heritage or your country's ideals." Roberto's tone was dismissive. "Your leaders say that they believe in human rights, but you politicians funded my country's government as death squads walked into Salvadoran villages to assault, rape, and murder my neighbors. Your leaders say that they reject classism, racism, and inequality, but your government continues to disenfranchise the millions from Latin America that labor in the fields of America's farmland."

Lee could hear the rhetoric of Farabundo Martí—the Marxist-Leninist revolutionary leader whose ideals helped shape the Salvadoran guerillas. Mexico may be Roberto's home now, but he still harbored those feelings that inspired his service in the jungles of El Salvador.

"I don't have time to worry about the reasons past wars were fought," Roberto continued, turning around in the front seat again. "Those with ideals lose to those that hold the power." Roberto stared back at Lee. "You have your own war to worry about now. The Collins family will not stop until they hold you accountable for the death of their son."

The SUV slowed to a stop, and Lee looked away from Roberto's gaze. One of Mexico City's grand avenues—*Paseo de la Reforma*—opened up ahead of the vehicle. A series of tall buildings lined the sides of the avenue. Not a single one was Lee's hotel.

"The Olivera family has done what you asked of them," Roberto began. "I have been instructed to deliver you to your embassy." The chief of security's tone sounded even, businesslike now. "Look over your shoulder, your suitcase is in the rear storage. We collected it from the hotel this morning and checked you out of your room."

"Hold on a minute, I need to talk to Alex. This was not the plan."

"Step out of the vehicle, Lee."

Lee persisted, "Roberto, let's talk about this. My government will take me into custody and put me on trial for this murder. You just said the Collinses won't stop until they hold me accountable for Jake Collins's death."

The shifter on the SUV clicked as the driver threw it into park. Both front doors opened, and the men stepped out of the vehicle. Lee considered bracing himself with something inside the SUV, but he knew it would prove futile. Roberto opened the rear door on the passenger side, and the driver opened the rear hatch to remove Lee's suitcase.

"Get out!" Roberto growled.

Lee hesitated, and Roberto's hand came inside the vehicle. Lee brushed the hand away. "I'll step out myself."

"*Vamos*, come on, then."

Lee stepped out onto the hot sidewalk and looked around as business types hurried by. He spotted an American flag billowing in the wind some sixty feet away. Though he knew the embassy would detain him, the sight of the flag gave him a feeling of relief.

"I want to apologize for what we are about to do," Roberto said, business as usual. "The Olivera family wants the message to be clear."

A blow hit the back of Lee's head and he fell, smacking his face on the concrete. Adrenaline coursed through his veins as he pushed up with his hands, but a boot caught his rib cage with a force that knocked the wind out of him. Another fist drove his face into the concrete, and he felt dazed. Lee made a move to roll to his left side, away from the damaged ribs. Another boot caught him in the gut. Another caught him in his lower back. Lee heaved and gasped for air. He wheezed as he took another boot to the body. Pushing up once more, he felt a heavy blow to his temple.

With the same intensity that it began, the onslaught ceased. Lee tasted the blood in his mouth as he lay facedown on the concrete, listening as the doors to the SUV slammed shut and the vehicle pulled away from the curb. Bystanders screamed calls for help. Lee waited. Then, at last, the blackness claimed him.

BOOK II

31

Charlotte pushed against one of the tall wooden doors that led to the main courtroom. Her legs ached from the morning's run, and she felt a twinge in the muscles as the weight of the door pushed back, urging her not to enter. She thought about turning away from the courtroom, from the controversy. No. Hiding was not an option. Her father needed her there for him. She would not let him down. With that in mind, Charlotte pressed against the heavy door and stepped into the unknown.

The noise from the crowd in the gallery enveloped her as she stepped into the large room. The high ceilings of the courtroom could not contain the energy as reporters readied their cameras along the back wall, while onlookers, crammed in the benches that lined the gallery, chatted excitedly. Charlotte scanned the room, looking for a familiar face. She hadn't seen her father since he disappeared for Mexico six weeks ago. There had been news articles that appeared on social media. She'd caught video of her father in custody as he left the US embassy, bound for a flight back to the United States. She'd refused to visit him since he'd returned home to the county lockup. She knew that today, seeing him in that orange jumpsuit, that would make it real.

"All rise!" hollered the bailiff near the front of the room. Those seated in the pew-like benches rose with the call. The wooden benches creaked with the mass movement of bodies, and the crowd momentarily obstructed Charlotte's view from the back wall. She heard the bailiff's call continue with, "This court is now in session, the Honorable John Balk presiding."

"Please join me in the Pledge of Allegiance with your attention on the flag at the front of room," called a different, deeper voice from the front of the courtroom. Most of those standing near Charlotte placed their hands on their chests; she did the same. With a choppy start, the large group recited the patriotic pledge with a tempered enthusiasm. "I pledge allegiance to the Flag of the United States of America, and to the Republic for which it stands, one Nation under God, indivisible, with liberty and justice for all."

The room went silent for a moment, and the same deep voice from the front of the room bellowed, "Thank you, everyone, please be seated." With the judge's permission, the creaking of benches resumed, and the bodies of the curious onlookers returned to their seats. For the first time that morning, Charlotte had a clear view of the black-robed man seated at the front of the courtroom. He bore a classic haircut, and the knot from his red tie provided the only bit of color on his stoic figure. He sat up tall on the bench, now garnering the room's full attention, and greeted the excited courtroom with a warm introduction.

"Good morning, ladies and gentlemen," Judge Balk began. "I see we have a full courtroom today, welcome. I'd like to remind everyone here today that these proceedings are open to the public, but I will expect those in attendance to maintain order while the lawyers and the court's personnel are working today."

The judge looked out at the large clock on the back wall; it read 9:45 a.m. He noted something with his pencil on the notepad in front of him and then directed his attention to the attorneys seated before him.

"Counsel, are there any housekeeping matters that need to be addressed before we bring in the defendant?"

Charlotte, still standing in the back of the courtroom, watched as both of the attorneys stood to address the judge for the first time that morning. A deputy standing nearby tapped Charlotte on the shoulder, momentarily taking her attention away from the conversation taking place at the front of the room.

"Are you Miss Charlotte Acker?" the deputy asked. He wore a beige uniform with patches on the shoulders from the local sheriff's office. She recognized the young deputy from somewhere.

"Yes, sir," she replied.

"I saw your momma come in the courtroom earlier this morning. She is seated on the first row of benches, kind of center-left behind your daddy's lawyer."

"Thank you," she replied. "How do I know you?"

The young deputy readjusted his duty belt and said, "I came out to your family's home the night the GBI searched the place. You, me, and your momma stood out in the front yard while they performed the search."

"That's right," she replied. "The night this whole nightmare began."

"We were just doing our job."

"You don't believe my dad did this, do you?" Charlotte's voice was pointed, ready for a challenger.

The deputy shifted his feet and looked away toward the front of the room. "I am, well, you know, not really sure what to believe," he stuttered. "My job is to arrest those that break the law and leave it up to the court after that."

Unsatisfied with the response, Charlotte turned away from the young deputy and started walking toward the open seat next to her mother. As she walked down the aisle that cut between the lines of benches, she felt the eyes on her. Charlotte reached the front row and eased by the knees of those seated. She sat next to her mother, and they held hands, waiting for the morning's proceedings to begin.

"All right, let's go ahead and bring the defendant in," the judge announced as the attorneys turned to walk back toward their respective tables.

Maggie Reynolds eyed Charlotte as she made her way to the defense table. Maggie smiled, and, as if choreographed, made her way toward Charlotte. She leaned over the bar that divided the gallery from the area where the lawyers worked and stretched her arms out. "I'm so glad you are here this morning," she whispered, encouraging Charlotte to stand and reciprocate the gesture. Charlotte's mother gave a deft nudge, and Charlotte stood for the embrace.

"Remember, every single camera in this courtroom is fixed on you and your mom right now," Maggie whispered in her ear.

They separated, and Charlotte nodded.

As Charlotte went to sit, a door on the opposite side of the courtroom opened with a clank. A deputy entered first, followed by the man she'd been both dreading and longing to see. The man who'd rocked and held her when she felt scared at night. The man that taught her to ride a bike and shoot a basketball in the driveway. The man who loved her with all his heart and always would.

He strode across the room, still confident with shackles on his feet. In county-issued orange, socks, and flipflops, he still looked handsome. Not as handsome as he was in the pictures from their daddy-daughter dance, but, from across the room, hands cuffed in front of him, he still smiled the smile she'd seen thousands of times. She remained standing, eyes filling with tears.

"I've asked the judge for a few minutes after the hearing for you all to chat in the courtroom," Maggie whispered over to Charlotte. "You can go ahead and sit down. We will all talk once the hearings are done."

As the deputy unlocked the cuffs on her father's hands and shackles on his feet, Lee whispered, "Hey there, love you both."

Charlotte wiped her eyes, sat, and waited for the inevitable.

∽

"Is the state ready to proceed on the Petition for Bond in this matter?" Judge Balk asked, his eyes looking to the prosecution.

Maggie turned to look over at her opposing counsel, Michael Hart. Hart's head was down, reading some paperwork in hand. The two had spoken once over the phone when Maggie filed her entry of appearance with the clerk's office, and they'd met once last week in person to discuss the case. Hart, a career prosecutor, showed little in the two interactions. He'd prosecuted cases in Columbus, Georgia, for the last fifteen years and appeared eager to begin his work in Blakeston. Appointed to step in and handle the prosecution's duties, Hart opposed the court granting Lee Acker a bond. He believed Acker to be a flight risk that could not be trusted on pretrial release. Given the fact that Maggie's client had been located in Mexico, after weeks of the local authorities attempting to contact him for questioning, Maggie felt the state's argument was not too far out of bounds.

Michael Hart stood from his seat and said, "We are ready, Your Honor."

"And the defense?" Judge Balk asked.

Maggie stood. "Ready for the defense, Your Honor."

Judge Balk nodded at both parties, and Maggie returned to her seat.

Hart remained standing. His dark blue suit, tailored to his long frame, was complemented by a maroon tie and pocket square. His black dress shoes and short haircut looked fit for a military inspection. A lawman through and through, Hart looked ready to portray the image of law and order to the cameras rolling behind him.

"Is there anything you'd like to add, Mr. Hart?" Judge Balk said, staring down at the representative for the state.

"Yes, Your Honor."

There would be few surprises, if any, during the bond hearing. The parties discussed most of what would be presented that morning with the judge in his chambers. He knew the identities of all the witnesses, and he knew, generally, what the parties would argue. It was a simple bond hearing. One that would only be complicated by the pressure from the various news organizations covering the story, and maybe a few strategic calls from Maggie.

"Judge, I understand the defense has asked that all witnesses be sequestered from today's hearing. As the court knows, this tactic is often used by attorneys that represent criminal defendants. It helps them break up the orderly presentation of the state's case or score cheap points by embarrassing the hardworking members of our law enforcement that will testify today."

Maggie gave an imperceptible shake of her head at Hart's use of the words "tactic" and "cheap points" as they bled out into the onlookers in the full courtroom.

"My lead case agent, Tim Dawson, will be my first witness this morning," Hart said, covering a topic already addressed by the judge in chambers. "I ask that he be permitted to stay in the courtroom during the rest of the morning's testimony."

"Any objection, Ms. Reynolds?"

Maggie stood. "I'll object to Special Agent Dawson being permitted to sit in on future evidentiary hearings or the eventual trial. That is if the state is brazen enough to take this matter in front of a jury. Today, however, I have no objection."

"Very well, Ms. Reynolds, call your first witness."

In the majority of criminal cases, as long as the person arrested has some money to pay a bondsman, he or she can be released within twenty-four to forty-eight hours of arrest. It is one of the realities of the criminal justice system. In Maggie's first year as a public defender, she argued the issue often in front of judges. Statistically, her poor clients faced a stronger likelihood of being arrested, and on average spent more days in the county jail because of their inability to make bail. It had infuriated Maggie as she watched her clients wait days, weeks, or months without freedom because the price was too high. Then, after months in jail with little prospect of release, those same clients would start to consider pleading guilty to defensible charges. It pained her to think about those men and women taking responsibility for something they shouldn't have to, just to go home.

Maggie's days in indigent defense were behind her now, though. For the first time in her career, the lack of money would not be the main problem her client faced. No, Lee Acker had other problems—he faced a murder charge and was a flight risk. A heinous crime, coupled with the resources to flee the jurisdiction of the court, made for a challenge. Nothing is impossible, though, and Maggie knew there was only one witness that could tip the scales in favor of the defense.

"The defense calls Bill Collins to the stand, Your Honor," Maggie said, waiting for the reaction from the courtroom. She heard the whispers and gasps in the gallery behind her as she stood, waiting.

"Ms. Reynolds, would you please approach the bench?" the judge barked. He slammed the gavel on the desk in front of him and called for order in the courtroom as the conversations in the gallery rose an octave.

Maggie stepped away from the defense table and walked toward the judge. Her opposing counsel, standing across the aisle, turned to follow her. As she neared the judge, she rehearsed her argument in her head.

"Ms. Reynolds, what stunt are you trying to pull with this witness?" the judge said in a low voice, in an attempt not to be overheard by the clerk and court reporter seated nearby. An impossible task.

"It is not a stunt, Your Honor," Maggie responded, a little louder than intended. "Bill Collins has known my client since he was a child. He can testify to all of the relevant information Mr. Acker needs for you to consider a bond in this case."

"This is highly unusual, Your Honor," Hart interjected. "This is the victim's family, and I think the court should keep this from becoming a spectacle today."

"There is nothing prohibiting the defense from calling Bill Collins as a witness. Hell, he was listed as a potential witness for the state's rebuttal."

The judge looked up from the two attorneys bickering in front of him and saw Bill Collins step through one of the tall wooden doors of the court-room. The issues in a bond hearing are limited to consideration of four factors. First, whether the person charged with a crime is a flight risk. Second, whether there is a likelihood that person will intimidate witnesses or hinder the investigation in the case. Third, whether the person to be released poses a threat or danger to the community. Fourth, the likelihood that the person will commit another crime while on bond. All four factors call for speculation, and the judge saw no reason the senatorial candidate could not testify as to each.

"I'll allow it, Ms. Reynolds," the judge whispered. "Next time we discuss the outline of your case in chambers, though, I expect you to be more forthcoming."

"Thank you, Judge."

"I'd like my objection noted on the record, Your Honor," Hart said.

"That'll be fine, it'll be so noted on the record, Mr. Hart."

Judge Balk looked again toward the congressman and beckoned him forward. The politician began a slow walk down the center aisle of the courtroom. His black suit and dark tie looked appropriate for a funeral. Collins had been in campaign mode for the last month. Spending every day in front of the cameras as he inched closer to a seat in the United States

Senate. This morning would be no different. He stopped short of the seat behind the microphone and greeted the judge as if they were old friends.

"Madam clerk, please swear the witness," the judge ordered.

"Do you solemnly swear that you will tell the truth, the whole truth, and nothing but the truth, so help you God?" the clerk said, reciting the standard oath.

"I do."

"Please go ahead and take a seat," the judge said. He looked as if he was about to apologize for some reason. "It's your witness, Ms. Reynolds. You may proceed."

Maggie walked to a lectern at the center of the courtroom and rested her notes in front of her. She looked at her witness and listened to the deafening silence around her. She could feel the attention of the gallery lock onto her. She had control of the room.

"I'm sorry for your loss, Mr. Collins," Maggie began.

The congressman shifted in his seat. "Thank you, Ms.—"

"It's Ms. Reynolds, and I, as you know, represent Lee Acker."

First rule of questioning a witness on the stand—control the pace of the questioning. Maggie, always nimble on her feet when questioning a witness, had no problem cutting a witness off to establish control. Even the grieving father of the victim in a murder case.

"I knew your son, Mr. Collins," Maggie continued. "We worked together and tried cases against each other in this very courtroom."

Bill watched as his interrogator stepped away from her notes, making use of the space around her as she spoke. The sudden call to the witness stand surprised him. Something the old veteran of Washington politics rarely encountered in his more seasoned years in office.

"I know," Bill replied. "I poked my head in for the closing arguments in a case that you handled against my son."

Second rule of questioning a witness on the stand—never ask a question you don't know the answer to. Maggie tried a number of cases against Jake Collins. Jake stole some wins from her in front of juries. He was creative, well-spoken, and oozed charisma. A dangerous combination in any trial lawyer. Her success rate against Jake, in front of juries, was around fifty percent. She and Jake used to joke that they might as well flip a coin before the first witness was sworn. She was not about to ask the congressman which case he'd observed.

"The jury acquitted your client," Bill added. A smile on his face that implied some level of judgment.

"Your son was a good trial lawyer and a friend," Maggie replied, unsure how to wrangle with the congressman's compliment.

"Well, thank you for saying that, Ms. Reynolds."

The congressman poured a glass of water from the pitcher in front of him. As he sipped from the glass, he made eye contact with Grace Acker. She was seated directly behind Lee. She held the gaze until he refocused his attention to defense counsel.

"Now, you know my client well, don't you, Mr. Collins?" Maggie said as she redirected the conversation to the questioning relevant to the bond hearing.

"Yes, Ms. Reynolds. I've known Lee most of his life."

"You knew his parents?"

"That's right."

"Would you say Mr. Acker has deep roots in this community, Mr. Collins?"

"Lee was born and raised right here in Blakeston. His family is from here. They have farmed, run timber, and harvested oysters to our south, in Apalachicola, for as long as I can remember. I myself am getting a little older, so my memory goes back quite a while, Ms. Reynolds."

Bill smiled at the onlookers in the gallery as he waited for the next question. Ever the politician.

"And you know he started a family here in Blakeston?"

"That's right. I know his wife, Grace, and I have met his daughter. They both live here in Blakeston."

"And some of the companies and farming that Mr. Acker is involved in, they are here in this area?"

"As far as I know," Bill replied. "Here, Alabama, Florida, and Mexico."

Third rule of questioning a witness—recognize when they set the bait, never take it. Maggie noted the trap and moved on. The congressman wanted her to challenge the comment; she would let the prosecutor run down that rabbit hole.

"I assume you have not spoken with Mr. Acker since the passing of your son?"

"I have not," Bill replied, feigning impatience.

"Would you be intimidated by having to sit down and have a conversation with Mr. Acker?"

"No."

"You aren't concerned he could attack you?"

"Not any more than the next man."

"Would you be worried about our community here in Blakeston if Mr. Acker were to be allowed out on bond? So that he can work in his local companies. So that he can spend time and support his family while awaiting his trial in this case."

"No. Lee cares about this community. His companies employ a number of the residents here."

"In fact, Lee is a baseball coach here in town, right?"

"That's right. He helps coach a travel team here in the area. Lee was an excellent ball player. I coached him when he was just a boy."

"Would you be fearful of Mr. Acker working with these young men, passing along that wisdom you imparted on him?"

The congressman smiled, recognizing the well-placed compliment. "I don't see him being a danger to those young men, if that's what you are asking. He loves the game of baseball. He is a good baseball coach. The only thing he loves more than the game is his family. He gave up his eligibility at Vandy, maybe a shot at the big-time game, to come home to grow his family."

Maggie paused. This was too easy.

"Now, let's switch gears a moment. The election is tomorrow, right?"

"That's what they tell me," the congressman replied, spurring a few chuckles in the gallery.

"You currently serve in our United States House of Representatives?"

"I do."

"And now you are running for a seat in the United States Senate?"

"That's right. Vote if you have not already."

"I plan to," Maggie replied. "But you'd agree that everyone who isn't a felon should be given the opportunity to vote, right?"

The congressman smiled and looked up at the ceiling of the courtroom for a moment.

"I think every man and woman that has the right to vote in this country should."

"Does that include my client?"

"Of course, assuming he has the right to vote."

The congressman smiled again at Maggie. A nice smile. One she knew served him well in politics.

"I know what you are doing, Ms. Reynolds."

Maggie ignored the bait. "If the county won't permit Mr. Acker to vote from jail tomorrow, he should be released so he can do so, right?"

"Right," Bill replied after another pause.

"Assuming they supervise him while he does so, right?"

"Yes, ma'am, whatever they need to do."

"Because really the court needs to just know where he is?" Maggie said, taking a step closer to the congressman. She had him trapped.

"I don't know what the court needs to know," he replied, deflecting.

"Well, you said it yourself, Mr. Acker isn't a danger to the community?"

"Right."

"He doesn't intimidate you?"

"That's correct."

"So, if the court just needs to ensure it knows where Mr. Acker is at all times, it could do that with an ankle monitor, right?"

"If that's what the court decides."

She wouldn't push him any further. Maggie stepped back to the lectern and reviewed her notes for a moment. She didn't have any other questions, but she wanted the judge to think about the testimony he just heard.

"That's all I have for this witness right now, Your Honor," Maggie said, collecting her notes to sit down.

The judge looked up from his notepad. "Any follow-up, Mr. Hart?"

"Yes, Your Honor."

Hart popped up from his seat without a notepad in hand.

"Mr. Collins, the man seated across from you in this courtroom, dressed in an orange jumpsuit, is charged with murdering your son. Are you telling the court you are fine with him being on bond?"

"No, that's not what I am saying," Bill replied.

"Then what are you saying?"

Hart made his first mistake of the morning. He asked a question he didn't know the answer to.

"I am saying I want Lee to be held accountable for what he did. I'll do whatever needs to be done to make sure justice is accomplished for my son, for my family."

Maggie made a note on her pad and circled it with a highlighter—*He will do whatever needs to be done to ensure justice for his family.*

"So, keeping him here in jail is the safest for this community, then, right?"

"Look, Mr. Hart, I want the court to keep him in jail as much as you do."

Hart stepped away from the lectern, frustrated. His own witness, the father of his victim, was bucking the plan and going rogue on the witness stand. A prosecutor needs his witnesses, especially family members affected by violent crime, to tell the judge that they want an offender locked away without the prospect of release.

"Judge, if you decide to let Lee out," Bill continued, looking up at the bench. "If you have him wear some kind of an ankle monitor, I'll accept it. I swore to uphold the Constitution when I took office, and I won't violate my oath. Our country decided a long time ago that men and women are presumed innocent until proven guilty. It's only fair that I let the process run its course."

"Then what is it you want?" Hart asked in disbelief.

"A trial, Mr. Hart. An opportunity for the people of this community to hold Lee accountable."

Hart stood there, dumbfounded.

"That's all I have, Your Honor," Hart said, turning to sit down.

"Anything further with this witness, Ms. Reynolds?" Judge Balk asked.

"Nothing further, Your Honor."

Bill Collins stepped off of the witness stand and walked toward the short wooden gate that divided the gallery from the front of the courtroom. He looked at Lee, and then Grace, as he pushed through the gate to take a seat directly behind the prosecution's table.

"Call your next witness, Ms. Reynolds."

32

Lucy Collins stood in front of the hotel suite's bathroom mirror, touching up the makeup around her eyes. She listened to her husband's voice through the bathroom wall as he rehearsed a few of his remarks for that evening's campaign event. He had certain routines, like all people do. An adequate speaker and a better politician, Bill Collins led all to believe he was a natural at his craft. Lucy knew the truth, though. In fact, she preferred the truth. Bill's cavalier and charismatic demeanor on the stage was not at all a gift from God. Sure, he was a gifted conversationalist. He was the son of a farmer, after all. His public speaking, though, no, that took work, and she knew her husband took great pride in his preparation.

Tonight's remarks would be sincere and inspiring. They were meant to appeal to those last voters that were undecided, but as Lucy listened to words of the speech, she thought about how they might tie in with their victory remarks. As was their tradition, Lucy and Bill wrote the victory speech the weekend Bill announced his candidacy for the United States Senate. They started the tradition twenty-two years earlier, when Bill made his first run for public office. It worked then, and she felt confident their record in elections would remain perfect. Lucy lined her eyes with eyeliner and thought about the first night they drafted a campaign victory speech.

The two stayed up all night drinking wine in their pajamas and scribbling remarks on legal pads. It was all so exciting. They were younger then and naïve to the world of national politics. She remembered how they laughed at the absurdity of it all—leaving their lives in South Georgia for Washington, DC.

It turned out to be very real, though, and they stood on the verge of another victory. If polling numbers held true, Bill Collins would win by a slim margin. For the first time in twenty-two years, Lucy had a feeling the victory remarks would be scratched. Written before Jake's death, Lucy knew her husband would rework the speech. He wouldn't declare victory without mentioning the hole in his heart.

She waited until he finished his run through the speech and called into the other room.

"Bill, what do you plan to tell reporters that ask you about Lee Acker's bond hearing today?"

Lucy heard the ruffle of papers on the coffee table in the hotel suite's sitting room. "The same thing I told them this morning while leaving the courthouse."

His voice sounded terse. She considered confronting him later, once the politicking was out of the way for the evening. She raised her voice so that it could be heard clearly through the wall, "Lee is sitting at home tonight with a monitor around his ankle because you wouldn't urge the judge to keep him in jail."

"Lucy, it's done. I don't want to rehash this with you."

She snapped a mascara pen shut and stepped through the bathroom door into the sitting area. "I don't understand, Bill. Why can't you see that you should have done more?"

"I'll tell the media what I told the judge. I want Lee Acker on trial for our son's murder. It's that simple."

Bill walked toward Lucy and put his hands on her waist. The Republican-red dress had a black sash around the waist. He held her gaze and looped a couple of fingers under the sash. He could tell she was upset as she brushed his hands from her hips.

"You promised me that you would make this about justice for our son."

"And there will be, Lucy."

"Letting him out on bond, how is that fair? The murder weapon was found in his truck. I don't see how the judge can let this happen. We have known John Balk for years. We supported him when he ran for his judgeship years ago."

"The ballistics have to match," Bill said, looking down at his notes for the night's speech.

Lucy stepped back and shook her head, aghast. Tears welled in her eyes, ruining the makeup she just applied.

"Damn it, Bill, why can't you just accept that Lee is going to have to go to jail for this?"

"This is me accepting it. If I become emotional, I'll make mistakes. The ballistics have to match. That's what the agents with the GBI told me on the last conference call."

"Well, it sure seems like you hope they don't match," Lucy said as she glared at her husband.

"I'm sorry, Lucy! I'm struggling with this. Does that make me a terrible father?"

Bill threw the notes against the wall as he turned his back to his wife. He stepped across the room to the mini fridge that hummed against the sitting room wall. The notes fell in a clutter behind the sofa. The aggression surprised Lucy, and she watched as her husband pulled a beer from the cool interior of the fridge. He popped the top on the can and stared at the wall as he took a long swig.

"You are not a terrible father," she said, her voice soothing now.

"You know I care for Lee. Those boys were like brothers until that girl split them apart."

Lucy nodded at the nameless mention of Grace Acker. "Yes, they were like brothers, and you know even love can tear brothers apart."

Bill waved off the comment as Lucy stepped closer.

"Something happened to our son, though, Bill. It started when he began investigating Cliff Acker for racketeering and those dealings with the Mexicans. Jake suspected Lee was somehow involved. He suspected everyone. Jake became obsessed. He became reckless, you know that."

"Jake was right to do what he did," Bill added. "And he wasn't done investigating."

Bill shook his head and took another sip of the beer as he sat down on the couch. He leaned back and watched for a reaction from his wife. Nothing. She looked measured, beautiful.

"Who knows what happened," Bill began again. "Deese and the boys found boxes of information that Jake had been collecting on the Acker boys. Even information he gathered together on our companies. He was up to something. I suppose Lee found out."

"He must have," Lucy replied after a short pause. "Did he talk to you about the investigation?"

Bill rubbed his head and thought about the question. He and Jake argued twice about the issue. The Mexican labor company would begin fulfilling contracts with the US government come 2017. Jake confronted his father about the deal with Fronteras Force as soon as he found out. They'd argued about the arrangement for the second time only three weeks before the murder. Jake threatened to take the details of the deal to the public.

"No," Bill replied, lying. "I wish he would have."

"Well, I wish he would have, too."

Lucy stepped forward to her husband and kissed him. She could taste the beer on his lips.

"Get focused on closing out this campaign, soon-to-be Senator William Collins."

Bill grinned. "Yes, ma'am, Mrs. Collins."

~

A black SUV with a Blake County Sheriff's Office emblem pulled in front of the Acker home at 8:15 p.m. Lee Acker sat alone in the back seat of the vehicle and waited for the deputy to step out and open the rear door. As he waited, Lee reached down and readjusted the monitor around his ankle. The rubber bracelet and small black box that monitored his movement would be required until Judge John Balk decided otherwise. It did not bother Lee. He was glad to be returning home. Tucking the monitor under the cuff of his jeans, Lee stepped out of the vehicle.

"Curbside service," the deputy said, holding the door open like a wiseass.

"Thanks, Bubba," Lee replied with a nod.

"The judge may have let you out of jail, but the sheriff has told us not to hesitate to bring you back in if that ankle monitor starts going off. No funny business. You tamper with it, you are heading back to lockup. Understood?"

"Relax, I am not going anywhere."

"You better not," the deputy replied with a sneer. "It'll be on the six o'clock news faster than you can say, 'Not guilty.'"

"All right, well, good talk. I'm going inside. Do you need me to sign anything?"

The deputy shook his head and slammed the rear door shut. A line of news vans sat parked along the edge of the property, and Lee had no doubt the boys at the station drew straws on who would be tasked with handling the escort. No one wanted to play the local chauffeur. Lee thanked the deputy again as he stepped into the running SUV. Waving as the vehicle pulled away, Lee gazed at the taillights until they disappeared around the corner of the drive.

As Lee turned back to his house, he noticed that no lights were on in the upstairs of the home. A single lamp illuminated the front living room, but Lee saw no one waiting. He stepped to the front door and checked the knob. It was locked. Opting not to knock, Lee walked down the front path to the garage. One of the three roll-down doors stood open, and Lee made his way to the interior door. The door was locked as well. He knocked, then knocked again. No answer. Lee glanced around the garage and noticed Charlotte's vehicle was gone but Grace's SUV was accounted for. She was home, somewhere in the house.

Locked out of his own house, Lee peered around the garage for options. There were few other than to wait. He opened the door to an old dusty fridge that sat in the corner of the garage and scanned the selection. He pulled a Diet Coke and a bottle of water from the door before making his way around to the backyard of the home. With some finesse, he popped the handle on the backyard's gate and continued around to the rear patio. The sun descended slowly behind the tall pines in the woods, providing the last light of the day. Lee could hear birds chirping in the trees and the gurgling of the pool as he walked down the stone footpath. It felt good to be home.

"Welcome home," the familiar voice said as Lee rounded the corner of the house.

"Thank you, baby," Lee replied, slowing his walk to a saunter. His bride sat at the patio table, a glass of red wine resting in her left hand.

"There is a pot of vegetable soup on the kitchen stove, in case you're hungry."

Lee nodded. "I'll get a bowl in a little while."

Grace took a sip of her wine and exhaled.

"Charlotte is out with some friends from school. I tried to convince her to wait until you got home. So that you could see her and—"

"It's all right," Lee said. "I understand she is upset."

Grace stood from her chair, and Lee stepped to meet her as she turned to go inside. He wrapped his arms around her waist and kissed her on the forehead. She leaned into the embrace and wrapped her arms around him.

"Are you upset?" Lee asked after a long pause.

Grace nodded her head up and down against his chest, not saying anything. She slid her arms from around his back and grabbed his hands with hers. Still quiet, she led him into the house and through the kitchen. He could smell the soup that sat simmering on the stove, the bread long cooled from the oven. She led him past the family photographs that hung on the wall in the front hallway, his light jacket still hanging by the door. Up the steps they went, and he followed her without saying a word.

Lee admired her slender figure from behind as it turned the corner to their bedroom, the bed's covers and sheets still unmade. Grace pulled him onto the bed with her, and the two embraced for a long kiss. His hands went to her body, a body that he had explored time and again. He slid them under her shirt and rubbed his hands along her stomach, around to her back. She went to work removing his belt, then his pants.

"I missed you," she whispered, breathing heavy as Lee continued to remove the clothes that remained on her body.

"I missed you, too," he replied. "I love you and—"

She stopped him. "Let's not talk about it tonight," she said, rubbing a cut on his face that hadn't yet fully healed.

Lee obliged, and the two wrapped themselves in one another again. Her hands tugged against the soft sheets, and the monitor on his ankle rubbed against her strong calves. In that moment, their minds cleared. The trial, Jake Collins, the reporters, his trip to Mexico, it could all wait. Tomorrow was as good a day as any to deal with what would come.

33

"The ballistics match," Tim Dawson said as he handed a thin tablet across the table to his boss, Don Malone.

"Good," Malone said as he scrolled through the report. "Have you delivered it to the prosecutor yet?"

"No, I wanted to discuss this with you before we took it to Hart."

"What's to discuss? It is a match on the murder weapon that we found in our primary suspect's pickup truck."

Dawson nodded as he thought about how to broach the subject with the acting director. A ballistics report in most cases helps identify a weapon by the markings left on a bullet or bullet casing after a firearm is discharged. The reports, and experts that prepare them, can help identify where the gun was fired by reviewing the depth of the wound, angle of entry, caliber of the bullet, and a number of other factors. Dawson's ballistics guy would work closely with the forensic pathologist to map out the scene in the woods where Jake Collins was found dead. They would be able to reconstruct the scene of the shooting and location of the shooter. If Dawson was lucky, they would be able to give him a solid opinion on the height of the shooter and other clues that could shore up issues in the case.

"Have you reviewed the fingerprint analysis?" Dawson said, pointing to the tablet.

"Not yet, what does it say?" Malone replied, setting the tablet down in front of him to meet the gaze of his lead investigator.

"We pulled prints out of the truck, and they of course match the prints supplied by Acker when he was booked two weeks ago at the jail."

"Good again," Malone replied. "What did they find on the weapon?"

"There were two sets of prints on the Beretta found in Acker's truck's toolbox. Well, a set, and then a partial set."

Malone nodded, listening.

"One set matches our guy that found the Beretta, José Valdez Bisbal."

"The farmhand," Malone added. "We assumed the guy's prints would be there; he admitted to picking up the gun and looking at it." Malone shook his head. "Stupid."

"I agree, but the partial set of fingerprints found on the weapon aren't a match for Acker."

"The Mexican told us he wiped the gun down," Malone replied dismissively. "That explains why the shooter's prints are gone."

"That's one way to look at it."

Malone leaned back in his seat, folding his arms in front of him.

"Care to elaborate, Dawson?"

"Something doesn't smell right, sir."

"That's because you are overthinking the issues involved."

"So, you agree there are issues, sir?"

"What am I on the witness stand here? No, I don't believe there are issues with the case, Dawson. The farmhand's dumb decision to wipe the weapon is a plausible explanation for Acker's prints not being found on the Beretta. The weapon matches, bullets match, and it was located in the killer's truck. Jesus Christ, son, what more do you need to build your case?"

Dawson leaned back in his chair. He looked up at the ceiling fan clicking above them and could feel his boss's eyes studying his every move.

"Did you review the report they put together at the embassy in Mexico?" Dawson said, returning his gaze across the table.

"I did," Malone replied. "Sounds like Acker got his ass whooped and was left for collection at the front door of the US embassy. My cat does the same thing with birds and lizards."

"They performed an inventory of items found on Lee Acker, though. Did you notice he had a Beretta 92FS on him that day?"

Dawson watched for some reaction from his more experienced counterpart. Nothing.

"I saw it," Malone replied, curtly.

"The weapon they took off of him in Mexico City was the same model, size, caliber, weight, everything matched the—"

"Yes, Dawson, it matched the weapon we found in the truck. The Beretta 92FS is probably Acker's favorite piece to carry with him," Malone said in a calm, controlled voice. "Where are you going with this, Tim?"

Dawson stood from his seat and walked over to the coffeepot in the corner of the conference room. He grabbed a disposable cup from the cabinet and poured the coffee.

"Why wouldn't Acker take the murder weapon with him to Mexico?" Dawson said as he stirred a packet of sugar into the coffee. "I mean, the guy decided he needed to take a heater with him on the road, right? Why intentionally leave behind the one piece of evidence that ties him to this case. If he already had the clean Beretta with him, why not leave it in the truck? Why not take both weapons with him and ditch the murder weapon?"

Malone smiled from across the room. "People are stupid, Tim. You know that. Killers are just people, too. Ipso facto, killers are people that make stupid mistakes." Malone looked pleased with himself in his attempt at humor.

"My gut tells me it's wrong, sir."

Malone paused and tapped his fingers on the conference table. In his short time as acting director with the GBI, he'd already started to miss the mentorship aspect of working investigations with younger, less experienced agents. Tim Dawson was in need of guidance at the moment. Then and there he made the decision that he would need to stay involved in the investigation of the murder.

"Everything may not make perfect sense, but you leave those questions to the criminal defense attorney."

"Is it not our job to solve this case, sir?" Dawson responded, immediately regretting the retort.

Malone raised an eyebrow. "We have solved this case, and next week the grand jury will hear the evidence. They will return an indictment for Lee Acker for the offense of murder, and the prosecutor will take this case to trial."

"Are you not interested in—"

"Tim, I am going to stop you right there. This case may still be develop-ing, but the investigation has a clear direction now. You have done some nice work here, and I expect you to continue to lead the charge. If that is an issue for you, or you have too many questions, just let me know. It won't be the first time two investigators have different approaches to catching a murder suspect. I'll just take the case over myself, though, so you just say the word and I'll get us across the goal line."

Tim nodded, indicating he understood the veiled threat.

"Good, good. Well, that settles it. Let's nail this son of a gun."

~

Lee Acker's legal defense team, Maggie Reynolds and Bruce Tevens, stood on the front steps of the Acker home. They rang the doorbell and waited. Within a few seconds, the door opened, and Lee Acker came into view. He wore shorts and a faded polo. Even in bare feet, Lee stood tall and had the body of an athlete. He greeted them both with a handshake and waved them into the house.

"This is a beautiful home," Maggie said as she entered the foyer.

"Thank you," Lee replied. "It's good to be home. I have you both to thank for that."

"That was all Maggie, Lee," Bruce said. "She did a tremendous job at the hearing. I want to be involved in discussions around your defense, but Maggie is lead counsel."

Lee nodded at the two standing in the front hallway of his home.

"Well, let's get to it, then," Lee said as he led his lawyers down the hallway to the back of the house. "I say we use my home office for today's meeting. It'll give us plenty of space."

"Wherever you would like to meet is fine, Mr. Acker," Maggie said as she followed.

Lee smiled. "It's Lee, just Lee. I told you the first time we met in jail that you don't need to call me Mr. Acker. My future is in your hands, so let's at least be on a first-name basis."

"That'll work, Lee."

The three gathered around a coffee table in Lee's study. Maggie set two files and her laptop on the table. Bruce fell into a leather couch facing the door and pulled his cell phone out to run through emails. Lee offered coffee, and both attorneys declined.

"It sounds like the prosecution is going to be pretty aggressive with their timeline," Maggie began. "Your case will be presented to the grand jury next week. Michael Hart, the lead prosecutor, will be pushing to have your case added to the earliest trial calendar available."

"What will the grand jury decide?" Lee asked.

"They'll listen to some evidence presented by the prosecution and decide whether to return an indictment. That'll formally charge you in this case, and it'll allow the state to push this thing toward a trial."

"You will be indicted, Lee," Bruce added. "It is not that difficult for Hart to accomplish."

Lee nodded, listening as the two lawyers walked him through the procedural timeline of a felony criminal case.

"When do we tell our side of the story?" Lee asked, leaning forward in his wide leather chair.

"Well, of course we will at a trial, but we will keep our cards close for now. The most important part at this stage of the case is to collect as much information as we can. The prosecution will have to give you a packet of discovery; this is the evidence law enforcement and other agencies collected while investigating the case. That discovery packet doesn't have to be handed over for another few weeks, though."

"So, right now, we just wait?" Lee said, frustrated.

"Yes, sort of. I am in discussions with the prosecutor and have my connections in law enforcement."

"She knows the lead investigator extremely well," Bruce blurted from his seat on the couch.

Maggie turned to Bruce Tevens, who still stared down at his phone, tapping away on the screen as he prepared a response to an email. His eyes flicked up from the smartphone, and he caught Maggie's stare. Bruce grinned and returned to the screen.

"How do you know the investigator?" Lee asked, noting the awkward gaze exchanged between his lawyers.

"He and I were, uh, seeing each other, briefly," Maggie replied cautiously. "It ended abruptly when I decided to come on board as your defense counsel."

Bruce stood as he answered a call on his cell phone. Maggie looked over at him as he motioned that he was stepping outside. Bruce Tevens had little expertise in criminal defense. His absence would not be much of a loss.

"What's the investigator's name?"

"It's Special Agent Tim Dawson. It's important you know this prior fling does not affect my ability to represent you."

"I'm not concerned," Lee replied after a short pause. "Bruce says you are who I need in my corner. I trust Bruce, and he has always provided sound guidance. He doesn't know a damn thing about a criminal case, though."

Maggie smiled. "I'm glad we are on the same page."

Lee crossed his left leg over the right and leaned back in his chair. They sat in silence for a moment, considering how to proceed. Maggie studied the pictures of motorcycles, baseball stadiums, and family portraits that dominated the wood-paneled walls. She scanned the bookshelves of the home office, waiting for her client to speak again.

As a public defender, Maggie was always crunched for time. Always a line of clients waiting to talk to her and a string of phone calls to return. She'd press her clients to tell their story so she could evaluate the case and formulate their defense. Sure, she found success in the chaos, but it never felt as though she had the time to put her maximum effort, her undivided attention, into a person's case. Now, Maggie had the chance. Her one client sat across from her on furniture that cost more than her car. He demanded her full attention, and she would not rush him. He would tell his story when ready.

"I assume you would like to know why I went to Mexico?"

Maggie nodded. "If it is relevant to your defense, which I imagine it is, then I need to know."

"I was not running from the situation here," Lee began. "I went down there to meet someone."

"Okay," she said as she leaned over to her bag to remove a pen and legal pad.

"As you may know, my brother, Cliff, is in prison."

Maggie nodded. "Conspiracy to violate the Racketeer Influenced and Corrupt Organizations Act."

"That's right. Years ago, my brother began working with businesses owned by a family out of Mexico."

"The Olivera family," Maggie added again.

"You have done your homework," Lee said, impressed. "Well, during Cliff's last year of college at the University of Texas, he met Alex Olivera— the oldest daughter and successor in power to the Olivera family's businesses. The two hit it off and so began their ten-year working and romantic relationship."

Lee leaned forward in the chair and rested his elbows on his knees.

"Alex Olivera is the CEO of a Mexican company that facilitates labor contracts for governments and private companies all over this part of the world. She and Cliff used to work in some of the family's more questionable lines of business, but now she appears to devote her time to leading and growing a more legitimate venture, Fronteras Force, S.A."

"While researching the family, I found a few articles on the company," Maggie said. "If Fronteras' financial reporting is accurate, the company is a rising star. Alex Olivera is being heralded as a member of the new generation of Mexican leaders. Still in her thirties, ambitious, and publicly critical of the cartels."

"And female," Lee added.

"How progressive," Maggie quipped. "She is impressive, though, and it looks like she has negotiated some large contracts with both the Canadian and United States governments in just the last year."

"She has," Lee replied with a nod. "These are megadeals to work on public works projects that are already over budget. Fronteras will ship workers into Florida, Georgia, Louisiana, Texas, New Mexico, Arizona, and California by the thousands. The US government pays the contract price, and Fronteras handles everything else. These people will be housed in temporary buildings near the work sites, and they will be tagged with tracking devices. Food, tobacco, beer, and the other bare necessities will be supplied with the housing."

Maggie exhaled as she considered the legal dilemma surrounding the placement of tracking devices on employees. She made a few notes on the notepad in front of her and returned her gaze across the table.

"They sound like they will be a step above prison work camps," she said.

"That's pretty accurate. They are paid at a wage above what they would earn in Mexico, but well below federal minimum wage standards."

"I assume the room and board is considered a part of their compensation."

"Exactly," Lee replied. "And it gets better. The workers that are brought in by Fronteras have to agree by contract to a waiver of extradition and to all their constitutional rights. If a dispute arises or if they try to walk off the job, they will be headed straight back to Mexico."

"I read a few articles on Fronteras' deals with the US, but none of this information made the cut."

Lee nodded and stood from his seat. He walked to a small fridge and pulled a bottle of water out.

"One of Fronteras' first major projects would be to seal the entire Mexican-United States border. They would erect a wall along the southern borders of Texas, New Mexico, Arizona, and California. Fronteras will do the job for a bargain, too." Lee took a sip from the water bottle and continued. "The wall is supposed to curb the flow of undocumented workers coming into the country and create jobs here for US citizens."

"I imagine that's at least how they will try to sell it," Maggie added. "Depending on the outcome of this upcoming election, funding for the project could go through the roof."

"Bingo. And if the wall is built, Fronteras will just keep bringing people over the border under the guise of contract labor for more US government projects or work for private companies. It is win-win for them."

"You think their business will take off?" Maggie asked.

"It already has. Fronteras has found success with the model in other countries that are wary of immigrants, and they will do the same in the US."

"So, to curb the flow of immigration, the US government is going to start letting private labor companies tag and track the immigrants that do come to our country to work?"

"That's right."

"Seems like a lot of work for Fronteras," Maggie said, a note of skepticism in her voice. "This will be profitable?"

"The sky's the limit," Lee replied in a serious tone. "And on top of the money they make off the backs of bargain labor, it'll pave the way for the Olivera family to corner the drug trade in the US. Fronteras will have control over the people coming from out of the country for contract work, and they'll be loading the buses, trucks, ships, and planes that carry those workers over the border."

"That's incredible," Maggie said. "The Olivera product will just walk right over the border while the other suppliers, their competitors, will have a much harder time due to the increased border security."

Lee nodded and sat back in his seat, waiting for questions from his attorney.

"What does this have to do with your case?" Maggie asked, setting her pen and notepad on the coffee table. "And second, how did you come across all of this information?"

"It has everything to do with my case, Maggie," Lee said after a long pause. "And I learned it all from the man I'm accused of murdering."

34

Maggie climbed into the driver side of her Saab 900 and turned the ignition to get the air going. She laid her purse, files, and laptop on the passenger seat before noticing that Bruce stood by the window of her car. He knocked twice on the glass, and she mashed a button on the door to roll the window down.

"How do you feel about our guy's chances so far?" he asked, loosening the knot on the tie around his neck.

"It's tough to say at this stage. I have some real questions about the defense theory that he wants to use. I'll think on it a few days before going back to him with recommendations."

Bruce nodded. "Lee is a smart guy, but he won't tell you everything. That's his way. I have fussed at him in the past over some decisions he made with his family's businesses."

"Anything illegal that I should be worried about the prosecutor dredging up?" Maggie asked.

"I don't think that prosecutor would know where to start looking," Bruce replied, sidestepping the question with a grin.

Maggie felt the cool air begin to fill the car, and it felt nice on her skin. She was a South Florida girl, and running the AC during the month of November was not an unfamiliar concept.

"Have you talked much with his wife about this yet?" Maggie asked.

"I was in and out of the study where we were meeting today. I spoke to her a few minutes, but nothing to do with the case. Just 'how you doing' and 'how are the kids' stuff."

"I think Grace is the next step in building the defense. I know she met with Tim Dawson a few weeks ago. Tim told me about the meeting. He came over here to the house, and they sat on the back patio discussing their history. I can almost guarantee you he recorded her every word without her knowing."

"They won't be able to make her testify against Lee, though, right?"

"That's right," Maggie replied. "The prosecutor cannot compel her to testify against him. She could voluntarily, though."

"That won't happen," Bruce replied, leaning against the convertible roof of the vehicle. "That marriage is strong, and they are a tight-knit family."

"Well, I'll talk to Grace. I might as well talk to the daughter, too."

"Keep me posted," Bruce said, his tone casual. "I'm here to help with the case however I can."

"Thanks. I'll see you at the office tomorrow," Maggie replied. "Running by my precinct to vote and then heading out to the Sandbar."

"Presidential race will be interesting tonight."

Maggie nodded. "I sure as hell hope so. Collins will probably win his race, too."

"A local boy that makes it all the way to the United States Senate. What's not to love?" Bruce said with a smile.

"A lot, Bruce. Plus, he was dead in the water before this all went down."

"Maybe so," Bruce replied. "The country loves him now, though."

Bruce patted the hood of her vehicle before walking away. He climbed into a newer-model pickup truck and pulled slowly out the driveway. As Maggie watched, she removed the high heels from her feet. She stretched out the toes on her liberated feet and pressed down on the clutch with her left foot. She could manage a straight shift in heels, but she liked the feel of her bare feet on the pedals.

～

He spotted her during the last set, sitting at the same table they'd flirted at over a month ago. The lights above illuminated the sandy volleyball pitch, and Tim Dawson redirected his attention to the play at hand. A group of onlookers held beers and talked trash as they waited for the next match.

"Let's see if you can put this game to bed, champ," a guy from the local bank yelled as Tim stepped to the end line to serve.

"This should look familiar to you, big guy," Tim shouted back in the heckler's direction. "It was my ace that ended your team's shot at the Hooch this year!"

Tim tossed the volleyball high into the air and executed the serve with finesse. The ball sailed to the back corner of the opposing team's side of the pitch. It landed in bounds with a thud on the sand and ended the match. Tim looked back over his shoulder at the high deck of the Sandbar and saw her brown hair still seated on the other side of the railing.

Hands were slapped. Fists were bumped. Tim declined to continue on playing in the next match. On drop-in nights, players would come and go. There were no set teams, but the winners always stayed on the sand until they suffered a loss.

"You done for the night, Dawson?" the banker said as Tim walked off the sandy pitch.

"Yeah, I'm out. The shoulder has had enough for one night."

"Depriving me of another shot at you?"

"Next time," Tim replied, grabbing a pair of slides from the sideline.

Tim slapped his sandals together as he walked across the grass toward the wood steps that led up to the high deck. The grains of sand fell with each step. Stopping at the outdoor shower, he hosed his sandy feet off with cold water and climbed the steps to the deck. As he climbed, he considered whether he should just cut around the building to his SUV parked out front. It would avoid an awkward hug and conversation, but, no, he wanted to see her. He wanted a look at those gorgeous eyes gazing back at him.

"Hey, Tim," she said as he walked by the end of her table. Maggie sat with Jenny Marsh, her former colleague at the public defender's office. Jenny greeted him with a smile and scanned back to her friend's face for some reaction.

"Hey, Maggie," he replied, trying to convey some surprise in his voice.

The televisions positioned outside of the bar all ran election coverage. CNN played on two screens, muted. The remaining three screens showed the coverage on Fox News—the presidential election dominating the conversation. At 8:00 p.m., there were still polling locations closing across the country, and it would be a while until the final results were called.

"Is the volleyball league still going on?" Maggie asked, trying to make conversation.

Tim shook his head. "No, it ended a little while back."

"Boys in Blue won the championship, right?" Jenny said.

"That's right. The Hooch went home with us this year."

"Does that mean the team picture goes on the wall and everything?" Maggie asked, smiling.

Tim nodded and looked toward the front of the restaurant, debating how to make a smooth exit.

"I am going to grab another round," Jenny said, overemphasizing the empty wineglass in her hand. "Tim, can I get you anything?"

"No, thank you," he replied. "I have to run in a few."

Jenny excused herself and headed toward the indoor bar. No doubt looking for some separation from the palpable tension.

"I've tried to call you," Maggie said, looking up at him with those eyes.

"I know. I'm not much for talking on the phone," he replied. "I had a pretty good idea what you needed to say."

Maggie nodded and ran a hand through her dark brown hair. She looked beautiful.

"I saw you on the news the other day," Maggie said with a smile. "I thought you didn't do interviews with the press. Especially not on an active investigation."

Tim laughed. "Well, I have seen your cute face on a few networks trying to get the media to chase rabbits. I, we, thought it would be a good idea to make sure the reporters hear the truth every once in a while."

She could hear the ease in his voice. It lacked an edge in it, a harshness she was sure she'd find.

"You know who I talked to the other day?" Tim said.

"Who?"

"Your old client, Eli Jones."

"Really? Don't tell me Eli got in trouble while locked up?"

"Nope, that's not it," Tim replied. "Eli apparently got hooked up with some bad boys a while back. They robbed a gas station near the Alabama line, and we haven't had any real leads on it."

"You investigate small-time stickups now?" Maggie chided.

"No, but I am handling a murder investigation in Albany where a gas station clerk was shot in the face. Thankfully the Albany store has some decent surveillance footage. I brought it to your guy, Jones, so he could take a look at it."

"What did he say?"

"He told me he wanted to talk to you first."

"You trying to offer him a deal if he knows anything?"

"That's how these things tend to go, Reynolds. There is a murderer on the loose, and the shooter threw up a gang sign on video that I think your boy will recognize."

Maggie sipped the last of the red wine in her glass. She spotted Jenny making her way back from the bar.

"I'll talk to him," Maggie replied. "What's the deal?"

"County time and felony probation. I'll have to clear it with the DA, but that's what I think is fair."

"You can do better than that." She smiled.

"I can't recommend a dismissal of his pending charges, Reynolds."

"You can't or you won't?"

"Both."

"Well, that's a shame. Seems like if he can help solve a murder, he should get a hefty benefit for his troubles."

Jenny approached and sat back down on the other side of the table. She handed Maggie another glass of red wine, and the two clinked glasses. The temperature had dropped considerably, and both women wore light jackets. The wine would help add an extra layer of warmth as the night wore on.

"Most of the Georgia polls haven't reported yet, but it's already looking good for Collins," Jenny said as she sat down. "Incredible turnaround."

"There is a lot of red on that map," Maggie added, glancing over at one of the large television screens by the outdoor bar. The election coverage was predicting polling outcomes across the country with maps in red, blue, and purple.

"Most of the races look the same to me," Tim said. "I'll leave you ladies to it, though."

"You sure you don't want to stay?" Jenny prodded.

"Next time," he said with a glance at Maggie.

She nodded.

"You ladies be safe tonight. Call a ride if you need one."

"Yes, Dad," Jenny said with a smile.

"See you later, and I'll get back to you on the Jones case," Maggie added.

Tim made his way for the door, resisting the urge to look back over his shoulder. As he walked through the indoor dining area, the local news channel predicted a historic night for Blake County. A local would soon be elected to the United States Senate—another chapter in a historic family's legacy.

~

He woke at 5:00 a.m. Leaning over to the bedside table, Tim silenced the alarm on his cell phone and rolled out of bed. It was leg day, and he laced up his shoes with reluctance. By 5:12 a.m., Tim was out the door, jogging the neighborhood streets. He breathed in the cool November morning air as he made his way down the dark road. The sun would not be up for another hour, and most of the town still slept around him. Running without headphones in his ears, he focused in on the quiet of the morning.

Streetlights illuminated sections of the neighborhood road, each pole some thirty yards apart. After his legs felt warm, Tim began running intervals between the poles. Alternating between sprinting and jogging, he counted each interval between the amber light that streamed down from the lamps along the road. His speed always intimidated opposing players on the football field, baseball diamond, and basketball court—it had not left him yet.

Reaching the end of his running route, Tim began to circle back toward home. He passed a few vehicles backing from their driveways and waved, showing as much outward friendliness as possible. Though an agent with the Georgia Bureau of Investigation, Tim was also a Black man running a dark neighborhood street. The world was changing, but, in South Georgia, some things took time. He considered whether he was willing to wait— whether that patience made him a coward or a realist.

Tim pushed down the last stretch of the run and turned at his driveway. He breathed heavily as he checked the watch on his wrist: 4.2 miles in just under thirty-eight minutes—not too bad for only four hours of sleep.

Flipping the garage radio on, he turned his attention to the morning lift. Loading bumper plates onto a barbell, Tim began a set of squats, followed by core work and various plyometric exercises. The music from a local hip-hop station played the latest chart toppers as Tim completed set after set. His body felt healthy, apart from the shoulder, and he pushed through each exercise without straining the muscles past their breaking point. When he finished his final set, he racked the weights and straightened up the workout area in the garage.

Tim looked out on the neighborhood street; the morning sunlight now swathed the small single-story houses that dotted his road. He knew this town was as good a place as any to live, but he missed the coast. Breathing in one last breath of the crisp morning air, he hit the garage light and headed inside of the house. Strong and focused that morning—he knew what he wanted out of life.

"Good morning," Maggie said as he entered the kitchen area.

"Morning," he replied. "I was thinking you might be up."

Drenched in sweat, he removed his shirt and tossed it in the nearby hamper that sat waiting by the laundry room door. She watched him carefully from her seat on the kitchen counter. She wore only his T-shirt, a ratty old thing from a football camp some ten years ago. He liked the T-shirt on her, he liked anything on her.

"I didn't hear you get out of bed this morning."

"I'm like a ninja."

"That you are," she said, a tired smile on her face.

"When do you need a ride back to your car at the Sandbar?"

"I can wait for you to shower, and then we can go."

"You sure?"

"Yeah, I only have one client at the moment. I can get to the office a little later than usual."

"You mean two," Tim said as he walked to the fridge to pull out a carton of eggs. "You have two clients. Acker and Jones."

"Yes, my two clients. I'll go see Mr. Jones today if I can."

"You can just call me later on it," Tim said. "I understand things can get complicated with you and me working a case from different perspectives."

Maggie paused as she thought about the appropriate response. Tim nodded at the extended pause. He understood.

"I am going to have to disclose our relationship to my office," Tim began. "They will take me off of the Acker case, and I am not sure what will happen from there. I know we have not spoken much about where things are going with us, but I have a responsibility to let my superiors know my judgment could be compromised in this investigation. I need to do that even if we don't see each other again."

"Do you believe it is compromised?"

Tim paused for a moment to think. The eggs started to bubble in the pan, and Tim continued scrambling them with a spatula.

"To be honest, it might be."

"So, you will be off the case?" Maggie said, feeling her stomach begin to knot.

"Most likely. Seeing how our acting director, Don Malone, operates, he will probably try to take over the investigation himself."

"I'm sorry, Tim."

Tim flipped the burner off and removed the pan from the heat.

"When you texted me last night, I knew what I was doing. I wanted to pick you up from the bar. I hoped you wanted to come home with me."

"Last night was great," Maggie added with a smile, though she felt the pangs of guilt.

Tim nodded. "I knew if we hooked up again, it would end my involvement in the Acker investigation. I am good with that. I have my doubts, and the Collinses deserve someone that is going to pursue Acker with more conviction."

"You have doubts?" Maggie said, surprised.

Tim shoveled a forkful of eggs into his mouth and raised the other hand in protest.

"I don't want to get into it, Reynolds."

"Okay, okay. So, what happens next?"

"I'm not sure. How about a shower?"

35

John Deese sat in a leather armchair reading a copy of the *Blake County News*. It was 9:25 a.m., and he held his second cup of coffee in hand. As he waited, John admired Bruce Tevens's well-appointed office space in downtown Blakeston. It met John's approval, and he considered himself a man of good taste. The office's dark walls bore colorful artwork balanced by professional pieces of black-and-white photography. It smelled clean, but also of leather and coffee. The office reminded John of the boutique consulting firms that took over portions of historic buildings in the nation's capital. Buildings that had been renovated to suit the clandestine business of Washington, DC.

John moved to the capital fourteen years ago, starting on Bill Collins's staff as an intern. He entered the pool of lowly staffers on Capitol Hill and found ways to make himself indispensable. He abandoned his accent and disregarded his illusions of a future in the South. It took time, but he left behind his Southern skin—trading up for a better life.

With his new life in the District came lunches adjacent to powerful people and meetings with other underlings at restaurants on Barracks Row. He worked long hours, but John liked the work and he loved the city. He enjoyed walking from his place in Georgetown to the trendy coffee shops and bars that dotted each corner. He ate at great restaurants and grew to appreciate the music at the buttoned-up political parties. Though he'd lived his entire life in the South, he soon realized there was a better, more exciting world out there waiting for him. Now, the only reason he enjoyed coming back to the South was to remind himself why he'd left.

As John looked around the lobby of the small law office, he considered what life would have been like if he'd stayed in Georgia. Would he have been forced to hustle the people of rural towns and strategize with small, irrelevant politicians? Maybe. Would he have been happy? Probably. But only because he wouldn't have known any better. He shuddered at the thought. Still, had he been forced to live in a backwoods town, he imagined himself in an office much like the one that surrounded him.

As he continued to scan the photographs in the lobby, John's eyes rested on a small portrait of Arthur Kelley. Kelley was a local legend. John had a copy of the same portrait at his home in Washington, Lucy Collins having gifted it to him some years ago as a birthday present. The caption under the sepia-toned photograph read, "Never underestimate the potential of a boy from South Georgia." John smiled at the image and the absurdity of the statement. Where you are born does not make you special, he thought. Being born into a family with wealth and connections is what makes you special.

"Mr. Deese," the receptionist's voice called, breaking John's train of thought. "I spoke with Ms. Reynolds, and she will be at the office in a couple of minutes."

"That'll be fine," he replied with a smile.

"Do you want some more coffee?"

"No, I'll float away if I have another," he replied, overemphasizing his old Southern accent.

A door from the back wall opened, and out stepped Bruce Tevens with a large smile on his face.

"Johnny Deese, I thought I heard your voice up here in the lobby area. What are you doing loitering in here? This is private property, Bubba!"

"How are you doing, Bruce?" John said, standing from his seat and extending his hand. "I'm only in town for a couple of days, but I like to visit old friends when I am here."

Bruce kept the smile on his face and waited for his guest to begin shoveling the day's manure into the conversation.

"Twice I've seen you in Blakeston this year, John. The funeral, and now here in my office. This is too much!"

"I know, I know. The Best Western here may make me join the rewards program. The benefits sound awful."

"Well, you should have called. I'd have put you up at the pool house at my place."

"I'll call ahead next time."

"You do that. So, what can I do for you?" Bruce asked, starting in on business.

John shifted his stance and decided to dodge the question. He looked back over at the portrait of Arthur Kelley on the wall and pointed to it with his right hand.

"Where did you pick this portrait of Arthur Kelley up?"

Bruce paused. He didn't remove his gaze from the man standing in his lobby. "That was a gift. Every boy from Blakeston knows the quote there inscribed at the bottom."

"Who gave it to you?"

"Some old friends of mine."

The receptionist stood from her desk and called out to the men standing in the reception area.

"Ms. Reynolds has just arrived. She can see you now."

"Thank you, ma'am," John replied, the twang emphasized again.

"I'll show Mr. Deese back to her office," Bruce added. "Come on, Johnny. You can follow me."

Pushing through the rear door that Bruce exited from minutes earlier, John followed the lawyer down a narrow hallway. The hardwood floors were cherry pine, and they shined from the continual upkeep. More artwork covered the walls, and John continued to be impressed by the small law office's décor.

"Who does your decorating?" John asked.

"I do," Bruce replied. "During my time in Charlottesville, I studied a little art history while picking up the law degree. I also travel to Italy a couple of times a year and have made friends, mostly beautiful women, that I welcome input from."

John nodded. "You are truly a backwoods renaissance man, Bruce."

Bruce ignored the comment and knocked twice on an open office door. He walked through the doorway and motioned for John to follow. Maggie Reynolds sat behind an oak desk with her laptop open in front of her. She stood from her chair and extended a hand.

"I apologize for the wait, Mr. Deese."

"John here doesn't mind. He came without an appointment," Bruce added before John could respond.

"That's right, Ms. Reynolds. Thank you for making time to see me."

"Sure, I assume you want to talk to me about the defense of Lee Acker."

Maggie wasted no time. She knew why the man was in her office, and she wanted him to know it. Bruce leaned against the doorframe, a fly on the wall.

"That's right. Do you mind if I sit?"

"Not at all. Now, I want you to know I am not at liberty to discuss strategy, and I am recording everything that we discuss today. Your boss, Bill Collins, and his family have singled out my client as the sole suspect in the murder of Jake Collins. He is innocent, and we intend to pursue civil action tied to defamation claims as soon as the criminal matter is resolved in his favor."

"Well, let's just pump the brakes a moment," John said. He turned to check if Bruce was still in the room, and Bruce met his glance with a bounce of the eyebrows. "Yes, I work for the congressman."

"Recently elected senator," Maggie added.

"Correct, recently elected senator. Yes, the Collinses are of the opinion that their son's brutal murder was a tragedy."

"As are we, Mr. Deese. Defending Lee Acker in this misplaced prosecution does not make us any less sympathetic to what the Collinses are going through."

John cleared his throat and acted as though he were thinking a moment. After years of tense meetings with political foes, he felt qualified to negotiate with hostiles.

"What would you like from us?" Maggie asked.

"The Collinses want this case over with, Ms. Reynolds. With Bill's recent election to the Senate, he should be focusing on that new endeavor, not trouncing back and forth from Washington to relive his son's murder."

Maggie nodded. "We want the case over and done with as well, by dismissal or acquittal."

"I think we know these things take time," John replied diplomatically. "Trials are messy, and it could take a year to get to that point. We can agree that something without the public spectacle could be good for these families, right?"

"Mr. Deese, I have worked out my fair share of cases over the years. There is always exposure to a verdict of 'guilty' when you take a case to trial, but that will be my client's only option if the prosecution does not choose to dismiss the case."

"You are aware, then, that Mr. Hart, the prosecutor, has told the media that he will try this case before Christmas if the defense can be ready?"

"I keep tabs on what statements the district attorney's office releases to the press."

"And you will be ready?" John said, leaning back in his chair.

"Mr. Deese, with all due respect, I do not want to get into strategy today."

"Then I think we could all agree that this case will only be further delayed when the lead case agent, Tim Dawson, is removed from the investigation."

"If that happens..." Maggie paused, mindful of the recording in progress. The insight this man had into her personal life shocked her. "It'll be the choice of the GBI or prosecution to remove him. Unneeded delay only prejudices my client, though. We will continue to ask for a trial as soon as possible."

"What if the unneeded delay is caused by Lee's own defense attorney?"

"Let's just get to your point, Mr. Deese."

John smiled at Maggie. The smug expression signaled to her that he knew more.

"You are sleeping with Tim Dawson, right?"

"Let's keep this professional," Maggie replied.

"I'll take that as a yes, then."

"No, you can take that as a non-answer because the question you asked was inappropriate," Maggie remarked. She could feel her body tensing up. "I'm not sure why you feel you can—"

"What?" John interjected. "Ask you about your love life?" he said with a shake of his head. "I wouldn't hesitate to broach this subject with a male adversary. I won't change my tactics with you, Ms. Reynolds."

"Where are you going with this, John?" Bruce said from his spot in the doorway.

"I am going to the GBI's acting director after I finish meeting with you two, and I am going to make sure he knows his lead investigator on this high-profile murder investigation is sleeping with lead defense counsel. Then, after he decides to throw Dawson off the case, I am going to the district attorney's office to talk to Michael Hart about calling a conference with Judge Balk to discuss this highly unprofessional tactic you two put together."

"Tactic?" Bruce said.

"Yes," John replied, turning around to look at Bruce. "I think you two decided that Ms. Reynolds here would seduce the GBI's primary investigator so that he would be compromised as the key witness in this investigation."

"That's bullshit."

John spread his fingers and shrugged the shoulders on his thin frame. The smugness on his face remained as he returned his gaze to Maggie.

"Now, we are all adults here," John continued, his voice calm and controlled. "I personally don't have a problem with your little tryst with the investigator. He is a handsome Black man, and you are an attractive woman."

Maggie felt the need to cover her bare arms as his eyes leered at her. She sat still, though, listening to her guest's increasingly reptilian voice.

"This could cause some trouble for your client's defense, wouldn't you agree?" he said with a smile. "I felt, the Collinses felt, that an expeditious resolution of this case may be the best option for everyone."

Maggie stood from her chair and extended her hand. The abruptness of her move startled the men in the room.

"Thank you for coming by today, Mr. Deese. You have given me something to think about, and I certainly wish you could have kept this meeting professional today."

John stood and shook her hand. "This is all a discussion, Ms. Reynolds. You are a skilled attorney, and I certainly don't think your future lies here in Blakeston. I just want your reputation to remain intact. You know how the media can take a story and run with it."

"Kindly leave," she replied.

"I'll show you to the door, John," Bruce added.

"Thank you, Ms. Reynolds. I'll get going, then. I have more appointments to get to today. Bye for now."

As the two men walked out the door, Maggie stood staring at her office wall. Her diploma and other framed certificates still sat stacked in the corner. The only frame that hung on the wall was a piece Jim Lamb, her old boss from the public defender's office, gifted her on her last day in his office. The painting was an Edward Hopper knockoff. Though she and Lamb joked about the cheap motel artwork that filled the public defender's office, Maggie secretly liked the gift that now hung on her wall.

The painting depicted a woman standing alone in a bedroom. The slender woman wore a green dress and stared out the window. Maggie liked the woman's facial features, the simple lines drawn around the subject's mouth. She often looked at the painting and wondered what the artist meant to convey in the woman's expression. Some days, Maggie thought the woman looked confident. Other days, the woman looked worried or anxious. Maggie knew that this was, at least partially, a projection of her own emotions. The artist's image doesn't change over time, the viewer does.

Today, though, as Maggie stood staring at the simple painting on her office wall, the woman in the green dress did not look worried or anxious— she looked angry.

36

Charlotte Acker knocked on her father's study at 6:00 p.m. and opened the door. Lee sat on the leather couch in the center of the room, a stack of paperwork beside him. He lifted his eyes to the door when he heard it open and grinned at the sight of his only daughter.

"Dad, flip the news on. They're running a story right now that you should see."

"Okay," he replied, leaning over to the coffee table to find the remote for the study's television. "What network?"

"Probably any of them," she said. "My phone always sends me a notification when there is breaking news in your case. This one looks like it could be a big deal."

Lee turned the television on and found one of the local news stations first. The image on the screen showed a reporter standing in front of the GBI's Region 15 Investigative Office. The bottom line of the screen read, "Breaking News: GBI Removes Lead Investigator in Acker Case." The blonde on screen used large gestures with her hands as she explained the latest wrinkle in the local case. "In a shocking move, the GBI announced today at four p.m. that, effective immediately, Special Agent Tim Dawson would be removed from the investigation into the death of Jake Collins. He will be placed on administrative leave for the foreseeable future. The GBI's acting director, Don Malone, stated in a short press conference this afternoon that he would be taking the lead in the ongoing investigation into the murder of Collins."

Charlotte settled in next to her father on the couch as two photos appeared on the screen.

"Pictured here on screen is Special Agent Tim Dawson and Maggie Reynolds, Lee Acker's lead defense attorney. Sources have indicated that Dawson and Reynolds have been engaging in a romantic relationship over the course of the entire murder investigation. The GBI was made aware of its investigator's relationship with Reynolds late this morning and made the decision to remove Dawson from his post. Dawson's nondisclosure of the relationship with Reynolds violates the GBI's professional code of conduct, and sources within the GBI cite concerns with the level of influence Reynolds may have been able to place on Dawson during the course of the investigation. The GBI is considering its options, including an investigation into Reynolds that may lead to evidence of witness tampering."

Charlotte had on running shorts and a pair of bright neon running shoes. She propped both feet on the coffee table in front of her and leaned back on the couch. Lee liked her being there, sitting with him.

"Did you know anything about this?"

Lee exhaled. "Maggie called me this morning around ten thirty to fill me in. She told me a man came by her office this morning and threatened to take her relationship with the investigator public."

"Was the guy like a private investigator?"

"No, the guy's name is John Deese. He is a sort of loyal gofer that works for Bill Collins in Washington. He and Jake were cousins."

"John Deese?" Charlotte muttered as she listened. Her head began to spin at the mention of the man's name, the creep that nearly spotted her while she was running from Jake Collins's home in the woods.

The reporter on screen told viewers that the grand jury would convene within a few days and that sources expected Lee Acker to be indicted. She then sent the news coverage back to studio, and the local news anchors began recapping the election results from the night before. The results of the presidential election were the national story, but Bill Collins's surprising victory in his bid for the United States Senate was a particularly special story for the viewers of Southwest Georgia.

"So, this guy Deese, he wanted to make a deal or something?" Charlotte said, watching her father's expression.

"That's right," he replied. "I don't know what kind of a deal. Maggie told me she never entertained a discussion on the matter."

"Good," Charlotte remarked.

"Oh yeah?"

Charlotte nodded. "I like Ms. Maggie, and I've already read a few of the comments online about today's news story. Just because she is a woman, now people think they can call her a slut."

"Easy with the language," Lee replied, though smiling. "But I agree. I expect people to paint her as a conniving character in all of this. She and Bruce know what they are doing, though. She has a meeting with the judge tomorrow, and I know Maggie Reynolds isn't going to take this treatment lying down."

"I hope not!" Charlotte remarked.

Lee flipped the television off and looked at the flashy running shoes on his daughter's feet.

"You wearing those shoes for fashion, or can you manage to shoot some hoops with your old man?"

Charlotte smiled. "Are you going to blame that ankle monitor you're wearing when I beat you at one-on-one?"

"It does kind of keep me off-balance."

"Well, let's go out in the driveway and see, hotshot."

As they headed toward the basketball goal in the driveway, Charlotte debated telling her dad about her encounter with that weasel, John Deese. Maybe it could help the case in some way. Her dad would know what to do with the information. Something in her gut told her to wait, though. There was a reason she ran to Jake's house that morning. She needed to find out for herself how her father could do such a thing. There had to be an explanation.

Charlotte decided against telling him, at least for now. She would need to find out more about Deese and the thumb drive before discussing the little "breaking and entering" incident with her parents. And though she hated keeping a secret from him, wasn't he doing the same to her?

~

As Tim Dawson stepped out the back door of the building, he felt raindrops begin to fall. The heavy drops landed on the cardboard box he carried. Picking up his pace, he jogged from the building to his SUV parked in the back row of the parking lot. The cardboard box held little. The few picture frames inside bounced around as Tim hustled along the wet asphalt. Per office policy, Tim left his computer, cell phone, sidearm, and all files on-site for inspection by the GBI's Office of Professional Standards, or OPS.

The GBI tasked the men and women within OPS with the unpopular responsibility of investigating allegations of misconduct within their own ranks. Tim never expected to have to deal with OPS, at least not in an investigation directed at him. He knew that by being a subject under investigation, the inquiry would place all of his work on the Collins murder under a microscope. OPS would comb through everything that Tim generated during the course of the murder investigation. They would look at his calendar, phone calls, text messages, emails, voice recordings, and any other correspondence they could get their hands on. OPS had the reputation of being thorough in their approach to investigating the internal affairs of the GBI, but Tim felt comfortable with the integrity of his own investigation. Other than his relationship with Maggie Reynolds, he did everything by the book.

As Tim slammed the hatch to the SUV, he looked back at the office building one last time. Everything changed today, he thought as he stepped into the vehicle and turned the key. Just before lunch that day, Don Malone called Tim into the main conference room and notified him of OPS's impending investigation. Things then began to happen quickly. Within hours, the team from OPS arrived in Blakeston and conducted Tim's exit interview. They spent three and a half hours walking through each step of

Tim's investigation into the murder. He handed over his notes and explained his organizational methods. The duo from Atlanta came with a script, and they drilled Tim with questions about every aspect of the investigation.

After Tim felt he'd answered the same questions ten different times, the team from OPS turned their attention to Maggie. They asked about how Tim met Maggie and wanted a detailed timeline of when the relationship turned from professional to unprofessional. They asked intimate details about his sex life with Maggie, and they wanted a list of Tim's partners over the last three years. Tim expected some blowback from his decisions, but he did not anticipate being labeled a sexual deviant by his own office.

In close to eight years with the GBI, no one ever accused Tim of mishandling an investigation. He received top marks from every supervisor he'd been assigned to, and Tim was quick to point that out to his interrogators. When asked for references, Tim handed over the letter he'd received from Don Malone only two months prior. The letter said, in part, "Special Agent Dawson, you are being assigned as the lead investigator on the murder investigation and/or suspicious death of Mr. Jacob Collins, former district attorney in the Southwest Circuit. I believe you are the right agent for this assignment. Your leadership and track record of unwavering commitment to the high standards of the Georgia Bureau of Investigation are invaluable to our agency."

The two investigators appeared impressed as they read the letter from the very man responsible for ushering Dawson out the door. They recognized the irony, and their demeanor only softened as they familiarized themselves more and more with Tim's impressive track record. When the questioning ended, they all shook hands, and assurances were made to Tim that OPS would be fair in its evaluation.

Tim thanked them both. They all knew how things would play out, though. Tim Dawson's time with the GBI had drawn to a close.

As he pulled into the driveway of his single-story home, a familiar Saab 900 sat parked on the front curb. The rain fell in steady sheets, and Tim sat in the vehicle, watching the raindrops beat on the windshield. He and Maggie had not yet spoken about this latest development in his career. As soon as he was notified of the investigation into his relationship with Maggie, his cell phone and other electronics were confiscated. Maggie expected this, and she knew better than to text him about the news. As he listened to the rain tap on the roof of the vehicle, he wondered what would come next. Though he would be on administrative leave for ninety days, he expected to be fired. He would receive his pay during the ninety-day term, and that would give him enough cushion to make plans for his next phase in life. A new chapter in life, somewhere away from Blakeston.

Stepping out into the rain, he jogged up to the front porch of his house. She'd left the front light on. Rubbing a hand across his face and through his short hair, he wiped the rainwater away and entered the house. She looked up from her seat in the living room and smiled as he entered. The news played low on the television, and her laptop sat open on the couch. She'd been crying.

"Well, this is unexpected," Tim said, setting his keys down by the door.

"Me being here?" she said, a scratchiness to her voice.

Tim smiled as he crossed the room. "Everything, Maggie Reynolds. All of it is unexpected."

"Are you okay?"

"Don't you worry about me," he replied. "I'll be fine. I made my choices."

She stood from the couch and kissed him. A reporter on the television recapped the latest developments in the investigation into the murder of newly elected Senator Bill Collins's late son. The shocking revelation of the romantic relationship between the criminal defense attorney representing the accused and the agent running point on the investigation would give the talking heads plenty of content for the next few nights.

"We are the scandal of the week now," she said, hugging his neck.

"You have a way of getting a guy in trouble."

"No, that's not the case at all. Boys that are in trouble seem to have a way of finding me," she replied. "Even a handsome lawman like yourself."

"Handsome, huh?"

"That seems to be the consensus on social media," she said with a smile. "How could a girl resist herself?"

Tim leaned over and picked up the remote. He turned the television off as the reporters switched gears to the implications of the recent presidential election. He picked Maggie up and carried her to the bedroom.

"Let's see where this goes, then."

"I like the direction already."

37

The lawyers sat around a mahogany conference table waiting for the judge to arrive. He was late. Though that was not uncommon for a judge, it was certainly unusual for Judge John Balk. Michael Hart sat across from Maggie with a stack of paper in his lap, and he drummed his fingers on the table as he waited. He already looked uncomfortable with the agenda for today's conference with the judge. She was uncomfortable, too, but she wouldn't show it.

"Has the judge told you his story about this conference table yet?" Maggie asked, looking across the table at the prosecutor.

"Not yet," Hart replied, not looking up from the paperwork in front of him.

"The judge inherited it from the estate of his uncle, an old sugar baron that hailed from New Orleans. The table, so the story goes, was constructed in Havana, Cuba."

Hart lifted his eyes to hers, listening.

"The uncle made his money importing sugar from the plantations on Hispaniola and Cuba," Maggie said.

"Hispaniola?"

"That's an island in the Caribbean that the Dominican Republic and Haiti share."

"I've been to the DR on a cruise. It's beautiful," Hart added, setting the stack of papers on the shiny table.

Maggie nodded. "The old uncle did plenty of business in that part of the world during the forties and fifties. He had excellent relationships with the sugar refineries and plantation owners. He spent half the year working on deals and playing the casinos around Havana. The other half he'd spend back home in the Big Easy."

"Not a bad way to live," Hart said with a smile. "Apparently that casino scene in Cuba was something back then."

"That's right, and places like the Tropicana or Montmartre nightclub were filled with mafioso types from the US. The American gangsters started to run their own muscle in the Caribbean and infiltrated the larger casinos like the Riviera, Capri, and Havana Hilton."

"This was all before Castro, right?" Hart asked.

Maggie nodded. "Fulgencio Batista, president in the forties and again after a coup staged in the fifties, was running the country."

"I read somewhere that the casinos and tourism were big money at that time," Hart added, touching his fingers to his chin. "At least before Castro shut the place down and kicked all the American businesses out."

"Yes and no," Maggie replied. "The gambling brought money, but the sugar industry generated more than three times what gambling could do for the Cubans. It's just not as glamorous for historians to write about."

The door opened, and Judge Balk's judicial assistant poked her head into the room. The judge was running even later than expected, and she apologized on his behalf. Everyone agreed to continue to wait, though there was not much of a choice. The door remained open, and Hart turned his attention back to Maggie.

"So, what's with the table?" Hart asked, rubbing his hand across the top of it. "Did the uncle win it gambling or something?"

"The judge says it was a gift," Maggie replied with an eyebrow raised. "You see, if you wanted to do business in Cuba during the forties and fifties, you needed to know the right people. Judge Balk's uncle knew all of the right people. He partied with the likes of Meyer Lansky, Santo Trafficante, Jr., and Bugsy Siegel. He knew the government types that had to be greased to move his shipments in and out of the Caribbean. He knew it all."

"The Sinatra of the sugar game," Hart replied with a grin.

"You could say that. Now, when the judge tells the story, he explains that his uncle never married. He invited women to travel with him to the Caribbean, or he kept his social calendar full while working on the islands. But, at some point during the mid-fifties, it started to become apparent that the perpetual bachelor had a love interest in Havana."

As Hart listened, he stood and walked over to a window in the conference room that looked out onto the street. He peered down to the parking area that ran alongside the courthouse, searching for some sign of the judge that was now close to twenty minutes late.

Maggie continued, "By the summer of 1958, the Cuban Revolution was nearing its end. The rebels would oust Batista later that year, and American business owners were unsure what the future of the sugar industry would look like under the new regime. The uncle made plans to back away from the Caribbean, and he decided to take a stowaway back with him to New Orleans."

"The love interest?"

Maggie nodded. "Fulgencio Batista's second daughter, Elisa."

"Get out of here," Hart said, still standing by the window. "Sounds like this story has been embellished by our old judge."

Michael Hart turned from the window to look back at Maggie and realized Judge Balk was standing in the doorway to the conference room.

"What have I embellished, Mr. Hart?" Judge Balk said, taking a seat at the head of the rectangular table.

"Judge, Ms. Reynolds and I were discussing the history of this beautiful conference table."

"I was doing my best to tell the story of how your uncle came to be the owner," Maggie added.

"It's an incredible story, sir," Hart said, his face burning from embarrassment.

The judge opened his briefcase. He began removing files and placing them in stacks on the table in front of him. Each file, bound by large rubber bands, had colorful tabs poking out from the edges.

"My uncle Jack stood on the docks of one of the largest ports in Havana, waiting for a woman that promised to return with him to his home city of

New Orleans, Louisiana," the judge said, removing a rubber band from a large green file. "The two agreed that she would meet him on a summer evening in 1958, and they would board a vessel scheduled to slip out into the waters of the Gulf of Mexico, destined for the Louisiana coast. She was the daughter of a man that faced removal from political office by Cuban rebels. By the late fifties, only a small group of loyal government troops remained, and they could barely hold their own. Jack knew it was time to leave."

Hart resumed his seat at the table and listened to the judge continue the story in his baritone voice.

"The presidential election had been scheduled to take place that summer, but it was delayed due to the ongoing conflict in the country. Cuba was, and still is, a poor country with citizens desperate for changes. My uncle Jack was an opportunist, but he loved the people and culture of Cuba. He had no interest in standing in the way of the revolutionaries that sought power of their own."

The judge focused his gaze on the prosecutor as he spoke. Maggie watched from her seat at the table. She noticed flecks of gray spreading through the judge's dark hair. Though not a handsome man, he held unique qualities in his face that made him attractive for a man past middle age. As the judge told the story, she pictured Jack Balk waiting by the boats moored in the Cuban harbor.

"My uncle Jack could hear the sounds of gunfire going off in the outskirts of the city. The rebels neared the capital, and Jack knew he would not return to Cuba after that night. Two hours past the agreed-upon meeting time, four men in green military uniforms with helmets began making their way down the very dock that Jack Balk stood waiting on. The captain of the small vessel signaled to my uncle, but one of the soldiers instructed them not to move. In the dark, he could hear the sound of casters rolling along the dock."

The judge crossed his legs and leaned back in his chair. He patted the table with his right hand and smiled at the two attorneys seated in front of him.

"The soldiers rolled this beautiful piece of furniture right up to Jack's boat. When they approached my uncle, one of the soldiers trained a rifle on

Jack while another handed over a letter with a long legal document attached to it. The letter was from his love, Elisa. The document was a bill of sale for all of Jack Balk's assets left in Cuba. The soldiers pointed to a spot to bear down on the table and handed Jack a pen. Without reading the letter, he slid it into the front pocket of his shirt. He laid the bill of sale on this very table and penned his signature. The green clad soldiers loaded the table onto the small vessel and instructed my uncle to never return to Cuba."

"Wow," Hart said. "What did the letter say?"

"My uncle Jack claimed he never read the letter," the judge said, shaking his head. "He knew she'd already made her decision. Either she, or her father, decided to leverage his love for her. He had no other choice but to sign over his holdings in Cuba and leave the country."

"Then why give the table as a gift?" Hart said.

The judge smiled at the question. He, too, wondered the same thing when his uncle Jack first told him the story.

"My uncle Jack refused to speculate on the matter. My father, Jack's younger brother, assured me that his brother never discussed it with him." The judge paused again, then asked, "Why do you think she would give him such a gift, Mr. Hart?"

Maggie remembered the day that Judge Balk told her this story about his uncle's table. She remembered reaching the end of the anecdote and this very question being posed to her.

"I don't know, sir," Hart replied. "Maybe it was a family heirloom. She could have been worried about whether it would be destroyed once the Cuban rebels arrived at the home of the president."

The judge nodded; it was as good a guess as any. "As you know, Mr. Hart, the revolutionaries attacked the Presidential Palace in 1957. They tried to kill Batista, unsuccessfully. The group intended to infiltrate Batista's study that was located on the second floor of the Palace."

"Was this table in the study?" Hart asked.

"Reports suggest that it was."

"So, it's possible the daughter wanted the table protected."

The judge steepled his fingers in front of him and looked over at Maggie.

"Ms. Reynolds, do you remember what your theory was about this enigmatic gift?"

"I do, Your Honor."

"What was that?" Hart interjected.

"This is Cuban mahogany, Mr. Hart," Maggie replied. "This piece is handmade and is harvested from new world timber that would be impossible to find in modern-day Cuba. It was simply overharvested by the island's opportunistic visitors, like the judge's uncle Jack. You can find mahogany on the Ivory Coast in Africa and in the rainforests of Honduras, but it would be difficult to find a piece of furniture that matches the quality or craftmanship in this table."

"So, it is an heirloom?" Hart asked, frustrated by the game.

"Now it is," the judge said. "When Elisa gifted this table to my uncle Jack, though, it was a symbolic gesture."

"Okay," Hart said, nodding along. "So, the table represented the value received for the assets signed over in the bill of sale?"

The judge frowned. There was little he could do for a man that had no imagination.

Maggie continued, "Judge Balk's uncle would always be an outsider in Cuba, a foreigner. He'd come to the island for years to enrich himself and enjoy the Cuban resources, but those days were coming to a close. He was no longer welcome in Cuba, and this gift was Elisa's way of making that abundantly clear."

"It sounds like a consolation prize," Hart said.

"Let's call it more of a memento," Maggie replied, folding her hands in front of her.

Judge Balk nodded to them both and picked up the file in front of him. He flipped to the first section of papers and found the set of articles he'd printed out that morning. He handed the articles to the lawyers and began with the substance of the day's meeting.

"These are all news articles that appeared in newspapers across the Southeast. As you can see, this case is turning into even more of a media circus with the firing of the GBI's lead investigator, Special Agent Tim Dawson."

Hart, grateful for the change in topic, said, "My understanding is he was placed on administrative leave, Your Honor."

"Regardless, he is off the Acker case," Judge Balk responded. "It appears the reason for this removal is because of a personal relationship with you, Ms. Reynolds."

"That's correct, Your Honor," Maggie said. "I asked for this meeting today because I wanted to assure you, and Mr. Hart, that my relationship with Tim Dawson began before I had any involvement in the representation of Lee Acker. In the last twenty-four hours, my personal life has been thrust into the news cycle around this case, and much is being said that is untrue."

Judge Balk nodded. "I have read some of what is being reported, and I am concerned with the conclusions that are being drawn. I have never had a reason to question the decisions an attorney makes in his or her personal life. I hope that I don't have to start doing so with this case."

Maggie could feel the level of discomfort begin to rise in the room.

"I am going to be the bad guy in all of this," Hart began. "I am concerned about the ethical implications here."

"You should not have any concerns about my professionalism or commitment to defend Lee Acker in an ethical manner," Maggie replied, a firmness in her voice.

Hart nodded. "And that's what makes me the bad guy. I believe you when you say this relationship began when you were at the public defender's office. You carried on with the relationship, though. You never disclosed it to the court or to my office."

"Are you accusing me of hiding this relationship with your lead investigator?"

"What happened, then?" Hart replied, answering the question with a smartass question of his own.

"The report I received from Dawson's exit interview says you slept over at his house the night before last. How is this not carrying on a relationship, Ms. Reynolds? How is this not hiding a conflict from the court?"

The judge raised a hand to silence the two attorneys beginning to bicker in front of him.

"Loyalty and independent judgment are essential elements in a lawyer's representation to a client," the judge said, rubbing his forehead as he spoke. "This relationship with the investigator would have to be disclosed to the client, which I am sure it has. However, I am not convinced that this was a conflict that Ms. Reynolds was required to disclose to the DA's office or my court." The judge paused, then added, "Though I do believe this relationship could have been disclosed to the court as a matter of professional courtesy. This case continues to be a matter of national interest, and I would like the facts reported on this case to be as close to the truth as is feasible. I hope this is the last of surprises like this."

"This relationship was not ongoing when I got involved in this case, Judge Balk. It began before Mr. Acker hired me, but I did not continue my relationship with Special Agent Dawson after I notified the court of my appearance as counsel of record. We did not see each other in a personal capacity until the night of the election."

"That does not settle anything," Hart said, a harshness returning to his voice. "You were sleeping with the lead investigator in my case. This will affect everything gathered to date."

"Watch it," Maggie said, glaring back across the table. "I'll bet there—"

Judge Balk raised his hand again to stifle the ensuing argument.

"We are not going to do this. I want to be clear that I disagree with how you have handled this situation, Ms. Reynolds."

"Thank you, Your Honor," Hart added, emphasizing the point scored for his team.

"However, this does not affect either party's ability to move forward in this case."

Hart shook his head. "Ms. Reynolds should recuse her—"

"Please do not interrupt me, Mr. Hart."

Hart stopped talking and leaned back in his chair, fuming. The judge pulled another set of documents from the file in front of him and handed it to the attorneys. It was a scheduling order, and it would be used to establish the deadlines for the approaching trial of Lee Acker. The representatives for the parties looked down at the document, reviewing the proposed timeline.

"This is aggressive, Your Honor," Maggie said, looking up from the document. "My client has yet to be indicted, and you are proposing a trial week that will take place before Christmas."

"He will be indicted tomorrow," Hart said, regaining his composure. "The State can be ready, Your Honor."

"I have yet to see the full discovery from the State," Maggie added, beginning to formulate her argument.

"The State will provide you full discovery tomorrow," the judge said. "Any experts you need to retain, please go ahead and do so. We will hold the hearings on pretrial motions or other challenges you may have to the State's evidence the Monday and Tuesday of the week of Thanksgiving."

The shortened timeline surprised Maggie, and her mind began to run over her client's Constitutional challenges that could be made to such a proposal. In most cases, it took at least a year to get to trial because of plea discussions, pretrial motions, and the general backlog of cases. The judge's scheduling order pushed Lee Acker to the front of the line, and Maggie started to question his motives.

"I'll have the discovery ready, Your Honor," Hart said as he jotted a note on the scheduling order.

The judge nodded in reply, pleased with the answer.

"I am not sure that the defense will be ready, Your Honor. I want to just—"

"That is nonsense, Ms. Reynolds. You must first review the evidence that the State has in its possession, and then you will be able to make your argument to my court. I believe if we have the understanding that this case will be tried before Christmas, we can avoid any unnecessary delays."

Maggie knew her time to argue her points to the judge would have to wait. "Yes, Your Honor."

The judge dismissed the lawyers, and the two combatants stood from the table. He thanked them both for their patience and added that he would be fishing in the Gulf of Mexico all of next week. He assured them that he could be reached on his cell phone to resolve any issues. As the lawyers exited the room, Michael Hart turned to look at the judge still seated at the head of the table.

"Did you ever consider the table a slap in the face to your uncle?"

The judge's face reported no expression. "How do you figure that?"

"The woman he loved, she took everything from him. All the assets he owned on the island, all that money he stood to earn by taking his product to market. He signed it all over on this very conference table." Hart paused, then cautiously added, "She conned him."

The judge, pleased with the prosecutor's renewed and more imaginative perspective on the story of his uncle, replied, "I have wondered the same, Mr. Hart. I actually once asked Jack if he ever felt slighted by the lopsided trade."

Hart shifted his stance. "What did he say?"

The judge patted the table with his hand again and gave the prosecutor a short nod.

"He said she was a shark, Mr. Hart. That he knew what sharks were capable of when he fell in love with her."

38

On the morning that the parties were set to argue pretrial motions, Judge John Balk assumed the bench at 9:30 a.m. He greeted those present in the courtroom and asked everyone to return to their seats. As he removed files from his briefcase, Judge Balk scanned the terrain of the large wood-paneled room. The courtroom's gallery looked to be a mix of reporters, curious onlookers, *pro se* parties, and a few local attorneys looking for his signature.

"I have a few uncontested matters on the calendar this morning," Judge Balk announced. "I will take those up first, and then we can continue with your motion to suppress, Ms. Reynolds."

Maggie stood from her seat. "Certainly, Your Honor. We will be ready to move forward after those matters are heard."

"Can you ensure your witnesses are here, Mr. Hart?" the judge said, directing his attention to the prosecutor.

"We will, Your Honor."

The judge nodded and began calling the uncontested civil matters on the morning's calendar. Michael Hart leaned over to Don Malone to review the witness list. Maggie watched the men from her seat at the defense table. Covering his mouth with one hand, Malone appeared to argue with his prosecutor until noticing Maggie's gaze from across the aisle. He stared back, holding the eye contact with her until she looked away. The two men returned to their hushed debate until Hart pushed his chair away from the table. The lean prosecutor popped to his feet and handed the list across the aisle to Maggie. She tried to discern whether there was some frustration in her opponent's face as she accepted the paper with a smile. With her approval, Hart handed the list to the courtroom deputy and asked that all witnesses subpoenaed for the day's hearing be marked present on the list.

"How many more are you calling?" Maggie said, looking across the aisle.

"There are ten witnesses on the list," Hart replied with a wink. The non-answer did not surprise her, but the attempt at humor did. She considered this as she watched a young couple, both no older than twenty-five, approach the bench to finalize a divorce.

She looked back at Hart. "Please call all ten. Balk will rule against you after your fourth takes the stand."

"I'd put the over-under closer to three."

"That's pretty close," Maggie said with a wink of her own. "I'll have to let you know if I am going to call anyone after your witnesses go."

Hart nodded as he returned to his notes. "That'll be fine."

While the visitors to the courtroom waited for the morning's main event, they watched the machine of the court system churn. Most of the individuals that Judge Balk called to the front of the courtroom were there *pro se*, meaning they were unrepresented by counsel. They sought divorces, name changes, and orders on unpaid child support. The judge took his time with each matter, unhurried by the spectators or journalists seated in the courtroom. A less experienced judge might have felt pressure to accommodate those members of the press or lackeys sent by the newly elected senator. Not Judge Balk, though. He understood the importance of his role in the judiciary, and he gave no special treatment to the high-profile case waiting before him. It was his courtroom, and he would run it how he saw fit.

After granting the third divorce of the morning, Judge Balk looked over to the prosecution's table for some sign that they would be ready to move forward with the meat of the calendar. The deputy tasked with confirming the presence of all witnesses returned with the marked-up list and handed it back to the prosecutor.

"They are all here, Mr. Hart. Everyone except this fella." The deputy pointed to a name on the sheet of paper. "I called for a José in the hallway and even walked the entire courthouse looking for any Hispanic-looking guys. No one here by that name."

"I met with him on Friday of last week," Hart said, more to himself than anyone within earshot. "He knew when to be here today."

"Maybe he is late, sir. You know how those—"

"Thank you, deputy," Hart said, interrupting the deputy's commentary. "That should be all we need right now."

The deputy readjusted the utility belt around his waist and asked, "You want us to go pick ol' José up?"

"Not without an order from the judge," Hart muttered.

The deputy paused as he realized the number of eyes in the room that were watching, listening.

"Yes, sir, Mr. Hart."

Judge Balk looked toward the parties and asked for an update on the availability of the prosecution's witnesses. He planned to take a short break and wanted to move forward with the remainder of the hearing as soon as he returned.

"We are missing a José Valdez Bisbal, Your Honor. I met with him last week and explained to him when to be in your courtroom. I am confident he understood his responsibility and the information on the subpoena. My office is going to reach out to him now to see when he can be here."

"Is he a necessary witness, Mr. Hart?"

Michael Hart did not get off the bus from law school last week. Pausing to consider the question, he responded with a calmness that came only from experience.

"Judge Balk, Mr. Valdez worked for the defendant for years. He found the murder weapon in the defendant's pickup truck. For purposes of today's hearing, he is essential."

"Does he still work for the defendant?"

"He does, Your Honor," Maggie replied, jumping into the discussion.

"He handles the management of one of Mr. Acker's larger farms in Alabama."

"Well, figure this out. We can't wait all day, Mr. Hart. We can figure out a way to get a deputy out there if your office cannot contact him. Is that your only witness today?"

"No, Your Honor. I have two or three more witnesses to call. They are each members of law enforcement in Alabama."

"Well, let's get them on the witness stand before lunch. They need to get back to work on the other side of the river."

"Yes, Your Honor."

The judge looked over at the courtroom deputy standing to his left and gave him a signal of sorts.

"All right, everyone, let's take a fifteen-minute break. Mr. Hart, locate your witness. Ms. Reynolds, we will return to hear the remainder of the evidence presented in connection with your client's motion to suppress after the break."

"Yes, Your Honor," the attorneys said, almost in unison.

"All rise!" the deputy called out as the judge rose from his chair. As everyone clambered to their feet, Maggie turned to Lee and said, "We need to talk."

～

Maggie and Lee took seats in a small conference room located two doors down from the main courtroom. Lee loosened the knot on his tie and undid the top button of his dress shirt. He ran a hand through his hair and flashed the same smile that the news cameras loved to run with updates on the case. In her five years of practice, she'd represented clients facing all manner of offenses. They all had to deal with the pressure that comes with being charged with a crime. To grapple with the unknowns of potential incarceration is not easy for a person, but Lee always seemed to maintain his composure through each step of the process. It impressed her. He never appeared flustered or anxious. For some reason, that control concerned her today.

"Let's talk about this witness that the prosecution is trying to track down," Maggie began.

"José?" Lee replied.

"That's right. When is the last time you spoke to him?"

Lee pulled his cell phone out of his coat pocket and pressed the button on the side to power on the device. A white icon shaped like an apple illuminated the smartphone's screen.

"I'll have to check, but it was probably Monday or Tuesday of last week," Lee said, waiting for his phone to turn on. "He needed to purchase supplies for the farm, and he wanted to interview a new set of hands to work the cattle side of the operation."

"Did you talk to him on the phone or text with him?"

Lee punched in a security code on the screen of the phone and scrolled through his call history.

"I talked to him last Monday at ten a.m. for twenty-five minutes. That would be nine a.m. over in Alabama."

"What about texting or email? Do you send him any kind of written communication?"

"We text every now and then," Lee replied, a confused look on his face. "It's mostly over the phone or in-person meetings with José, though."

Maggie nodded. "You can't travel to the farm anymore because of the bond restrictions. Who handles the in-person meetings?"

"Grace drove over once last week to drop off some documents that needed my signature, but José and I have been able to handle everything over the phone. We just do a video call if he needs to show me some issue with anything on the property."

"Did you tell him not to appear today?"

Lee shook his head. "I understand what you are getting at. I don't have anything to do with it."

Maggie paused and studied his face. "Lee, this is one of those moments where I need to be sure you are being straight with me."

Lee nodded. "I am, Maggie. I've been straight with you from the beginning."

Lee handed the phone over to Maggie and encouraged her to scroll through his text thread with José.

"You can go through anything on the phone," Lee added. "I don't have anything to hide in there."

Maggie took the phone and began scrolling through the message history. With a notepad in front of her, Maggie began taking notes about the dates and contents of the communication over the past month. It all appeared to be harmless.

"If this witness does not show up today, the prosecutor is going to blame his reluctance to appear in court on us," Maggie said, trying to make her tone as serious as possible. "He will do everything he can to convince the judge that we would benefit the most from José deciding not to appear in court."

Lee nodded, listening.

"At a trial, you normally can't use the testimony of someone that isn't there in the courtroom to testify live. However, if a party makes sure that witness is unavailable, or scares that witness into not testifying, the judge has options on how to deal with the testimony. Do you understand, Lee?"

The cell phone in Maggie's hand vibrated, notifying her of an incoming text. She looked down at the screen. The message from Charlotte Acker read, *Dad, I found something that might help*. Maggie stared at the message for a moment before handing the phone back to her client.

"I understand what you are saying, Maggie. I don't have anything to do with José being late to court today. Yes, he has worked for me for years now and I can assure you that he is loyal. I have not asked him to do anything with this case, though."

Maggie studied her client some more. One of the talents that made her a skilled trial lawyer was the ability to anticipate problems in her cases. Hurdles other attorneys didn't see until it was too late. She felt a problem brewing, and she needed to be ready to improvise.

"Check that message from your daughter," Maggie said as she stood from her seat. "I did not mean to snoop, but the text came in as I was holding your phone. It read like she had something that might help your case."

"She is a smart kid. I'll let you know if she has the case solved."

Maggie grinned. "I'll hire her for a summer internship next year if she does."

"So much may change by then," Lee replied, a hint of concern in his voice. The first crack of worry in her client's façade.

"They have to get through me first," Maggie replied. "Let's get back out there."

~

The first of the prosecution's witnesses was an investigator by the name of Jesse Hernandez. With seventeen years serving the Henry County Sheriff's Office, he looked to be in his mid-forties. Most in the courtroom recognized Hernandez's face from a series of political ads that ran nonstop the month before. Though his voter base was across the state line in Alabama, they were still within miles of Blakeston. The campaign's commercials crept into the market of Blake County. The ads asked viewers to "Vote Jesse Hernandez for Henry County's Next Sheriff."

From what Maggie had heard, Hernandez lost a tight race to the incumbent sheriff. He'd run a better campaign, but his opponent had labeled Hernandez as a first-generation immigrant that sought to change the character of rural Alabama. Hernandez had an unblemished career and took an aggressive line on the current sheriff's outdated policies. Still, it was not enough to overcome the conservative white vote that feared influence from outsiders.

As Hernandez walked to the witness stand, he still had the shine of a candidate ready for an impromptu political appearance. He wore a slim-cut blazer along with black boots and tapered slacks. When he raised his right hand to take the oath, he stood with his shoulders back and nose slightly in the air. There wasn't a hint of humiliation in his demeanor. Hernandez would run again, and Maggie had a feeling that he would win.

The investigator explained to the judge that Lee Acker's truck had been located in Henry County, Alabama. That "we"—a term officers often used on the witness stand in an attempt to circumvent hearsay and other evidentiary issues—believed evidence tied to the murder of Jake Collins would be found inside the truck. Hernandez described the process he used to obtain a search warrant for the vehicle and did so with the skill of an experienced state witness. He was polite, and he provided Michael Hart with concise answers to each of the questions that supported Hernandez's involvement in the investigation. Hernandez was the infallible witness. When Hart sat down at the prosecution's table, the investigator directed his attention to Maggie and waited with a pleasant smile.

"The information that you used to obtain this warrant for Mr. Acker's truck, it all stemmed from an interview with a man by the name of José Valdez Bisbal, correct?" Maggie asked, stepping to the lectern without any notes in hand.

"Yes, ma'am," Hernandez said. "I reviewed a video interview that showed Special Agent Tim Dawson questioning Mr. Valdez. Agent Dawson sent the video over, and I was then able to obtain the search warrant for the defendant's truck based on that interview."

Maggie smiled as the investigator tiptoed around speaking directly to the statements in the video interview. Hernandez waited for her next question, unwilling to fill the brief silence with any testimony that did not correspond to her questions.

"This information, as you stated in your direct examination with Mr. Hart, indicated that there was a firearm in the toolbox of Mr. Acker's truck?"

"That's correct."

"Why didn't you have Mr. Valdez just bring the weapon in to your office?"

"Well, I like to do everything by the book, ma'am. Special Agent Tim Dawson appeared to be the same way. We wanted to avoid any allegations that the evidence could have been tampered with."

"Do you think it could have been tampered with?"

Maggie could see Hart rising from his seat out of the corner of her eye. "Objection, Your Honor, the witness would be speculating."

Maggie nodded her head as if she agreed with the objection. Though Judge Balk had let the investigator speculate all he wanted only moments before during the prosecution's direct examination. "What about Special Agent Tim Dawson, was he concerned with tampering?" Maggie asked.

"Same objection, Your Honor," Hart added, this time from his seat.

Judge Balk instructed the witness to focus on what he himself knew about the case. Maggie folded her hands in front of her waist, hoping Judge

Balk might notice Hart's voicing of an objection normally reserved for the defense. It was an unusual position, and Maggie wanted to set the bait.

"Now, at that time, you were already aware that Mr. Valdez had touched the weapon, right?"

"Yes, ma'am, I was aware of that."

"That he'd grasped the weapon with his own bare hands and then supposedly wiped the weapon down after that?"

"That's correct. That is my understanding."

"And you don't know when this touching, grabbing, and wiping of the weapon occurred, right?"

"Well, I believe Mr. Valdez said—"

"Let me stop you right there," Maggie said, grabbing hold of the witness to avoid another intrusion from Hart. "You don't exactly know when he touched the weapon, right?"

"No, ma'am, not exactly."

"Now, we don't want to speculate or guess about these things, so it's safe to say that the only person that knows when that weapon was touched by Mr. Valdez is, well, Mr. Valdez, right?"

Hernandez paused. "That's correct, ma'am."

"You don't know when he wiped the weapon down either, do you?"

"Again, no, not exactly the date and time. I don't want to guess about it either."

"Does that not concern you?" Maggie asked after an intentional pause in her questioning.

Hart stood at his table again, prepared to voice his objection. Judge Balk raised a hand and spoke first, "The witness can answer, Mr. Hart. Take your seat."

Hernandez looked to the judge and then back to Maggie, "It does somewhat, ma'am. It can create a number of problems with an investigation."

Maggie nodded—the trap was set. Now she would let Hart explore that minefield. If Hart punted, Maggie would pick the questioning back up once a jury was seated in the courtroom.

"That's all I have for questions right now, Your Honor," Maggie said as she thanked the investigator and turned to her seat at the defense table.

"I don't have any other questions," Hart said, the speed in his decision evidencing his unwillingness to touch the aforementioned minefield.

"Investigator Hernandez, you can be excused."

"Thank you, Judge," Hernandez said, stepping down from the witness stand.

"Do you know if anyone from your office has been out to check on our missing witness today?" Judge Balk added.

"No, sir. I'll step out of the courtroom and make a phone call to check."

Judge Balk nodded and instructed Mr. Hart to call his next witness while they waited. Hart obliged and called another member of the Henry County Sheriff's Office. The deputy walked through the process of cataloging into evidence one Beretta 92FS, the alleged murder weapon, that was found in the toolbox of Lee Acker's truck. The deputy explained that they ran a trace on the Beretta and confirmed that it was registered to Lee Elmer Acker of Blakeston, Georgia. The dry testimony was necessary for the prosecution's argument around adequately handling the chain of custody for evidence purposes. Maggie had few opportunities to score any points with the witness and asked only a few questions on cross-examination. The testimony mattered little to her. She hoped by the end of the day, Judge Balk would have other reasons to believe the Beretta should be excluded from trial.

The testimony of the prosecution's "chain of custody witness" took thirty minutes. The deputy stepped off the witness stand and looked relieved to be leaving for the day. As the judge excused him, Jesse Hernandez walked back into the courtroom. His fashionable blazer was off now, revealing a trim physique. His sleeves were rolled up on the tailored dress shirt, and it was obvious that the phone calls back to Henry County revealed some issues locating Mr. Valdez. Hernandez stood at the front of the gallery and looked for direction from the judge or prosecutor.

"Investigator Hernandez, were you able to find anything out about our missing witness?" Judge Balk asked, looking up at the clock on the wall of the courtroom. "I'll let us all break for lunch if Mr. Valdez is going to take more time to get here."

Hernandez paused, looking over at Hart with some apprehension.

"Judge, we sent a couple of deputies out to Mr. Acker's farm. They were able to find another employee there working and asked about Mr. Valdez."

"Were they able to locate him?" Judge Balk said, his tone growing impatient.

Hernandez shook his head. "The house Mr. Valdez stayed in on the farm is empty. The employee let the deputies inside the house. Apart from a few pieces of furniture, the entire house is completely empty. The whole family is gone."

Maggie's stomach sank as she began to recognize the conundrum her client would soon face. The courtroom stayed deathly quiet as the entire gallery listened to the handsome investigator's update. Maggie could almost hear the journalists in the room spinning their next articles for the Acker trial.

"Did the employee have a number for your deputies to call?" Judge Balk asked, his eyes flashing to Lee and back to the investigator.

"The man did, and the deputies called Mr. Valdez's cell phone number and then the one that Mr. Valdez's wife used. They are both disconnected or turned off."

"I see," Judge Balk said, thinking.

"That's all I have at the moment, Judge. We are trying to gather information about their appearances and vehicle information. We will also check the local U-Haul dealerships to see if anyone matching Mr. Valdez's description would have come by in the last few days. I just need the bench warrant or some sort of green light to push the investigation forward."

Maggie did not move. She did not want to even lean over to Lee to discuss the issue. The simple appearance of any knowledge about witness tampering would set the judge off and initiate an investigation that she did not want to become a part of.

"Counselors, I am going to have the bench warrant prepared. I need to make a few phone calls, and then I want us all to meet in chambers. It is 11:45 a.m. now. I want you all back no later than 12:45 p.m."

Hart jumped to his feet. "Your Honor, this has all the elements of witness tamp—"

"Mr. Hart, we will discuss this in chambers," Judge Balk barked. "Get

Investigator Hernandez's cell phone number, as I will call this afternoon for an update on the progress in his investigation."

"Certainly, sir," Hernandez said.

"I can assist with that process, Your Honor," Don Malone said, speaking for the first time after what seemed to be a deep hibernation at the prosecution's table.

"I'm not going to tell you how to run your office, Director Malone. It sounds like you have your own investigation to worry about, though."

With that, the judge disappeared through a door at the back of the courtroom. His anger left with him, and the entire room erupted in excited conversation.

39

As soon as the judge broke for lunch, Grace Acker slipped out of the courtroom to grab a table at the downtown deli. Maggie asked Lee to hang back a few minutes to speak with her about the upcoming meeting with the judge. He invited her to lunch, but Maggie declined. She was not sure if the prosecution would argue that Lee's bond should be revoked. That would mean Lee would have to return to the county jail until trial. Maggie wanted her client to enjoy a lunch with his wife just in case. She also wanted to do some quick research so that she was well prepared for the inevitable finger-pointing.

Lee listened as Maggie explained to him how José's unavailability would become a major problem for today's hearing and the prosecution's entire case. He nodded along, trying to conceal his reaction to the new development. The Beretta had already been identified as the murder weapon, but Michael Hart needed José's testimony. Without it, the State would have a difficult time tying the weapon to Lee. It would create a mountain of arguments for Maggie to make in front of the jury, and she assured Lee that with the right jury, she could convince a group of twelve that reasonable doubt was present.

"The State is going to argue that you must have paid José to leave town.

That you must have threatened him or his family. Do you understand that?" Maggie watched her client's face closely. Nothing.

"I understand," Lee replied.

"If they find anything, and I mean anything, that suggests you had something to do with José moving out, the judge will let that evidence into your trial and the prosecution will hammer you with it."

Lee nodded. "They won't be able to. There is nothing to find."

Maggie wasn't convinced, but she was satisfied with her client's responses. The two agreed that Lee should come back by 1:00 p.m. and that he could wait in the hallway's conference room until Maggie exited the meeting with Judge Balk.

"Be prepared for the prosecutor to argue that your bond should be revoked so more witnesses don't go missing," Maggie added. "Michael Hart is going to be pissed, and he will tell the judge to keep you in jail."

"Can the judge do that?"

"He can do pretty much whatever he wants, he's the judge," Maggie smirked. "If there is no evidence of witness tampering, then I think you are safe."

Lee nodded and turned to walk out of the courtroom doors. Bounding down the steps two at a time, he headed out of the courthouse and into the warm afternoon sun. Each time he exited the courthouse grounds, his thoughts wandered. They led him to the islands or some foreign country that did not have an extradition treaty with the US. Somewhere miles away from Blake County, Georgia, and the terrible murder of one of his oldest friends.

~

Grace looked up from her cell phone as Lee entered the deli's back door. She'd snagged their favorite table in the place, a two-top stuck in the back corner of the local eatery. He kissed her before taking a seat, and she assured him that his turkey club was already put in with the kitchen.

"I talked to Alex," Grace said, her eyes watching him from across the table.

"Oh yeah? What did she say?"

"Not a whole lot," Grace replied, peering down the row of tables to ensure no one was within earshot. "Apparently she bought a racing team?"

"Really?"

Grace nodded. "She mentioned something about inviting us to a race sometime. It sounds like fun to me."

"Let's get past my murder trial first," Lee said with a wink. "What else was going on?"

"She asked about your brother."

The server arrived with two baskets of sandwiches and sides. He placed both baskets on the table before asking if there was anything else he could bring out from the kitchen. They shook their heads, and he hurried away to attend to his other tables.

"Cliff doesn't have too much longer," Lee said, picking up the sandwich in front of him. "I'm sure those two are communicating somehow."

"On the telephone lines? Aren't those recorded?"

"No, a lot of prisoners have cell phones these days. Cliff probably has one stashed away to make calls to her."

"Kind of risky, but it makes sense."

Grace cringed at the thought of her and Lee talking on burner cell phones in the middle of the night. It couldn't come to that.

"Do you think she still loves him?" Grace said, her appetite waning with an image coming to mind of Charlotte visiting her father in a room divided by protective glass.

"If she does, I'm not sure Cliff would feel the same way. He seems to be pretty well ready to move on with his life once he is released from prison. Taking a charge for someone isn't easy."

"I don't blame him," Grace replied after a long pause. "Still, if they love each other, hopefully they can figure it out."

Mindful of the time, Lee checked his watch.

"Did she call for any reason?" Lee said, returning his attention to his wife.

"She wanted to make sure that we were happy with her efforts to help out."

Lee took a sip of his tea. "I don't know what you're talking about, but I'm listening."

Grace smiled. "Alex and I talked at length the night you stayed at her ranch in Mexico. We talked about the investigation, and we put a plan together to help with the case."

Lee chewed on the sandwich as he tried to recall the events of that night with Alex. He remembered the excitement of the Mexican rodeo. He just couldn't remember what happened when he made it back to his bedroom.

"They call it *La Finca*," Lee said, snapping himself away from his thoughts. "And what exactly did the two of you discuss?"

"You were passed out. She was buzzing hard. I proposed a way to get us out of this mess."

"You wait until today to finally tell me about this?" Lee replied, more surprised than frustrated.

Grace rubbed his leg under the table with her foot. The way she always did when trying to cheer him up. "It was for your own good. If you knew, you would have told Maggie."

"How much does Alex know?" Lee asked in a hushed tone.

"Everything," Grace replied. "I had to tell her what was going on so that she could understand the problem."

"How can you keep this from me, Grace?"

"You've kept things from me, too," Grace replied, deflecting. "I'm just trying to handle damage control as best I know how. It was the smart play."

They locked eyes and made an unspoken agreement not to have this argument in public. Lee looked away to the television hanging in the corner of the deli. SportsCenter played on the screen, and Lee noticed the day's breaking news out of racing scrolled across the ticker at the bottom. Fronteras Force, a Mexico-based labor group, would go from a premium partner with Williams Racing to a 65 percent shareholder. The historic announcement was the news of the day in the racing world. Lee pictured Alex Olivera celebrating and toasting to her family's latest accomplishment.

"So, she found a way to get José to move back to Mexico?" Lee said, turning back to his wife.

Grace nodded. "That's right. She told me he is already back across the border and that his family will have enough money to begin a new life there."

Lee rubbed his forehead as he thought for a moment. The stakes would only be higher now.

"Maggie believes the judge might throw me back in jail over this," Lee said, slightly changing the subject. "Everyone is going to believe I tampered with a witness."

"They won't prove it," Grace said, a confident smile on her face.

"I know, Grace. Because I didn't do it. I didn't do any of it."

The server returned to the table with the bill, and Lee handed him twenty dollars. As Lee stood from the table, a few people noticed him in the restaurant and realized they had just lunched with the country's most recognizable murder suspect. With the trial nearing, Judge Balk had modified Lee's bond conditions to allow him to travel within Blake County. The previous restrictions that came with house arrest had the unappreciated benefit of helping Lee avoid the judgmental stares and shakes of the head. He would have to get used to it. Still, without another thought, Lee and Grace slipped out the back door, holding hands and hustling toward the courthouse.

~

"Tell me something good," Lee said as Maggie entered the small conference room.

"You aren't going to jail today," Maggie replied with a quick smile.

"I'm glad to hear that I won't spend Thanksgiving on the inside. I imagine the jail's turkey is not the best cooked bird in the county."

"It might surprise you," Maggie replied with a chuckle.

Maggie knew that everyone was hesitant to send Lee Acker back to jail. It seemed cruel to put an upstanding citizen in lockup for the approaching holiday season. The poor, the Blacks, and the other undesirables would be having Thanksgiving in the jail, though. No one seemed to care about that. No one seemed to care about people like Eli Jones—another young Black guy doing time for looking like a gang member. A guy that hadn't killed anyone or interfered with the judicial process. Eli just looked guilty, and for some reason unbeknownst to Maggie, that was Eli's problem—not the criminal justice system. Maggie shook her head at this thought as she sat down at the end of the table—maybe she too was starting not to care.

"Grace, I need you to step out of the room," Maggie said, looking over at her client's wife. "I need to talk to Lee about something important. You two can talk about it later, I know you will. I just prefer all attorney-client communication be between Lee and I."

Grace stood from her chair. "Are we done for the day with the hearings?"

Maggie nodded. "The judge is going to take everything under advisement, so there won't be anything more today. You can go on home if you prefer, and I'll drop Lee by the house on my way out of town."

Grace looked from Maggie to Lee. Lee nodded and assured her that he would be home soon. The door closed behind her, and Maggie turned back to her client.

"I want you to know that the judge is furious. I did everything I could to convince him not to put you back in jail. You are technically entitled to a bond revocation hearing, but I would not have been shocked if the judge insisted on holding the hearing on the spot."

"Thank you for making this happen, then," Lee said, breathing out a sigh of relief.

"I have never been involved in a case where a key witness goes missing like this. I have seen eyewitnesses to crimes make themselves hard to locate or give false names to the police. Nothing like this, though."

Lee nodded. "It is pretty wild."

"It's more than wild. It's borderline illegal, and the judge is going to issue search warrants for your cell phone, computer, and anything else you could have used to contact José Valdez Bisbal."

"Fine, they won't find anything," Lee quickly replied. "I didn't threaten José or pay him to leave the state."

Maggie stood from her seat and opened the door to the hallway. She peered out into the empty corridor, making sure no one was nearby to eavesdrop on their conversation.

"When does the judge make a decision about keeping the Beretta out of evidence at trial?" Lee asked, beginning to get the hang of what was important to his case.

"Well, it's going to be all or nothing. The judge has already indicated that if there is no evidence of someone paying José to go into hiding, then he isn't going to let the prosecution comment on his unavailability to the jury. No video interview, nothing."

"That's great news. Anything else?" Lee asked, sensing there was more.

Maggie did not like to oversell her position with clients. She learned early on in her career that discussing best-case scenario with a client facing criminal charges could be dangerous, even borderline cruel. It allowed that person to get their hopes up, to feel the weight of the system lifted off their chest for just a moment. She preferred to underpromise and overdeliver.

"Lee, let's take this one step at a time. I don't want us to get ahead of ourselves."

Lee persisted, "Is the judge thinking about keeping the firearm out of the trial? I need to know."

"He told us in chambers that he may have no other choice if the prosecution doesn't bring José in to testify. Judges change their minds, though, and I expect there will be some pressure on Judge Balk to keep the weapon in play."

"That's incredible," Lee said, a jolt of adrenaline rushing through his body. It was the best news he'd heard in months. "So, the jury would just make a decision based on these bogus arguments by the prosecutor?"

"I am not sure the jury would end up making the decision if the prosecution can't get José's testimony or the gun into evidence."

"How's that?" Lee said, watching his attorney closely.

"Are you familiar with the use of the term 'directed verdict' in a criminal trial?"

"I've heard it before," Lee responded. "I couldn't tell you what it means."

"Well, you obviously know that in a criminal trial, the prosecution has to go first. They have to stand up and give their opening statement first, put their witnesses on first, and present all of their evidence to the jury first."

Lee nodded. "They have the burden of proof."

"That's right. What people don't realize, though, is that all criminal cases don't have to make it to the jury. The judge can take the final decision away from the jurors and enter a verdict once the prosecution is done presenting its case."

"Do you think that could happen in my case?"

"I've asked for one in every case I have ever tried before a jury. A judge has never agreed with me."

"So, what makes you think this case is any different?"

"Because the judge hinted at it in chambers fifteen minutes ago."

40

She left the office at noon. It would be Thanksgiving tomorrow, and Maggie needed to get out of town for a while. She followed her GPS across the Alabama-Georgia line and then into the panhandle of Florida to catch Interstate 10. Heading west, she listened to the radio and made the long drag across rural Florida. A local station took a break in its music lineup to provide a brief weather update. The meteorologist forecasted clear skies with a high of seventy-one, the typical fall climate on the Gulf of Mexico.

Exiting the interstate, Maggie began to follow the road signs that directed drivers to the white sand beaches of Gulf Shores, Alabama. Traffic slowed as two-lane roads became the only means of siphoning the cars and trucks splitting off from the interstate. With no schedule, Maggie eased along with the tractor-trailers and vehicles packed with families. She hadn't called ahead, nor had she made any hotel reservations in the beachside town. All Maggie had was a short speech prepared and the address for the seafood restaurant owned by the Dawson family.

At 6:30 p.m., Maggie pulled her Saab 900 into a gravel parking lot, and her GPS announced that she'd arrived at her destination. The restaurant clearly had a wait as Maggie noticed crowds of guests congregating on the porch of the establishment. They held glasses of sweet tea or bottles of beer, chatting away while waiting for a table. The packed parking lot held vehicles with license plates from all over the country, and Maggie carefully maneuvered her vehicle into a tight space at the end of a row of pickup trucks. Taking in a deep breath, Maggie flipped the vehicle's visor down and touched up her makeup in the dimly lit mirror. She was ready.

The smell of fried seafood hit her before she walked through the front door of the restaurant, and she could almost taste the crispy golden-brown batter from the thick smell that hung in the air. Springsteen played over the speakers, but the conversations at the rows of tables drowned out the lyrics. Maggie waded through the crowd, bypassing the hostess's station to find a spot at the bar where she could plan her assault. Surveying the packed bar area, Maggie found the perfect barstool for the reconnaissance and hunkered down behind a large laminated dinner menu.

Her bartender approached, and Maggie ordered a glass of red wine. The special for the night was a smoked red snapper with collard greens and hush puppies. Maggie's stomach reminded her how hungry she was as her tattooed bartender described the menu items. When he returned with her glass of pinot noir, Maggie placed her food order and thanked him before he slipped away to tend to his other customers.

As she waited, Maggie listened to the conversations nearby and admired two photographs that hung on the back wall behind the bar. They were both photos of Tim. In one image, he stood smiling on a high school football field with his arms around his adoptive parents. In another, he was lined up for action in Auburn's defensive secondary. He looked leaner in both images, and she wondered how many pounds of muscle were added on once Tim left the game of football.

"One snapper special," the bartender said as he placed a plate in front of Maggie. He handed her a set of silverware and glanced at her nearly empty glass of wine. "Can I get you another glass of the pinot?"

Maggie shook her head. "I'll stick with water with my meal."

He nodded. "Well, let me know if—"

"Do you know the guy that is in those pictures on the wall?" Maggie said, pointing to the two photographs behind the bar.

He turned and looked at the photos. "That's Tim Dawson. His parents own the place. He played ball up at Auburn and works in law enforcement somewhere in Georgia now. I actually saw him earlier tonight. Probably in town for Thanksgiving."

Maggie nodded. "What about the owners, are they around tonight?"

"Yeah, Mrs. D is around here somewhere," he replied, eyeing her suspiciously. "Is everything good with the meal, or do you want me to see if I can find her?"

"That would be great," Maggie said, ambiguous in her reply.

The bartender nodded as he stepped away. He grabbed a couple of orders from his bar patrons and went back into the kitchen area. Maggie took a bite of her smoked snapper and cut into her hush puppies as she waited. The food did not disappoint, and the large crowd on a holiday evening began to make perfect sense. Within a few minutes, a tall woman appeared from the kitchen doors beside the bar and made her way over to Maggie's seat.

"I am Marie Dawson," the woman said. "One of my employees mentioned that you wanted to speak with me. Is everything all right with your meal tonight?"

"The food is wonderful," Maggie quickly replied. "I just wanted to meet you. I know your son, Tim."

Maggie could tell the woman was studying her, trying to place her.

"You are Maggie Reynolds. The lawyer representing that man charged with murdering the politician's son. I've seen you on television."

"Lee Acker is my client, and yes, ma'am, I am Maggie. Nice to meet you."

The couple seated to Maggie's right stopped their conversation, obviously listening in on the discussion.

"And it's nice to meet you. You and my son have become quite the news story for the gossip magazines lately. It has created, well, an interesting challenge for my son."

Maggie nodded as she thought of the tabloids that undoubtedly lined the checkout areas at the beach town's groceries. She knew of a few that had featured articles making outlandish and salacious claims about the love affair that got Tim Dawson fired.

"How is Tim doing?" Maggie asked.

"He is doing okay. It's good to have him home. He came back two weeks ago, told us he'd lost his job. We'd already seen it on the news, of course."

Maggie winced at the comment. "Well, I know some reporters had been hounding him for an interview when he was at his house in Blakeston. He thought that coming home might help him avoid the press."

"It has helped some. A reporter will call the restaurant every now and then. Tim tells me not to talk to them. Have you two not spoken since he left to come home?"

"No, ma'am," Maggie replied. "Tim handed over his cell phone when the GBI put him on administrative leave. He decided to come home to think about the next steps in his life, but he never gave me another number to reach him at. I didn't press for one either. I assumed he would call me."

"That's typical of my son. He has never been one to nurture his relationships with girlfriends. That's probably why I don't see any grandchildren in the near future."

"Well, we haven't really talked about—"

"So, you drove all the way down here to speak with him?"

"Yes, ma'am," Maggie quickly replied, happy to change the topic of relationship statuses and grandkids.

"Well, I insist you stay for a Thanksgiving meal tomorrow. My husband is going to drop a turkey in the fryer, and I'll have the staples. Do you have a room booked somewhere for tonight?"

Maggie considered lying about the lack of a hotel reservation as she took a sip of her water. She paused too long.

"I'll take that to mean you do not have a hotel room reserved. I insist you stay at our home, then. I'll call Tim and let him know, and the both of you can find some time to talk before Thanksgiving lunch tomorrow. You two work this thing out."

"I'd like that," Maggie replied after a short pause.

"I'll give you the address. We live in Fort Morgan, on the bayside. It's just down the road from the restaurant."

"Thank you," Maggie said with a smile.

"Don't mention it, Maggie. Your meal is on the house tonight, too. Just tip my bartender."

"Yes, ma'am."

Maggie watched Tim's mother as she made her way back to the doors to the kitchen. Maggie tried to imagine Tim working the restaurant as a busboy and growing up with a mother as understanding as the woman she'd just met. It started to make sense.

~

Maggie left the restaurant and drove west toward the peninsula. Her headlights bobbed up and down as she followed a coastal two-lane that sliced between the Gulf of Mexico and the waters of the Mobile Bay. As instructed, Maggie slowed at the sight of a baby blue hand-painted sign on the right side of the road. The sign directed her down a sandy driveway that led to the bayside home of the Dawson family. The porch lights were on, as were the lights that illuminated the long dock that stretched out behind the three-story home. Slowing her vehicle to a stop, Maggie watched the home for any movement.

"Woof, woof, woof!" came the bellow of a dog as Maggie stepped out of the vehicle. She could hear the padded feet of a large dog running across the sandy terrain. Her headlights had not turned off yet, and she saw a black Lab come into view, happily warning his owners of the new guest in the driveway. She beckoned the dog closer and patted the gritty fur on his head.

A screen door slammed on the porch ahead, and a familiar voice called out into the night. She recognized the voice as it called, "Stacks! Come here, boy, come on!" The dog stopped enjoying his head massage for a moment to listen to the voice in the night, weighing the urgency in his owner's voice. The dog decided he would face the consequences of his decisions and leaned back into the scratching behind his ears. "Stackhouse! Where are you, boy? Come on inside."

"He's over here, Tim!" Maggie called up toward the porch. "He is serving as the sole member of the welcome party."

Tim came into view as she started walking toward the well-lit porch. He leaned against the railing at the top of the steps and had a curious expression on his face.

"Stackhouse doesn't like new people," Tim said with a grin now on his face.

"He seems to like me just fine," Maggie said as she stared up the wooden steps. "I think I may have a new friend."

"Well, I am not sure how many more friends you will make around here. I've told everyone that you cannot be trusted and to run you out of town at the first sight of daylight."

"Is that right, Mr. Dawson?"

"That's right," Tim replied, smiling with his arms crossed.

"Your mother must not have gotten the message because she invited me for Thanksgiving lunch tomorrow, even offered me a room here tonight."

"I know. She called me here at the house."

Maggie still stood at the bottom of the steps as she waited for some indication as to whether Tim wanted her to be there.

"Is that fine by you?" Maggie finally said.

Tim nodded. "I am happy you're here. I just know you came for more than turkey and my company."

It did not surprise her that Tim met her appearance with skepticism. The trial was coming up in a couple of weeks, and she needed him.

"Can a girl not have it all?"

"If anyone can, it's going to be you."

"Can I come in?"

Tim nodded. "I'll grab your bag from your trunk and set it inside. Then, let's go out on the dock and talk about what you need from me."

~

Adirondack chairs sat at the end of the dock, and Tim pointed them out to Maggie as they walked across the backyard. They both held mugs of coffee, and Tim carried a thick blanket over his shoulder.

"The temperature has dropped quite a bit," Maggie said, her bare feet choosing a path carefully through the grass.

"It can get pretty cool down here at the end of the fall, especially if the wind is whipping off the bay."

Tim handed the blanket to Maggie as he scooted the two wooden chairs closer together. They sat, and she cozied up under the heavy fleece, tucking her bare feet up close to her body. The heat from the mug felt good on her hands, and the coffee warmed her with each sip. Shrimp boats passed in the distance, and Tim pointed to their lights. Maggie listened as Tim laid out the methods and seasons for harvesting shrimp in the coastal waters around Alabama. He explained how the otter trawls are attached by towlines to a boat's outriggers and then dragged alongside to capture the shrimp. He'd been fishing and diving around the coast of Florida and Alabama since he was seven years old. She enjoyed sitting with him, talking about his childhood. He was relaxed, and she knew that his decision to leave Blakeston had been a good one.

"Are you going to leave law enforcement to run a shrimping outfit?" Maggie said, grinning from behind her coffee mug.

Tim shrugged. "The Alabama market brought in over twenty million pounds of shrimp last year. It had a dockside value of over sixty million dollars. I know some of the players in the market, and I probably could get some partners in starting up an operation. I'm not serious yet, just weighing my options going forward."

"From all-around badass investigator to shrimp boat captain," Maggie said in a voice out of an action movie trailer. "Bringing law and order to the waters of the Gulf of Mexico."

"I am facing a major career change and you are over here making jokes?"

"You will be great at whatever you do. The marine life will be impressed with your credentials, too."

"Well, I sure hope so," he replied. "Besides, I can't live at home with my parents forever!"

"It's a nice view at least," Maggie said with a laugh.

They sat in silence for a while until Tim reached over to hold Maggie's hand.

"Maggie, this trial will be the last time I testify as an investigator. I don't plan on going back to police work."

"The prosecution is calling you to testify?" Maggie said, surprised.

"No," he said, taking another sip of his coffee. "You are here to ask me to testify for the defense, though. I am telling you I will."

Maggie squeezed his hand and looked up at the night sky. There were no lights from high-rise condominiums nearby, nothing to block out the stars in the sky.

"Did you know as soon as your mother called from the restaurant?"

"I knew the night they put me on administrative leave that I would still have to testify at trial. I figured the prosecution would call me, tell me they wanted to talk about my testimony. They still haven't called."

"You have to leave a phone number with people so that they can call you."

"I left a phone number with Don Malone and the people at OPS," Tim replied. "They know how to find me."

"Well, I'd like to call you as a witness for the defense. Are you comfortable with that?"

"I don't like this business with the witness going missing. I think someone got to this José guy and paid him to leave. I still don't think Acker murdered Jake Collins, though."

"I don't like José going missing either," Maggie said.

"Do you think your client murdered Collins?" Tim asked. "If I am going to testify for the defense, I want it to be in a trial where at least the defense attorney believes her client is innocent. I don't mean not guilty, I mean innocent. There may not be a difference to you, but there is to me."

Maggie smiled as she thought about the question.

"Are you going to let me stay for Thanksgiving tomorrow?"

"My mother thinks you are the most beautiful girl that's ever asked about me. She managed to squeeze that into our two-minute phone conversation meant to warn me of your arrival. I am pretty sure she will be disappointed if I run you off."

"You trying to run me off, Tim Dawson?"

"Stay for turkey tomorrow. I want you to meet my whole family. Now, what about your client?"

"I know my client is innocent," she replied. "I am sure of that."

"But?" Tim said, sensing there was more.

Maggie hesitated, then said, "I am confident he didn't do it, but I am pretty sure he knows who did."

41

On the morning of Monday, December 5th, two hundred potential jurors reported to the Blake County Courthouse for jury duty. Rows of news vans parked outside, grabbing footage of the jurors lined up in the brisk morning air. Most were bundled up and talking amongst themselves, fighting off the chill laid down the night before. The cold snap was not unusual for the time of year, but it added a sense of urgency to the courthouse security as they worked to get the jurors out of the cold and into the building. Each potential juror looked relieved as they stepped into the warm courthouse, passing through the metal detector and security screening with great anticipation.

Inside the courthouse, Maggie Reynolds sat huddled with her team at the defense table. The jurors filed in behind them. They looked like students on their first day of school, looking around cautiously before selecting a seat. Each person in the jury pool wore a number, and the defense had a file dedicated to potential jurors one through two hundred. Each file included a questionnaire prepared by the court, social media information, and various items found through public record searches. The defense spent hours reviewing the list of potential jurors, scouring the names to find any troublesome connections to witnesses or the subject matter in the case. For attorneys that pick juries in large cities, they demand jurors with no connection to the witnesses or the parties. In a small town, the concept is laughable. Every potential juror on the list had some connection to either Jake Collins or Lee Acker, and the trick would be to find out whether that connection could be leveraged for an acquittal.

Sitting next to Maggie were Jenny Marsh and Chris Owens. When they were all together at the public defender's office, they picked close to forty juries together. Maggie wasn't about to break tradition. Chris knew everyone in town, and Jenny had a keen eye for jurors that hid their biases in plain sight. They huddled together over a large grid that matched the courtroom's seating arrangement and readied a stack of cards with each juror's number and picture taped to it. Bruce Tevens and Lee Acker sat together at the end of the defense table, and they surveyed the room full of familiar faces and waited for day to begin.

"All rise!" called the bailiff.

The packed courtroom stood with the bailiff's order and watched as Judge Balk entered the courtroom. As usual, the deep voice of the jurist greeted those in attendance with warmth. He explained that the clerk would soon call the roll to ensure everyone summoned for jury duty was in fact present and then they would begin with some preliminary questions from the court. He pointed out the parties in the courtroom and explained that there would be only one criminal case on the trial calendar—*State of Georgia v. Lee Elmer Acker*.

Judge Balk told the group that his jury selection process was efficient. Maggie knew this to be true, and she'd warned her client that Judge Balk would insert himself often throughout the jury selection process. She'd explained to Lee that the judge wanted a jury impaneled by the end of the day Wednesday. That meant that the trial would begin with opening statements on Thursday morning. The aggressive timeline was not unusual for a trial in one of Judge Balk's courtrooms, but Maggie suspected that it would shock the television pundits that were used to weeks of jury selection and trials that puttered along for months on end. The jury would be sequestered during the trial, but Judge Balk wanted everyone home by Christmas.

∽

"Jury selection is an art to some lawyers, and it is a game to others," Maggie said as she stood at a lectern in the center of the courtroom. "For me, though, I look at jury selection as my only opportunity to get up here in front of you all and simply have a conversation about some of the issues that may come up in this case."

Maggie stepped away from the podium and started to walk toward the center aisle of the courtroom.

"Let's get into your questions for the panel, Ms. Reynolds," Judge Balk prodded from his seat. It wasn't even lunch and the judge's patience was waning. "Mr. Hart was fairly efficient in his presentation today, and I expect the same from you. I don't want to waste time with too much chitchat."

Maggie did not turn around to face the judge. She paused, as if considering an argument. She knew the judge's words were only for show, at least for now. Still, she wanted to get her most important questions in front of the panel before the judge really decided to rein her in.

"Mr. Hart stood in front of you all earlier this morning and asked you some questions about your familiarity with the news coverage in this case." Many of the jurors nodded their heads and made eye contact with her as she scanned the room. "A lot of you, most of you by our count at the defense table, were familiar with at least some part of the investigation into the death of Jake Collins." More heads nodded back at her. "How many of you have watched any news stories about me and my relationship with Tim Dawson, though?"

Silence hung in the air. Maggie panned the room, looking for raised hands, and three shot up in the back few rows. Maggie pointed to the closest woman with her hand up.

"Yes, ma'am, what have you seen?" Maggie said, walking closer to the center of the gallery. She wanted to be close to the jurors; she wanted them to feel comfortable with her.

"Well, I—"

"Ma'am, please stand and give us your name," Judge Balk barked from his seat.

"Of course," she said as she stood from the wooden pew. "Sandra Beal, Judge. I have watched some of the news stories that talk about your relationship with Mr. Dawson, and I saw that he lost his job with the GBI because he was seeing you. You make a handsome couple, by the way."

The crowd of potential jurors responded with a muffled laughter, and Maggie noted that there was a hint of charisma in Ms. Beal. Humor could be a valuable tool for those that chose to lead.

"Thank you, Ms. Beal. Did you see anything else?"

"Well, reports say that he was kicked off the investigation into Jake's murder as soon as his boss found out. That they were worried him being involved could compromise the case."

Maggie nodded, letting the words marinate in the minds of her potential jurors.

"Who else has seen anything on my relationship with Tim Dawson?" Maggie said as she walked back toward the podium. "I saw a few other hands go up earlier."

A man close by had his hand up, and Maggie pointed in his direction.

"Dan Claussen, Your Honor. I have seen some stories that mention the relationship. I also saw the *Saturday Night Live* episode where they did a skit on the trial and your relationship with Mr. Dawson."

A few other members in the gallery chuckled, recalling the episode from the late-night comedy show. The jury was in a good mood, and Maggie wanted that loosening-up to translate into honest feedback.

"Mr. Claussen, what was that skit about?" Maggie asked.

The potential juror blushed. "Well," he said, giving a cough into his hand. "The whole piece revolved around Mr. Dawson clumsily hiding evidence or changing his police reports in exchange for, well, you know—"

"Sex," Maggie said, cutting him off in a tone that reverberated around the wood-paneled courtroom. She continued. "The comedian that plays the part of Mr. Dawson runs around frantically trying to tamper with the investigation so that he can get laid. Is that more or less the gist of the skit?"

"It was all a joke, of course," Mr. Claussen said, defensively. "That would be ridiculous."

Maggie turned to look at the other faces in the gallery. Each tried to avoid her eye contact now, not wanting to engage in the awkward questioning.

"Who else agrees that would be, as Mr. Claussen here stated, ridiculous?"

Almost every hand in the gallery shot up. Maggie caught the gaze of Michael Hart and winked at him. He just shook his head in response.

Standing at the podium, Maggie said, "Let's switch gears a little bit. Who in this room has heard anything about a government project to build a wall along the US-Mexico border?"

Maggie waited for the judge to call her to the bench for a discussion on relevancy to a murder investigation, but he did not. Looking out onto the gallery, she saw about a third of the hands raised. She pointed to a young man in the second row and asked him what he knew about the border wall.

"My name is Floyd Peterson, and I know that our new president, when he takes office, is going to step up efforts to wall off the entire border. There is already some fencing down there, but he is going to beef it up. It will keep those people coming up in caravans from crossing our border illegally. It should keep the Mexican gangs and illegal drugs from coming across the border, too."

Maggie nodded at Mr. Peterson. "Thank you, sir."

Another hand shot up nearby, anxious to get her opinion into the fray.

"Yes, ma'am, what have you heard about the wall being built?"

"I know that there is—"

"Ma'am, we need you to stand and to give us your name first," the judge bellowed from his bench. "And frankly, Ms. Reynolds, I am not sure I see much need to go further into this line of questioning."

Maggie turned to the judge this time and assured him that she only had a few questions on this issue. He gave her a begrudging wave of the hand and told her to move it along, then. Maggie nodded at the potential juror, prodding her to answer the question.

"Kelly Davis, Your Honor. I've heard about the project to fund the wall. It was one of Mr. Bill Collins's key talking points on the campaign trail. He talked about it pretty regularly and seemed to know a lot about what it would take to build. I know he intends to be instrumental in the planning process when he gets back to Washington."

"Thank you, Ms. Davis," Maggie said, pleased with the juror's answer.

"Who else in the room is familiar with soon-to-be Senator Bill Collins's work on the border wall?"

Over half of the hands in the gallery were up in the air now, and Maggie paused, giving the team at the defense table time to mark the responses on their large grid of names and photographs. Maggie debated the next question in her head, unsure what the reaction might be like in the courtroom. She looked at the clock on the wall and expected the judge to soon recess for the day. She wanted the jury panel to ponder things when they went home.

"In Bill Collins's bid for the US Senate, did anyone in this room ever see Jake Collins on the campaign trail with him?"

No hands in the room were raised. Maggie panned the room and felt her heart rate rising with excitement.

"Anyone in this room, raise your hand if you ever saw an interview where Jake Collins spoke out in support of his father's bid for the United States Senate?"

Still no hands.

"What about Jake Collins speaking out on his father's support for the border wall project?"

Maggie let the silence hang in the air. It would not be unusual for someone in the crowd to misremember an event in politics. Still, no one in the group could recall a time that Jake Collins publicly endorsed his father's most recent political campaign. No one. Not one hand was lifted in the air.

42

After three days of pushing the lawyers through the selection process, Judge John Balk had his jury. The clock on the wall read 4:00 p.m., and the judge dismissed the jurors for the day. They would be sequestered during the trial, so the jurors were transported to the local Holiday Inn Express to get settled into their rooms. The judge wanted the jurors fresh for tomorrow's opening statements and ready to dive into the substance of the trial itself. He explained this to them in a stern, fatherly voice. A few jurors' eyes drifted over to the defense table as they listened to the judge explain the rules of juror sequestration. Lee Acker made eye contact with those that chose not to avoid his gaze. A few gave him a short nod, and Lee did the same in return. He knew family members of those that sat on the jury, no one close, but kinfolk, nonetheless. He hoped that those that knew him knew to pass along the word. Lee Acker would not murder a man in cold blood.

Once the jury exited the courtroom, Judge Balk turned to the attorneys and asked that they hand up the final version of their witness lists. Michael Hart and Maggie Reynolds approached the bench, handing the stapled lists up. The judge flipped through both packets as the lawyers returned to their positions. The judge turned his attention to Maggie.

"You have listed here some forty-five witnesses, Ms. Reynolds. Do you intend to call even a third of this list?"

On the defense witness list were thirty-one names of individuals that Maggie had never even spoken to, witnesses she never intended to call at trial. The defense theory would only need four witnesses on the list, but she saw no reason to share this information with Judge Balk, much less her opposing counsel.

"The defense will make an attempt to whittle down the names on that list after we have heard the State's presentation of its case," she replied. "I exchanged this list with Mr. Hart's office over two weeks ago."

"Mr. Hart has ten witnesses on his list, Ms. Reynolds. There are only four witnesses that your two lists share—Tim Dawson, Don Malone, Bill Collins, and one Antonio Barrea. How can there still be so many other individuals with information relevant to this case? Individuals the State has no interest in calling."

"Your Honor, I have no hand in the prosecution's theory of the case nor the strategy for proving it. My client is entitled to a defense, and I intend to mount one."

Hart stood from his chair and inserted himself into the discussion without invitation.

"Judge Balk, this list provided by the defense is full of names that have no plausible connection to this case."

"Your investigators have spoken with all of the names on the defense's list?" Judge Balk snapped as he turned an eye to the prosecutor.

"Well, quite a few," Hart replied, sheepish. "There are witnesses on this list, Your Honor, that my investigators have found difficult to contact. Twelve names on this list are people that are Mexican nationals."

"They have phones in Mexico, Mr. Hart. I don't want to hear about your troubles contacting witnesses. The defense does not have to hand-deliver their entire defense on a platter."

"I understand, Your Honor. Still, even the most notable of the witnesses in Mexico, Alex Olivera, has refused to return our calls."

"She is the CEO of a large company," Judge Balk replied. "I am sure she is busy, and you will have an opportunity to talk to her if the defense calls her to the witness stand."

Bill and Lucy Collins looked on from the gallery. This was the first they'd heard of Alex Olivera appearing to testify at the trial. Lucy laced her hand into that of her husband's and gave it a squeeze. They watched as the judge rubbed his head, reviewing the names again on the defense's list.

"I want this list cut down significantly, Ms. Reynolds."

"Yes, Your Honor."

"We will take it up again as soon as the State finishes its case."

Maggie nodded again to the judge and took her seat beside Lee. Judge Balk looked out toward the rest of the courtroom, already growing weary of the cameras that seemed to remain constantly trained on him.

"Ladies and gentlemen, I know that tomorrow we may have a full court-room because of the interest that this trial has garnered at the local and national levels. Please remember that this is a court of law, not a source of entertainment. Opening statements will begin promptly at nine a.m., and I will not tolerate any outbursts during the course of this trial. If you are here as a spectator, you will be respectful of the court and its personnel. These are public proceedings, and I will do everything in my power to provide you all, along with the outside world, access to this judicial process. With that being said, anyone that acts inappropriately will be asked to leave immedi-ately by one of the deputies posted in this courtroom. If you refuse to follow those directions, you will be held in contempt. I hope that is clear."

With the gallery properly admonished, Judge Balk looked back to the attorneys.

"Are there any other matters the parties need to take up before we adjourn for the day?"

Both tables shook their heads and started packing their briefcases.

"Perfect. See you all tomorrow morning, then."

~

Charlotte Acker stood in the doorway of her father's study. Her parents sat together on the leather couch, talking quietly with one another. The trial would officially begin tomorrow, and Charlotte assumed they were talking about what was to come next. As she started into the room, her parents looked up at her and smiled.

"We were just talking about you," Grace said, setting her glass of wine down on the coffee table. "Come over here and sit down for a minute."

Charlotte walked over toward the couch and sat at the end closest to the door. She'd just iced her right ankle after a long road run; it still looked red from the chill of the ice pack. She draped both of her bare feet across her dad's lap, hoping he would give the ankle an impromptu massage.

"Is this going to be another conversation where you try to convince me to take the scholarship at the University of Florida?" Charlotte asked, eyeing her mother on the other side of the couch. "I am leaning toward Oregon. I've told you that."

Lee headed that discussion off at the pass. "We think Eugene, Oregon, would be a great place to go to school. Whatever you decide, we support your decision one hundred percent. This isn't about that, though."

"Oh," Charlotte replied. "What's this about, then?"

"This trial, well, this is all going to be a stressful few weeks, Charlotte. We don't want you to feel like you have to be in the courtroom all day, every day. Don't feel like you can't step out or stay home."

Waving them off, Charlotte reached into the pocket of her running shorts.

"I'll be there with you every minute, Dad. You know that. Let's not talk about it anymore."

"Charlotte, I think you might be underestimating the stress that this process—"

"I have to tell you both something, and I don't want you to be upset," Charlotte said, interrupting her father's attempt to shield her from the trial.

She handed the thumb drive over.

"What's this?" Lee asked, turning the device over in his hands. He stared at the label "Collins III" as he inspected it.

"It's a thumb drive that I found in Jake Collins's place. I sort of broke in and found it."

"You did what?" Grace exclaimed from her side of the couch. "When did this happen?"

"It was a while ago. Dad was still in Mexico. I used a key to get in, so I did not technically break anything to get inside."

"That does not matter," Lee said. "That was dangerous, and I can't believe you didn't tell us sooner."

Charlotte paused and waited for her parents to collect their thoughts. Though they both looked tired, Charlotte knew that they needed to hear her story. She told her parents everything that happened that day in the woods. The run to Jake Collins's house, finding the house keys in the old farm truck, the close encounter with the pair of unknown thugs.

"So, you were in Jake's house and these two men came inside to box up his home office? How do you know they were not law enforcement?"

Charlotte shook her head. "I know they weren't cops, Dad. One of them kept urging the other to call the police because they realized some things were out of order in the study. They wanted to know if the investigator, Tim Dawson, was the one that would have moved the stuff."

"Who were they, then?" Grace interjected. "Friends of Jake's?"

"I don't know, Mom. They did not seem very friendly though. I think they were sent down here by someone else to pack everything up. The only name I heard was 'Deese.' I never caught another name."

Lee looked over at Grace as soon as Charlotte said the name. They both could not believe what they were hearing.

"You know him, don't you?" Charlotte asked after the noticeable pause. "It's the same man you told me threatened Ms. Maggie's reputation, before the stuff came out about her and the investigator being in a relationship."

"You don't miss much, little one," Lee replied affectionately. "And yes, I know him. He was Jake's cousin, and he is now Bill Collins's right-hand man. He has a reputation for doing the dirty work when politics demand it."

"He is a sleazebag," Grace added.

"Is he dangerous?" Charlotte asked, beginning to grow worried again.

"Nothing we can't handle," Lee lied.

Charlotte hesitated, then continued on with her story of how she retrieved the thumb drive by detailing her escape from the house. Both of her parents were on the edge of their seats as Charlotte described how she crept up the stairs when the men pulled into the driveway, stepped out onto the awning of the roof, and jumped to the ground below.

"I think this John Deese might have seen me," Charlotte added. "He was standing at the kitchen window looking out onto Jake's backyard when I made a run for it. In fact, looking back, I am almost certain he did see me."

"He never reported it," Lee said. "Maggie would have told me about it."

"What's on the thumb drive?" Grace asked.

"I can't access it. The drive is password protected, and I haven't tried anything because I didn't want to lock us out."

Grace snapped her fingers as she shot up from the couch. She went for the desk, leaving both her husband and daughter surprised by the sudden burst of energy. She began rummaging through the messy desk, searching for something.

"What are you looking for?" Lee asked.

"One of the sheets of paper that was included in your discovery packet. There was a page of handwritten notes that they included. It was in Jake's pocket the day he died. I think there was a password on that sheet of notebook paper. Don't you remember seeing it, Lee? Never mind, here it is. I found it."

She stood there reading the notebook paper and extended her hand out for the thumb drive, snapping her fingers again. Lee handed it to her, and she went to the computer on the desk. Sliding the drive into the back of the monitor, Grace took a seat in the leather swivel chair. Both Charlotte and Lee stood from the couch and walked around behind her to see the screen of the monitor.

"I remembered thinking that it was strange that Jake had this piece of paper in his pocket. It wasn't a to-do list or a grocery list. To me, it looked more like a note with a password on it."

"Like a message?" Charlotte said.

"Exactly," Grace replied, typing away on the keyboard in front of her.

Lee picked the piece of paper up and stared at it. He'd paid it little attention when reviewing the discovery packet. He and Maggie discussed it at one point but decided it was only a piece of scratch paper.

"These numbers at the bottom are coordinates," Lee muttered. "I don't know how I didn't recognize this earlier."

Grace typed the series of numbers into the password field on the screen. After a few seconds, a window opened on the screen revealing a series of folders. Charlotte's heart began to beat harder as she leaned over to look closer at the names on the folders. Before her mother clicked on the first in line, Charlotte stopped her.

"Before we do this, I have to know something."

Both Lee and Grace looked at their daughter, surprised at the forceful-ness in her voice.

"Dad," Charlotte said, tears welling in her eyes. "Mom told me that you killed Jake. She told me the night the agents first searched our house. She told me I couldn't tell anyone else, and I haven't. I have to know, though."

The room was silent as the tears began to stream down her face. Lee said nothing as he went to hug his daughter. She was shaking.

"No, I have to know," Charlotte said again, pushing him away and looking at her mother now. "Why would you tell me that, Mom?"

"I lied," Grace quickly replied. "I had to lie."

"Why?" Charlotte replied. "Why tell me my dad is a killer?"

Lee could feel the tears welling in his own eyes as he listened to his daughter's words. Now was a time that she would remember for the rest of her life, and to lie about something of this magnitude would be unfor-givable.

"Your mother had to lie," Lee said, wiping his shirt sleeve across his eyes. "She knew they would be after me, and she didn't want you to be in danger, too. Have a seat, and I'll tell you all about it."

43

Michael Hart stood before the jury and delivered an impressive opening statement to start the morning. The jury looked well caffeinated and eager to begin the trial as they listened to the prosecutor walk through his roadmap to conviction. Hart was methodical in his approach, but he had just enough flare to keep things interesting for the jury. Maggie Reynolds sat up straight in her chair with her legs crossed, a notebook resting on her knee for the occasional scribble. Every so often, a juror flashed his or her eyes to the defense table to gauge reactions. Maggie gave away little in her expression.

The judge dealt a crucial blow to the defense's case weeks prior when he issued an order denying parts of the pretrial motion to suppress. The decision was clearly an attempt to even the playing field for the parties. It permitted the introduction of the Beretta 92FS into evidence and limited discussion about the interview with the man that located the firearm—José Valdez Bisbal. The decision by Judge Balk to let the murder weapon into evidence did not surprise Maggie, but it did surprise the members of the media covering the case. José was still nowhere to be found, and that presented a number of problems that could be explored on appeal. Though Maggie always tried to pad a case with arguments to use at the appellate level, she never planned to lose a jury trial. She believed the jurors picked up on the subtle body language of someone that expected to get beat. The Acker case would be no different.

When Hart sat down, Maggie picked up a yellow legal pad from the defense table and walked toward the jury box. Like athletes, trial lawyers can be somewhat superstitious. Some attribute past success to rituals, knowing good and well that the ritual has little to do with their performance. Though experienced and polished in her approach to trying a case, Maggie had her own ritual, and she performed it as she walked in the direction of the twelve jurors. She knew the name of each person selected to sit in the box, and she scanned the rows of faces. As she passed each face, she said the person's name in her head until she reached the end of the row. She knew the silly ritual had no bearing on the outcome of her trials, but there was no reason to risk it in the biggest case of her career.

After placing the legal pad on the wooden lectern, Maggie walked within feet of the first row of jurors and greeted the group with a warm smile. She planted both feet on the ground below her, and she began to tell the story of an innocent man. She said the words with a practiced calmness, and she assured the jurors that the evidence presented by the prosecution would not support a conviction. With tact, she pointed to the evidence of the firearm found in Lee Acker's truck—the only evidence linking her client to the murder itself. She did not linger on the troubling evidence. Instead, she pivoted to the testimony that the jury would hear from the defense's primary witness, Tim Dawson. Testimony that would show the jurors why credible and reasonable doubt already existed in the case. With thanks to the jury, Maggie returned to her seat and waited for the onslaught to begin.

~

The State began the presentation of its case with the testimony of Jake Collins's legal secretary, the woman that discovered Jake's body lying in the woods. She explained to the jury that she'd worked for Jake the past couple of years. She became concerned the morning of Jake's murder because he missed two of his morning appointments. Overlooking one appointment was unusual, but blowing off an entire morning without so much as a call to the office was unheard of. So, she decided to run by Jake's house during her lunch hour to check on his well-being. When she arrived, she found Jake's pickup truck in the driveway. She knocked on the door and rang the doorbell. Hearing no one inside, she walked around to the back door of the home and grabbed a spare key from under a flowerpot. Once inside, she checked every room.

She set the scene of the empty house beautifully for the jury. As Maggie listened to the woman's testimony, she contemplated asking the legal secretary if she'd considered making a change to a career in acting. The jury seemed transfixed on the petite brunette as she followed the prosecutor's line of questioning. Maggie listened, beginning to feel as though she'd missed something.

"I walked back downstairs to the kitchen, and that's when I noticed his cell phone sitting on the windowsill by the sink. That's where he tends to leave his phone when he is home."

"Did that concern you?" Hart asked.

"Yes," she replied. "I felt like he had to be home. Who leaves home without their cell phone these days?"

The jury nodded along in agreement as they listened to the doll of a witness.

"I certainly don't," Hart said. "So, you've checked the entire house. You know Jake's cell phone and truck are still at his place. What did you do next?"

"I stepped outside to make a phone call to my brother. He works as a deputy with the Blake County Sheriff's Office."

"Why?"

"I was worried about Jake. I thought he might be in some kind of trouble, and I figured my brother might know what to do."

"What did y'all decide on?"

"Well, I was only a few seconds into the conversation with my brother when I saw the body, Jake's body. I knew it was him right off because he wears bright-colored running shoes. I could see the fluorescent yellow Nikes from where I was standing."

"Did you tell your brother what you saw?"

She nodded. "And the operator with 911, while I waited at the scene. My brother wanted it called in—he wanted everything by the book."

Hart handed a couple of photos to Maggie. She took both images in hand. They were photographs she'd seen countless times now, lifeless images of her friend and former adversary from the courtroom. Maggie nodded at the prosecutor, and he turned back to his task at hand.

"Do you recognize these photographs, ma'am?" Hart said, handing the images to his witness.

She grimaced. "I do, Mr. Hart. This is how Jake looked the day I found him dead in the woods."

With a tearful witness, Hart walked through a set of questions to establish his foundation for admitting the photographs into evidence. He then showed them to the jury with the judge's permission. The jury stared at the photographs of the dead body—the most powerful image in the prosecution's arsenal.

"She is with the court, Your Honor," Hart said as he handed the witness off for questioning by the defense. He left the gruesome images on the courtroom's large projector screen. Sounds of sobbing from a few individuals in the gallery could be heard as Maggie stood to approach the lectern. She had to admit, the images were hard to look at. She picked up the remote that controlled the courtroom's video system and took the images off the screen. Maggie did not want the jury looking at the dead body any more than necessary.

"Did you know Jake liked to go for runs in the woods behind his home?" Maggie said, directing her attention to the dark-haired witness.

"Yes, ma'am, he mentioned that from time to time at the office."

The woman was close to Maggie's age and wore a suit jacket with a conservative blouse. Her hair was pulled back, and she'd applied her makeup sparingly that morning. It was a small town, though, and Maggie had seen her before at the gym. The young woman was in excellent shape and dressed fashionably when out of the courtroom.

"Are you a runner?" Maggie asked, already sure of the answer.

"I enjoy working out and staying healthy," the witness replied. "I'll go for a run, occasionally."

Maggie handed her a photograph. It was taken off of the witness's social media account. Maggie asked her to identify the image.

"When is this photograph from?"

"It's from a local five K. Some people from the district attorney's office ran the race together as a team building event. It would have been sometime this past year."

"Is that image from your social media account?"

"It looks like it."

"And is that Jake there in the middle of the photograph?"

"Yes, ma'am, it is."

"That's him with his arm around you?"

"That's correct, and his other arm is around Sharon Sloan. Sharon is another coworker of ours, well, mine now."

Maggie paused and pretended to look down at the notepad in front of her. She'd planned a brief cross-examination of this preliminary witness in the State's presentation. Her only role was to set the scene for the prosecution's case, but Maggie's gut told her there was more.

"I gathered from your testimony earlier that you had visited Jake's home a number of times."

The witness paused and glanced over at the prosecutor. Maggie caught the glance and knew she was on the right course.

"Let me rephrase that," Maggie said. "How many times have you been to Jake Collins's home?"

"I've been to his home quite a few times, ma'am."

"Have you eaten meals there?" Maggie said, prodding the witness along.

"Yes, ma'am."

"Breakfast?"

The prosecutor stood from his seat and objected to the question. Maggie could feel that this witness was hiding something. Hart was trying to protect her.

"Overruled," Judge Balk said. "Please proceed, Ms. Reynolds."

Maggie looked from the judge to the jury, acting as if she was considering her next question.

"How long had you and Jake been sleeping together?"

Maggie waited for the objection from Hart, but it never came. Maggie wondered if the prosecutor had simply missed the question.

"We had been seeing each other off and on for the last year," the witness said after a long, arduous pause. Tears began to well in her eyes as she stared back at Maggie.

"Did you ever disclose this relationship to law enforcement?"

"No, no one knew about us. I've told a few people since he died, but I never told the investigator when he interviewed me."

Maggie's heart pounded. This was unbelievable. She pressed forward, eager to delve into this shocking admission right in the presence of the jury. When there is a murder, law enforcement looks to rule out the spouse or significant other as a potential suspect. The legal secretary's decision to hide that information from law enforcement created problems for the State's case. Maggie had enough information for an interesting argument to the jury, but she wanted more.

"Why didn't you disclose this information to law enforcement?"

"I was scared, and Jake never wanted anyone to know about us in the first place. I wanted to honor our promise to one another."

Maggie caught the witness's eyes glance to the prosecutor again, as if she wanted to say something else.

"Any other reason why you didn't disclose your relationship with Jake to Special Agent Dawson?"

"Well, he didn't love me, and I knew that."

"And your feeling that Jake Collins did not love you was enough reason for you to hide this relationship from the people investigating the murder?"

"He loved someone else, Ms. Reynolds. That was always the way it was going to be with him."

Maggie knew she'd dug too far with this witness, and she began to back away from the podium.

"Thank you, ma'am. Your Honor, I don't have any further—"

"He loved your client's wife, Grace Acker," the witness spouted out before Maggie could conclude the examination. "I knew he loved her, and that's why he could never love me."

Maggie turned to Hart, who was seated at his table, smirking. He had not objected because he knew where the questioning of this witness would lead. He'd baited Maggie with this testimony, knowing she would fall right into his trap.

"I don't have any other questions for this witness, Your Honor."

"Any redirect, Mr. Hart?" Judge Balk asked.

"No, Your Honor."

With the first witness of the trial, Maggie knew the prosecution had begun to establish an important component of the case—motive.

~

At 5:00 p.m., Judge Balk dismissed the jury for the day. The entire defense team stood as the jurors exited the rear doors of the courtroom. They would board the county vans that would take them to their hotel. The jury looked tired and ready to leave for the day. Maggie attempted to look as pleasant as possible, but she too was ready to get home.

She had to admit, Michael Hart drove his side of the case in an efficient manner, and he'd scored some valuable points in the first day of the prosecution's case. He carried his momentum from the morning's first witness into the testimony of the coroner and those witnesses tasked with collecting the evidence from the crime scene in the woods. Their testimony was much drier than the legal secretary's. But it was necessary in proving the elements of the case. Maggie questioned each witness sparingly, still reeling from her misstep that morning. She would bounce back.

"Who are you calling tomorrow?" Maggie asked, looking across the aisle at the prosecutor as he packed up his things.

"A few of the guys that searched your client's house, and I'll try to get Antonio Barrea out of the way. He has a flight back home to Mexico in the evening."

Maggie nodded. "Are you calling Don Malone before the weekend?"

"Not planning to. We can get into that next week with the jury."

Hart looked to be in a good mood, and he left the courtroom almost skipping. Maggie didn't blame him. The media coverage tonight would be brutal. Every station would run wild with new theories around Jake's long-held love for Grace Acker. Their coverage would include old photos from when Jake and Grace were fresh-faced high schoolers, attending prom and football game afterparties. The news anchors would help weave the prosecution's narrative, and the analysts would chastise Maggie for her poor job questioning the witness. She planned to watch none of it.

As Maggie turned to finish packing her files, she noticed her old boss, Jim Lamb, was still seated in the gallery. He was reading a book with his arm draped over the back of the wooden pew. He wore a worn-out olive-colored suit with a blue tie. Maggie carried her bag down the center aisle, then tapped on the edge of the pew to get Lamb's attention.

"Tough start for the defense," Lamb said, placing a bookmark between the open pages in his hardback. "Killing Jake over jealousy. It's a nice, believable theory for the jury. A tale as old as time."

"Even if it's a manufactured theory?" Maggie said, sliding down the row to sit next to her old mentor.

"Aren't all our theories manufactured to some extent?" he replied. "I've certainly seen worse."

"I guess so," Maggie replied.

"What's on tap for tomorrow?"

"Don't you have a job? You can't spend all day critiquing the trial."

"It's all constructive feedback, Reynolds."

"Uh-huh," Maggie said with a grin. "Well, tomorrow Hart is calling his witnesses that'll show Lee took off and ran for Mexico. The deputies that searched the house will show the jury he was gone the night they came looking for him. Antonio Barrea will show Lee was in a shootout just north of Monterrey, Mexico, a few days later."

"Do you think Hart has anything else up his sleeve?"

"He has to have something more," Maggie replied. "He will want to leave the jury with something juicy for the weekend."

Lamb nodded. "Jesse Hernandez would be my bet. That's what I would do. Get the jury thinking about that gun registered to Lee Acker."

"You are probably right."

"I might be. I'm not the hotshot defense lawyer, though," Lamb replied with a wink. "You go with your gut."

44

The next day, Bruce Tevens had lunch delivered to his office. The defense team sat together in the well-appointed conference room and discussed the strategy for that afternoon. Lee Acker sat at the end of the table. He chewed his sandwich and reviewed the translated statement from Antonio Barrea, a member of the State Police in Nuevo León. In the statement, the officer described the shootout at the gas station north of Monterrey. He pointed out in the statement that "an unknown white male assisted in fending off the gunmen but refused to stay on site to provide a statement in connection with the event." Lee remembered the cocky young officer. He remembered the way the lawman shook his hand and called him 'cowboy.' He thought there was an understanding there. That would not be the case, though, not with the young man flying up to testify on behalf of the prosecution.

"Michael Hart is going to use Barrea for three things," Maggie said, working through her thoughts out loud. "First, he wants to show the jury that Lee knows how to use a gun and is willing to shoot one at another human being. Second, the prosecution wants to establish that Lee was on the run in Mexico while local law enforcement and the GBI were looking for him. Third, they want to show Lee being uncooperative with law enforcement in Mexico."

"That way they can infer that Lee has been uncooperative with law enforcement in the US," Bruce added, shoveling a forkful of salad in his mouth.

"Exactly," Maggie said. "It'll all be on video, too."

"I'm not sure the video hurts us," Bruce countered.

Maggie shrugged. "The video is not terrible on its own, but I think Hart can twist it to his advantage if Barrea sets it up right."

Lee's cell phone vibrated in his coat pocket, and he pulled it out to check the number. The screen showed the incoming call was being placed from a blocked number. Lee excused himself and stepped into the law office's hallway. Lee could hear Bruce and Maggie continuing their debate as he pulled the conference room door shut behind him.

"Hello," Lee said as he put the phone to his ear.

"General Lee, how are you?" began a heavily accented greeting.

Lee recognized the voice of Roberto, head of Alex Olivera's security. He had not heard the voice since moments before being badly beaten on the streets of Mexico City.

"I think you meant to ask how my ribs are doing," Lee replied. "Last time I saw you, you and your little sidekick were getting plenty of cheap shots in."

"Yes, how are your ribs?" Roberto said with a laugh. "And your face, how is your face?"

"They're great. Thanks for asking, asshole."

"I was taking orders, and you can appreciate that. I am sorry about how we left things—"

"No, you aren't," Lee snapped. "What do you want?"

"We are coming to visit next week," Roberto replied after a brief pause. "I am bringing my boss. She wants to see you so that you can talk about this request that she testify at your trial. She is not yet comfortable with the idea."

Lee took a few paces down the hallway. His black dress shoes tapped against the hardwood floor as he took in the news. He did not expect her to entertain the idea of testifying at his trial.

"Okay. She doesn't strike me as the kind of woman who calls to ask for permission to visit. Why are you calling me?"

"She wanted me to tell you she was coming."

"That's it?"

"That's it."

The advance notice struck Lee as odd. The defense team added Alex Olivera to the witness list to scare Bill Collins. They never expected to have her stand in support of Lee's defense.

"Call me when you get to town, then," Lee said, beginning to walk back to the conference room door. "Anything else?"

"Don't tell the media, General."

Lee slid the cell phone back in his coat pocket and rattled off a few obscenities as he pushed the door open to the conference room. Maggie and Bruce were on their feet using a whiteboard now, still discussing trial strategy.

"She is going to fly up for the trial," Lee said, interrupting the lawyers midsentence.

Maggie looked over at him. "Olivera is?"

Lee nodded. "I just spoke to her head of security, and he confirmed that they would arrive sometime next week."

"This is big, Lee."

"She wants to talk about her testimony before she agrees to testify, but I think we can convince her. I need you to check on something, though."

"What's that?" Maggie asked.

"Let's see what we can do about getting my brother, Cliff, involved in that discussion."

"How closely involved are we talking?"

"As close as we can get."

～

The trial continued to move along at an efficient pace. Michael Hart was a skilled quarterback for the prosecution's offensive attack, like a game manager that knew how to control the clock to his advantage. He stood from his seat and called the second witness of the afternoon at 2:45 p.m. If he squeezed Antonio Barrea's testimony into an hour window, he'd have time to call one more witness for the day. Maggie's gut told her that the prosecution's final witness of the week would be the charismatic investigator from Alabama, Jesse Hernandez.

"The State calls Antonio Barrea to the witness stand," Hart said, standing at the prosecution's table.

The tall wooden doors at the front of the courtroom opened, and the Mexican officer strode into the room. He walked like a young rooster, shoulders back and chin up high. He wore a dress uniform that looked crisp from the dry cleaner and had a round police cap tucked under his left arm. Lee glanced at the jury as the foreign officer took his seat at the witness stand. The twelve looked intrigued. Barrea was by far the most well-groomed witness that had appeared thus far, and the smell of his cologne must have snapped the jury out of the afternoon's lull.

A translator stood near the witness's chair in a plaid pantsuit. As Hart approached the lectern, he pointed out the interpreter to the officer and asked that she introduce herself to the witness. Hart assured his proud officer that the interpreter was only there as a backup. He then asked that both raise their right hands, and the oath was administered. Hart then dove into questions about Barrea's background in law enforcement and gave his witness an opportunity to endear himself to the jury. Barrea handled the opportunity wonderfully, showing no signs of nervousness. Though it was clear to the jury that English was not his first language, Barrea spoke in a clear and concise manner. He stepped around complicated vocabulary and only asked the prosecutor to repeat his questions on a couple of occasions.

"I am going to show you a video clip from earlier this year, and I want you to tell me if you recognize the location," Hart said as he clicked play on surveillance footage from the gas station shootout.

The parties had stipulated to the admissibility of the footage. This allowed for Hart to move through his questioning without the delay of authenticating the video itself for evidence purposes.

"This is a fuel station north of Monterrey," Barrea said. "It is in Nuevo León, a state in Mexico."

"Have you been to this location that is depicted in the video?"

"Yes," Barrea replied with a nod. "It is where I met Mr. Acker."

Hart froze the video and looked over at Lee as if it was the first time he'd seen him in the courtroom that day.

"Now, are you familiar with the substance of the charges that Mr. Acker is facing?" Hart said, building the anticipation of the jury by keeping the surveillance footage on the large projector screen paused.

"Can you repeat?" the witness replied with a confused look on his face.

Hart rephrased his question. "Do you know what crime Mr. Lee Acker is charged with here in the United States of America?"

"Yes."

"What crime is that?"

"Murder."

"Do you know when this crime took place?"

Maggie stood from her seat and objected to the question. Judge Balk swung his gaze to the prosecutor and sustained the objection.

"Fine," Hart said, feigning frustration in the presence of the jurors.

Hart pulled a copy of the indictment from his file and asked the judge for permission to approach the witness. He handed the paper to Barrea.

"Do you see on this indictment the date that this murder took place?"

"Yes."

"Do you know if this surveillance footage is from before or after that date?"

"After," Barrea replied, setting the paperwork back on the wooden rail of the witness stand.

"How do you know that?"

"Because I was there at the fuel station," Barrea replied. "I remember the day."

"Did you know that members of law enforcement in the United States were looking for Lee Acker at that time?"

"No."

"Now, we are about to watch this surveillance footage from a shooting incident at this fuel station, correct?"

"That is correct."

"A shooting incident that Mr. Acker was involved in?"

"I was involved in it, too," Barrea replied, not wanting his valiant efforts to be excluded from any mention.

"Of course. Now, did you ask Mr. Acker to stick around to give a statement after this shooting?"

"I did," the officer replied with a nod. "He did not wish to stay, and we let him go. I knew nothing about this here in the US."

"So, Mr. Acker chose not to cooperate with your investigation?"

Barrea paused as he appeared to think about the question.

"I could have made him stay to cooperate with the investigation. I chose not to."

"Fine," Hart replied, not wanting to press the subject. "Let's take a look at the tape, then."

The jury turned their attention from the witness stand to the projector screen as soon as the prosecutor pressed play on the video. Hart walked over to one side of the jury box to watch the screen from the jurors' perspective. He looked as though he wanted to hand out buckets of popcorn as the images moved on the screen. No audio accompanied the video, so the courtroom sat quiet as the scene from the gas station shooting played out. When the footage reached the end, Hart paused the video with an image of Lee jogging away.

"No further questions at this time," Hart said as he headed to his seat.

The jury stared up at the projector screen—the image of a man on the run. Maggie stood from her seat and made her way to the podium. She rewound the video and pressed play as the windows in the gas station exploded.

"When did you find out that Lee was being investigated for murder?" Maggie asked, picking up her pace in questioning as the video ran.

"I read about it in an article in *El Norte*, a newspaper in my home state."

"Did that article discuss my client's involvement in this incident?" Maggie said, pointing to the screen.

"Yes. It reported on the shooting and identified Lee as a fugitive from justice in the US."

"Were you interviewed for that article?"

Barrea shook his head and smiled. "No. The journalist should have called me. His story would have been better. He made mistakes about the facts of what took place. It is typical of the reporters in my home country."

The jury chuckled at the comment from the cocky officer. They appreciated his noted disdain for journalists that failed to gather all of the facts.

"What would you have said in an interview?"

"That Lee acted like a hero," Barrea replied after a long pause. "He saved my partner's life, and he helped defend the people hiding inside of the gas station. It was all very brave. Things could have ended badly."

Maggie paused the video. She left the image of Lee supporting the weight of Barrea's partner, the older Mexican police officer injured by the unknown gunmen. With the action paused, the jury zeroed in on Barrea and his words. He unfastened the top shirt button of his crisp uniform and pulled a necklace out with a gold cross. He held it out in front of him for the jury to see.

"God intervened in my life that day," the young officer said, his voice calm as he spoke to the twelve. "I have prayed, and I know now that it was part of God's plan. Lee served a purpose on that day."

Maggie held her breath as she listened. She had her back to the prosecutor, but Maggie knew Hart was considering an intervention of his own by way of objection.

"I know how it sounds," Barrea said, still looking over at the jury. "Amado Nervo wrote that '*De todas suertes, me escuda mi sed de investigación, mi ansia de Dios, honda y muda; y hay más amor en mi duda que en tu tibia afirmación.*'"

The interpreter stepped forward and nodded at the witness.

"He says, 'Notwithstanding, I am shielded by my thirst for inquiry—my pangs for God, cavernous and unheard; and there is more love in my unsated doubt than in your tepid certainty.'"

The jury stared back at the interpreter and the officer. They had no idea whom the young officer had just quoted or what he meant. Still, it was obvious from the jurors' faces that the officer's words were heartfelt.

"That statement you just made, what does that mean to you?" Maggie asked the officer.

"People should try to have faith. They should want to know why things happen in life. That even if you have doubts, you should not believe the grand moments in life—moments like those caught on this recording—are just random events." The officer turned to face the jury. "Keep asking the questions, keep inquiring. This Lee is a good man, a brave man."

Maggie let the words hang over the courtroom like a blanket. She knew which churches the twelve jurors attended. Maggie wanted those men and women that walked by faith to grapple with the young officer's words. So, she waited and let the twelve reflect.

"Is there anything else you would like the jury to know?" Maggie said as she watched the officer move his gold necklace back inside his dress shirt, fastening the top button.

"Pray about this and know that this man is innocent. He—"

"Objection, Your Honor," Hart said, finally popping to his feet to try to stop the bleeding. "That calls for—"

"I'll sustain the objection," Judge Balk said without listening to an argument. "Mr. Barrea, please refrain from commenting on the accused's innocence or guilt. Move it along, Ms. Reynolds."

"No need, Your Honor," Maggie replied.

She thanked the witness and left him with the court. Looking deflated, Hart stood and resumed his questioning. He tried to piece together a few additional points, but his efforts were futile. Maggie watched the faces of the jurors as the flustered prosecutor attacked his own witness's knowledge as to the facts around the death of Jake Collins. Barrea never wavered on his support of Lee, and by the end of the examination, the clock on the wall read 3:50 p.m.

"Thank you for being here, Mr. Barrea," Judge Balk said as the officer stood from the witness stand.

Barrea nodded. "You're welcome, sir."

"Have a safe trip home."

As Barrea left, he passed the defense table and leaned over to Lee with a hand extended. He winked at Lee and shook firmly.

"Good luck, cowboy."

～

The prosecution stuck to the game plan and called Jesse Hernandez to the witness stand at 4:05 p.m. The judge looked surprised by the decision to squeeze another witness in before the weekend, but he allowed it. Judge Balk assured his jury that they would call it quits at 5:00 p.m., and the twelve let out a collective sigh of relief.

Hart started fast out of the gate. He moved through the questions about

Hernandez's background and qualifications, pushing toward the meat of his witness's testimony. In his haste, he gave the jury little opportunity to get comfortable with the investigator. It was obvious to Maggie that Hart planned to get the image of the Beretta 92FS, registered to Lee Acker, on the projector screen before quitting time. He wanted that image to burn in the minds of the jurors during the weekend ahead.

"Do you recognize this photograph?" Hart asked, handing an image of a pickup truck to his witness.

"This is a photograph of the defendant's pickup truck. I located this vehicle on a piece of farmland in Henry County, Alabama. Farmland that is owned by the defendant."

"Where exactly did you find this truck?"

"Tucked behind a barn on the property," Hernandez replied. "It was not covered up or anything, but it was parked in a place that was not visible from the road or main driveway."

Hart entered the photograph into evidence and was granted permission to show the image to the jury. The prosecutor pulled a laser pointer from his pocket and placed a red dot on the truck's toolbox.

"Did you search this vehicle?"

"I applied and obtained a search warrant first. I then searched the entire vehicle."

"Did you search the toolbox on the vehicle?"

"I did."

"Did you find anything of interest there in the toolbox?"

"Yes, I found a semiautomatic pistol, a Beretta 92FS."

Hart then handed another photograph to the investigator. Hernandez confirmed that the handgun in the photograph was the same as the one he'd located in the defendant's truck. With permission from the judge and a click of the remote, Hart displayed the image of the firearm to the jury. He let the jurors stare up at the image on the projector screen as he flipped through his notes. He was right on time; the wristwatch on his arm read 4:49 p.m.

"How did you handle this firearm?"

"Like it was potentially the murder weapon used on Jake Collins. I had someone on my team tag it, bag it, and place it into evidence. We followed standard procedure."

"Once a weapon is in evidence, how do you determine who the owner of the weapon is?"

Hernandez was conscious of the time restraint outlined by the judge. "Do we have time to get into this?"

Hart nodded. "Go ahead, we have a few more minutes."

"Well, when my office finds a firearm at the scene of a crime, we run the weapon through a tracing process. That involves us sending out a trace request to the folks over at the ATF, or Bureau of Alcohol, Firearms, Tobacco and Explosives. They take serial number information to track the weapon through retail and wholesale points of sale to determine owner-ship. The tracing process is just another tool, it does not always settle the question of gun ownership when dealing with a criminal investigation."

Maggie looked down at her watch—4:55 p.m.

"In this case, did the trace reveal the owner of the Beretta 92FS that you located in the defendant's truck?"

"It did. The Beretta was purchased a few years ago at a sporting goods store in Columbus, Georgia. The only owner listed on the firearm's history is the defendant—Lee Elmer Acker."

45

Cliff Acker heard the footsteps of the guard coming down the pathway that ran alongside the row of cells. Shift change would not take place for another hour, but it was not unusual for the guards to make their rounds early in the morning. Cliff stared at the empty ceiling of his cell, listening as the tap of the guard's boots echoed off the walls of the caged hallway. The boots stopped at the doorway to his cell, and Cliff heard a key ring tap on the metal bars.

"Get on up, Acker. We are putting you on a transport this morning."

Cliff lifted his head off the pillow and looked at the guard. A dim light illuminated the passageway outside; he could only see the outline of the plump jailer.

"Since when?" Cliff asked. "No one told me anything about this."

"You are property of the federal government, boy. They'll send you where they like."

"The fuck they won't. My release date is in two weeks. I have the paperwork right here."

The guard shifted in his shoes. He knew Cliff Acker well, and he wasn't worried about the backtalk. You put a bunch of men in cages, you are bound to get some lip every now and then.

"Come on, Acker, you know the drill. Pack your shit, and I'll walk you down to processing. I'm going to finish my rounds, and I'll come back to get you. Bring your paperwork."

Cliff looked around at the cell. There wasn't much he cared to take with him, a few photos and his Bible would make the cut. He packed his belongings into a cloth bag and reviewed his release paperwork. The date on the front page clearly stated his release date was tentatively set for December 23, 2016.

"Let's go," the guard said when he returned to the door of the cell. "I'll get a cup of coffee and a donut for you to have while you wait for the van."

"How many you had this morning?" Cliff replied with a grin.

"Didn't your momma ever teach you not to bite the hand that feeds you?"

"Yeah," Cliff replied with a shrug. "I went pretty hungry as a kid."

The guard laughed as he unlocked the cell door. Cliff was a good four or five inches taller than the guard, and he weighed in at a shredded two hundred twenty pounds. Putting both hands out in front of him, Cliff waited for the cold metal and click of the handcuffs.

"Where are they transporting me?"

"Not too far. Paperwork says the local jail in Blake County, Georgia."

Cliff nodded at the guard's response, as if he expected to be going home all along. His emotions were hard to conceal, though. Cliff turned back to the dark cell where his bunkmate still laid prone on the thin mattress. Peering into the darkness, he took the opportunity to wipe his wet eyes on the sleeve of his jumpsuit. His bunkmate sat up and gave Cliff a short salute with two fingers. Cliff was going home.

"I'm out of here, brother."

~

John Deese walked up the brick steps that led to the front door of the main house on Kelley Hill Plantation. There were a number of cottages and buildings peppered across the property, but they all paled in comparison to the main house. Waiting for the door to open, John admired the view from the wide front porch. A view of privilege handed down through generations of wealth.

"Hello, John," said the familiar voice as the door opened. "Come on inside."

Bill Collins stood at the door, holding it open with a smile. John always envied that smile. It was a wonderful tool, as important as any in a politician's arsenal.

"Yes, sir," John replied as he made his way into the house. "Do you want to meet in your study?"

"Let's meet on the back patio instead. We have a fire going in the outdoor fireplace."

"We?" John asked as he walked through the grand foyer.

"Lucy is going to join in the conversation. She enjoys sitting outside on these late fall evenings."

As John walked through the Collinses' plantation home, memories of his visits as a child rushed to mind. As a boy, he'd always felt like the poor cousin when visiting Jake. They would explore the woods around the mammoth house by four-wheelers and horseback. They hunted, fished, and swam until the sun dipped below the trees. They ate meals of fresh vegetables and meat at the kitchen bar, listening to the Collinses' dinner guests conversing in the dining room next door. Though John always loved his visits to Kelley Hill, they reminded him of the life he never had.

"Come sit over here by me," Lucy said as the men stepped onto the patio. She scooted over in her spot next to the fire to make space for John.

"Can I get you a drink?" Bill asked as he picked up a glass of his own. "I have a nice bottle open from some small outfit in Kentucky. It's an early release of their small-batch rye."

"Bill and the judge got quite a bit of visiting done earlier this evening. I imagine that bottle is getting close to being gone. You'd better help him out, John."

"I'll take one," John replied, noting the mention of the Collinses' meeting with Judge Balk.

Lucy smiled and sipped from her mug of hot tea. Her eyes studied him as they waited for Bill to return from the patio's wet bar.

"Here you are, John," Bill said, handing over a generous pour. The two men clinked glasses, and Bill returned to his seat.

"What do you have for us?" he asked, sipping from his refreshed glass.

John took a moment to collect his thoughts. His report today would not be well received.

"I am certain that the Ackers have a copy of the files, sir. I personally went through every record recovered from Jake's house, and there are items from his research missing."

"How do you know what's missing has any bearing on the project?" Lucy asked.

"We know that Jake was aware of the deals with the Mexicans. He didn't know anything about it when he started investigating Cliff Acker, but he found out not long after. His notes on Fronteras Force go back to about this time last year."

Bill nodded, listening to the information as if it was news to him.

"In his notes, he keeps going back to an argument you two had about it, sir," John said, his eyes focused on the senator-elect, looking for a reaction. "A confrontation that ensued after you invited Jake to join the endeavor."

As he said the words, John noticed Lucy's gaze shift to her husband.

"You asked our son to work on the project with you?"

"I did," Bill quickly replied. "Jake expressed interest in taking on a larger role in politics. The project was an opportunity to introduce him to a group of powerful people. You know how important that is."

"I can't believe you tried to bring him on board. This explains everything."

"You are overreacting, Lucy."

"You told our son about your plans to hand government-funded contracts to a company that is run to specifically benefit the Olivera family, a family name soaked in organized crime. You think I am overreacting? All this ridiculous discussion around Jake being targeted by the cartel. The theories pushed by that haughty defense lawyer representing Lee. It all makes sense now. It turns out they knew more about my son and his relationship with his father than I did."

There was no appropriate way to intervene in a married couple's argument. John took another sip from his glass and considered how they might redirect the conversation to his report. Then he could leave and let the Collinses hash it out.

"Here I was, assuming that Jake was investigating all of this because of

Cliff Acker. I thought Jake had come across damaging information that connected our families to one another, but that wasn't it at all. He was investigating you, Bill."

"Calm down, Lucy. That is not entirely accurate."

"Don't try to politick with me," Lucy snapped. "Why didn't you tell me about this argument? And how much did you tell him, Bill?"

"Everything, Lucy. I told him everything. He was my son, and I trusted him. I explained how the contracts would work and where the camps for the workers would be located. We discussed the advantages of cutting off the flow of illegals coming across the border, controlling the ones that are already here, and the other political advantages to the project. It's still going forward, and it will be a good thing for the country, Lucy."

"Did you tell him the investors would all receive a percentage of the profits?"

John shifted in his seat. All of the investors with an interest in the project knew the Olivera family would move contraband into the US, using the camps as unofficial distribution points. It was never specifically discussed in the negotiations with Fronteras Force, but the contracts contemplated a percentage of "ancillary profits" being allocated to investors. If one could ever wade through the shell companies, they would find the investors were really just a group of politicians and businessmen. Politicians that would campaign on a commitment to increased border security and the continuing war on drugs. Businessmen that wanted their networks to believe their millions were made through hard work and ingenuity.

"I did not explain how the percentage would work, Lucy."

"He wasn't stupid," she scoffed. "That's what he was investigating, wasn't it?"

"Yes, ma'am," John added, finally seeing an opportunity to regain some involvement in the conversation. "His notes and records indicate he was curious as to how the other members of the investment group would make any profits. He suspected it would come through illegal activity. I believe any missing files will discuss that aspect of Jake's investigation."

"I knew it was trouble when that lawyer announced that she was going to bring Alex Olivera up from Mexico to testify."

"She won't exonerate Lee," John replied. "In fact, she won't shed any negative light on the partnership between her business and the US. It would jeopardize her company's relationship with our government."

"She will be able to clarify the fact that Lee was not an investor in the endeavor, though," Lucy pointed out. "She will be able to confirm Bill and others in places of power are involved in the project. That's all Maggie Reynolds needs so that she can spin things to the jury."

"Well, she needs evidence to do that, ma'am," John said, setting his glass down. "I believe we have most of that information."

"Most of it?" Bill said. "I don't like the idea of not having all of it."

John agreed, but he let the tension marinate a moment as he thought about how to proceed. He looked to Lucy.

"What did you believe he was investigating?"

"It's not important," Lucy replied with a wave of the hand. "He was investigating his father, and the defense knows about it now. That's all that matters."

"Is there something I need to know about?" John said, looking back to his boss's eyes. "It sounds like there is something more that Lucy believes is compromising to the family, compromising to you, sir."

Bill shook him off. "You know everything you need to know, John."

John nodded at them both. He still sensed there was more.

"Okay. Well, I work for you. I can't help with something I don't know anything about. I can't protect you if I don't know where the attacks may come from."

"There is nothing else to tell. There is nothing else to protect. Now, how are you going to retrieve the files?"

"Well, Lee's daughter was most likely the girl I saw in the woods behind Jake's house. I've looked at a few pictures and have seen her in court. She's a perfect match. Best-case scenario, she got away with a few pages of records. Worst-case scenario, she made it out with a digital file. Something with all of Jake's most recent findings in his investigation."

Lucy stood from her seat and started toward the patio door.

"Go talk to her, John," she said as she walked away. "Charlotte Acker is just a girl, but she needs to understand the way things work in this world."

"Are you sure about this?"

"Why wouldn't I be?" Lucy replied, stopping where she stood.

"I just thought there were familial lines we weren't going to cross anymore. I thought we agreed that—"

"That won't happen again," Bill assured him. "Go get it done, John. Don't be stupid about it, though."

John pulled out his cell phone and scrolled through one of Charlotte Acker's social media pages. CharlieGirl18 posted her whereabouts fairly often, and she tended to train around the same time each day.

"I'll visit her tomorrow and pick her up. Based on her recent posts on social media, I have a pretty good idea where she will take her afternoon run."

46

Lee pulled his truck up to the chain link fence and rolled the windows down. He zipped his jacket up and felt the early December air drift inside the cab. The radio played the sounds of Monday Night Football. It was half-time, and Washington led Pittsburgh by a field goal. Lee breathed in the night air as he listened to the commentators recap the first half of play. Buzz continued to surround Washington's rookie quarterback. He'd accounted for three touchdowns in the first two quarters of play, two on the ground and one in the air. With Washington atop the division, there were rumblings that the fifth-round pick could win Rookie of the Year.

As Lee stared out at the white lights running along the edges of the airport runway, he smiled as he listened to the commentators describe the rookie quarterback's style of play. It reminded him of his old friend.

The whine of a jet's engines grew in the distance, pulling Lee away from his thoughts. He stuck his head out the window of the truck to search the night sky. He could see the flashing lights of the small aircraft as it made its approach to the uncontrolled airstrip. Lee turned the key to the truck and started the engine back up. The heater blew warm air on the floorboards, working to warm the cab that had acclimated to the December night.

The jet touched down on the airstrip, bouncing twice before beginning to slow itself on the rural tarmac. Lee shifted the truck into drive and began his route around the edge of the fencing that surrounded the airport. The jet taxied alongside the fence, and Lee drove in line with the aircraft. Hanging a hand outside the window, he waved and then sped ahead to the hangar located at the end of the airfield.

Alex Olivera would step out of her jet and onto the terrain of Southwest Georgia. If she wouldn't get on the witness stand to help rescue Lee from a murder conviction, he would understand. Maybe her presence would at least strike fear in those that knew the truth.

~

"I've reserved two rooms at a local hotel," Lee said as he maneuvered the truck out of the airport's front gate. "You are also welcome to stay at my home. We have plenty of space."

The lights around the airfield began to fade in the distance as Lee drove toward town. He looked over at Alex and tried to gauge her expression. The darkness of the truck cab made it difficult.

"Where are we going now?" she asked.

"We are going to see Cliff."

If the news was a surprise to her, Lee would never know.

"So, we are going to the jail to see him?"

"That's the only place we can meet with him right now. He won't be released for another couple of weeks. Have you spoken to him since he was transferred?"

"No," she replied. "Have you?"

Lee shook his head. "Not yet. The crazy thing is, tonight will be the first time I've seen my brother in our home county in almost two years."

Lee felt a pat on his shoulder. Alex's head of security, Roberto, sat in the seat directly behind Lee. The pat was as much about getting Lee's attention as it was a reminder of the bully's position. Lee glared into the rearview mirror at the Salvadoran. He had no plans to forgive the cheap beating handed out in Mexico City.

"Will I be permitted in the jail?"

Lee shook his head. "It'll just be Alex and me, along with Maggie Reynolds, my attorney."

Alex placed her hand on Lee's thigh. She squeezed the middle of his quad twice and returned the hand to her lap. Lee recognized the gesture.

"That will be acceptable," she quickly added, not giving Roberto an opportunity to protest. "I'll be able to take my mobile phone inside?"

Lee nodded. "I don't expect that to be a problem."

"Good," Alex replied, turning around in her seat to look at her bodyguard. "I'll call you if there is a problem."

"Are you sure?" Roberto replied.

"You will be fine," Lee added, glancing again at Roberto in the rearview mirror. "I'll crack the window in the truck."

Alex gave a small laugh, prompting what Lee hoped was only the knee of the old guerilla soldier pressing against the back of his seat.

"Here we are," Lee said, turning the truck onto the county jail's property. "Temporary residence of Mr. Clifford J. Acker."

A dark, half-lit sign read "Blake County Sheriff's Office Detention Center." The sign was nearly hidden behind a mass of kudzu, but the facility was not hard to miss. It looked depressing, intimidating even. Concertina razor wire was draped along the fencing that surrounded the property, and the aging cinder block buildings could be used for nothing other than the caging of men.

Lee eased the truck past the first building on-site and selected a spot at the front of the nearly deserted parking lot. He turned the radio back on low. Ten and a half minutes of play remained in the Monday night game. Another touchdown on the ground had Washington leading by ten points now. They sat in silence, listening to the commentators praise the play of the rookie quarterback until a pair of headlights pulled through the main gate of the facility. Lee recognized the Saab 900 as it came into view and gave the vehicle a wave as the headlights flashed across his windshield.

"This is my lawyer," Lee said as the vehicle pulled alongside the pickup truck. "Are you ready, Alex?"

"That is what she drives, Lee?"

Lee smiled. "Maggie is damn good."

They all stepped out of the vehicles, and introductions were made. Lee looked over at Alex and could tell by her face that she was sizing his lawyer up. Maggie had her hair pulled back and wore tight blue jeans with a sweater. She pulled a blazer from the back seat of her vehicle as she explained her thoughts on the meeting that evening. Even in her casual attire, she had the aura of an advocate. It burned in her eyes and gave Lee comfort as they walked toward the jail. Maggie explained that the arrangements for the late-night meeting with Cliff had been made hours earlier. She knew the jailers working the night shift and they had agreed to give her the large conference room so that they could review the case in private. Maggie pressed the button on the intercom, and the large metal door on the exterior of the facility buzzed. She yanked the door open and held it as Lee and Alex walked through.

"We have a forty-five-minute time block. Let's be efficient with the time."

$$\sim$$

Cliff hugged Alex first. The two held the embrace long enough for Lee to feel a slight cough was appropriate to move the reunion along. As they stepped apart, the magnetic energy between the two seemed to ripple around the room. Lee was next. He received a bear hug from his little brother with hearty slaps on the back. Tears welled in the younger Acker's eyes as the two men separated. He'd not expected the meeting that night and was obviously thrilled by the visit.

"This is Maggie Reynolds," Lee said, directing his brother's attention to the third visitor in the room. "She is trying to save my ass."

"Not much worth saving," Cliff laughed, walking toward Maggie and wiping his eyes on the sleeve of the jumpsuit. "Oh, what the hell? I'll hug you, too!"

They all laughed as Maggie hugged him, reluctantly. She could smell the faint body odor and musty jumpsuit material. She thought of Jim Lamb and his theory of physical contact with his clients. "They go so long without seeing their loved ones," Lamb would say. "Even if the courts don't believe it, inmates are human beings, too. We must honor that." It was hard not to agree with Lamb's philosophy as she witnessed a scene that, even for Maggie, a woman that had defended hundreds of men and women jailed for various stretches of time, was powerful.

"Let's get to it," Lee said. "Maggie here tells me we only have a small window of time to meet on this. This may be the only time I get to see you for a while without a recorded line hanging over our heads."

Cliff nodded. "Let's hear it."

"Dad's death wasn't a suicide," Lee responded. "Jake told me. He came to visit me before he died. He told me he had proof that someone covered it up, made it look the way it did."

Cliff fell into one of the conference table chairs and crossed his bulked-up arms in front of him. He stared at Lee, and they studied each other. Lee waited for his little brother to respond.

"Bullshit," Cliff finally said, breaking the silence in the room. "Dad shot himself, point-blank. The case was open and shut. I went back and read all the reports ten years ago."

"No, I have the original report. There was an eyewitness in the woods. Another hunter trespassing on our family land. He was walking back to his truck parked off the shoulder of Columbia Highway. That spot right along the creek."

"I know the spot," Cliff responded. "Dad only ran a single strand of hot wire along that creek bed. He thought the ravine and running water made enough of a boundary for the cattle held over there."

Maggie looked across the table at Alex, then Lee. Both had their eyes fixed on Cliff, waiting for a reaction.

"Who was the witness?"

"Kevin June's daddy."

"No shit?"

"Kevin's a restaurant owner these days. He has a place in town called Juno. It's fancy for your standards, but our investigator knows the owner well. Kevin's daddy granted an interview on the topic."

Cliff leaned forward on the table, listening.

"His daddy has cancer and is pretty bad off now," Lee continued. "He might die any day, and he wanted to set the record straight. We have a video-recorded statement now."

"Kevin's daddy is an old drunk."

"I know he is," Lee replied. "He wasn't drunk the day he was hunting our land, though."

"Who did he see in the woods?"

"Bill Collins."

Cliff looked down the table at Alex, and the two appeared to exchange thoughts without the benefit of words. Then he looked at Maggie.

"Do you believe that old drunk's story?" Cliff asked in the direction of the lawyer.

"That's not the question I care about right now," Maggie replied. "My priority is to defend your brother. This new evidence helps us do that."

"Is the investigator that interviewed June's daddy your boyfriend?"

"You mean Tim Dawson?"

"That's the one," Cliff said with a smile. "Is he running down this lead for you?"

"Yes. He is going to be a key witness in our side of the case, Cliff. He will present his findings on the buried report and interview with Mr. June. He is expertly qualified to do so."

"Bill Collins didn't kill his own son, though." Cliff said this in a matter-of-fact tone. "No jury in Blake County is going to believe that he did either. Don't y'all know that?"

"We know that," Lee replied. "That doesn't mean someone within his orbit didn't. Someone that wanted to protect his office, his business interests."

"What did Jake know that his own daddy would have wanted him dead?"

Alex stood from her seat. The others in the room looked over at her as she walked to the conference room door and peered out the window, as if looking for eavesdroppers. She turned back to the table and began to explain.

"Jake knew enough, Cliff. I have read over some of the materials that Jake collected while researching my family's businesses." Cliff leaned back in his chair, all ears. "He paid serious money to look into Fronteras Force, especially its projects in North America. He pieced together business entities tied to his father and a group of investors that began brokering contracts with us eighteen months ago."

"Labor contracts?"

"We are planning to build the rest of the wall along the southern border, cutting off half the trafficking that comes into the US."

"The other families will find a way to move their product across the border," Cliff replied.

"Not the traditional way, and my family will keep that exclusive access."

Cliff stood from his seat and began to pace. He looked up at a clock hanging on the wall, mindful of the time left in the meeting.

"Alex can't testify to any of this," Cliff said, directing his comments at the only lawyer in the room. "You know she will be admitting, under oath, to facts that will lead to a laundry list of offenses. I know you represent my brother, but this is the type of thing that could get Alex locked away for a long time."

"So does murder," Maggie replied.

"So, put June's daddy on the stand. Explain the conspiracy there. Weave reasonable doubt and all that garbage."

"We will try to put him on the stand, but it doesn't make sense without Alex's testimony. June helps us establish that Collins has killed in the past and would do it again. Alex helps us establish the legitimacy of Jake's investigation. She helps establish motive for Jake's murder. There would be no motive to kill Jake without evidence of him uncovering the agreements with Fronteras Force."

Cliff turned his attention back to Alex. "You are not really considering this, are you?"

Lee pulled his phone from his pocket and noticed the notifications on the screen. He had eight missed calls from Grace and a text message that read, *Call me now. Charlotte is missing.* Lee's heart fell to his stomach, and he shot up from his seat.

"I have to go," Lee said, walking toward the conference room door.

"What the hell, Lee? We have to talk about this, figure this shit out. You aren't leaving just like that."

The phone was held to Lee's ear as he pulled the door open to the empty hallway.

"Alex, catch a ride with Maggie. I need to take Roberto with me."

"Where are you going?" Cliff shouted, standing from his seat now.

"Charlotte is missing."

47

Lee jogged from the exterior door of the jail in the direction of his truck. He saw Roberto leaning against the hood, smoking a cigarette.

"Load up, Roberto!" Lee shouted. "I need your help tonight."

Roberto flicked the cigarette to the pavement. He never hurried, always slow and calculated in his movements. "I am not leaving without Señorita Olivera."

Lee had the cell phone to his ear, still waiting for Grace to pick up on the other end. It worried him she wasn't answering. He ended the call, frustrated, then pressed a button on the screen to phone Maggie. The phone was on speaker and rang once; she picked up.

"Put Alex on the phone," Lee demanded. "Roberto here isn't leaving without permission."

Roberto still leaned against the truck, examining his fingernails now as he waited for his boss to get on the line. Alex picked up the phone and explained to Roberto that he needed to help the Acker family out for the evening. *"Oiga, su hija fue secuestrada*—someone has taken his daughter." Roberto nodded along as he listened to her words. His facial expression and body language changed with each syllable. Roberto looked at Lee and pointed to the driver's side of the pickup, signaling for Lee to get going. The call ended, and Roberto made his way to the passenger-side door. He didn't say anything, he just climbed in and handed the cell phone back to Lee. With the windows down, Lee peeled out of the parking lot and headed in the direction of home.

~

No one from local law enforcement was parked in the driveway when Lee pulled up to the house. The garage door was open, and he could see Grace's vehicle still parked in her spot. As he pulled the truck to a stop, he spotted her sitting on the front steps of the house. He exited the truck and hurried over to her. Roberto took his time stepping out of the vehicle, cautious not to intrude on the delicate moment ahead. He'd seen kidnappings on too many occasions in his home country of El Salvador, and now in his work in Mexico. Many, if not most, did not end well.

"What is happening, Grace?" Lee said. "I have been calling and you didn't pick up."

"Whoever it is, they told me to stay off of the phones. I did not want to risk anything. I knew you would come find me."

Roberto approached quietly. He stood a few paces behind Lee, listening.

"What did the police say?"

"I haven't called them, Lee." Her voice sounded monotone, defeated. "The voice told me no cops. I am not going to anger these people. They have Charlotte, wherever they are."

"How long has she been gone?"

"She went for a run around four thirty this afternoon. The eight-mile loop that she likes to take. You know the one, down to the river and back."

Lee nodded and tried to map the route in his head.

"It got to be close to suppertime and she still wasn't back. I started to worry, so I got in the car and drove the route. I didn't see her anywhere, and it was getting dark."

"Did she take her phone on the run?" Lee asked, certain he already knew the answer.

"No," Grace said with a shake of the head. "I received a call around eight p.m. from a blocked number, though. The voice told me they had Charlotte and we were going to do what they wanted. I tried to get their name, but the coward wouldn't give it to me."

Roberto stepped another two paces closer, and Grace's eyes locked on his for a moment. She didn't say anything to him or even ask who the stranger was.

"The voice told me Alex Olivera had to go back home if I ever wanted to see my daughter again."

"Done," Lee quickly replied. "I can ask her to go home tonight. She is here as a favor, and I am sure she will understand. I'll serve the rest of my life in prison if it means Charlotte can come home unharmed."

"You need assurances first," Roberto said, chiming in for the first time. "Señora Acker, I work with Señorita Olivera and her family. I have seen kidnappings take place my entire life, and I understand how these wolves think when they steal a child from a family. They will act irrationally if we give them what they want right at the beginning. Let me talk to them."

Grace and Lee both locked eyes. Lee motioned for her to step inside the house and they would talk a few minutes alone. Lee turned to Roberto and asked that he wait a few minutes while he and his wife talked privately. As Lee turned to head inside, a set of headlights came rolling down the driveway. It was Alex and Maggie returning from the visit at the jail.

"Do you mind updating them?" Lee asked. "Remember, no law enforcement can be involved."

Roberto nodded. "That's the way I prefer it."

Lee walked inside the house and found Grace waiting in the living room. She was crying now. The sobbing would only take place in private. Grace would never share her raw fear or grief with the outside world. In the darkness, he made his way to a spot beside her on the couch and wrapped his arms around her. They did not say anything to one another for a few minutes, and Lee just listened to their breathing and the low murmur of voices that were in conversation outside.

"Did the voice sound like John Deese?" Lee asked, breaking the silence.

"It was distorted, meant to sound like a robot."

"Did the voice say anything about going to the judge?"

Grace shook her head. "Not specifically."

"That's what we do first, then."

"Lee, are you sure?"

"No, but someone kidnapped our daughter to influence the trial. The judge needs to know, even if we keep it private."

"We have to call the kidnapper back before five thirty tomorrow morning."

"I'll ask Roberto to do it," Lee replied. "The voice is already demanding that Alex Olivera leave. It will make sense for her head of security to place the call."

"Do you trust him?"

"No, but I think we need someone that is less invested handling the negotiations. I believe Roberto has more experience with these types of things. I heard his boss explaining to him that he should do everything in his power to help. He is a mercenary that will do as he is told."

Grace nodded and stood from the couch.

"All I care about is getting her home safe. You make that happen."

"I'll talk to Roberto. Maggie will get in touch with the judge."

48

The prosecution rested at 11:35 a.m. For the benefit of the jury, Maggie feigned surprise and looked over at Michael Hart. When she did, she noticed the tightness in his face. He appeared to struggle with the words as he informed Judge Balk that the prosecution would not call any additional witnesses and would present no other evidence.

"Very well," Judge Balk said, looking from the prosecution's table to the defense. "Does the defense intend to present any evidence?"

Maggie stood from her chair. "The defense will, Your Honor."

Maggie looked across the aisle at Hart. He'd played fair, and she respected that. Trial lawyers strive to represent their clients' interests, but above all they want to win. The *State of Georgia v. Lee Elmer Acker* had captured the nation's attention. Maggie knew that her opponent did not want to just play ball in the highest-profile case of his career, he wanted to put it to the jury for judgment. Maggie doubted that would happen now.

"At this time, ladies and gentlemen of the jury, the prosecution has concluded its case in chief. I am going to go ahead and release you for an early lunch so that the parties can discuss this afternoon's calendar."

The jurors stood from their seats and began filing out the rear door of the courtroom. A few of the twelve looked pleased by the announcement. The trial was moving along at a faster pace than was expected.

Many of the jurors were no doubt concerned with missing the holidays with their families. The conclusion of the prosecution's case lifted their spirits.

After the jury exited the courtroom, Judge Balk looked out onto his packed courtroom and informed those in the gallery that he and the lawyers would be meeting in chambers to discuss matters. An audible groan could be heard from a few journalists seated in the room as the judge explained that he hoped to resume the bench by 3:00 p.m. All rose, and the judge exited through a rear door of his own.

Maggie looked over at Hart again, and the two met eyes. He nodded at her and returned to collecting his files strewn about the prosecution's table. Don Malone was talking in his ear, glancing over at Maggie as he spoke. She expected Malone to seek an interview with her client as to the circumstances of Charlotte Acker's disappearance, a request that would complicate things due to the ongoing murder trial. With a wave of the hand, Malone motioned for Maggie to come over closer.

"What's up?" Maggie said as she approached the two men. A chattering in the courtroom still echoed around the large room as those in the gallery exited the doors to find lunch.

"I need to interview your client and his wife," Malone said in a low voice. He looked behind him at the front rows and noticed both Lucy and Bill Collins's eyes were locked on the trio. "I know you said no law enforcement, but I won't be reaching out to the kidnapper. At least not yet."

"It's up to my client," Maggie whispered.

"Advise your client, Reynolds," Hart said, as if he had decades of experience counseling individuals in the midst of crisis. "We can enlist the GBI to help. I just need a statement or something other than the word of his lawyer."

"This girl is missing," Maggie hissed back. "Let's meet with the judge first. If Balk declares a mistrial, I'll advise my client to interview with Don here."

"I need to tell my victims something."

"No way," Maggie replied. "They could have orchestrated this kidnapping. If they hear it from you, they will know my client let this slip to law enforcement."

"You don't really believe a US senator orchestrated the kidnapping of a seventeen-year-old girl, do you?"

"I don't know," Maggie replied. "I just don't want Charlotte harmed."

They all nodded and went their separate ways. The Collinses' eyes were zeroed in on Maggie as she stepped back to the defense table. She ignored the stares and focused on her client. Lee leaned against the table, looking surprisingly handsome in the brown suit he'd selected for the day's proceedings. Though he looked polished, his eyes could not hide the worry.

"We need to get back to the judge's conference room. Are you ready?"

Lee nodded. "As ready as I'll ever be."

"Let's go."

~

Roberto stood outside the courthouse and made another call to the kidnapper. He listened to the phone ring while he smoked and sipped his third coffee of the morning. Reporters in a line down the sidewalk gave hurried takes on the morning's court proceedings, hoping to make the midday time slots on their respective networks. He chuckled to himself. The hottest news story of the day was merely feet away, but they would never know.

On the fourth ring, the voice picked up. The electronically enhanced words first asked for an update on Alex Olivera's whereabouts. Roberto knew from his experience dealing with kidnappers that the timeline for the return of a hostage would be set only by the kidnapper. There was no use jockeying for control of the conversation, so he informed the stranger that his boss would be returning to Mexico that day.

"Why the delay?" the synthesized voice asked after a noticeable pause. "If you want the girl to go home, get the Mexican woman gone. That was our deal this morning."

Roberto took a pull from his cigarette. He wanted to tell the voice to go to hell, but he chose diplomacy instead. Old guerilla soldiers have a unique characteristic that makes them especially dangerous to deal with —patience.

"As I mentioned this morning, Señorita Olivera rented the private jet that flew her in from Mexico City. We have requested another flight, and the company informed us that an aircraft would arrive at the local airfield by three p.m. The trial itself will not resume until three p.m. today. There is no way for her to testify at the trial now."

"Where is she, then?" the voice snarled.

"I hope you can appreciate the position you put me in when asking a question of this sort, being that I am Señorita Olivera's head of security."

"I have no plans to harm anyone."

"How is Señorita Charlotte?" Roberto asked, pivoting somewhat on the subject. "This morning you mentioned she had not slept yet. Is she resting?"

"I gave her something to help," the voice replied.

The comment made Roberto's veteran stomach churn. He hated animals that drugged young girls, and he knew what could happen once the drugs kicked in.

"I hope she is resting, undisturbed."

"Once you Mexicans are gone, she will be home with daddy and mommy. Until then, she is mine."

The phone clicked, and Roberto pulled the phone from his ear to check the call time. Scrolling through the few contacts saved in the phone, he found Grace Acker's number. She picked up on the second ring, diving right in.

"Any news?"

"I spoke to the kidnapper," Roberto said. "We will have until three p.m."

"What about Charlotte?" she asked. "Did you ask about her?"

"She is fine," Roberto quickly replied. The half-truth sounded convincing enough. "He told me he has no plans to hurt anyone."

"Do you believe him?"

Roberto did not respond. He stared down at his boots and waited for Grace to ask another question. Silence waited on the other end of the line. He knew a mother would hold out hope until the very end.

"She is going to be okay, Señora Acker."

"And if she isn't?"

"Then you do what people do when they lose someone they love."

"Don't even talk to me about grieving right now."

"I didn't say anything about grief," Roberto replied. "But, yes, grieving would be inevitable."

"Then what do people do?"

Roberto smiled into the cell phone. "They kill, Señora Acker. They hunt down and kill the person who took that loved one from this world."

Roberto could almost hear the gears turning on the other side of the phone call. He had no doubt that the Ackers would retaliate if their daughter was not returned home. He'd met a number of wealthy people in his work for the Olivera family. Men and women that put their families first, acting as though they were above reproach. He knew those people could be just as dangerous as the person with nothing to lose. Encroachment on a wealthy family's child never goes unnoticed either, a fact the kidnapper would be wise to recognize.

"Let's hope it doesn't come to that."

49

Maggie Reynolds took the lead on the discussion. She leaned forward, her elbows resting against the mahogany conference table. There was no court reporter in the room, as this meeting would not become a part of the trial's record. Lee Acker sat to her right. Michael Hart sat across from her with his lead case agent, Don Malone. At one end of the table, Judge John Balk sat with his robe off and sleeves rolled up. At the other end, Alex Olivera sat with her arms folded across her chest.

As Maggie looked around the table, she could feel the anticipation bubbling. It was the moment, in her mind, that the case could turn the corner and her legacy could be built upon. Rarely can one recognize momentous events in their professional life. The steps toward greatness are often so small that it takes personal reflection to appreciate the progress made. Still, every now and then there are bursts of progress. Opportunities that present themselves as pivotal moments in one's professional life. Maggie was in the midst of hers. The defense was now the aggressor, the truth seeker meant to bring justice. Maggie held the power now, and she did not plan to give it up.

"As you know, Charlotte Acker was kidnapped yesterday evening."

Maggie paused, considering her words. She had spoken at length with Judge Balk and Michael Hart by phone in the morning's early hours. She'd updated them on the kidnapping, and they'd agreed to listen to the witness's testimony before making any decisions.

"The only demand that the kidnapper has made to the Acker family is one that would affect the integrity of this trial. The kidnapper, whoever he or she is, gave the ultimatum that if Alex Olivera testifies at trial, Charlotte won't come home."

"What are you asking me to do, then, Ms. Reynolds?" Judge Balk said, scratching the stubble on his neck. "I can't in good conscious let Ms. Olivera testify for the defense. None of us can go along with that, not knowing what we know now."

"I agree, Your Honor, and my client certainly does not want that," Maggie replied, looking over at Lee's face for a reaction. "It's fair to say that he does not really want us to be having this meeting right now."

Lee nodded. "That's right. The kidnapper told us not to involve law enforcement or the press. Agent Malone here sitting across the table has the entire Georgia Bureau of Investigation at his fingertips. I'd say this conversation puts my little girl's life at risk."

"I agree, Mr. Acker," Judge Balk added.

"Then these are grounds for a mistrial," Hart said, his words hesitant.

"These may be, Mr. Hart," Judge Balk mused. "I'm not sure what else we can do at the moment. The implications of this kidnapping, the influence it has on the trial, creates a number of reversible issues that I cannot let fester for appeal."

"Maybe so, Your Honor," Maggie said, urging the conversation along. "I'd like you to hear what Ms. Olivera has to say, though. It will change Mr. Hart's and the GBI's perspective on this murder. It may even change your perspective, Judge."

A silence blanketed the room as the judge appeared to consider his options. Frowning, he pulled a pen from the chest pocket of his dress shirt and scribbled a few lines on the legal pad in front of him. The scratching of the pen sounded forceful, frustrated.

"Let's hear from your witness," Judge Balk said, exasperation in his voice. "Do you have any issue with this, Mr. Hart?"

"No, sir. I think this is the right thing to do." Hart's demeanor surprised

Maggie, and she appreciated his support. "Whoever kidnapped Mr. Acker's daughter needs to be located and prosecuted. This might help us do that."

"Very well," Judge Balk said with a nod in Maggie's direction. "Swear your witness in."

~

Roberto climbed into the passenger seat of Tim Dawson's SUV and introduced himself with a handshake. Dawson pulled away from the curb of the courthouse and began the trek toward the river. Though he was on administrative leave, Dawson still enjoyed his speeding privileges. It was one of the perks of the job he would miss the most.

"I need a weapon," Roberto said as he stared out the window. "Can you lend me anything?"

The men rode in silence for a while as the vehicle picked up speed. Doing eighty-five down a rough county road, Roberto buckled his seat belt to settle in for the ride. The brick buildings of the city's quaint downtown were out of view, and they began to pass small houses and single-wide trailers with unkempt yards.

"I have a tactical rifle, two Glock handguns, and a less-lethal shotgun. I'll give you a handgun and the shotgun," Tim said, one hand draped over the steering wheel. "I also have an extra Kevlar vest if you want it."

Roberto kept his eyes fixed on the road ahead as the SUV made an abrupt turn off the pavement. The vehicle crossed onto a steep clay road that led toward a wood line. The SUV fishtailed slightly as it climbed the road to a gate that blocked the entrance to the path into the woods. A sign on the gate read, "No Trespassing—Kelley Hill Plantation." Dawson hopped out of the SUV and grabbed a set of bolt cutters from the rear of the vehicle. A sensor in the SUV dinged as Roberto watched the agent cut the chain at one end of the gate and kick it open. He liked this guy already.

"This is a plantation?" Roberto asked as Dawson returned to the driver's seat in the vehicle. "A plantation is something different back in my home country."

"Well, they used to be something different here, too."

Roberto nodded. Both men understood that exploitation and oppression of people was not unique to any one country.

"We are going to park up here," Dawson said, pointing to a clearing. "We can hike the rest of the way in."

"Do you know if they have any security?" Roberto asked.

"They have a few bodyguard types, and I'm guessing there are some surveillance cameras as we get closer to the main house." Dawson paused, then said, "I am not looking to get into a gunfight, though."

"No one ever is," Roberto replied. "I'll make the call once we get stopped."

Dawson reached under his seat and pulled a bottle of water out to take a few swigs. He edged the SUV off the path and onto the grassy clearing. Roberto stepped out of the passenger side and put the phone to his ear. Dawson pulled out his own cell phone and texted Maggie to let her know they were on the plantation now.

Roberto stood at the rear of the SUV, in conversation with the kidnapper. Dawson listened to the only end of the conversation he could hear. He noted the talent exhibited by Roberto as he kept the kidnapper engaged in a discussion. The way he discussed the hostage and kidnapping made Roberto sound more like a coconspirator than a negotiator for the Ackers. It scared him how effective that could be.

"I have to see the girl today," Roberto said into the phone. "My boss will be leaving on a flight in thirty minutes, but I am staying behind to make sure this is handled for the Ackers. The boss has directed me to do so."

Roberto pointed at one of the Kevlar vests in the SUV's rear storage and motioned for Dawson to hand it over. As Roberto listened intently to the voice on the other side of the phone, he began putting the vest on.

"Yes, I understand your concerns. These people are not savvy like you and me, though. They don't have any interest in retaliation right now. They are simple family people that just want their child. Once the girl is home, the Ackers will ask law enforcement to investigate. You know how inept these locals are. They botched the whole murder investigation already; you think they will be able to figure you out? No witnesses or cooperating parties. There will be no leads for them to go on with this situation."

Roberto gave Dawson a sharp wink. By the way he spoke, there was no doubt the old guerilla soldier had his fair share of experience living on the other side of the law. His authenticity helped forge a necessary connection with the kidnapper.

"Besides, I have killed hostages before," Roberto said, smiling as he continued to inure himself to the captor. "You don't want this on your conscience. It's terrible, I assure you."

After a long pause, Roberto pumped his fist slightly. He then looked at Dawson and gave him a thumbs-up.

"The exchange will be tonight, then. *Muy bien*. Yes, I will tell him to meet you there."

50

Lee slowed his truck at the entrance to the public landing and rolled the driver's side window down. He cut the engine and listened to the water rushing by on the riverbed below. It had been some years, but he'd put a kayak in at this spot on the river before. It was an area that proved simple to navigate at night, making it popular with the summer fishermen that chose to trailer their boats in for twilight fishing. There would be no one fishing tonight, though. At thirty-four degrees outside, few had much interest in sitting in a boat on a river, much less wading into the water with a flyrod in hand. For South Georgians, the spring and summer were for fishing, the fall and winter for hunting.

Lee checked his watch and decided it was time. He cranked the truck back up and followed the road down to the landing. With a hand hanging out the window, he felt the temperature drop a few degrees more as the roadway neared the Chattahoochee. The truck's engine and exhaust echoed through the forest, giving those that waited for him ample time to prepare for his arrival. Lee felt his heart rate increase as the road opened up to the dark parking lot. He slowed the truck, urging his eyes to spot something in the darkness. Swinging the headlights around the open parking area, he saw nothing but an abandoned boat trailer and the remnants of a high school bonfire.

With nothing to do but wait, Lee backed the truck into a parking space that faced the entrance to the landing. He opened the door and stepped out into the night air. The stars shined bright in the crisp night sky, surrounding the crescent moon. As Lee's eyes scanned the sky for familiar constellations, he heard a whistle in the darkness. He looked around the dark parking lot. Nothing. Lee whistled in response and started walking in the direction of the boat ramp.

As Lee approached the ramp, he saw a black inflatable boat waiting at the edge of the river. The faint light of the moon reflected off the water, barely allowing Lee to make out the outline of an individual clad in black.

"Let's go!" a voice said, calling out from the side of the boat. "Cut the monitor off your ankle and toss it in the woods before you get in the boat."

A pair of pliers landed near Lee's feet and skidded across the pavement. He picked the tool up and cut the rubber band around his ankle. He then lobbed the device well into the forest brush before taking another few steps toward the boat. He spotted the outline of a weapon in the man's hand, and as Lee approached, he began to make out the face of the individual.

"Where is my daughter?" Lee asked. "I've held up my end of the deal. Olivera is long gone back to Mexico."

"You haven't held up shit, Acker. Get in the boat. We are heading upriver."

"Is Charlotte there?"

The man paused, then motioned with the handgun for Lee to get in the boat. Lee obliged and stepped onto the air deck of the black watercraft. The small outboard motor started up, and the two-stroke engine idled as the two men shoved off from the bank and into the deeper water. Once they were out into the current, the man handed Lee a black sack.

"Put this on."

"This isn't necessary," Lee replied. "I grew up fishing this river and running along its banks. I'll be able to guess where we stop regardless of whether I have a sack on my head."

"I am not going to ask you again," the man said. "Put the mask on and shut up."

Lee slipped the bag over this head and settled into the seat. The engine hummed and then roared to life. They were heading upriver.

~

The engine slowed, and Lee could feel the boat begin to inch closer to the shoreline. The water was shallow in this part of the river, and Lee could hear a familiar set of rapids no more than a hundred yards north. He knew where they were.

"You can take that sack off your head," the man said. "I'll bring us in over by this clearing up ahead, and you can hop out to help pull us onto the bank."

Lee removed the stuffy wool sack and felt the cool breeze on his face. He scanned the tree line, searching the shore for Charlotte.

"Pull the boat in up there instead," Lee replied, pointing to the edge of a sandy bank some twenty-five yards up the river. "That'll save me from jumping waist-deep into this water."

The man nodded and maneuvered the boat to the spot. Lee rolled his pant legs up to his knees and pulled his boots off. When the boat hit the loose sediment with a thud, Lee swung both legs over the side. The water felt chilly on his ankles and the backs of his calves. He dug his toes into the riverbed and pushed the boat further onto the bank. He then grabbed the thick nylon cord at the nose of the boat and heaved.

"Are we good?" the man asked, deferring to Lee on the positioning of the boat.

"Yeah, come on," Lee replied, extending a helping hand to the man. "Let's give it one more pull when you hop out."

The man extended his left hand to Lee, leaving his rib cage exposed. Lee grasped the hand and brought a fist against the man's side. The blow hammered the man and knocked the wind from his lungs. Lee pulled the balled fist back again, swinging a second time as hard as he could. Connecting again, he felt bone break on contact. The man rolled to the ground, and Lee went for the sidearm tucked in the rear of his pants. Lee pressed the man's face into the dirt with one hand and mashed the barrel of the gun into the center of his back.

"Don't scream," Lee said, whispering with as much force as he could muster. "I'll pull this trigger if I have to."

"What the hell, Acker!" replied the man. "Are you nuts?"

Lee grabbed the nylon cord from the end of the boat and wrapped it around the man's wrists. He tied the knot tight and then set the man upright. Lee slipped the handgun in the waistband of his pants and took a few steps back. Lee's heart was banging away in his chest, adrenaline still coursing through his veins.

"Where is my daughter?" Lee said, breathing heavily.

"Acker, you are risking her life by pulling this shit," the man replied. "We were planning to make an exchange tonight. Didn't that Mexican guy tell you all of this?"

"Is she up at the main house?" Lee said, ignoring the question.

"I don't know yet. I was supposed to get a text with the location."

Lee stepped closer to the man again and dug into his pockets for a cell phone. He found the device and pulled it out. He turned it around to the man, allowing the facial recognition to unlock the keypad. The first unopened message was from "JD": *Bring him up to the top of Parker's Knoll. Graveside.* Lee typed a quick response: *On the way.*

"I assume you and John Deese are doing the Collinses' bidding now?"

The man didn't answer; he didn't have to. Lee shook his head and dialed Grace's number. She picked up on the third ring.

"This is Lee," he began, knowing she wouldn't recognize the unfamiliar phone number. "It's just like we thought. Deese has Charlotte. I am about to go meet him at the family cemetery on Kelley Hill Plantation."

"Do you want me to meet you over there?" Grace asked.

"Yes. Get in the car and head this way. Be careful."

"Lee, wait, should I bring anything?"

"Bring something for protection," he replied after a short pause. "I'll see you soon."

Lee slipped the cell phone into his back pocket and turned to the man on the ground. Lee grabbed the sack used to cover his head on the boat ride and twisted it around until it resembled a makeshift gag. Lee wrapped it around the man's head and mouth to stifle any yelling. As Lee turned to make his way up an elevated path to the cemetery, the angry murmurs of the man dropped an octave in defeat.

"Someone will be back for you eventually," Lee called back. "Don't worry."

∾

When Lee reached the edge of the trail, he pulled the confiscated cell phone from his back pocket and typed a text: *This is Lee. At Kelley Hill and looking for Charlotte. Calling you now. Listen and record what you can. We may need it later.* He mashed send on the text message, then dialed Maggie's number. She picked up on the second ring. He placed the device in his front pocket and kept moving toward the family cemetery.

Lee looked up at the grassy summit of Parker's Knoll and saw two individuals seated among the headstones. As Lee pushed his way up the trail, the smaller of the two finally came into view. It was his only daughter.

"Hold on, now," came a familiar voice from the taller individual. "Stop right there, Lee. Let's talk a minute before you get any closer."

Though Lee did have his suspicions, the words still took a moment to register in his mind. Shocked by the sound of the man's voice, he kept walking a few more paces before he realized what he was doing.

"I asked you to hold on, Lee."

Lee stopped on the spot—staring in disbelief at the face of Bill Collins.

"Did one of my employees get left behind at the boat?" Bill asked. "It seems I asked him to escort you over this evening."

"Charlotte, are you okay?" Lee said, ignoring the question. "Are you hurt? Tell me they didn't hurt you."

"I'm okay," she replied, her voice calmer than he'd expected. "I'm not hurt, Dad."

Lee looked up at the night sky and felt tears burning in his eyes. He knew his daughter was strong, but she looked so grown up from where he stood. The little girl was gone forever, replaced now by a young woman that had the iron stomach to act calmly in the face of danger. He returned his gaze to his daughter, and she gave him a reassuring smile, one that he would never forget.

"I've done what you asked," Lee said, directing his words at Bill Collins. "Alex Olivera is gone. She went back to Mexico hours ago."

"She testified, though, didn't she?" Bill replied. "She gave a statement to the judge. She told him everything she knew."

Lee paused, considering his response. It came of little surprise that the most well-connected man in the state was able to find out about their private meeting with Judge Balk. Lee wondered if the information came straight from the judge himself.

"I am just trying to clear my name," Lee replied. "Can't you understand that?"

"I can understand what you're doing, Lee. I had a family once, with a reputation to uphold for a child that loved me."

"Then you understand?"

"There was a time in my life when I certainly would have," Bill said, his words trailing off. "Now, I am not sure it matters all that much to me. A man's legacy is all he has, and your little stunt with Olivera testifying has threatened mine."

Light flashed across the edge of the grassy knoll, and soon Lee saw headlights bouncing into view. They all stared at the vehicle as it approached. Lee recognized the driver.

"Mom!" Charlotte yelled, waving her hands. "Over here!"

"What is she doing here?" Bill asked.

"She's here to take my daughter home. You have me here now. You can let Charlotte go."

Grace made her way across the field, stepping carefully around the headstones scattered around the cemetery. As she approached the group, another set of headlights crept up the path and pulled to a stop behind Grace's vehicle. Grace kept walking straight toward Charlotte and stretched her arms out wide as she prepared for an embrace with her child. Bill did not stop her, stepping to the side as Charlotte hugged her mother.

"It looks like we have everyone here," Bill said with a nod toward the second vehicle. "Let's all stay awhile and visit."

Doors slammed on the second vehicle, and the murmur of two individuals continuing conversation joined the sounds of the night. The two approached slowly, and Lee noticed a rifle slung over the shoulder of the man exiting the driver's seat. Within moments, he recognized the pretentious saunter of John Deese.

"Lucy!" Bill called out. "Bring John over here, and let's all talk a few minutes."

Grace's eyes cut over to her husband. Her expression was not one of surprise or anger. It was one of fear.

"John," Lee said with a stiff nod. "Mrs. Collins, how are you doing, ma'am?"

"Fine, Lee."

"You are all involved in this?" Grace said, interrupting her husband's cordial greeting. "This is insane."

Lucy ignored the question and walked the few steps left between her and Jake's headstone. She touched it cautiously with her hand, rubbing the smooth edges of the marble.

"Jake would agree that this is insane," Grace said, doubling down on her previous statement. "He would hate this."

"Don't you dare act like you knew anything about the man my son became," Lucy snapped back at Grace. "You were just a teenage girl when you knew my son. The world changed; my son changed."

"I know he wouldn't agree with you kidnapping my daughter."

"It was his daughter, too," Lucy fired back, her eyes zeroed in on Grace. The retort cut through the night like a knife. "You kept him from knowing, Grace. And by the time he found out, it was too late."

Grace shifted her feet and kept her eyes focused on her accuser.

"You don't know what you're talking about."

"Oh, yes I do. I've seen the DNA test. I found it in my son's study. I know she is my granddaughter. I know he confronted you over it and you hid it from everyone, even your own family."

"What is she talking about, Mom?" Charlotte said, her hand clasped in her mother's now. "Tell me what's going on."

Lucy stepped closer to Charlotte and reached out a hand. Charlotte ignored the gesture and kept her eyes on her mother, waiting for a response. The silence felt damning.

"My son, Jake, was your biological father," Lucy said softly. "I'm your grandmother, and this is your grandfather."

Charlotte turned her eyes to Lucy's outstretched hand. She was unwilling to take it, and her mother was trying to find the voice to speak.

"You aren't my family," Charlotte finally said. "I don't care what you say."

The anger did not surprise Lucy. In fact, she'd expected it. Her son had a temper when he was young, and he'd benefited from that fire at times. With a firm voice, Lucy used her words to exert control over the conversation. She did not want tensions to spiral.

"Charlotte Elmer Acker may be your given name, but my family's story runs through your veins. This soil under your feet is family land, and your relatives are buried in this very cemetery." Lucy paused a moment before pushing forward. "Our families have always been tied together by love and conflict. This chapter tonight is just another part of our shared history. You may consider yourself an Acker, but you are part of my family, too."

Lucy walked over to a headstone that was a row over from Jake's. She took a seat on it. Her strong voice travelled well in the quiet night air, and she began to tell the history of Colonel Nathan J. Parker. Her version, much like her husband's rendition at Jake's funeral, was told with the skill of a seasoned storyteller. As she approached the fateful hours leading up to Parker's demise, the story took an off-ramp.

"Nathan Parker's wife, Sarah, knew her husband's killer quite well. I have never been able to figure out how the two came to meet, but her journals indicate that Joseph Cobb would visit when Sarah's husband was away. As Parker's travel schedule increased, the passionate meetings only became more frequent between Sarah and Cobb. The two fell deeper in love with one another, setting events in motion that affect us to this very day."

Lucy paused and glanced over at Grace.

"One summer day, the couple's secret was uncovered. A man that had worked for Sarah's husband was walking through the woods. He came upon two horses tied up by the river, their riders sunning and making love alongside the waters of the Chattahoochee. The man watched from the tree line, then headed off to find Parker."

Charlotte listened from where she stood, studying Lucy as she spoke. Emotions swam through her mind and body, suspending her in a dream-like state.

"The man knew that the information he'd stumbled upon was invaluable. Cobb and Parker already feuded over the manner in which their timber businesses should operate. Cobb believed that the Black laborers that worked in his camps should be treated the same as the whites. He paid them according to their skill and dealt with the men based on that alone. Because of this position, Cobb's wages were higher, and he employed the best laborers in the area. Northern financiers took notice and began to invest in Cobb's outfit, allowing it to grow. Cobb started to amass more land, and he built more camps for turpentine work. He cleared acreage with motivated employees and drove logs downriver to the mills with an efficiency that threatened Parker's operations. For those that knew Nathan Parker, the threat of losing Sarah would only push him to the breaking point."

Bill Collins stood off to the side and admired his wife's ability to command the attention of a group. He'd always found her natural ability as a speaker to be impressive, even intimidating at times. It always puzzled him that she'd conceded the spotlight to him, opting to stand by his side. It was only one of the many sacrifices that she'd been forced to make as a wife and mother—sacrifices he would never understand.

"Nathan Parker was well-connected and ran a sophisticated timber business for the times. He approached Cobb with a proposal that would help the men control a large market share of both the Alabama and Georgia timber industries. An endeavor that would allow the men to push into Florida and eventually Louisiana."

"Cobb rejected it, though," Charlotte said, finally cutting into Lucy's narrative. "I'm familiar with the story. We spent a week learning about Arthur Kelley in a high school history course. This conflict over the merger of their operations led to the death of Parker. It also led to the appearance of Arthur Kelley in our local history."

"Do you know why Cobb rejected the proposal?" Lucy asked.

"I am sure there was more than one reason," Charlotte replied, her arms crossed. "After what you just told us, it probably had more to do with Sarah than anything else."

"Smart girl," Lucy remarked.

"Our history teacher told us that Joseph Cobb didn't want to use the political power of the state to create an unfair advantage, and he didn't want to disenfranchise his Black neighbors any further. He was progressive for his time and paid a price for his views."

"Color me impressed," Bill said from where he stood.

Charlotte ignored the comment.

"Cobb left the service of the Confederate Army because he did not believe in the cause, Mr. Collins. He'd read the words from the Emancipation Proclamation and chose a different path. I've always admired his story, even if others don't."

"What else did you learn about this storied rivalry between Nathan Parker and Joseph Cobb?" Bill asked.

"Cobb didn't trust the terms of the venture with Parker. The proposal was not a partnership. It required Cobb to hand over key decision-making in his operation to Parker. Cobb did not want to do that. He'd built something of his own and he didn't want to give it up, even if that meant political repercussions."

"And?" Lucy asked with a smile.

"And, so it seems, Joseph Cobb was in love with Sarah Parker. He'd most likely asked her to leave her husband to be with him. That's not exactly the recipe for a successful working relationship."

John Deese began a slow clap from where he stood, the rifle leaning against a headstone nearby. Deese had a large smile plastered on his face and started to speak. Before he could say anything, Lee pulled the pistol from his waistband and trained it on Deese.

"Easy, John. Don't make any movements toward that rifle."

"I'm not going anywhere," Deese replied, his hands in his pockets. "You don't need the weapon, Lee. We are all friends here."

"I wouldn't exactly call us friends, John."

"How about family, then?" John said with a smile. "Hell, we were all close as brothers until that fishing trip to Costa Rica. You remember that trip, Lee?"

"I remember the trip," Lee replied. "Best news of my life came through the phone on that trip."

Lee turned his attention to Charlotte, placing his free hand on his heart while speaking to her.

"Your mother called me frantically in the middle of the night. She'd been searching for me to tell me the good news. The news that I would be a father and she a mother. It was a wonderful—"

"You remember your fight with Jake?" Deese asked, interrupting the moment.

Lee refocused his attention on Deese. "I was there."

"Jake told you he'd slept with Grace quite a few times that summer, too. I remember the fight because you, old buddy, didn't know the two of them were still hooking up. Jake told you they hadn't been using protection, and he thought the baby might be his."

"And I remember telling him she had picked me. That she wanted me to be the father, not him. There was nothing else to it."

"Now you know the truth, though, don't you, Lee? You were wrong all those years ago, and so was Grace."

"I wasn't wrong, nor would I trade the last seventeen years for anything."

"Maybe not," John said. "That'll never fly in front of a jury, though. They'll think you killed your old friend once he told you about the DNA test."

"There won't be another jury trial," Lee replied calmly. "At least not one that puts me in the crosshairs for Jake's murder. They could end up judging you, though."

"We will have to see, won't we?" Deese mocked.

Lee looked over at Grace and motioned toward the vehicles parked nearby.

"Go ahead and take Charlotte home. I won't be far behind."

"Come with us, Lee," Grace urged him. "This has already all gotten out of hand."

"Yeah, Lee," Deese added. "You go on home. Don't you worry about us. We will be here tomorrow."

"Go home, Grace," Lee said, ignoring the comment from the man on the other side of his pistol. "Trust me."

"When did you find out?" Deese chided. "Please tell me it was tonight."

Lee continued to ignore him as Grace pulled Charlotte along with her toward the vehicle. Bill and Lucy Collins watched from where they were. They appeared unsurprised by the turn in events.

"Did you tell him, Mom?" Charlotte asked, digging her feet in as she waited for an answer.

"Sweetie, this is complicated."

"Don't lie to me!"

"Charlotte, this is—"

"Dad, did you know?" Charlotte screamed, spinning in the direction of her father. "Did Mom tell you about Jake? Did she tell you about this DNA test?"

Lee's eyes moved from the end of the pistol to his daughter. She was standing some twenty yards away now.

"I found out from Jake," Lee said, his words coming out slowly. "He and I met one night not long before his death. He told me everything he knew. We've talked about that conversation, Charlotte. I explained everything in my study a few nights ago."

"You told me grandpa had been murdered," Charlotte snapped back. "You told me about the plans to wall the southern border off to exploit foreign workers and better control the illegal drug trade coming in. You didn't tell me anything about you and Jake discussing a DNA test! You didn't tell me that he was my real father."

She was angry, and she had the right to be. The words—*real father*—burned Lee's heart as soon as they were uttered.

"You are right, Charlotte. I didn't tell you the part about the DNA test."

"So, what, you planned just to keep this from me?"

"I'm not sure. I wanted to tell you about it, though. I wanted to tell you it didn't matter. That I would always be your father and would love you forever."

"You didn't, though, did you?" she replied, a chill in her voice. "You thought if I knew Jake was my real father that I might still not believe your story about grandpa or the wall. That I might suspect you killed him."

"I didn't kill him!" Lee shouted, the pistol shaking in his hand.

The words carried through the woods that surrounded them, their earnestness unmistakable. They hung in the air, like a hawk prepared to strike its prey.

"Then, who did?" Charlotte whispered. "Who killed him, Dad?"

"Charlotte, let's go," Grace said, putting a hand on her daughter's back.

"Don't touch me," Charlotte said, raising her voice again. "You lied to me, Mom. I'll never forget that."

Grace turned to look over at John Deese. He gave her a smirk and looked back toward the pistol trained on his chest.

"Who did it?" Charlotte asked, walking a few steps toward her father. "Someone here knows, and I am tired of the lying. If Jake was my biological father, then I deserve to know."

Charlotte's eyes scanned around the circle. She looked like a bull in the ring, waiting for a challenger.

"You are right," Lucy said, stepping forward. As she did, she pulled a handgun of her own out and pointed the barrel at Lee. "You do deserve the truth, Charlotte."

"Then tell me the truth," Charlotte quickly replied. The appearance of the second weapon did not faze her. "Someone here knows."

"I can promise you this," Lucy said, her hands steady as they pointed the pistol in Lee's direction. "I'll always be honest with you, Charlotte."

"Then tell me."

"I had to shoot him," Lucy said softly. "I had to protect the family's legacy, our family's legacy. My son had changed, Charlotte. He'd forgotten that family is everything."

Charlotte's hands covered her mouth. They all stood there in silence, letting the confession surround them. Lee looked at the faces of both Bill and John, trying to gauge their expressions in the darkness.

"Now you all know," Lucy said, her words slow and somber.

"Grace, take Charlotte home," Bill added from where he stood. "Enough has been said in front of the girl for one night."

Grace turned to look at her husband.

"I won't be far behind, Grace. Now, go."

∾

The vehicle's interior dome light faded once the doors shut. Charlotte sat in the front passenger seat and buckled her seat belt. She rubbed her hands together, looking forward to the heater that might thaw her from the cold. The engine cranked, and they started back down the path that led away from the grassy knoll. Charlotte rolled the window down and looked back toward the group. She gave her father a small wave as the vehicle pulled away. He waved back. She was angry with him, but she looked forward to seeing him when he got home.

Once the vehicle reached the bottom of the hill, the sound of the road under the tires changed as the rubber met gravel. The roadway would lead them to the plantation's exit. The cold night air started to rush by the open window as the car picked up speed. A quiet hung in the air, making Charlotte uneasy.

"He will be home soon," Charlotte said, looking over at her mother. "We can figure this out."

Her mother's eyes remained fixed on the road ahead, and the quiet returned. As Charlotte waited for her mother's response, the unmistakable crack of a gunshot cut through the night. A second and a third rang out soon after, sounding different than the first. Charlotte looked over at her mother and waited for her to say something, for her to turn the car around. The vehicle never slowed as Grace simply mashed the buttons on her door to roll the driver and passenger windows up. Cheeks glistening from the tears, eyes fixed on the road ahead.

51

She felt mud from the wet ground speckle her calves and running shorts as she made the last push up the hill. Digging deep, she ignored the burning in her legs and maintained focus on the makeshift finish line ahead. Charlotte could see her coach standing some fifty yards uphill, her rain jacket's hood up and stopwatch in hand.

"Push it, Acker!" cried the coach. "All the way through the line!"

Rain had fallen in steady sheets the entire five-kilometer run. As Charlotte crossed the finish line, the coach called out the final time. She was under nineteen minutes. A solid showing for the day's sloshy conditions. Charlotte's coach looked over at her and flashed a big smile.

"Beautiful day for a run in the woods, right?"

"Wouldn't want to be anywhere else, Coach."

"That's what I like to hear, girl. You are leading the freshmen pack today!"

The coach turned her attention back to the other young runners on the team that were making their way up the hill. Charlotte stood at the edge of the trail and watched her teammates navigate the slippery incline. She shouted words of encouragement as each finished the time trial. They were all stand-out runners back home. All the type of top-tier talent that flocked to Lane County, Oregon, to run for the Ducks.

"It doesn't rain like this back home in Arizona," complained a teammate nearby as she sucked wind. "I'm pretty sure I'm ten pounds heavier when all this water and wind is knocking me around on the trails. It killed my time today."

"Leave those excuses in Arizona," the coach yelled back at the group. "The conditions sure didn't affect Acker today."

"She is a Georgia girl, Coach. They get raised running in the woods!"

The rain slackened as the freshman women huddled around their coach for a few words on the day's training session. Most still had their hands on their heads or hips, recovering from the day's run. The coach expressed her displeasure with the team's overall effort and outlined her plan for improvement. The criticism was harsh, but the newly minted college athletes listened intently and vowed to work harder. They were some of the best freshman runners in the nation, and their coach expected them to start acting like it.

"You are all dismissed," the coach said. "I'll see you in the morning at five thirty for practice."

The group gave a collective nod and started downhill toward their parked vehicles. As Charlotte made her way down the trail, she admired the redwood and cedar trees that lined the Jory soil path. Sunlight peeked out from behind the clouds and cut between the towering trees. A humidity hung in the air, moisture left over from the heavy rain showers. When the water droplets caught the afternoon sunlight, colors flashed in the tiny prisms. Charlotte enjoyed the beauty in her new state. The new zip code made her feel like she had a chance at distancing herself from the past she feared would forever define her days ahead.

"Can you hang back a second?" came the coach's voice behind Charlotte. "I want to talk to you about something."

"Yes, ma'am," Charlotte said, turning back toward her coach. "I know I was dragging at the end of the time trial today; I am going to focus on my training more. I'll improve, Coach. I promise."

"That's not what this is about," the coach said, dismissing the comment with her hand. "You have been impressive this first month on the team. I have high expectations for your career here as a Duck."

"I hope to meet those expectations, Coach. What can I do you for you, then?"

The coach paused a moment and looked down the trail as the other women on the team distanced themselves further from the conversation.

"I saw that *60 Minutes* will be running the special tonight that focuses on your family."

"That's right," Charlotte replied, shifting her feet as she answered. "They interviewed me for a portion of the story."

"How much have you told your teammates or classmates about the murders?"

"Not a whole lot. Most people, once they hear my name, put two and two together. No one has really asked me to talk about it here at school, though."

"Well, if you want to talk about it with me, I'm always available to do that."

"Thank you, but I'm getting through things. Deciding to come out here for school was the right choice for me. The only thing I miss from back home is my family, what is left of it, at least."

The coach nodded, and they started down the trail together.

"How is your mother doing?" the coach asked. "I remember meeting her the week you moved in for school."

"She is getting by. I have an uncle that was released from prison a few days after everything happened with my dad. I know that makes us sound like a bunch of rednecks, but my Uncle Cliff is a good person. He has been there for us. He works in the family business and checks in on my mom from time to time."

"That's good to hear," the coach replied. "I received a call not too long ago from a man that told me he was your uncle. I remember the call well. A man with a thick Southern accent asked me to keep an eye on the best athlete to ever leave South Georgia—'Charlie Acker.'"

"That would be my Uncle Cliff," Charlotte replied with a grin. "He thinks I'll be running in the Olympics one day."

"That's the dream," the coach replied. "You have to put the work in to make it a reality, though."

Charlotte nodded. "Yes, ma'am."

They stopped at the bottom of the path. Charlotte watched her team-mates loading up into their vehicles. They were all strong and confident runners, their bold futures ahead of them.

"Do you know if there will be a trial this fall?"

"It's set to begin in a couple of weeks," Charlotte said. "I may have to go back to testify. I assure you I'll keep up with my training and schoolwork, though."

"I have no doubt."

"Maybe I'll be able to let it all go once that woman gets what she deserves."

52

When Maggie opened her eyes, she lay in bed for a while listening to the sounds of the boat as it creaked and groaned with the Gulf waves underneath. They would arrive in Key Largo later that morning, and there the boat would stay for the winter, or at least until it was sold. The sailboat's aging owner could no longer navigate the trip from southern Alabama to the Keys, so Tim offered to take the helm as a favor. Maggie tagged along so she could disconnect for a few days from her practice. The trip also gave her the opportunity to spend quality time with her fiancé, a man that continued to surprise her.

Maggie's eyes searched around the cabin and found the digital weather monitor on the wall. The temperature outside registered at fifty-five degrees. She wrapped the bed covers around her body and rolled out of bed to search for her travelling companion. She found him seated at the rear of the boat, drinking coffee. He wore a pair of swim trunks and a waterproof jacket. A radio played from a speaker near his seat, and she listened for a moment as Tim whistled along with the tune. She couldn't remember ever asking if the former lawman could play an instrument.

"Sounds like you might be able to carry a tune there, sailor," Maggie said as she stepped up onto the deck.

A gusty breeze passed over the boat and caused the sail above to clap as it shifted with the changing winds. Tim's eyes moved from the horizon to the sound of her voice. The expression on his face told Maggie he hadn't heard what she said. Still, he stopped whistling the tune and smiled at the sight of her.

"It's going to be a nice one today," Tim hollered over, eyeing the bed covers wrapped around her body. "We should be off the water by eleven. Did you bring a jacket up with you?"

"You told me clothes were optional on this trip."

Maggie walked over to take a seat next to him. Tim scooted over to make room and put an arm around her shoulders after she sat.

"I assume that under this blanket you are wearing the same thing I left you in last night?"

"Those investigative skills haven't left you yet," Maggie replied with a grin.

Tim reached under the bench seat and found a thermos. He handed Maggie a mug and unscrewed the top to the metal container of coffee. The black liquid steamed as he poured coffee into the waiting mug. Its aroma struggled against the salt smell in the morning air, a battle it would ultimately lose.

"The *60 Minutes* interview was last night," Tim said, a hint of caution in his voice. "How do you think you came off?"

"Who knows," Maggie replied with a shrug. "I'm glad we didn't watch it. I didn't get a good vibe from the producers when they came over to interview me. It felt like a hit piece."

Tim and Maggie hadn't talked much about the interview. They'd both made efforts to stay out of the spotlight when it came to the feuding families of the county they'd left behind. Plenty of offers came in after Lee Acker's death and the arrest of Lucy Collins. Offers that carried monetary incentives and exposure for Maggie's burgeoning law practice. In some ways, Maggie regretted their decision to not make attempts to manage the narrative around the trial. It was too late now, though. Bill and Lucy Collins had made significant progress in shaping public opinion around the charges levied against Lucy. Maggie only assumed that the interviews the night before were another example of that growing bias toward the Collinses.

"What did you tell them about the night of Lee's death?" Tim asked, eyes fixed on the horizon as he steered the boat.

"I told them I wasn't there."

Tim nodded. He knew Maggie had listened in on the final minutes of Lee Acker's life. She'd told him that much.

"Did you tell them about the recording?"

Maggie thought about the question. The interviewer hadn't asked her about a recording from the night of the killing on Parker's Knoll. No one had. Tim knew it existed. Nothing more.

"No," Maggie finally replied.

"Don't you think people should know what was said that night?"

"Even with the recording, I'm not sure a jury will convict Lucy Collins in Blake County."

"That's for the jury to decide."

"We've talked about this, Tim. I can't hand over the recording without Lee's permission."

Maggie waited for Tim to respond, but he stayed quiet. They'd argued once over the matter, and that was it. He respected her decision to not share the recording with anyone. She'd explained to him that attorney-client privilege applied. A rule that required lawyers to keep certain communication confidential. The rule didn't allow her to share secrets, disclose legal advice, or gossip about sensitive client information. There were exceptions to the rule, but Maggie didn't feel right sharing what was on the recording.

"You will testify at the trial," Maggie said after a long pause. "You saw everything from the wood line."

"People won't know what was said, though."

"You're right," Maggie said with a nod. "And they won't."

Tim steered the boat slightly back toward the coastline. They listened to the waves slap the hull and eyed the waters ahead. Maggie thought about the words captured on the muffled recording. A recording she'd safe-guarded on a thumb drive now tucked away in the safe at her office. She still couldn't shake her late client's final words.

"Those families have feuded for over a hundred years now," Tim said, breaking Maggie's train of thought. "I'd be willing to bet good money that this trial won't settle anything."

Maggie nodded, still mulling the words over in her mind. Words heard only by those that stood over Lee's body as he died. She murmured the words. Testing them out for the first time.

"This isn't over."

"What's that?" Tim asked.

"This isn't over," Maggie said again. This time more forcefully.

"What do you mean?"

"I dug into this feud between the Collinses and Ackers while preparing for Lee's trial. I came across the Acker family tree. Every generation going back to Joseph Elmer Cobb has had at least one child named after Cobb."

"Well, this generation won't," Tim countered.

"No, this generation carries on the legacy," Maggie replied, pushing back. "Charlotte Elmer Acker is just the next in line to continue the fight."

"Hopefully we won't be there," Tim said with a smile. "I've had enough of their fight."

He stood to adjust the main sail as the boat approached a marina on the south side of Key Largo. Groups of people stood around dive boats readying themselves for a day exploring the reefs around the long key. Tim waved at the excited divers. They returned the wave, smiling in their wetsuits and sunglasses.

"What day is our flight back to Mobile?" Tim asked, turning back to Maggie.

"We have three days left down here," Maggie replied as she finished the last of her coffee. "The flight isn't until Thursday morning."

"Let's not worry about the Ackers, Collinses, Cobbs, or Elmers of the world. At least not for the rest of the trip."

"I'd like that," Maggie said with a smile. "I'm not a Dawson yet. Let's talk about when that's going to happen."

53

Charlotte walked out onto the track at Hayward Field and looked up into the stands. The stadium looked to be about half full, and spectators were still walking in from the entryways. The Pacific Northwest air pierced her lungs as she inhaled deep and began working through the flow of her warmup routine. Her legs felt fresh, and she'd been injury-free for the entire training season. She looked forward to her first opportunity to race against Division I competition and expected those around the sport to take notice. As she stretched, Charlotte spotted her small fan section. She popped up from her stance and jogged toward the railing that fronted the stadium seats.

"Hey, Charlie girl!" yelled Cliff over the hum of the crowd in the stands. "Looking sharp in that green and yellow!"

Her mother sat beside him, decked out in the latest Ducks apparel. They waved and whistled from their seats like many of the other families waiting for the competition to begin.

Charlotte yelled up into the stands, "Does your probation officer know you are out of state?"

Cliff smiled back as he felt the eyes of innocent onlookers cut in his direction. He couldn't be prouder of the wiseass track star that stood before him. His brother loved her more than anything in the world, and he intended to be ever present in her life, if only just to remind her of that love.

"You just worry about running fast today!" Cliff hollered back down to his niece.

Charlotte grinned at her loved ones and turned back to the track to continue her warmup. She bounced up and down, energized by the familiar faces that flew up to show their support. She would compete in the 3,000-meter steeplechase and the 1,600-meter relay. Charlotte was one of the few freshman women that OU expected to be competitive that day—Charlotte hoped to make her family proud.

As she looked out on the historic field, she tried to appreciate the moment and honor her own strength, perseverance. With the world falling down around her, many expected her to veer off course. Many mentioned the prospect of Charlotte taking some time away to recalibrate herself emotionally. "Why not a gap year?" they had asked. "You could stay home and keep your mother company in this strange time," others had urged her. Charlotte had no interest in staying home to wallow in the loss of the only man she'd ever known as a father. She needed to move forward. He would have wanted her to move forward. It was time to etch her story into the history books. Others would write her history for her if she did not get started. Charlotte knew that with power came the privilege of shaping history. Lucy Collins would shape her family's legacy, and Charlotte would have to do the same for her own.

She expected a jury would acquit Lucy Collins later that year. Blake County now marinated in the theory that the killing of Lee Acker was done in self-defense. No potential juror discussed the trial of Lucy Collins without also debating whether he or she believed it was Lee or Lucy that shot first. The seed of doubt was sown by the Collinses' powerful machine that had once been built to conquer political foes. That machine was unstoppable, and Charlotte wanted that power.

Charlotte jogged around the track, kicking her feet back to loosen the last twinges of tightness in her legs. She nodded at her competitors as she passed them on the track. Charlotte wondered if they knew who she was. If they realized they would soon compete against the strongest runner to ever come out of the South. A descendent of men and women that were revered for their tenaciousness. The offspring of families that were willing to disregard the rules and do whatever was required to win.

Charlotte knew her father would worry about her path to retribution, but she had seen her roots firsthand. She knew of only one way to shape her family's legacy. It would begin on the track and in the classroom. She would then make her move to DC. Those who did not know her eventually would. Those that underestimated her would pay a price. Charlotte Elmer Acker would soon write her family's history—she would set the record straight.

IN DEFENSE OF CHARLOTTE

The national exposure of the Lee Acker case put the trial skills of Maggie Reynolds on full display. Now she is intent on pursuing more profitable victories in the courtroom. Leaving behind her work as a criminal defense lawyer, Maggie is hot on the tail of her highest-profile job yet: a personal injury case with the potential for an incredible paycheck. Maggie hopes that a win will give her the recognition—and the bank account—that she deserves. Even if it means contending with shady lawyers who are willing to cut corners and backstab anyone for easy money.

But when Blake County native Charlotte Acker is accused of murdering Lucy Kelley Collins, the wife of a Georgia senator, Maggie is pulled back into the world of criminal defense...and immersed in a local drama, generations in the making.

Charlotte's guilt seems undeniable. Her hatred of the victim is well-known; a product of bitter and longstanding tensions between the Acker and Collins families. In a case that appears to be open-and-shut, Maggie must unravel the complicated history between the two families in order to clear Charlotte's name...all against the ticking clock of a senatorial election.

Torn between the lucrative payout of a personal injury case and the satisfaction of a career-defining murder trial, Maggie must reconcile her ambitions with her calling.

**Get your copy today at
severnriverbooks.com/series/blake-county-legal-thrillers**

ABOUT THE AUTHOR

Joe lives in Thomasville, Georgia. When he is not writing in the early morning hours, he devotes his attention to his family and law practice. The love he has for travel, sports, and the practice of law play a large part in shaping his stories. If the sun is shining, you may find him holding tight to his Triumph's handlebars.

Sign up for Joe Cargile's newsletter at
severnriverbooks.com/authors/joe-cargile

Printed in the United States
by Baker & Taylor Publisher Services